CELESTE
Book Three: The Faceless

For Christophe and Kara, who brighten my days and make me feel loved.

CHAPTER 1

February 2000

The shadow man stood at the foot of the bed.

Riley's body lay heavy and limp, unable to move. The bitter wind outside slammed snowflakes against the window, obstructing it and darkening the room even more. Yet the outline of the shadow was clearly visible, thick and threatening as it towered above her.

Celeste.

The sound of his voice grated at her nerves and jolted her body into motion. Riley shot upright and fumbled for the bedside lamp, heart in throat. When she swiveled back, her room was empty. Just another nightmare that left her panting, with sweat sticking her dark hair to her cheeks. Riley wished she'd screamed. If she had, Rudy would have come rushing to comfort her, but his sleeping energy downstairs was steady and undisturbed.

She waited a moment, willing her heartbeat to slow down as she took deep breaths. She had to be brave. She had to be strong. She had to face her fears. She was Riley Winter, future paranormal investigator, like Rudy and Grace.

No. You're weak and scared. You'll never be like them.

How could she? The terror she felt each time she dreamed of the shadow man was like glass shards piercing her throat. Not even in her wildest fantasies would she be a ghost and demon hunter. She would have to settle for working at Winter's Attic and selling special objects, if that.

Tears pricked her eyes. Her throat burned.

The soft glow of the bedside lamp didn't do much at cutting through the shadows clinging to each corner of the room, potentially hiding a monster ready to grab her ankles if she stepped out of bed.

After debating for what felt like hours, she finally swung her legs out of bed and tip-toed to the door. The hallway was shrouded in darkness, and the staircase resembled a black tunnel leading into the guts of a cold abyss. It was stupid, of course. Just childish fears. She loved her house, and she had been loving living with Rudy for the past nine months. She had never been happier, but the dark still threatened her.

Riley stepped down the stairs. Once on the first floor, she opened the door to the right. She could make out Rudy's shape on the left side of the bed. After hesitating again, she rounded the bed and buried herself under the covers in the empty space next to her new dad, curled up in the fetal position. He would probably be annoyed. She would turn twelve next month. In other words, she was *way* past the age of sneaking into her dad's bedroom at night. Not that she ever did it with Lance, the so-called biological father that never acted like a proper dad. He would have beaten her up real bad.

In the reassuring warmth of the covers, Riley felt Rudy shift next to her. A second later, the blanket was lifted off her head, and she blinked at the soft light and the pale blue eyes looking at her.

"Sorry..." she mumbled.

Rudy smiled and laid his head on the pillow, facing her. "Nightmare?" he signed.

Riley nodded.

"The shadow man?"

She nodded a second time. "I think you were right. Maybe I should be a beekeeper or something."

"Why?"

"Because I'm not brave like you. I'll never be a paranormal investigator. I'm too scared."

"You can do anything you set your mind to, pumpkin."

"I don't think I can do that..." Riley hugged the blanket a little tighter around her shoulders and wiped the tear rolling over the bridge of her nose.

"Hey. What did I teach you?"

"Do what I say, not what I do."

Rudy chuckled. "Not that. The other one."

"Trust your instincts."

"The other, other one."

Riley thought about it. "Being scared isn't a good reason not to do something?"

"Yes. If you're telling me you don't *want* to be a paranormal investigator, then don't become one. But if that's what you want to do, you've got to fight for it and face your fears. Don't let them slow you down."

"But you're scared of demons too, aren't you? Since the shadow man."

"Yes. But I keep doing my job. Because it's important to me, and I think Grace would have liked that."

"Do you think Grace would have liked me to do it too?"

Rudy brushed a strand of hair away from her face. "I think she would have been proud of you, whatever you decide. I will be too, no matter what you do. But the good news is you don't have to decide now, kiddo. You've got a few years to make up your mind."

Sleepiness returned, making Riley's body and eyelids heavy. The fears were muted for now. Tamed. He was right, she didn't have to decide now, but something was bright and clear in her mind. "I think maybe I can do it. I can do it as long as you're with me."

Rudy smiled again, seemingly pleased.

"You'll stay with me, right?" Riley asked, her heart aching at the single thought of having to battle her own demons alone.

He nodded. "Of course. I'll always be by your side."

CHAPTER 2

Riley stands in front of the Russels' house, the afternoon sun unpleasantly hot on her back and exposed arms. She brings the cigarette to her lips and takes a long drag, staring at the building in front of her. The house sweats sadness. Trauma. Anger. Much like her own house back when she lived with Lance. Only this time, it's not a little girl who needs help.

Riley turns to her dad's growing energy. His truck is not in view yet, but it'll be here in a few seconds. She waits until that old, green Ford truck he's had for as long as she can remember strolls down the street. She thinks about what Grace said when Riley was just a little girl. They were sitting next to each other on the floor in a quiet corner of Winter's Attic. Riley was saying that sometimes Rudy's energy was spotted with red when the truck broke down and he was trying to fix it.

Grace had laughed. *'That truck drives him crazy, but he loves it anyway and will never part with it.'*

Boy, was she right. Riley draws on her cigarette again as the truck comes into view and stubs it before Rudy parks. He's been trying to quit smoking, so it wouldn't be nice to dangle a cigarette in front of him. She bites back on a laugh at the sight of his red plaid jacket, the one with the gray hood that he's also had for as long as she can remember. It's draped over the driver's seat, as though Rudy's keeping it there just in case the temperature drops suddenly. Riley wishes it *would* drop already. She's thoroughly sick of the humid heat constantly coating her skin with a thin sheet of sweat that makes her jeans stick to her legs.

She tightens her loose, low ponytail, feeling her hair brush the middle of her back, and walks to Rudy. "Hey, Dad."

"Hey, pumpkin." He kisses her forehead. "Ready for this?"

"Always."

Rudy grabs a demon lockbox and locks the truck. After all these years, he stopped carrying amulets and UV light sticks to the extractions. He used to take them, just in case, but Riley doesn't need these things to weaken a shadow or exorcise it.

Together, they walk the path leading to the front door. Riley's stomach twists into knots. She takes a deep breath, trying to distance herself from the toxic feelings that saturate the house. They don't belong to her, she has to let them wash over her without letting them in.

Rudy pushes the doorbell.

"You have your phone, right?" Riley asks.

He nods. "Will I need it?"

"Yes."

The door opens, revealing a frightened-looking woman with wide, scared eyes.

"Mrs. Russel. W and W Paranormal Investigation. I'm Rudy Winter, and this is my daughter and partner, Riley Winter. You called us about your son?"

The woman lets out something that could either be a sigh of relief or a sob. "Yes, yes. Please, come in."

They both step into the foyer, and Riley looks up the staircase to her right. The boy is up there, and he's in pain.

A man appears in the living room doorway, his face hard and cold. Riley stares at him, looking him up and down and taking in the bad vibrations coming from his aura. He freezes for a moment, probably getting that feeling people have when Riley looks at them this way–that feeling of being seen *through*. Although uncomfortable, he pushes through and walks up to them.

"I'm Henry. This is my wife Corinne. Thank you for coming on such short notice."

He shakes Rudy's hand, but when he turns to Riley, his hand held mid-air, she doesn't budge. She keeps her eyes locked on him, giving him the Death Stare until he looks down.

Her dad watches her out of the corner of his eyes, reading her cues, as always. He hands her the lockbox and signs, "Social services?"

Riley nods once.

Corinne looks confused for a moment, then starts toward the staircase. "Aiden is in his room–"

"I'll find him," Riley cuts off. "Stay here, please. I need a few minutes with him."

She climbs the stairs, briefly glancing at Rudy to make sure he's texting Stella for her to call social services. She'll also send one or two officers over here. Social services can take up to twenty-four hours to start the investigation, Riley knows that by now. Law enforcement, however, will respond immediately. Using sign language in these situations has often proven useful. They don't want Mr. Russel to freak out and throw a fit, which he'll do if he suspects anything. He's a dark, gray man, who probably doesn't just beat up his son, but his wife as well.

The headache he gave Riley fades as she crosses the hallway upstairs, passing doors she knows lead to empty rooms. She unlatches from the energies of the people in the foyer, distances herself from her dad's, and searches for the shadow. It's weak. Small. Barely a newborn for it to possess a child. It can't even make the kid move. It's probably just feeding on what it can before growing strong enough to possess the dad. If that happened, it would lead to carnage.

But it *won't* happen. Because Riley's here now, and it'll be a piece of cake.

She stops in front of a closed bedroom, the lockbox in one hand, and rests her other palm against the door. The shadow's in there. Riley turns the handle and steps into the dark room. Her heart sinks. Poor kid. Possessed and lethargic on his bed while a demon is eating him alive. The space reeks of sulfur. The curtains are closed. The parents probably thought it was better to keep him in the dark to allow him to rest. The shadow is so weak that a bit of sunlight would have done the job at extracting it, but it would have been a little more difficult to catch it then. For other investigators, of course. Not for Riley. She's a shadow magnet. It would have come rushing as soon as it smelled her, eager to feast on her celestial soul, and all she would have needed to do was pluck it like a flower and put it in the lockbox.

The child moans and moves his head. A trickle of black ectoplasm comes out of his nose and runs down his cheeks, soaking his blond hair. The demon is stirring inside of him, probably picking up on Riley's energy. She walks to the bed and sits next to Aiden, setting the lockbox on the nightstand. When she looks back at the child's face, his black eyes are wide open and fixed on her.

"What... are... you?" the entity inside his body asks, its raspy voice over-lapping the child's, before licking its lips in anticipation.

"Out of your league."

The thing lets out a feeble groan, very much like the shadow man roaming her bedroom when she was a child. It still manages to send a shiver crawling down her spine.

"You really are a small, miserable imprint for possessing a little kid, aren't you?" Riley says. "Couldn't get your hands on something bigger, could you? Sorry to burst your bubble, but you're being evicted."

The demon opens a mouth coated with black goo and shrieks, the sound loud and piercing.

Riley grits her teeth against it and presses her hand on the boy's forehead. *"Shut up."*

The screech dies down, and the child's eyes close. Then, Aiden stirs, coughs up the black liquid out of his mouth, and blinks at Riley confusedly. His breathing kicks up a notch as he starts whimpering.

"Help me... The monster wants to eat me..."

Riley bends over him and brushes his cheek, taking in as much of his fear as she can. "Shh... It's gonna be okay. The monster won't hurt you anymore."

9

Aiden calms down after Riley works her magic on him, and his sobs die down to soft sniffles. His lips still tremble a little. "I want my mom."

"She's downstairs. I'll call her in a minute. But first, I'm going to chase that monster away."

"You can do that?"

"Yes."

"Are you, like... a monster slayer?"

Riley Winter, Monster Slayer. I like the sound of that.

She smiles, brushing his hair with her fingertips, absorbing the bad feelings. "Something like that, yes. But I need you to be brave, okay? I'll go as quick as I can, but it might feel a little uncomfortable."

Anxiety spikes through the child, and tears prick his eyes, but when Riley presses her hand against his cheek again, his body relaxes more, and he nods. "Yes. I'll be brave."

"Very good."

Riley opens the lockbox and fetches her pocketknife—the one James bought her for her twenty-first birthday—from her jeans pocket. She pops the blade open and cuts her finger, just enough to draw a few drops of blood. Demons are bound to the last vessel they possessed and will follow their blood into the lockbox, but Riley's energy is a lot stronger and more tempting for any shadow. She prefers it. That way, she doesn't have to hurt Aiden.

She brushes her bloody finger inside the iron box, staining its insides, and turns back to the kid. "Ready, buddy?"

He nods shakily.

Riley places her hands on both sides of his face and closes her eyes. She reaches out with her mind, searching for the demon. When she finds it, she seizes it easily, and drags it out of the boy. She hears Aiden gag as the ectoplasm comes out of his mouth and slithers to the lockbox. That's the worst part. When the liquid fills your throat, and you feel like you'll never breathe again.

Fortunately, the entity is weak and small, and soon, it's trapped inside the box Riley closes and locks. Aiden gasps and coughs, then starts crying again. He shuffles to his knees and surprises her by throwing his arms around her, sobbing into the crook of her neck. These are tears of relief more than anything, but Riley still soothes him the best she can, stroking his hair and shushing him, much like her dad has done for her countless times.

She turns her head to the empty doorway, feeling Rudy approaching. She's looking at him before he even sees her.

"The mother wants to see him," he signs.

"You can send her in," Riley says. "Keep the dad downstairs."

A glint fleets through his icy blue eyes. "That shithead won't go past me."

No doubt about that. Even in his mid-fifties, her dad is still very much intimidating. His height alone does the trick.

Riley listens to his footsteps backtracking to the staircase, as others, lighter but hasty, pound the floor. Corinne appears in the doorway and lets out a cry of relief at the sight of her healthy son, who turns to her and scrambles off Riley to jump in his mother's arms.

Riley rests her elbows on her knees, feeling exhausted after all the sharp fear she absorbed from the boy, and looks at the two of them cuddling and crying.

"Thank you..." Corinne says, sobbing. "Thank you so much."

"He won't hurt you anymore," Riley says.

Corinne appears confused for a moment. "Was it a... male?"

"I'm talking about your husband. He won't hurt you. We won't allow it."

Even though Corinne stays frozen, her mouth hanging open, Riley feels an intense sense of relief blooming through her.

Aiden pulls away from his mom's arms and looks at her. "The woman in black killed the monster, Mommy. She's a monster slayer!"

Corinne smiles and holds her boy tightly against her chest before her eyes find Riley again. "Yes, sweetie. That, she is."

CHAPTER 3

"For your collection," Riley says, handing the lockbox to Rudy. It will join all the others in the basement.

Rudy puts the box on the driver's seat. "How do you feel?"

"I'm okay. Aiden's emotions jarred me more than the extraction. But I'm glad we could help them." She glances at the house, now quiet. Luckily—sort of—Henry threw a rage fit at the sight of the police officers, which ended up with him being taken away, at least for now.

"You did good. As usual. I'm proud of you."

"Thanks, Dad. I have to go home. I'd like to take a shower before my show tonight. Will you be there?"

"Of course."

Riley hugs him before walking back to her car. There are no words in any language to translate how grateful she is to have him in her life, the only constant in a world full of disappointment.

She hops in her car and starts the engine, quickly opening the window. The air inside is as sizzling hot as the fiery pits of hell. She drives away, the warm wind barely doing anything at refreshing her.

Before she opens the door to the small condo she's renting with Kelly, she already knows her roommate is waiting for her on the other side. And she's not happy.

What now?

Riley steps inside, quickly glancing right, where Kelly's sitting on one of the kitchen chairs. "Hey, Kell."

Kelly rises, twisting her fingers together. "We need to talk."

"Now? 'Cause I have to get ready for my gig—"

"Yes, *now.*"

Riley can almost feel the lump in Kelly's throat choking her. She sighs, accepting that she might not be able to take that shower after all. She'll stink on stage. Oh well. "Sure. What's up?"

"I thought a lot about something, and I need you to be honest with me."

"Um, okay."

"Sit down."

Riley joins Kelly in the kitchen and sits with her, pretending she isn't stressed at the idea of being late to her gig.

Kelly takes a deep breath, trying to calm her nerves. "Will there ever be more?"

"What do you mean?" She's acting like a dick. She knows the answer perfectly well.

"More between us. More than an occasional one-night stand."

Finally. The question Riley wished Kelly would never ask has been asked. After breaking up with Daniel, she found out she was attracted to both men and women. And Kelly's pretty. She always has been. But with them being friends, and now roommates for a while, Riley shouldn't have given in to the temptation, especially since most of the physical interactions she's had in the past few years were sought out of loneliness. And now she's made a mess, possibly ruining a precious friendship she's had for nine years.

"I want *more*. Don't you understand that I have feelings for you?" Kelly says.

It's not that Riley doesn't know. For years, she's made herself blind to what people feel toward her. It's just easier not to be emotionally involved. That way, she doesn't get hurt.

But that was before. Something's changed in the past few months, helping her move on, even if she's not ready to face it yet. "I'm sorry, Kell… I can't give you what you need."

"You're emotionally distant."

"I'm not."

"You are. Since you broke up with Daniel, you can't let anyone in. It's all you ever talk about—or should I say *complain* about. It's always Daniel this and Daniel that. You are *incapable* of making an actual connection with anyone. You're-you're *emotionally impaired.*"

Riley grimaces. It was true for a while. "I—"

"I know you're not doing it on purpose. It's just…" Kelly swallows, searching for her words. "The more I think about it, the more I realize that us living together isn't a good idea."

"Oh…"

"It's not healthy for me to have you around all the time. Even if we hung out less, we'd still see each other pretty much every day, and I just… can't."

Riley nods, her chest a little heavy. "Yeah. I understand."

"I'm sorry…"

Riley's phone vibrates in her pocket. She ignores it. "Don't be. I get it. Really. I... I never meant to hurt you, Kell."

Kelly nods, trying to smile but failing at it. "I know. It's gonna sound bitchy or selfish but... my name is on the lease..." She stares at Riley, waiting for her to fill in the blanks.

"So, you'd like me to move out."

"I'm not throwing you out or anything. But the sooner you can find a new place, the better, I think."

Riley lets that sink in, not knowing how to respond. Her phone vibrates again, irritating her, but she refuses to reach for it. "I can crash on James's couch for a while. I don't mind."

"Okay... I probably won't come to your gig tonight."

"It's fine."

The damn phone vibrates once again, and this time Riley takes it out, grunting. It's James. Three texts.

Help.

Emergency.

I need you, like, yesterday.

"What is it?" Kelly says.

"Nothing. It's James. He needs help with... something."

The phone vibrates in Riley's hand.

ANSWER. No calls. Just texts.

"It's fine, answer him. I said what I needed to say." Kelly stands up and walks away.

Riley rises too and calls after her. "Kell."

Kelly turns, eyebrows raised. Her soul is spotted with dark blue, making Riley's heart ache. "Are we still friends?"

She shrugs, her eyes shimmering. "Yes, of course. I'll just need some time."

Riley watches her as she turns away and walks to her bedroom, guilt filling her, and sighs in frustration as she replies to James.

WHAT

Need help. Was supposed to cleanse a house haunted by dead husband. Widow won't stop crying in my arms. I need you to help her calm down.

Just use your natural charm. Take your shirt off and flex your biceps or something. I have a gig tonight, and I can't be late, or Liam will lose his mind again.

Please, she's heartbroken. I don't know how to handle it.

Riley rolls her eyes, her shoulders dropping. She lifts her arm and briefly smells her armpit, nodding to herself. "Could be worse."

Okay, on my way. Send the address.

Something strikes her suddenly, and she types another text. Wait, she's crying in your arms now??

After only a handful of seconds, a reply pops up on her screen. *I'm texting behind her back. Literally.*

This makes Riley chuckle. What an idiot. A second later, he sends her the address, and she's off again. Hopefully, she can take care of this quickly and not be late for her show. Having another friend be upset at her is the last thing she wants.

Riley parks in front of a pretty white house surrounded by other pretty Victorian houses on a quiet street of Auburn. With each second ticking away from her and making her dangerously close to being late, she strides to the front door and knocks loudly. The vibes coming from the house don't match what James said. There's some sadness, sure, but it's pretty mild and certainly not what a 'heartbroken' person would be feeling.

Riley waits, barely containing her impatience as the late afternoon sun heats her shoulders. The door flies open, revealing a woman in her sixties, her smooth, white hair tied into a tight bun. She smiles politely at Riley and seems quite composed, her face relaxed and her eyes neither puffy nor red.

"Yes?"

Riley fights to bite back on a sigh of irritation. "Hello. I'm Mr. Williams's partner."

James appears in the doorway, his relief blooming through Riley. "Mrs. McCarthy, this is my partner Riley Winter. She's here to help."

Mrs. McCarthy turns to him, taking on a fake saddened expression. "Will she cleanse the house in your stead? I very much need your company. I know I'm asking for a lot, but I'm just..." She wipes an invisible tear from her eye. "Pardon me, I'm such a mess."

"That's quite all right," he says.

Riley gets a glimpse of the living room behind them. On the coffee table lies a familiar object. A Ouija board. She presses her lips into a tight line and signs to James, "You haven't cleansed the house yet?" He's still clumsy with signing, but he's made a lot of efforts these past few years to learn it, and he can understand it pretty well.

The woman looks at her with huge eyes as though Riley had given him the middle finger, and James beckons her to the couch. "Will you excuse me for a second? I'd like to have a word with Riley. I'll be right back."

She sits down and shakes a finger at him like a teacher talking to a child. "Don't be too long."

James gives her a tight smile and steps onto the porch with Riley, closing the door behind him.

"You're such an idiot," she says, grinning.

He chuckles, a little embarrassed. "She literally threw herself at me almost as soon as I got here. That's why I couldn't cleanse the house. If you could calm her nerves, I could do the job and get the hell out of here."

Riley grins wider, shaking her head. "Jamie-bear... So naïve... Her nerves don't need to be soothed. She's not even sad. A little blue, at most."

James frowns, opens his mouth, then closes it. He knows better than to doubt Riley's instincts by now. "Then, why would she—*oh...*"

He starts nodding to himself, and Riley nods with him. "Yeah."

"She wants a piece of that, huh? I mean, I can't blame her," he says.

"Very modest, as usual. Now, if you'll excuse me, I need to go."

She turns away, but James catches up to her. "Woah, wait, don't leave me alone with her."

"Dude, she's faking her sadness. You can handle it. And by the way, I feel no ghost vibes coming from the house. It's not haunted."

"Yeah, my EMF sensor didn't pick up anything. I brought a Ouija board because she insisted on it. That séance was ridiculous."

"I suppose no dead husband contacted you, and the planchette didn't move."

He scoffs. "Oh, it did. Because *she* moved it."

Riley bites back on a laugh. "You can probably just flail around her house with some sage for five minutes and then get the hell out. You don't need me."

"Come on, stay with me. It won't take long. If you go, she'll never let me leave. Once she wraps her arms around me, she's like a Boa constrictor." He leans forward just a little, cocking his head. Strands of black hair brush his raised eyebrows, and his dark eyes fix on her, imploring her.

"Don't do the sad puppy eyes..." she says, looking away because she knows she'll go to the end of the earth for that look.

"All right. I wish I didn't have to do this, but you give me no choice." He pauses and crosses his arms. "Kelly's last birthday party."

Warmth instantly rises to Riley's cheeks. She looks down and pretends to wipe invisible sweat from her forehead, hoping that James will blame the crushing heat if her face turns red. The fact that he can bring up this night without batting an eyelid is borderline shocking.

"You said you'd owe me big time," he says, leaning forward to catch her gaze.

"Come on..."

"I shaved for you that night."

"You barely trimmed your beard."

20

"I hadn't even planned on taking a shower."

"Gross."

"But I did it, and within minutes, I was at that party, surrounded by a bunch of people twelve years younger than me, to keep you company because you were awkward as hell."

"I'm not that awkward..."

He tilts his head, looking at her with an expression that means *please...* "Your paternal likes to say that no one is as self-aware as they think–"

"Don't quote my dad to me."

Riley nibbles on her lip. She *really* needs to leave. Every chance she gets, she throws herself into work. The library, the extractions, various haunting cases, treasure hunting. She's been late to several of her shows, and Liam and Miguel are starting to get tired of it. The fourth member of their group, Keenan–who happens to be Miguel's boyfriend–has replaced Daniel because he not only plays the guitar but sings quite well too. One time, Riley was so late that they started playing without her, Keenan taking the lead and singing in her place. They sounded good. Good enough for her to feel frightened by it. They could play without her if they wanted, and Riley has no intention of being kicked out of her band.

On the other hand, James always does anything she asks of him, no questions asked. That night at Kelly's birthday party, Riley felt stupid. She felt self-conscious in front of some of the girls there who remembered her from high school and liked to tease her because, *of course,* her and Daniel would break up, eventually. They also had a nice time reminding Riley she was a bit of a freak and *are you still hitting people? Ha-ha, you were such a weirdo!*

21

So, she asked James to fly in to her rescue, which may not have been the best idea.

"Come on, lovie," James says, snapping her out of her internal battle and back to reality. "You know I don't like to ask for help. Don't make me beg. Which I'm already pretty much doing."

"All right. Five minutes. *Tops.*"

His hand falls on her shoulder and squeezes it. "You're the best." Before she can reply, he opens the door and pushes her inside.

Mrs. McCarthy springs from the couch, her face going from happy to falsely sad. "James! I was afraid you had left."

James smiles and pushes Riley next to the woman. "Of course not. Riley will sit with you while I cleanse your house. It'll be done in no time."

The disappointment staining her soul gets to Riley, and she almost feels bad for the lonely woman. If all she wants to do is hug a strong, young man, let her have it, damn it. Riley's about to offer to switch places, but James has already taken a sage bouquet out of his bag. He lights it and disappears upstairs, leaving her and the woman to stand awkwardly together.

Mrs. McCarthy clears her throat, clearly uncomfortable. "Would you like some tea, dear?"

"I'm all right. Thank you."

"Well... sit down."

Riley sits down and almost gasps when the old couch sinks in under her weight, half-swallowing her. Mrs. McCarthy settles too and glances around as if looking for something to say. She might be a bad actress, hungry for some young blood, but she has lost her husband, nonetheless. If Riley's here, she might as well do what she does best.

"When did your husband die?"

The woman's eyebrows shoot up all the way to her hairline, as though she had forgotten she had initially called W&W Paranormal Investigation to get rid of her late husband's lingering spirit. "A few months ago. Heart attack." She turns to the small table next to the couch, grabs a picture frame, and shows it to Riley. On it, the two of them sit on the porch's swing outside, beaming. "That's him."

"I'm sorry for your loss," Riley says, putting her hand on the woman's hand and soothing her.

Mrs. McCarthy looks at it, smiles softly, and squeezes back. "Thank you, dear."

James tumbles down the stairs and heads straight to the kitchen, a cloud of white smoke trailing behind him.

"He's quite handsome, isn't he?" Mrs. McCarthy says.

Riley glances at the picture. "Sure."

"I was talking about your partner."

"Ah, yes. Quite the Casanova."

A playful grin plays on the woman's lips as she watches him. "He's a sight for sore eyes. I don't mind living in a haunted house if he's the one cleansing it."

Riley chortles, suddenly delighted by this conversation.

"Is he single?" Mrs. McCarthy asks.

"Yes. And I know for a fact he likes mature women."

"Oh, really?" She lets out a little giggle. "I think I knew that. He couldn't keep his hands off me earlier."

"You don't say!" The urge to laugh is powerful and tugging at her lips, but Riley summons all her willpower to keep it under control. Willpower is a limited resource, though. To help herself, she presses her fingers to her mouth, hoping it looks sort of casual.

"Mm-hm," Mrs. McCarthy says. "I have met many men in my life, young lady. I recognize those things."

"He definitely has a kink about white hair."

Mrs. McCarthy beams at her, and Riley realizes that after the extraction and the talk with Kelly, sitting here with this woman is the highlight of her day.

"All right," James says, back in the living room, his EMF detector in hand. As expected, it's deadly quiet and doesn't pick up anything supernatural. "Your house is cleansed and ghost free." He quickly places the Ouija board back into its box and the detector in his pocket.

Mrs. McCarthy almost looks disappointed. Riley imagines that her husband has probably moved on a while ago. She could tell as soon as she stepped into the house that there wasn't anything supernatural going on. Sometimes, the living want to believe so much that their loved ones haven't really left them that they'll interpret the creaking of the floor and a door slamming shut as paranormal activity. Other times, they'll misplace objects and be convinced a ghost is messing with them.

Riley rises from the couch—extracts herself from it, more like—and smiles at her host. "It was nice to meet you."

"Likewise, dear."

Mrs. McCarthy has barely let go of Riley's hand after shaking it when her gaze is swallowing James again, and she follows him to the front door, telling him she'll call again if anything comes back. Despite him assuring her that ghosts don't come back once they've moved on, she insists that it is an old house, and *you never know.*

Riley exits the house, followed by James, who gives an awkward smile to the woman as she watches him walk away. The two of them walk side by side, bathed in the increasingly coppery light announcing an early evening.

He clears his throat once they're far enough from the house. "Why do I feel like you have something to do with her grabbing my ass before I stepped out?"

The laughter Riley has been trying to suppress bursts out of her mouth, and James shoves her, almost making her trip, but she keeps laughing anyway.

"Give the woman a break," she says. "She's grieving."

"You didn't even like her at first."

"Well, I quite like her now. This short visit was highly entertaining. Thanks for sharing the fun."

"You can always count on me for some fun."

"Tell that to Mrs. McCarthy."

He laughs. "I'd rather not."

"I really gotta go now."

"All right. Thanks for coming to my rescue. I'll see you in a little bit."

She pauses halfway to her car. "Yeah... You know, or not. Don't feel like you *have* to come."

"What is that supposed to mean?"

"Nothing. Just, if you didn't want to come, just know that you don't have to."

James squints at her, registering this, then inhales. "I'll behave this time."

Riley tries to smile, knowing he means it, and also knowing he can't control himself. His bar fights have gotten completely out of control lately, and the last time it happened, she had to get his ass out of jail. "Will you, though? Because you say that every time."

"I'll do my best. I promise."

"All right. I'll see you later, then."

She returns to her car while he goes to his. If he loses his shit again tonight, she'll have to refrain from getting in the middle of it, or she'll get herself and her band in trouble again.

CHAPTER 4

Rudy opens the basement door and goes down the creaky stairs, the lockbox under his arm. The air down here is colder than upstairs. Maybe he should spend more time here to escape the fiery heat of summer. He heads to the high shelf against the wall on the right side of the basement and gazes at all the lockboxes tucked up there. Riley has extracted more demons in five years than he had in thirty. She's become known and talked about among other paranormal investigators, especially since they created W&W Paranormal Investigation. Investigators can't help but look her up and down when they walk into Winter's Attic. They ask questions. Some admire her. Others are misogynistic douchebags who look down on her and actively pretend not to be impressed.

Riley doesn't care about what they think. She does what she does best, which is help as many people as she can. She travels across the country if she has to, and Rudy likes to go with her when he can. No matter how good she is, and no matter that she's twenty-five and doesn't need her old man to follow her around, she's still his little girl.

Rudy slides the lockbox onto the shelf and quickly counts how many there are. Forty-three, the majority belonging to Riley. Shadows are still relatively rare compared to ghosts, but the more people talk about Riley's abilities, the more families in need reach out to her. Although Rudy's still old school and doesn't care for technology, Riley's idea to set up a website for their business has proved to work pretty well. People these days will go on the internet as soon as they're looking for something, and that's how most of them found Rudy, Riley, and James. They had a whole argument about what to name this business.

"Snowwight," Riley pitched in, smiling wide.

James almost slammed his beer onto the table, making some people in the bar turn to the sound. "Fuck no."

"Dude. Snow for Winter, Wight for spirits," she said, her eyes sparkling.

"Yeah, I get the word play."

"It's *genius*."

"Still sounds like a delicate princess. And what about *my* name? Rud, back me up here."

Rudy took a gulp of his own beer, chewing on this. "I don't think it sounds really professional."

"Damn right," James said, satisfied.

Riley shook her head at him. "Can't believe you'd let me down like that. Okay, how about Winter's Basement?"

Rudy shrugged. "Meh."

"W2 Investigators. For Winter and Williams."

James's thick eyebrows pulled into a frown over his dark eyes. "Are you hammered? Sounds like a tax form."

"Well, then *you* find something," Riley said.

"Metaphysicists."

She cocked one eyebrow, looking almost offended. "Are you serious?"

"Logicalmythologicals."

"Why you gotta be like this?"

"WilWinParanormal."

"No!"

"That's it, I'm putting my foot down," Rudy said. "Winters and Williams Paranormal Investigation. Clear and efficient."

Riley's shoulders dropped. "Dad, I love you, but that's a little lame, isn't it?"

"I like it," James said.

She did a double take. "Really? After pitching 'Logicalmythological,' you like this?"

"Yeah. You've got my vote, Rud."

"Two against one. Sorry, pumpkin."

She shook her head and brought the beer to her lips, mumbling, "I still think Snowwight was genius, but okay, I guess."

"Why does my name come second, though?" James said.

Riley grinned. "Because there's two of us and one of you."

"Exactly. One of me, so my name should be first. And alphabetically speaking, it makes more sense."

"I was there first," Rudy said. "You only started working for me later, you smartass."

"Hey. I work *with* you. Not *for* you."

Riley started giggling uncontrollably, making Rudy smile before he said, "When I see how Riley orders you around and sends you on missions, it definitely looks like you're working for her."

"Well, your daughter's really bossy."

Rudy put his beer down, meaning business. "How about this? W&W Paranormal Investigation. It's shorter, still efficient, and we don't need to bicker over whose name is first."

James considered this, nodding. "All right, I like it. But we know my name comes first."

"Whatever keeps you sane, boy."

James smiled, clearly satisfied, and jumped off his stool. "Gonna get another one. Anybody want something?"

They told him yes, and James went to the bar to order more beers.

Riley leaned forward, her signature mischievous smile playing on her lips. "His name doesn't come first, though, right?"

"What do you think?"

He winked at her, making her laugh some more.

Riley had business cards printed for them. She asked Daniel to design them, and Rudy must admit they look quite professional. Black with a silver-white lettering. During all those years working as a paranormal investigator, he never thought about having business cards. He always got a job by word of mouth. But it turns out that Riley is quite the entrepreneur, and since the website has been set up and they pass their business cards to the people they work for, their workload has increased quite a bit. They even met a guy who can build lockboxes for them—legit ones. That way they don't need to go around chasing them out.

Rudy climbs the stairs and reenters the stuffy air of the hallway, closing the door behind him. He should get ready before going to Riley's gig. Stella said she would join if she could get out of work early enough. Maybe he should fix her something to eat before taking a shower. He heads to the kitchen, cracks the window open, even if it does nothing but bring more hot air inside the room, and takes out what he needs to make a mac and cheese casserole. Riley always loved it. Make some mac and cheese and cook some bacon, throw the pasta into a casserole, mix the pieces of bacon in it, then add more cheese on top and shove it in the oven.

Once this is done, the clock tells him he still has time to clean up a bit before Stella comes home. Rudy looks around the place. It's mostly in order, nothing to make a fuss about. He used to have to put stuff away all the time when Riley still lived here. She would always leave a trail of books, sweaters, and candy wrappers in her wake. That might be the only good thing about her not living here anymore: not having to pick up after her.

The truth is, he misses her, and he's glad he gets to see her at Winter's Attic. He can't say he feels lonely. Especially not since he started dating Stella three years ago, and even less since she moved in with him.

Rudy heads to his bedroom, planning to take that shower now, preferably cold, when his phone buzzes in his jeans pocket. He stops halfway through the hall and takes it out. Stella's name shines bright on the smartphone's screen James and Riley assured him he needed when they bought it for his last birthday. Rudy would have gladly kept his Nokia for a few more years.

"Hey, you," he says, as he picks up, a smile hanging on his lips.

"Hey. I don't think I can make it to Riley's show tonight."

Her voice is clipped, and Rudy's smile vanishes. He knows what that voice means, but he hangs onto the belief that he's wrong this time. "Tell me it's not what I think it is."

She sighs, her breath blowing into the phone. "I'm afraid it is. We found another body."

After talking to Rudy for a minute, Stella hangs up the phone and takes a deep breath of stuffy air before going down the steep slope, walking sideways to avoid falling flat on her ass. Dry leaves and pine needles crunch under her shoes. A drop of sweat slides down her temple, and she brushes it away with the back of her hand. The high trees hide most of the burning sunrays, offering protection and shadow, but also trapping the foul air emanating from the corpse.

Stella breaks through the trees and reenters the clearing crowded with cops and forensic experts, all of them surrounding the body. The injuries are different. They're always different. Ranging from various broken bones, cuts, burns—small or widespread, but the end result is always the same.

Eyes clawed out.

Teeth pulled out.

Face stabbed, the flesh cut and slashed so many times it looks like a messy red pulp.

Hands and feet severed, nowhere to be found.

How many more are they going to find before catching the culprit? It sickens Stella. They have *nothing*. The victims don't have much in common. They can be male or female, twenty or sixty. This one, lying on a bed of leaves and pine needles, with dirt clogging her wounds and worms already festering on her flesh, seems young by the look of her skin.

They're not sure yet, but it could be the twenty-six year old woman who went missing five days ago, less than twenty miles away. It's impossible to tell for now, and body identification by the family is out of the question. Their only way of identifying the victim is through DNA, since there are no teeth and no fingerprints. They'll use the hair left on the missing person's brush and compare it to the body's.

Stella winces in disgust, the thought of someone capable of such atrocities making her stomach churn. The buzzing of the hundreds of flies fighting to get a piece of the cadaver fills her head, deafening and dizzying. Rudy can't be right. It isn't paranormal. She understands his reasoning. Only someone really strong could carry a body so deep in the woods without using any means of transportation. But the behavior of this killer is very much human. And whoever they are, they want to be noticed.

Stella lets her eyes sweep over the ground, looking for something she might have missed. The girl wasn't killed here. She was dumped, stripped of her clothes and humanity, just like the others. The murder happened someplace else, after the victim was tortured, probably for days before dying of her wounds. Then, she was dragged, as the track in the dirt, meticulously avoided by the police, clearly shows.

She follows it, making sure not to step on it. How can someone walk all these miles through the thick trees while dragging a corpse? The 'path' weaves through trunks and shrubs, unbroken, erasing the killer's footprints. But they *had* to walk back. They must have left something behind. But that's the thing, they never do. After finding nineteen bodies, Stella never found a clue. No hair. No piece of torn cloth. No broken nail or lost button.

She backtracks her steps, studying the ground closely. Her heart misses a beat. There are footprints there, past a flattened bush. They could belong to one of her colleagues, but the narrow path is overgrown. Not ideal when transporting material. Stella follows the footprints, not knowing what she's looking for. It could be the path the killer took to leave the crime scene, weaving through shrubs and trunks instead of taking the regular trails.

Something's strange. The footprints go straight, then disappear. There are no more tracks, neither left nor right. Stella stops, glancing around herself, trying to make sense of what she sees. To the sides are more shrubs and bushes, undisturbed. She looks in front of her, tilting her head and squinting at the burning light peeking through the branches.

The footprints vanish in front of a tree.

CHAPTER 5

Riley's car skids to a stop as she parks in an empty space in front of the bar. She made it. She just has to rush in there with her guitars and amp, plug everything up, and they'll start playing on time.

She reaches for the handle when her phone rings in her pocket. It's probably Liam again, sending her another text.

Don't answer it.

She quickly takes it out just to check who it is. Daniel's name flashes on the screen, giving Riley pause. It's almost 7:00 p.m., which means it's close to midnight in England. Daniel never calls her this late, not when his girlfriend, Caroline, doesn't appreciate Riley that much. Why would he call her at this hour? Is something wrong? Did something happen to him? Thing is, he's not just calling her. He wants to FaceTime.

Riley stares at the phone for a second, torn between wanting to race into the bar and fly to Daniel's rescue. Eventually, she picks up. "Danny?"

The image on her screen clears and focuses on Daniel's handsome face, although he looks a little disheveled. His white shirt is unbuttoned at the top, and his eyes sparkle. His smile widens at the sight of her.

"Hey, my darling. How's it going?"

"Good. Are *you* okay?"

"Yes, of course."

Riley lets out a small breath of relief. "Okay, good. I was wondering why you were calling me so late. Can I call you back later? Tomorrow? I have a gig, and I'm *this close* to being late, and–"

"I won't keep you long, Riley, I promise. But I really need to tell you something. It just can't wait."

If only she could say no to him, but she never could. Now that she thinks about it, she can never say no to anyone. "All right. Make it fast, Sunny Boy."

He opens his mouth as if inhaling and says, "I proposed to Caroline."

Riley stares at the phone, unblinking. "You... what?"

"I proposed to her. I know, I should have told you I was gonna do it, but you've been busy, and it all happened sort of fast."

Someone shoot me in the head.

"She said *yes*. We're celebrating with our friends. They're in the living room. I did this whole surprise party for her, and she had no clue this was gonna happen. Can you believe it? I'm getting married!"

Or bash my skull with a baseball bat.

"We already chose a date. A little more than a year from now. October eleventh."

Stab me in the gut. Because this will hurt less than this.

"I want you to be here, Riley. I want you to be my witness."

Is there a bridge nearby I can jump off?

"Darling? I think your image is frozen. Can you hear me? Riley?"

"Huh?"

"Did you hear what I said?"

Her mouth turns dry. She's parched and can't utter a coherent word for a moment as she tries to keep a straight face. "Y-yes..."

Some of his genuine smile vanishes. "Are you okay? I-I'm sorry if—"

"No! I mean, yeah, I'm okay. I'm great. It's... It's fantastic news. Congratulations, Danny. I'm really... happy for you."

"Will you be there?" The smile is completely gone now, leaving Daniel with hopeful eyes as he looks at her.

Riley swallows around the lump in her throat and nods. "Of course. Of course I'll be there for you. Is Caroline okay with that, though?"

He chuckles softly. "I can make a lot of compromises, but she doesn't get a say in this. It'd be wonderful if your dad and James could be there too."

"They wouldn't miss it for the world, I'm sure."

They stare at each other in silence, and Riley wonders if Daniel has the same thoughts as her swirling through his head. Is he thinking about the day they met? About how they'd said they were so perfect together? About how they'd thought they would always find their way back to each other? Maybe not. Maybe he's thinking, *You shouldn't have broken up with me. Now you lost me forever.*

"You deserve her," she says, as if answering her own thoughts. "You deserve someone who makes you happy."

A soft smile spreads on his lips.

"You should go back to your friends. And your fiancée."

"Yeah, I should. You should hurry up to your gig."

Her heart misses a beat as she remembers she's late. *"Fuck. I gotta go. Talk to you soon, okay?"*

"All right, my darling."

He blows her a kiss, and Riley blows him one too before hanging up. Her body feels heavy and hot and sticky, and her heart aches. If only she had time to stay here and feel sorry for herself, but she can't. Rock music seeps out of the bar, telling her Miguel, Liam, and Keenan have started playing without her. Because once again, she's late.

James is sitting alone at a small table against the wall. He received a text from Rudy a few minutes ago saying he and Stella can't make it. That's not good. At least when Rudy's here, he keeps James in check, and the chances of him getting into a fight are smaller.

But never zero.

Where the fuck is Riley? After all that fuss about not wanting to be late, James managed to get here before her. The band has started playing already, with Keenan singing in Riley's stead. He's good, but even if James likes these guys, it's Riley he came to see.

He finishes his beer and looks around at the women in the bar in an attempt to distract himself. He quickly loses interest—like he has for the past nine months—and turns his gaze back to the stage. He'd rather stay alone than try to fill a void with meaningless sex, which has already proved useless.

After the first song, Riley enters the stage, carrying her guitar and her amp. She gets disapproving looks, especially from Liam, who raises his hands in a *what the fuck* gesture. James feels bad now. Whatever it is that made her late, she probably wouldn't be in this situation if he hadn't called her in the first place.

"Oh, she's fine as hell."

James glances to his left, where two drunk assholes cackle like little kids and stare at Riley while she's getting ready. He can't lose his shit. He promised. Let them say whatever they want, it's not like they're gonna get their way.

Riley bends over to plug her guitar to the amp, and one of the guys whistles, making the other one laugh.

James brings the beer to his lips and is disappointed as he remembers it's already empty. He's nowhere near as drunk as he'd like to be, and hot anger is seeping through his guts.

"I'd tap that ass," the guy says.

Keep your cool. They're just dicks.

Thankfully, the band starts playing again, and Riley's voice steals James's focus, annihilating the conversation the two dipsticks are having.

He allows himself to fix his eyes on her. It's the only time he can stare without being completely obvious, especially when Rudy is by his side. But he's alone now, hidden by the muted lights of the bar, and he can look all he wants.

Guilt crashes over him once again. He met her when she was fourteen, for fuck's sake. He was already an adult then. They've been friends for years. Hatred and self-loathing have been clinging to his skin for months now. Since Kelly's birthday party. He never should have gone there.

A few songs later, the three guys take a break, and Riley sits on a high stool with her acoustic guitar. God knows James loves rock music, the louder the better, but these bits of her singing alone are his favorites now. If Rudy were here, he'd probably go up on stage with her.

Riley adjusts the mic and pulls the hair tie off her long, straight, dark mane. She runs her fingers through her roots and sweeps her hair to one side, the strands draping her shoulder and arm. James can't avert his eyes, mesmerized by the brown undertones shining in the lights around her. When she raises her head, her silver eyes quickly flicker to him, sending a little shiver through his arms, and a ghost of a smile plays at the corner of her lips before she starts playing "True Colors."

"Did you see the things in her ears?" one of the idiots next to James says.

"Yeah, it's a hearing... thing."

"Do you think she can hear herself scream without them if you fuck her hard enough?"

The two guys laugh while staring at Riley, and anger flares inside James's chest again, his grip on the empty beer so tight he thinks he could break the bottle.

"Not sure she'll be able to scream with my dick in her mouth."

"Shut up," James snaps, giving them a murderous stare. "Say one more thing, and I'll kick your ass."

The two guys turn to him, grinning and looking him up and down.

"Hey, we're just having fun, man. No need to get angry."

His jaw tight, James looks at the stage again, straining to listen to the two men talking.

Go ahead, say one more thing. Give me a reason.

One of them cackles. "I wish she'd run her fingers over my cock like she does on her guitar."

James pushes away from the table hard enough to make it topple and grabs the guy's collar. He throws a punch, his knuckles connecting pleasantly with the guy's nose.

CHAPTER 6

Riley's grip on the guitar stiffens. She hits the strings harder than she should. A knot in her stomach tightens. She forgets the lyrics and stops playing, looking confusedly at where the bright red spots are coming from. In the middle of the room, people are agitated. The rest of the crowd doesn't pay attention to her anymore. Another fight has started, and James is right in the middle of it.

"For *fuck's* sake, Williams," she says into the mic, which doesn't stop him.

When a guy grabs his shoulder, James lets go of another man's collar, spins around, and shoves him. The other one drops on James's back, but James quickly shifts his weight and swings him over his shoulder and on the floor. Tables are knocked over. Beer bottles are smashed. Two other guys join the battle, and they're not on James's team. Marvelous.

This shit day will never end.

He's taller than the rest of them, and probably stronger too, but there's little he can do against four guys jumping on him at the same time. Riley glances to her right and meets Miguel and Liam's worried eyes. They shake their heads no, knowing she wants to jump in, as usual, and knowing they'll get in trouble because of it. She turns back to the fight. The more people that get involved in it, the harder it is to see. Surely, the owner will haul their asses out of here, right?

James takes a punch in the stomach, then in the face. Riley stands, glances to her right again, where Miguel and Liam shake their heads more vividly.

Fuck it.

She sighs and mouths to them, *"Sorry..."*

Before they can say anything, she puts her guitar on its stand and jumps off the stage. She makes her way through the crowd, cringing at the small currents jolting her body every time she touches them. She breaks through the mass and gets a clear view of the fight. James is clearly at a disadvantage. A guy turning his back to her raises his fist, and Riley kicks him behind the knee, making him lose his balance for a second, then shoves him harder. The man falls to the floor, and that little intervention is enough for James to gain an advantage again. A guy picks up a beer bottle and raises it.

Oh, no, you don't.

Riley jumps in and grabs his wrist before he can hit James. She twists it hard enough to make the man whimper and let go of the bottle. She kicks his ankle, sweeping his leg from under him and making him fall. Before any of them can retaliate, Riley seizes James's arm and drags him away from the chaos.

Miguel comes out of the bar, his feelings telling Riley everything she needs to know.

"So?" Liam says.

"We're banned for life. Well, Riley is. James as well."

"Fuck…"

"That's the third one," Keenan says, his dreadlocks framing his face as he turns to Riley.

Everyone looks at her. Keenan is annoyed. Liam is straight-up pissed. Miguel isn't angry, but definitely disappointed.

Riley chews on her lip. "I barely did anything…"

"You should have stayed away like we told you to," Liam says.

"I know… You're right. I'm sorry. It won't happen again."

Liam looks down, hesitating. "No. It won't. Because this just isn't working, Riley."

Her shoulders drop. "Dude…"

"You don't have time for us anymore. For *this*."

"That's not true."

"It *is*. I get it, you know. You're super busy, and we've been getting a lot more gigs, and sometimes it's hard to make it work. But you're *always* late and always distracted, and we can't keep getting banned from bars because James gets himself into fights and you have to fly to his rescue."

Riley swallows, her mind racing to find something to say. "I–"

"We've had a talk earlier," Liam says, cutting her off.

"About what?"

"Whether you should be in this band or not."

Her heart sinks. This was bound to happen, but she still hoped they wouldn't do this to her. They've been playing together for *years*. Since high school. Before *her* dad started booking most of their gigs, they played in *her* garage. "Come on... I..." But the words die in her mouth, and she turns to Miguel for help, resistant to the idea that he also agrees with this. "Miguel?"

He attempts a compassionate smile as he shrugs. "I'm sorry, amiga. We're still friends, you know, and we still love you, but... you've become unreliable. We're lucky that Keenan knows the lyrics to all the songs, otherwise we would have been in deep shit every time we had to start without you." He puts a hand on her shoulder, and all the feelings she could already pick up flow through her body. Guilt, mostly. "You understand, right?"

Riley nods, her throat too tight to speak. How stupid of her to have thought that James getting into a fight would be the last shitty thing happening today.

The band is allowed inside the bar only so they can retrieve their instruments. They pack up everything silently, each one of them focusing on their own task. Riley probably would have cried a few years ago. Not anymore. She has to put on her big girl pants and stop feeling sorry for herself. Life will carry on, and that's that. She won't allow herself to fall apart every time she hits a minor bump on the road.

After she says an awkward goodbye to her friends and shoves her two guitars and amp in her car, Riley looks around for James. He's not in sight, but he's still pissed, and it'll be easy to find him, wherever he is. Before locking her car, she grabs a pack of tissues and a bottle of water from the glove compartment. She has learned to come prepared.

Riley rounds the bar and crosses the parking lot, following the pull of his soul. Sure enough, James is sitting on the sidewalk, smoking a cigarette. She pauses for a moment, peering at him while he doesn't see her. He's colored in red and purple, still angry and frustrated. Also somewhat sad, like he's been for a while.

She walks to him silently and crouches in front of him. He peers at her without saying anything, either. His cheekbone has a bleeding cut, and his knuckles are raw, but otherwise, he's in pretty good shape. Riley pours some water from her bottle onto a tissue, soaking it, and raises it to his face.

He recoils slightly. "Don't do that."

"Hey." She points a finger to his face, the way she does when she wants someone to shut up. "You started this. So, stop being a baby."

He sighs and lets her pat his cheek with the wet tissue.

"Are you banned from the bar?" he asks.

"Yep. So are you."

"I'm sorry."

"That's not your fault. I made a choice. I could have let your dumb ass get beaten up, but I guess I don't have it in me."

"Next time, I'll—"

"There won't be a next time, Jamie."

He frowns and cocks his head, causing her to stop patting his bloody cheekbone. "What do you mean?"

Riley grabs his chin and turns his head the other way so she can clean up the blood caking his black beard. "I'm not in the band anymore." James turns his head toward her again, shocked. She sighs. "Will you stop moving?"

"They kicked you out?"

She drops onto the sidewalk next to him, giving up. "I've had it coming."

"Lovie, I'm sorry."

His guilt is growing, filling her, but the thing is, she's not mad at him. The mess she's been making lately is her own fault. Not his. Something needs to be discussed, though. "What the hell, Jamie?"

He turns away from her, his jaw working as he plugs the cigarette between his lips.

"It's not your first bar fight, we all know that," she continues. "But lately, you've been out of control, man. I don't know what's up with you, but you need to start controlling your anger because one day, you're gonna kill someone. Give a guy a brain hemorrhage or something."

James draws on the cigarette, still not answering.

"What set you off this time?"

"These guys were talking shit about you."

"Then, let them talk shit."

"You didn't hear what they said."

"I don't give a flying fuck about what people say about me, Jamie. You shouldn't, either."

James looks at her, his expression dark and angry. "I can't. I can't listen to a bunch of horny douchebags talk about you like you're some kind of sexual object. It *pisses me off*."

He turns away again, and they both sit for a while without speaking. It's not unlike James to be so mad all the time, but there's something he's not saying. Something he buried deep.

Riley wishes he would just say it, but the thing is, she doesn't have the courage to talk about it, either.

She picks up the water bottle and takes his right hand. He doesn't move as she pours some water on his knuckles and wipes the blood with a new tissue.

"I'm sorry Mrs. McCarthy grabbed your ass," she says with a small smile. "It was my fault. I encouraged her."

"I knew that," James says, cracking a smile too.

"I told her older women was your kink."

He laughs, making Riley do the same.

"I shouldn't have done that," she says. "If an old schmuck had grabbed my ass, I probably would have wanted to punch him in the face. So, I'm sorry if you felt violated."

James chuckles. "I'll live."

Riley takes his cigarette from him and draws on it. "Hey, um... Can I crash on your couch for a while? I need to find a new place to live, and I'd rather avoid any further awkward interactions with Kelly. We decided to part ways, I guess."

He peers at her for a moment, then nods, and Riley's grateful not to have to explain herself. "You could stay at your dad's, though. Your old room would be more comfortable than my shitty-ass couch."

"I know, but I don't want to impose. You know, with him living with Stella and all, I don't think he wants his adult child to move back in."

"Are you kidding? He'd do the happy dance if you moved back in. But sure. You can stay as long as you like."

It's good to know she still has one friend left. Riley finishes the cigarette and stubs it on the sidewalk next to her. "The night is still young. Wanna have a drink? It's been a shit day, I need it."

"The bar near my place? You can park at my apartment, and I'll pick you up there."

"Sounds like a plan."

"Let's go, then," James says.

"Please, don't fight again. At least not tonight."

"I fucking pinky swear."

CHAPTER 7

James and Riley settle at the bar and order whiskey shots. His cheekbone throbs a little, but it's not too bad. It could have been a hell of a lot worse. He needs to make it up to Riley somehow. Even if she said it wasn't his fault she got kicked out of the band, he knows it is, a little.

"Need a wingman tonight?" Riley says. "Pretty sure the blonde over there likes you."

"I'm not really in the mood."

"Nope, never mind, I think she likes *me*." Riley winks at the girl on the other side of the bar, who giggles and turns away.

"You're quite the Casanova."

"I've learned from the best," she says, bumping her shoulder against his. "But yeah, I don't think I'm in the mood, either."

They clink their glasses and take a shot.

Riley puts the glass down, spinning it between her fingers and staring at it for a while. "Daniel's getting married."

James does a double take. "Holy crap, seriously? Wow."

"Yeah."

"How do you feel about that?"

"Um... I mean, he did what I wanted him to do, you know. He got over me, and now he's happy." She grabs another glass and downs the whiskey.

"You didn't answer my question."

"I'm okay. A little stunned. It's just... I don't know. It's been a bad day."

"Hey."

Riley meets his eyes, and James tries to smile.

"You made the right call by breaking up with him. You said it yourself. It wasn't good for him to be with you."

"I know."

"But I think... it wasn't that good for you to be with him, either."

Riley's eyebrows shoot up almost to her hairline. She tilts her head, half-smiling. "*Really?* Can you elaborate on that?"

"You know how much I like Daniel."

"Mm-hm."

"And you're right. Even if he loved you, being with you was just too hard on him. He was scared and anxious all the time. Not just scared for himself, but for *you*. Might have been hard for him to get over you, but it feels to me like he's happier than ever."

"Please, keep going on about how shitty I made him feel."

"*But.* I know you thought he was keeping you grounded, but the truth is, you were addicted to his energy. Like a leech. I know I can't possibly understand what it's like to be you. Having to feel everyone around you all the time. But hijacking someone's aura doesn't make the problem go away, and I think it's good that you're learning to live with it. We all know you're particularly attracted to the 'yellow people.' Like that girl you met last year in Maine. The one with the baby and the supposedly haunted house."

"Hayden. Man, she was pretty. She had this crazy, curly, ginger hair—"

"Would you have been so addicted to Daniel if you hadn't been an empath?"

Riley scoffs as if the question is stupid, but James knows her. She's chewing on this, considering it. "I mean... Some people are addicted to other people, and they aren't empaths... I don't know. Pretty sure I would have still loved him."

"Maybe. But this thing you guys had... I know it was very strong, and I know you have nothing but good memories of it, but now that I see how he's doing, I think it was borderline unhealthy."

"That is *not* true."

James shrugs. "He was so anxious he was seeking your comfort and your reassurance all the time. You were so hooked on his 'brightness' that as soon as he was with you, nothing else mattered and you used his energy to tune out the rest."

Riley sighs, shaking her head. "I still do that."

"Do what?"

"Channeling on one person. You're right, I shouldn't. It's the easy way, but sometimes I just can't focus with all the noise. Why do you think I jump into a fight with you half of the time?"

Realization hits him, making him feel stupid for saying all these things to her. "You mean... Oh..."

"Yeah. When my dad's not here, *you're* the target. Because I feel you guys stronger than the rest. Because I know you so well, and I'm so close to you, it's just easier to pick up your energy through the crowd. But when you're pissed, then *I'm* pissed, and I don't know how to get out of it."

"That's why you didn't jump into the fights when your paternal was there..."

"'Cause I was focused on him, not you. So, sorry to disappoint you, but I still didn't learn to 'live with it.' I'm still channeled on you right now."

She takes another shot, and James does the same. What a dick. After all these years, he still hasn't figured her out. And now he's made her feel worse, which wasn't the initial intent. He just wants her to understand that there's a life beyond Daniel. That she made the right choice. That she can be happy if she wants it.

"I'm sorry, lovie."

"It's fine."

"I understand it's hard. Him getting married. He was your first crush, after all."

"Yeah... Thanks. I used to think he was the light guiding me when I stumbled in the dark. Now, it just feels like..." She shrugs. "I can't see."

If only she could say that about him, but that will never happen. "Hey. You've got me. I know I don't shine, but... it's better than nothing."

She cracks a smile. "You and I can stumble in the dark together."

"Yeah."

After a moment of silence and a few more shots, James asks, "What does it feel like?"

Riley looks up. "What?"

"Being an empath."

"You've never asked me that before."

"I just... I wish I could understand. I know it's easy for me to say you have to learn to control it when I have no clue what I'm talking about."

She peers at him, her beautiful eyes seemingly seeing *through* him, and James has to fight hard to keep his composure under her gaze. "Look at this room and all its people. There are quite a lot, right?"

James looks around and nods.

"You can only hear them talk, which is already loud. But now imagine that each of them is playing a fucking musical instrument without any regards for anyone around them."

A small laugh falls out of his mouth. "Sounds like hell."

Riley chuckles. "Yeah. All these people around me, it's like they play their own tune. Like they have their own theme song if you will. Everyone's song has a different tone and pace. Some are loud and fast, others are really slow and quiet. Some are sad, some are happy, or angry, and they all affect my mood. Then, you have someone like Daniel, Grace, or your friend Elijah walk into a room, and all the other songs are suddenly muffled, completely swallowed by a beautiful melody that you can't get tired of listening to, and that, let's be honest, makes you feel sort of high. When I channel on you or my dad, it's like I turn your volume up. The others don't disappear, but I hear them less, and it helps me focus a little better."

"What's my theme song?"

"You? 'Highway To Hell.'"

James laughs and nods, forced to admit that it fits him pretty well. "All right. I deserve that. And that's a pretty good fucking song. What about you?"

Riley grabs another small glass and slides one to James. "I'm 'Stairway to Heaven,' baby."

James clinks his glass with hers before ordering another round. He looks at the people again. He listens to them chatting and laughing and yelling, trying to imagine the sensory overload Riley feels on a daily basis. He has a headache just picturing all these people singing their own song or playing their own instrument. "What about demons?"

"What about them?"

"What do you feel when you're in the same room as one?"

"You're quite curious tonight, Jamie-bear."

"Tell me if that bothers you."

"It never does. Demons are weird. They're pure energy. Raw feelings. And they always hit me right through my core. But when I see one, it's like I'm looking into a twisted mirror. It *looks* like me, but also, it doesn't. We're on the opposite sides of the same spectrum. Completely different, but within the same species." She chuckles apologetically. "Does that make any sort of sense?"

"A little. I think. Like me and my brother. Same family, but opposite people."

"Yeah." She drinks another shot and looks down at the glass, playing with it. After a while, she fixes her gaze on him again. "You were wrong about one thing before. Daniel was my first love, yes, but he wasn't my first crush."

"Seriously? You're shitting me."

"I'm not," she says, and if the lights weren't so muted here, James could almost think she's blushing.

"I *cannot* believe that someone got Riley Winter's attention before Danny boy came into the scene, and I've known you for ten years."

"*Eleven* years. See? You're not the only one who keeps secrets."

"I believe I've made a lot of progress in opening up these past few years, but we're not talking about me right now, so *do tell*. Who was it? A hot teacher or something?"

Riley shakes her head, staring down and looking like she regrets saying anything at all. "It was you, you idiot."

"What, really?"

"Please, don't rub it in."

He doesn't want to. If anything, it almost hurts. If she had a crush on him before meeting Daniel, then it was before she was sixteen, at a time when he was lightyears away from looking at her this way. In other words, wrong place, worst time. But he won't say that. Instead, he'll act like the smartass he always is. "What did you like about me?"

"Dude, come on."

"Was it my luxurious, black hair?"

She playfully punches his shoulder. "You're an idiot."

"My handsome smile?"

"You're so modest, Williams."

"I'm just messing with you," he says, chuckling.

"I liked that you were nice to me. You know, when we met you at that asylum. I liked that you didn't look at me weird because I had hearing aids. I liked that you repeated yourself when I didn't understand what you said and that you weren't bothered by it. And... I liked that you seemed to like me even if I was a brat asking you annoying questions."

He swallows, trying not to show how touched he feels by this, and looks at her expectantly. *"And?"*

That mischievous smile plays on her lips as she raises one eyebrow. "And I thought you were hot."

He laughs, slamming his hand onto the wooden bar. "That's what I'm talking about!"

Riley shakes her head at him but can't hold back a laugh. She hands him another glass, and they clink them together before taking the shot.

What she said isn't lost on him, though. She mentioned the asylum, which means she had that crush when she was fourteen. She was *barely* a teenager. And now that she's twenty-five, *he's* getting dangerously close to his forties. Thirty-seven. There's just no way. He has to get over this stupid thing for her.

He admires how easily she said this to him, though. Riley was always open about things. Her dark past, her struggles, her fears. She could always share the darkest details without shame. Unlike him.

"What about you?" Riley asks. "Who was your first crush?"

"Honestly? I don't remember."

"Bullshit."

"No, it's the truth. I was called 'emotionally impaired' once, and it was probably true. I remember my first girlfriend, though. She was nice. *Too* nice. She thought I was the tortured, bad boy who needed to be saved, and because I was an absolute prick, I used that to get my way with her."

"Huh. Kelly said I was emotionally impaired today."

"Then, that's one more thing we have in common."

She chuckles and props her elbows onto the bar, resting her chin inside her palms and staring at him. "Keep talking."

"Hm?"

"You're in the mood for sharing. I like it."

"Oh, come on..."

"Did you ever have a pet?"

The question steals a laugh out of him. "A pet? *That's* what you want to know about? You're obviously hammered."

"After knowing you for eleven years, I feel like I *deserve* to know about any pet at that point."

"Well..." There *was* one pet, although it was unofficial. James wants to smile at first, but the memory mostly brings bitterness and sadness. Something he doesn't want to remember.

Riley's gentle fingers brushing his arm almost startle him. "Jamie?"

She felt his mood drop, of course she did, so James tries to regain his composure. "When I was twelve, a few months after my dad died, there was this brown little rabbit crossing my back yard every day. I know it's stupid, but at the time, I wanted to believe it was my dad, reincarnated into this creature to visit me." He scoffs at himself, but Riley doesn't flinch and keeps her hand on his arm, making his heart beat a little faster despite himself. "So, I started giving it some food, and as time passed, it let me get a little closer, until one day, I could touch it. Day after day, it came back and let me pet it. It helped me through my grief, you know?"

Riley smiles softly and nods.

"I named it Fluffy."

She bursts into laughter, which is infectious and gets to him as well.

"I *cannot* believe James Williams just said the word 'fluffy!'"

"All right, shut up."

"Dude, 'fluffy' is the cutest thing to ever come out of your mouth," she says, still laughing.

"Cut me some slack, I was twelve. Anyway. One day, Charles saw the rabbit."

"*Fluffy.*"

"Yes, Fluffy. Charles was six at the time, but already a little shit. He got jealous that Fluffy would let me touch it but not him. You know how my brother couldn't stand me having something he didn't, right? He *hated* that I was close to our dad, and then, he hated that Fluffy liked me and not him. That's why he hogged my mother and later fucked my ex-wife."

"I know."

"But... since we had just lost our dad, I thought it was my job to take care of him even if he was a shithead. So, I showed him how to get close to Fluffy. I told him to feed it. Told him he needed to be patient. But honestly, no matter what I tried, that rabbit *could not* stand Charles. Eventually, he threw a tantrum and stopped trying." James pauses and drinks yet another shot in an attempt to numb the acrid taste the words he's about to say will leave in his mouth. "One morning, I woke up with Fluffy's body torn in half and his guts spread all over my bed cover."

Riley's face falls. "Oh my God, Jamie..."

"Charles was standing in the doorway, watching me with that sickly grin on his face. I don't know how he did that to that rabbit. Or how he caught it. Then, he ran to our mother to tell her I was the one to have killed it, and she believed it because I was the so-called devil child." He clears his throat and signals to the barman he wants another round. He's not drunk enough to tell this story. "I've never told that to anyone."

Riley threads her arm around his bicep and lays her head against his shoulder. That's what she does now. She doesn't openly show that she's trying to soothe him, and James pretends he doesn't realize she's doing it. The truth is, they're both fully aware of what the other is doing. But James has learned to let her help, and for now, he enjoys the warmth spreading through his arm and body as much as he enjoys the weight of her head against his shoulder. His chest loosens, and the memory of the rabbit's intestines spread over his bedsheets fades into a distant blur.

Riley tilts her head up, still resting on his shoulder. "When I was a kid, I would build little habitats and put the snails in there. I called it the 'Snails Institute.'"

James smiles down at her, finding himself closer to her face than he's comfortable with. "'Snails Institute' might be the cutest thing to ever come out of your mouth."

Riley returns the smile, and James knows he should look away, but he can't. She doesn't, either, her gaze boring into him. If he dipped his head just a little, he could kiss her.

Suddenly, she breaks eye contact and straightens up, letting go of his arm. She swivels around and squints, gazing at something—or someone—in the distance. Any hint of a smile is gone, and her face darkens.

"You okay?" he asks, a bit taken aback by her sudden movements.

"Right there," she says, pointing at someone.

James turns around and looks at a women walking through the bar, her long, disheveled gray hair covering her shoulders. "What about her?"

"It's a demon."

CHAPTER 8

The woman's head twitches, and she freezes on the spot. Her eyes turn black and fix directly on Riley. It's strong. *Really* strong. Riley hasn't felt such a strong shadow since Terrestre when she was sixteen.

She grips James's wrist without looking at him, unable to avert her gaze from the shadow. "Get the lockbox from your trunk. Now."

James leaves without a second of hesitation, leaving Riley with the pulsing energy of the entity pressing against her skin.

The demon breaks eye contact and advances through the mass of people. Riley follows it, actively regretting the number of shots she's just had. Because of the entity in the room, the alcohol doesn't sit well in her stomach, and the air around her is as uncomfortably sticky and hot as it's been all summer.

She loses the view of the woman, but it doesn't matter. She has locked her focus on the demon's energy and can follow it easily through the crowd. It's not trying to get away from her, either. It wants her to follow. Of course, it does. No matter how tasty the person it's possessing is, it's probably nothing compared to Riley.

She enters the narrow, stinky hallway leading to the bathroom just in time to see the back door close shut. Riley takes her phone out and quickly texts James.

Meet me in the back.

She takes a deep breath, dodging the few people gathered here, makes for the back exit, and pushes the door open. She finds herself in a small court with dumpsters jammed with trash. Wooden planks, empty cans, and bottles litter the ground. The demon stands motionless a few paces ahead, a crooked smile on the woman's face.

Riley winces as a chill crawls down her spine. "A demon walked into a bar... Sounds like the beginning of a bad joke, don't you think?"

The shadow cocks its head. "You're different than the others."

Its voice grates at Riley's nerves, as usual, but she shakes it off. "Want a little taste?"

The demon's smile fades away, and it lets out a hungry grunt of anticipation.

Riley squares her shoulder. "Then, come and get me."

The entity shrieks, and Riley has to brace herself not to stagger backward. It still splits her head open after all this time, but she's gotten better at handling it. The thing rushes to her, tendrils of black ectoplasm already crawling out of the woman's mouth. Riley channels on it, reaches out, grabs it. The woman abruptly stops a yard from her, bent forward as the demon tries to push through Riley's hold, snarling. It's even stronger than she'd thought. Stronger than Terrestre was, but she's stronger than she was back then too.

Riley's head throbs, her mental energy and alcohol-soaked brain unprepared for such brutality. Warm liquid trickles from her nose as she keeps the entity from advancing. The demon bends forward further, struggling to get through Riley's energy wall.

The dumpsters shake. The various trash on the ground clatters and trembles. They spin and shoot through the air, shattering against the walls. An invisible force—the demon's mind power—tugs at her clothes and hair, trying to move her closer. Objects and things are easy to move. They're dead things. Empty. Moving a body, full of its own energy and force, with telekinesis alone would require tremendous strength, and no demon is strong enough to do that.

Where the fuck is Jamie?

A glass bottle shoots in her direction, hitting her temple before she sees it coming. The sudden blast of pain makes her lose her balance, breaking the energy contact between her and the entity. By the time she swivels back to the thing, the woman slams her against the door and circles her hands around her throat.

Riley slaps her hand against the woman's mouth, willing the black tendrils of ectoplasm to stay inside. They push against her, fighting to crawl out and slide through her fingers.

A can hits her face. Then, another one. Riley clenches her teeth, powering through it all, until the broken shard of a bottle flies toward her and stabs her forearm. The sudden pain makes her cry out and drop her hand. The demon shoots forward directly inside her throat. It begins its descent through her, moving against her will, and slowly clouding her mind. It sees her memories, just as she sees its own.

Screams. Blood. Fire. Blades sinking into tender flesh.

The ectoplasm suddenly leaves her, and Riley falls to her knees, light-headed and gasping for breath. She blinks the bright flashes out of her vision until James comes into focus. He's holding the woman down and has fastened the glowing amulet around her neck. The entity fights him fiercely, clawing at him and trying to crawl back to Riley.

Still dizzy, Riley stumbles to her feet and drops down next to them, opening the lockbox. She pulls the glass shard out of her arm with a grunt and uses her blood to paint the inside of the iron box. Now angered by the images she saw, she plants her fingers on the woman's temple, reaching out to the shadow inside, and forces it out.

"Get the *fuck* out."

It doesn't leave the body without a fight. It claws at them, snarling and grunting, and even James has a hard time pinning it down. When it crawls out of the body, it still tries to slide to Riley. Its black tendrils stretch in her direction, curling around her arm and throat, but thanks to the UV light stick James is burning it with, they manage to drive it inside the lockbox. She slams it close and locks it, finally allowing herself to sit back and take deep, slow breaths.

The dizziness lingers, churning her stomach. Call it pride or call it being an ass, but after all the years she's spent saying she could hold her liquor, the idea of vomiting and proving she was wrong isn't appealing. She closes her eyes and keeps breathing through her nose, trying to ignore the ache on her temple and the hot pain in her arm.

"You're bleeding," James's somewhat distant voice says.

"Mm-hm."

A gentle pat on the cheek forces her to open her eyes and stare at James's dark irises.

"Hey, lovie, you with me?" His warm fingers cupping her face might be the only good feeling at the moment, except for the fact that his fear slashes through her. The rest is just nausea and pain and sweat.

"I may or may not have gotten too cocky on that one."

"No *shit*. You need to be more careful. You know that if you ever get possessed, we can't do anything to help you."

The lady on the ground moans and shifts. Riley gives James the lockbox and shuffles to her knees, close to the woman to help her up. "It's all right. You're okay now."

The woman blinks at Riley. Now that the demon has left her body, she looks even older, the creases around her eyes deep and her mass of gray hair limp on the ground. Acne scars cover her cheeks.

The dazed, unfocused expression only lasts a second. Riley feels a shift in the woman's feelings. Her face hardens, and her hand flies to Riley's face with baffling agility, striking her already bloody nose.

Blinded by the surprise slap, Riley stumbles backward and is quickly assaulted and pinned down by the screaming lady.

"You *whore!*"

Riley raises her arms in an attempt to shield herself from the rain of fists dropping on her, the woman's screams filling her head and her hatred stabbing her guts.

The weight pressing on her vanishes, and she gets a glimpse of James yanking the woman off her with one hand.

"*Knock it off,*" he snaps.

The woman staggers back, shocked, and glares daggers at him, her lips turned up into a snarl. "You *monsters.*"

"What the fuck, lady?" Riley says, sitting back up and wiping her bloody nose. Her voice shakes from all the hatred and nausea, and her vision hasn't come back into focus yet. Whiskey is also to blame for this. "We *saved* you."

The woman lunges at James. Unflinching, he raises his hand high to make sure he doesn't drop the lockbox, while she pounds his chest and shoulders, shrieking hysterically.

"All right, that's enough," he says, reaching for the gun tucked in his belt behind his back.

The woman takes a few steps back, eyes as wide as saucers, as he points the gun at her.

"You must be a giant piece of shit to have been possessed by a demon this strong and still have all your head," he says, his voice low and menacing. "I don't know who you are, but I'm gonna call the police if you're still here in ten seconds."

"You... How dare you..."

"Fuck off. *Now.*"

Riley, still sitting on the ground and too dizzy to get up, watches as the woman walks backward. Her jaw is clenched, and tears well in her eyes as she starts pulling her hair and pounding her head in frustration. She suddenly points a finger toward Riley, locking a murderous stare on her. "I will destroy you, you hear me? *Destroy you.*"

James doesn't flinch, still pointing his gun at her until she disappears around the bar.

Riley throws her hands up. "What the hell was that? That was super weird, right?"

James tucks the gun in his belt and turns to her, a playful grin stretching the corners of his lips. "You got your ass kicked by an old lady."

Riley's shoulders drop, and she presses her mouth into a tight line. "What was I supposed to do, punch her? I'm not gonna hit an old person. But apparently, you have no problem doing it."

"I pulled her away from you. I didn't hit her. Nuance." He crouches next to her and hooks an arm around her waist to help her to her feet.

Riley hangs onto him. The world spins, and she slowly breathes through her mouth as her stomach threatens to revolt.

"Please, don't puke on my shoes," James says. "I thought you could hold your liquor."

"It's not the booze, it's *her*. Man, she was, like, *really* bad. We need... we need to do something."

"Yes, we do. We need to get you to bed. You look like crap."

"I'm fine." An outright lie since her upset stomach is still doing unpleasant flips while her nose throbs and her arm pulses.

James lets go of her and picks up the amulet and the UV light stick. Tucking everything in his pocket, he stands in front of Riley and bends his knees. "Come on, I'll give you a piggyback ride to the car."

She'd like to say no, but they had to park across the street and two blocks away because the parking lot was packed. The demon's overpowering energy and the woman's hatred seep out of her body, leaving her legs feeling numb. She places her hands on James's shoulders and jumps on his back.

"Hold that for me," he says, handing her the lockbox.

She takes it and tightens her other arm around him as he hooks his hands behind her knees. Riley rests her chin on his shoulder, letting his colors fill her. They're a little brighter now. Calmer.

"Thanks, Jamie-bear," she mumbles, already close to falling asleep as he strides through the parking lot, seemingly unbothered by her weight on his back.

"You're welcome, lovie."

CHAPTER 9

The front door opens with a creak, and Rudy crosses the living room to meet Stella in the hallway.

"I was starting to worry," he says.

"I'm sorry. I wanted to call you, but, you know."

"Shitty day."

"Like you can't imagine."

He can. Her phone call has left him more anxious than he has any right to be. They need to talk about her case again. For now, he walks to her and wraps his arms around her. "How about you eat something? You probably haven't had anything today."

She attempts a smile as she pulls away, though her eyes are dark-rimmed with fatigue. "Not sure I'm hungry."

"Just sit with me, then."

Rudy plants a kiss on her mouth and leads her into the kitchen. He sits her down on one of the chairs before opening a cupboard and grabbing two whiskey glasses and the bottle that goes with it. Rudy settles them onto the table, pours them a drink, and slides one glass to her.

"You're too good to me," she says, taking the glass.

"That mac and cheese casserole's still warm, you know."

"Stop trying to charm me into eating." She tilts her head, eyeing the casserole. "Though, I must say it, *does* look good."

"I'll make you a plate. You don't have to eat it."

She smiles and downs half of her drink. Rudy knows she'll eat something if he puts the plate in front of her. After a horrible day, she needs fuel, even if it's nearly midnight.

He takes a plate out and scoops a spoonful of macaroni, making sure to put a lot of bacon bites and grilled cheese on top. He slides the dish in front of her and bends down to kiss the mass of brown curls on her head, his hand lingering on her shoulder. Before he can pull it away, Stella squeezes it, resting her head against his stomach for a moment.

"Are you okay?" he asks, knowing the answer.

"I don't know."

"Wanna talk about it?"

"I don't know what's left to say."

Rudy rounds the table and sits across from her. "It might help clear your head, so go ahead. Tell me everything like it's the first time."

She sighs, peering at him with dark green eyes. The same eyes he'd found himself attracted to the day he visited her after dropping Daniel off at the airport four years ago. He stayed away for a while. Because having lost Grace a second time had slashed through an unhealed wound that refused to close. Because he didn't see Stella as a one-night stand. Because he was afraid to fall in love again. Molly had helped him move on, yes, but it had left him a little stunned when she decided to go back to England.

But he and Stella seemed to be crossing paths constantly after the 'Alison incident.' She dropped by a few times at Winter's Attic–to Riley's delight and Rudy's as well, even if he tried to hide it–asking for info on paranormal stuff or books or EMF sensors.

"She doesn't care about that stuff, she came to see *you*," Riley always said, shaking his arm to stop him from rummaging into the back room. "Ask her out."

"She just got divorced."

"That didn't stop you from dating Molly."

After months of Riley and James's constant nagging, Rudy eventually picked up the phone and called Stella, finding himself more awkward than he'd thought he would be.

He smiles at her now, trying to look comforting, and nods to signal he's listening.

"Same thing as the others," Stella says. "We found the victim in the woods. Hands and feet severed. Eyes removed. Teeth pulled out. So many stab wounds in the face that it looks like it went through a shredder."

"Male or female this time?"

"Female. Has no connection to the others. Different age, different demographic, different social class. She wasn't killed in the woods, either. None of the victims have been killed where they were found. Whoever did this is always going out of their way to place them in some random location. The next body could pop up twenty or two hundred miles away."

Stella finishes her glass and exhales while Rudy watches her, speechless and disgusted that a human being could be capable of such brutality.

"It's the nineteenth body, Rudy. *Nineteen.* And we have no clue who it is."

"Do you have the pictures of the victims with you? I could take a look at them."

She scowls and shakes her head. "No."

"Maybe I can help."

"You can't do more than an army of cops and forensic specialists. I won't make you look at these pictures. I know you've seen messed up shit in your career, but trust me, it's nothing compared to these murders. And it's not like I have a right to show you."

"We've worked together a few times now. Sometimes you have to do things you're not supposed to if the case is a paranormal one."

She sighs. "It's not paranormal. I think I would know by now."

"I just wanna help. If anything, I can provide moral support. This case is weighing on you, and I'm worried."

Stella hesitates, chewing on her lip. "Of course you're worried. You always are."

"So, let me help and take care of you. Not that you need to be taken care of."

She smiles despite herself. Stella is a strong, stable woman who doesn't like to ask for help. Rudy knows she doesn't need anyone to carry her, but some support never hurt anyone.

"All right," she says, sliding her chair back and getting up.

She heads to the foyer to fetch her folder. When she's back in the kitchen, she stands next to the table, sliding the thick folder in front of him.

"It's gruesome. Be prepared."

Rudy nods and opens the folder. His heart makes an unpleasant flip in his chest just at the sight of the first picture. He swallows, trying to conceal his emotions. A handless and footless body is sprawled on a carpet of dry leaves and dirt. The mutilated, bruised, and swollen face looks up to the sky with empty eye sockets. Clothes are gone, showing the person suffered many injuries before being killed.

"What happened to her before she died?"

"Her knees were broken, most likely struck with a hammer. She was burned in several places with either some type of kitchen appliance or a curling iron, which would indicate she was killed in a somewhat furnished place and then moved into the woods ninety miles away from her home. That's the first one we found, and the only one who didn't have her hands and feet severed. No nails, though."

Rudy looks at the next picture. It's a man this time, missing his feet and hands and eyes as well. His mouth hangs open, showing nothing but a bloody pit with no teeth. His body has been propped into a sitting position, his naked back resting against the dark bark of a tree.

"They're always found in the woods, right?"

"Yes. Never the same woods, though. No matter where the killer lives or kills, they don't give off any clue of their location."

Rudy continues onto the next picture. He flips through them, more sickened and unsettled at each one. Stella *saw* them. She was there, in the woods, smelling the wafts of decay and hearing the buzzing of flies. A chill crawls down his spine. He's seen twisted shit in his life, but he doesn't envy her job. He admires her for having nerves made of steel.

Her hand grazes the back of his neck. "You don't have to keep going."

"How can you be sure it's a human doing these things?"

"Because what they're doing… it's human behavior."

Rudy sits back and looks up at Stella. "Walk me through your thought process."

Stella crosses her arms against her chest, gazing down at the pictures. "It's a signature. Always the same process. He wants to make sure we know it's the same person doing this."

"You think it's a man?"

"Most likely. Only because carrying a body deep into the woods would require strength."

"Maybe they had some kind of vehicle."

"He didn't. We didn't see any traces of one. Only footsteps." She rests one hand on the side of the table and points at the pictures. "He always makes sure they're unrecognizable. He clearly takes pleasure in torturing his victims before killing them, but disfiguring them isn't done randomly. He wants to strip them of their identity and dignity. Make them faceless. It's a statement. We still have unidentified bodies to this day, but for the ones we could identify, the only connection between the victims is that they were successful in some way. A big career, a loving family, or… esthetically pleasing."

Rudy raises his eyebrows. "He's angry at people he considers attractive?"

Stella nods. "Our killer is a nobody. An ugly loser who was probably belittled many times in his life. Someone with a strong inferiority complex who wants to take revenge on the same type of people who used to mock him and make him feel like a failure. Anyone better than him in some way is frightening to him."

Rudy lets his eyes sweep over the pictures again, his mind naturally wandering back to his daughter, as always. "Do you have the identity of today's victim?"

"Not yet, but we might have a lead on that. A woman was reported missing a few days ago in the area, and we think it could be her. We have to see if the hair matches."

"How old was she?"

"Don't go there, honey."

"How old?"

Stella sighs. "Twenty-six."

It doesn't matter how many years Riley has done MMA, or how she switched to Krav Maga last year, or that she's probably hanging out with her strong, six foot and four inches tall best friend right now, Rudy will always worry about her. Trouble always seems to find her, and he has to resist the urge to call her.

"Like I said, we don't know if it's her yet," Stella says. "This is why I didn't want to show you, by the way. You always worry too much."

"Worry's my middle name."

She bends over and brushes his cheek with light fingers. "She's okay. And like I said, this killer is probably human."

Rudy frowns. "Probably? You made it seem like you were absolutely sure."

"It's most likely."

"Not a hundred percent sure, then."

Stella gathers the pictures and shuts the folder before settling back in her seat across from Rudy. She finally picks up her fork, sliding the plate in front of her. "I told you there were no traces of any vehicle. The killer came on foot to hide the bodies, sometimes so deep into the woods it would have taken *hours*. All the bodies were found by adventurous hikers, which also means there could be other bodies that we'll never find. Others that might have been eaten by worms and wild animals already."

Rudy nods his understanding.

"The thing is," Stella continues, "I saw something weird today. A set of footprints near the crime scene. I tried to follow them, but..."

"But what?"

"They vanished."

"What do you mean they vanished?"

"I mean that we could actually follow those clear prints on the ground, until they... stopped. In front of a tree, as if... It's stupid, but as if they climbed it. Have you ever heard of a paranormal creature that would check all these boxes?"

Rudy slowly shakes his head, his mind scrambling to come up with something, but he finds himself clueless.

"And the behavior... it's just so *human*. He must have found a way to get away without leaving prints. Another way than climbing a damn tree. Some kind of device... I don't know." She plants the fork in the macaroni and eats a spoonful, exhaling at the same time. "I didn't know I was hungry until I started eating. This is delicious."

"Well, eat, then take a warm shower, and maybe things will be less foggy after a good night's sleep."

"I sure hope so."

CHAPTER 10

Riley drops onto James's couch, or rather, she's being dropped by him. She fell asleep in the car. Her mind is foggy, and some of the queasiness lingers. The faux-leather couch feels too hot under her. Not bothering sitting up or opening her eyes, she kicks her shoes off and unbuttons her jeans. She pulls them down, making it as far as her knees, but her groggy limbs won't move further.

"Jamie, pull my pants off."

His discomfort shoots through the roof and fills the room. "Hell no."

"*Please.* I'm too hot to sleep in jeans. And there's no way I can pull them back up anyway."

He grunts, his footsteps backtracking in her direction. The jeans slide off her legs, and Riley cracks an eye open. She bites back on a laugh.

"Don't make that face, I'm wearing boxers, not a G-string."

He shakes his head and disappears in the bathroom, coming back out ten seconds later with bandages, antiseptic spray, and sterile gauze. He sits next to her on the couch, and

Riley lets him bandage her arm while she pats her own nose with the gauze.

"It's not deep. You won't need stitches."

"Cool."

"Let me see that," he says, taking the gauze from her.

Riley keeps her eyes open despite how difficult it feels and watches him as he searches her face and makes sure there's no blood left. It's weird to be lying down like this with him hovering above her, and her heartbeat kicks up a notch.

"You'll have a little bruise there." He brushes her temple slightly in the spot she was hit by a beer bottle.

"Pretty lucky, overall."

"Yeah." James packs up everything and gets off the couch. "Don't fall asleep with your hearing aids."

"Right." She reaches for the devices in her ears and gently sets them on the coffee table. "Good night."

He says good night in sign language and flicks the lights off before heading to his bedroom.

She rolls over on her side, her clouded mind already conjuring chunks of absurd dreams. Blurred images of the demon's memories crowd her thoughts. The face of the hateful woman jumps back at her, quickly prompting a train of thoughts leading to the shadow man. Lance. Her old house. The closet.

When Riley opens her eyes, a gasp catches in her throat. The shadow man is here, standing next to the couch and looking down at her. Her body feels like lead, heavy and limp.

Close your eyes. It's sleep paralysis.

Riley breathes through it, feeling the shadow man bending over, his face hovering just inches above hers. Her eardrum vibrates as if someone breathes close to her ear. The dread squeezing her chest intensifies.

Her body jerks awake. She looks around, her heart pounding and her hair plastered against her face and neck with sweat. The shadow man's gone. Thin strands of moonlight seep through the window above the couch, allowing her to read the time on the clock hanging on the opposite wall. Three fifty-five. She's been asleep for more than three hours. It feels like three minutes.

Parched, her mouth pasty and her throat dry, Riley extracts herself from the couch and drags her body to the kitchen. She rounds the countertop and opens the fridge, desperate for some ice cold water. After drinking directly from the bottle, she presses it against her neck and chest, savoring the feeling of the fresh plastic on her burning skin. It's always so hot in this room. Why there isn't a ceiling fan here when there's one in the bedroom is a mystery.

Riley settles back on the too-warm couch, lifting her tank top in an attempt to refresh her stomach. It doesn't work. The air is too thick and hot. The faux-leather sticks to her skin. She tries to distract herself from the humid heat and images of the shadow man, hoping she can go back to sleep.

Think happy thoughts.

Today didn't bring anything happy, which doesn't help. Her sixth sense naturally channels onto James in the next room. It's peaceful, stable, dreamless. Her mind wanders to Kelly's last birthday in November. That's when something changed. The night itself was a good night. Well, it started being good when James showed up. It's later that shit hit the fan.

Although Riley doesn't mind crowded bars, she very much minded the karaoke nightclub with multicolored, blinding lights that make you feel like you'll have a seizure any time. Add to this the struggle to hear people talk and squinting to read their lips, and you've found yourself a wonderful, pounding headache.

Liam and Miguel showed up for good measure but left pretty early on, leaving Riley alone and standing awkwardly on the high heels Kelly had forced her to wear.

"They'll go well with your outfit," Kelly had said. "You need a feminine touch."

Because apparently, what the tight, black vest and skinny black jeans needed were a pair of evil shoes that felt like they were trying to shred Riley's feet with each move.

It's not the bitchiness of Kelly's friends that made her call James. Not even the comments on Riley being weird and a freak. It's when they started talking about Daniel and looked at Riley with fake pity and an exaggerated pursing of the lips. Despite Kelly's efforts to try to make her fit in, Riley could feel these girls' disdain for her, and the pompous satisfaction at seeing her single.

"I actually have a boyfriend," Riley blurted out, instantly regretting it.

One raised her eyebrows, another cocked her head, one chuckled, recognizing the cheap attempt to avoid embarrassment. Kelly was having an animated conversation with other friends of hers a little farther away, which Riley was grateful for. Her reaction would have given her away.

"*Really?*" the not so stupid one said, fully aware of the lie.

Riley broke eye contact and took a sip of her drink. "Yeah."

"Where is he, then?"

"He couldn't make it tonight."

The three girls eyed each other, grinning. "How convenient."

Riley reached for her phone in her pocket. "My phone's buzzing. Might be him."

She turned away to hide from the others the pitch-black phone that was definitely not ringing. She looked for James's number and called him, nodding briefly at the girls in a *I'll be back* gesture, and walked outside of the club. Freezing air bit at her exposed arms, but escaping the deafening pulse of the music felt good.

"What's up?" James said. "Aren't you at Kelly's birthday party?"

"I am. And I need you to come and be my date."

A beat of silence followed, and she could easily imagine him frowning, his body slumped on the couch as he watched TV and wore his AC/DC shirt, the one with a hole in it. "Say what?"

"I may have told Kelly's friends I have a boyfriend, which you already know is a lie."

"Why would you say that?"

"I don't know... A stupid defense mechanism against criticism. But of course, they saw right through me, and I just... I know it's dumb, but I need to prove them wrong."

"Even if they're right."

Riley sighed through gritted teeth. "Yes."

"You have nothing to prove to anyone, lovie. Don't let these assholes bully you. And why don't you ask Miguel or Liam? They're your age at least."

"They were here earlier. Miguel showed up with Keenan, and Liam left with one of Kelly's friends after making out with her the whole evening." She paused, waiting for an answer, feeling so awkward and embarrassed she was ready to run away any minute, even without her jacket to protect her from the early snow, and shredders at her feet. "Please, Jamie. I'll owe you big time."

He sighed. "All right. Give me half an hour. I need to shower. And text me the address."

"Thank you."

She hung up, texted him the address with increasingly numb fingers, and hurried back inside, her skin stinging. Maybe she could find a quiet place to wait, *alone* if possible, but that proved difficult when Kelly took her hand and pulled her back inside the circle of wolves. She stood there, not participating in the conversation if she could avoid it. Tuning them out was pretty easy with the loud music, at least until one of the girls from earlier planted herself in front of her.

"So, what's the name of this boyfriend of yours?"

Riley couldn't hear much but the lights were bright enough for her to read the girl's lips. "Uh, James."

"James," she repeated, nodding, her smile so pinched it looked like her lips would splinter. "And what does he do?"

"Um..." Talking about Winter's Attic is always easy. A good cover. Which is the truth for her and her dad. But aside from her close friends, Riley doesn't go around telling people about the paranormal investigation business. And the thing is, James doesn't work at Winter's Attic. "Pest control." It's not *that* far from the truth since many ghosts often turn out to be rats.

"Right..."

"Actually, his plans got cancelled tonight. He'll be here any minute."

This time the girl's eyebrows shot up to her hairline, her surprise pleasing Riley.

After a painful half hour of making small talk and staring at people's lips without blinking, James's energy finally pierced through the noise. Riley kept glancing at the front door, anxious to see him walk in and annoyed that Kelly's friends kept asking her when the imaginary boyfriend was going to show up and grace them with his presence.

Then, there he was, stepping in and searching for her. Riley did a double take. His beard was cleanly trimmed, his normally shaggy-looking hair was still a little wet and brushed back, and that gray jeans button-down shirt looked surprisingly good on him, the sleeves rolled up to his elbows.

Without a word to the others, Riley walked through the crowd on feet that felt like they were marinating in their own blood.

His face lit up at the sight of her, and he opened his mouth, but Riley didn't let him talk and jumped on him, throwing her arms around his neck, and wrapping her legs around his waist. Thankfully, he was used to her jumping on him—on his back usually—and quickly caught his balance.

"Woah, what are you—"

"Just play along," she said.

She planted a kiss on his mouth, shutting him up before he could talk. She hadn't thought this through *at all,* certain this was no big deal since they had known each other for so long. But their lips connecting sent a warm jolt through her body, unexpected and uncomfortably pleasant.

Riley pulled away, her body suddenly tense, while James stared at her, his body even tenser. She scrambled off of him, clearing her throat, and quickly glanced at the group of friends farther away. They were watching, their jaws dropping. Mission accomplished.

"Sorry about that..." she said, glancing back at James.

He waved her away as if it was nothing, but his discomfort was evident, his motion stiff. "It-it's fine. Let's go prove them wrong. I'll be the boyfriend of the year."

She chuckled, relieved that he didn't decide to leave after this. "Okay."

"You're surprisingly tall," he signed, as they approached the others.

"Five inches taller thanks to these torture devices."

She hooked her arm around his and introduced him to the others. Kelly cocked her head at the sound of the word 'boyfriend,' giving Riley an amused smile, but thankfully decided to play along. The others looked him up and down, appraising him. Riley had only wanted to make herself feel better by pretending she had a boyfriend, but she hadn't foreseen the feelings that were now emanating from some of these girls. They were impressed, painted with muddy, green jealousy that instantly lifted Riley's mood.

It reminded her of why she had been so attracted to James when she was younger. Sure, he was nice and funny, if a little gruff, but those almost-black eyes of his and handsome smile could have melted her. An unwelcome swarm of butterflies fluttered in her stomach as James wrapped an arm around her, playing the good boyfriend. A simple, innocent thing he had done many times before, which now felt entirely different.

Tired of making conversation and reading everyone's lips, they started focusing less on the others and began having more fun together. Drinking, talking in sign language, and laughing. The karaoke torture eventually ended to make place for *real* music, and when "Don't Stop Believing" by Journey came on, James dragged her to the dance floor, even though she knew for a fact he hated to dance.

"Come on, this is the best song."

Actively ignoring the nagging memory that he had once told her this song was great for a first kiss, Riley shook her head. "I can barely walk with these."

"Then, take them off."

"I'm not taking my shoes off!"

"Take. Your shoes. Off."

He was dead serious, so she proceeded to take the shredders off, letting out a gasp of relief.

They were together, having fun, and for a moment, it felt like nothing had changed between them.

It's what happened later that changed everything.

Dark blue sorrow seeps through Riley's skin, jolting her awake. She fell asleep thinking about that memory, and now tears prick her eyes. It comes from James. He must be having a nightmare. What is he dreaming about? Despite how much he tries to hide it, James has many unhealed wounds. But he's not scared or angry at the moment.

Grief.

. Whatever or whoever's in his head right now makes him deeply sad and full of remorse. Maybe it's a dream about Grace and how he had to put her down. Maybe it's about his unloving mother.

Restless from the sorrow, Riley rolls off the couch and heads to his bedroom. In the dark, she can make out the shape of his body, curled up to the side and clutching the sheets. She walks to the bed and stands behind him, bending over and putting a gentle hand on his shoulder. He's only wearing sweatpants. No shirt. And the feeling of his hot skin under her fingers sends a new jolt like an electric current.

"Jamie."

He doesn't stir, deeply asleep despite the nightmare he must be having. He might not even remember it in the morning. Still, the ceiling fan beating the air above her feels good, and the prospect of returning to the living room isn't appealing.

Riley rounds the bed and settles in the empty space, facing James. The moonlight floods the room, seeping through the window behind her and shining its silver glow on him. His body is tense, his fists tightly clenched, and his brow slightly furrowed. She rests a hand on his cheek, gazing at him while she takes as much of his negative feelings as she can.

"I wish I knew what you were thinking," she whispers.

Of all the people she's ever known, James has always been the hardest to read. Sometimes being an empath has its limits, and he's a master at hiding his feelings. She's rarely surprised by what people do or say, but James always does things she doesn't expect.

She brushes the side of his face, grazes his eyebrow with her thumb, and runs her fingers through his hair, still soothing him. He exhales, his body and face relaxing, his fists loosening.

Riley falls asleep, enjoying that little moment of peace she could offer his tortured mind.

CHAPTER 11

Sunlight pours through the window, piercing James's skull. His drunk ass forgot to shut the blinds last night, and the orange light of the early morning is too fucking bright for his liking. He blinks sleep out of his eyes, and his heart jumps in his throat as he finds himself face to face with Riley. He freezes and holds his breath as though he's done something shameful, then remembers he's in his own bed, in his bedroom, and *she's* the one who shouldn't be here. Still, for a moment, he can't avert his eyes. Her dark hair is sprawled all over the pillow, some of it spilling on his side. If he moved his fingers just an inch, he could touch it.

Riley shifts slightly. James breaks out of his paralysis and scrambles off the bed, flustered. It's not the first time Riley crashes on his couch, but she has never ended up in his bed, not with him in it, and waking up next to her like this, knowing he can't have her, fills him with dismay.

A freezing cold shower. That's what he needs. It'll clear his head. He takes clean clothes from his dresser and heads to the bathroom. Once he's done showering, feeling as though he washed some of his frustration away, he goes to the kitchen to make coffee. Before it's done, James hears the shower running in the bathroom. She's awake, then.

A few minutes later, she comes in the kitchen, her hair weighed down by moisture, wearing her boxers and his black AC/DC shirt that is three times too big for her. She has rolled up the sleeves and knotted the bottom. It looks pretty cute on her. Riley fetches her jeans and socks next to the couch and pulls them on. James turns away, pretending to look through the window.

"Don't worry, I'll give it back," she says with a smile, as she puts her hearing aids on. "My tank top reeks after spending the whole day and night sweating in it."

James slides a cup of coffee on the countertop as Riley sits down. "No worries." He wants to ask her what the hell she was doing in his bed but decides against it. Showing her how much that bothered him might make him look suspicious.

"I've been thinking about that lady," Riley says, holding her cup with two hands and drinking from it. "We shouldn't have let her go."

"Maybe, but there's nothing we can do about it now."

"Actually, there is."

James raises his eyebrows, waiting for her to elaborate, but all she does is stare back until the little light in his brain switches on.

"Wait, you don't mean—"

"Yes."

He sets his mug down. "Are you out of your fucking mind? Absolutely not."

"She was *dark*."

"I don't care. You're not doing this."

"I saw bits of the demon's memories. *Her* memories. It wasn't clear, but I think she did terrible things."

"Yes, probably under the demon's influence."

"Maybe, but..." She shrugs, sighing. "She was so angry afterwards."

"She was probably confused, lovie—"

"This is what we do, Jamie. We *help* people. And we might have put them in danger by letting her go." She pauses, her silver eyes swallowing him. "You promised you'd always trust my instincts."

James looks down, chewing on this. He *did* make that promise, and he meant every word. But this, what she wants to do, it's *insane*. "Your paternal will kill me if he finds out."

"We'll do it in the daylight. We'll secure everything."

"What do you mean by secure—"

"Tie me up."

That sends a set of mental images he'd rather not think about, and he shakes them away. After debating internally, he looks at her again. "We're gonna go see your dad and ask him what he thinks about it."

"Oh, come on. You know he'll never agree."

"That's my condition. If you really want to go through with this, he'll have to be on board."

Her shoulders drop, but she nods. "Okay. Come on. We should go now before we open the bookshop."

James downs the rest of his coffee and watches her as she takes the lockbox resting on one of the shelves. This is insane, and he hopes Rudy will convince her not to do it. But she's stubborn as hell, and she'd be capable of doing what she wants, with or without them.

James follows her out the door, into a day that's already too hot and humid, reinforcing the dread seeping through his chest.

The weather channel announces a thunderstorm coming. Strong winds and heavy rain. Thank God. Rudy can't stand this heat much longer.

"Riley and James are coming," Stella says, looking through the kitchen window.

Rudy turns the TV off and gets off the couch, peering through the window just in time to see the blue Dodge and the black Mustang rounding the house. What are they both doing here? He's working with Riley today, she has no reason to show up here this early. And James *never* shows up anywhere early.

He goes outside and stands on the porch, watching his daughter come to him with a bright smile on her face. She doesn't seem sad or worried, at least.

"Hey, Dad," she says, kissing his cheek.

"Is that a new shirt?" Rudy asks, his eyes flickering to James, who looks away at the same moment.

"I crashed on his couch. And I come bearing gifts." She raises the lockbox she's holding.

Rudy takes it, uneasiness spreading through him. "Is it empty?"

"No, it's damn full." She glances at James, then turns back to him. "We need to talk to you about something."

"Is that a bruise on your face? Did you get into a fight?"

"Sort of."

"What's that on your arm?" He takes her arm, looking the bandage over.

"Come on, we can talk inside."

"What's up, Rud?" James says, as he walks past him.

Rudy points at the bruise on his face. "I see you got into a fight too. You kids get crazy when I'm not around."

Riley lets out a little laugh. "Jamie definitely needs your supervision."

Rudy shuts the door behind them and follows them into the kitchen.

"Hey, Stella," Riley says.

"Hey, Riley," Stella answers. "Gotta get ready." She quickly disappears into the hallway in the bedroom's direction.

"Coffee?" Rudy says.

Riley and James sit down at the kitchen table and nod.

"So." Rudy settles in his chair once everyone has their cup and eyes the lockbox. "What happened?"

"We exorcized a woman yesterday, and get this: she walked into a bar," Riley says, half-smiling.

"What was she doing there?"

"Pft, who knows. Fact is, the demon saw me, tried to possess me, and when we extracted it, I could feel that this woman was really bad. Like, murder vibes."

"It's not that surprising," Rudy says, not understanding where this is going. "In fact, it's a lot more surprising when it's an innocent child being possessed by a shadow. What surprises me more is the fact that the demon travelled."

"Yeah, like Terrestre used to do."

James stays quiet, his jaw set. Rudy tries to read him. Something's clearly not sitting well with him.

He turns back to Riley. "What did you want to talk to me about, exactly? You exorcised a demon. You do that a lot."

"Okay, well..." Riley rests her hands flat on the table, choosing her words carefully and taking on her most diplomatic expression. "The thing is, I think it was a mistake to let that woman go. And I think we need to find her."

Rudy frowns. "How do you plan on doing that?"

A humorless smile tugs on James's lips. "Yeah, Riley. How do you plan on doing that? Tell your paternal."

Riley audibly swallows. "Well, the demon knows the identity of—"

"*No.*"

"Dad—"

"Absolutely not. Are you out of your mind?"

James brings the cup to his mouth. "Exactly what I said."

"This woman is a killer," Riley argues. "You know... probably."

"I understand," Rudy says, "but I won't let you get possessed *willingly*. This is insane. If you can't take control of it, we *won't* be able to help you. It's too risky."

Riley sighs, looking down at her cup. "Being scared isn't a good reason not to do something." She shrugs, looking back at him. "Just saying."

"You have no right to quote me to me."

"Jamie and I quote you all the time."

Rudy turns to James. "What do you think about this?"

"I think this is an insanely bad idea. Especially since she hasn't told you everything."

Rudy raises his eyebrows and looks at his daughter again, who drops against the back of her chair, crossing her arms.

"I feel betrayed," she says.

"What happened? I want the whole story."

"She almost lost the fight is what happened," James says when she doesn't answer. "The entity was so strong it almost got her. It would have if I hadn't been there."

Rudy's jaw drops. "You're kidding."

"I was completely hammered, okay?" Riley says, straightening back up. "Drunk and unprepared don't make a good combination."

"Was it as strong as Terrestre?"

"Well..."

He frowns. "Stronger?"

"Maybe, but I am myself a lot stronger than I was nine years ago. I *know* I can do it."

Rudy shakes his head.

"I think she wanted it back," Riley says.

"What?"

"The woman. After we extracted the demon, she attacked me. She *hated* me. She wanted the demon back."

James looks at her. "I told you she was confused, lovie—"

"She *wanted* to be possessed." Riley looks at Rudy, her gaze intent and dead-serious. "I saw bits of memories. Murders. Screams... Limbs being, I don't know, *severed*. And that crazy lady, she didn't want us to help her."

"Did you say severed limbs?"

Everyone turns to Stella, who's standing in the doorway, ready to go to work and wearing a professional, black suit.

Riley nods. "Yeah."

Stella walks to them and stands next to the table, crossing her arms against her chest. "Tell me more. What else do you remember?"

"It doesn't mean it's linked to your case," Rudy says.

"Let the girl talk."

Both Riley and James look confused as they glance back and forth between Stella and Rudy.

"I mostly remember horrible screams, and, like, a lot of blood," Riley says, now talking to Stella. "I think I saw a hatchet cutting a limb."

"Like a hand? Or a foot?"

"Yeah."

Stella nods, prompting her to go on. "What else?"

"Um... Fire, slashing..."

"Slashing?"

"Yeah, like a blade slashing and digging through skin. It's really blurry, it happened really fast, and like I've already stated, I was shitfaced."

Stella turns to Rudy. "This might be the best lead I've gotten in weeks."

"Stella—"

"She might have met the killer we're looking for."

"What killer?" James asks.

Stella explains to James and Riley the case she's been working on for the past few weeks. Rudy hates that these two might be connected. Yes, they want to protect people. Yes, he would hate for someone to die the way the others did, and there might be more bodies hidden somewhere that the police will never find. But if Riley gets overpowered by this entity,

Rudy won't be able to save her, and she'll end up killing them all.

Riley leans forward, staring into his eyes. "Dad. I know you're worried. And I know I get too cocky sometimes. But I need you to trust me on this one. If Stella's right, and this is connected to her case, we'll catch a freaking serial killer."

Rudy sighs in defeat. "Not 'we.' You get her identity, give it to Stella, and then your involvement in this case is done."

Riley nods, a satisfied smile stretching her lips. "Deal."

CHAPTER 12

Riley follows her dad down the basement stairs, James and Stella at her heels. Their footsteps thunder and make the wooden steps groan. Rudy pulls on the chain, illuminating the room. He's tense, so is James. Stella, a little less. Mostly, she's impatient, eager.

Riley's not scared. She's quite calm, even, mentally preparing herself to fight a shadow. Her anxiety mostly comes from the people surrounding her, and from the hazy memories she saw a glimpse of. Who knows what other atrocities she's about to see?

Rudy sets the lockbox down and drags a dusty chair, placing it in the middle of the room. "Sit."

Riley does what she's told and settles in the chair, resting her forearms on the armrests.

"Here," Rudy says to James, as he hands him a ten pound bag of rock salt. "Go crazy."

James nods and opens the bag. He pours a thick line of salt onto the ground, making a circle around the chair Riley sits in.

"The house is warded," Stella says, watching them. "If the demon is already inside, it shouldn't be able to get out, right?"

"Correct," Rudy says. "It's mostly to block—or weaken—its telekinetic powers, or it'll throw shit at us and destroy this place even if it can't get out of the chair."

"That's where that bruise comes from," Riley says, pointing at her face. "I got attacked by a beer bottle."

Her dad grabs a roll of duct tape and kneels in front of her.

She cocks her head at him. "No rope? That thing's gonna rip my hair out."

He chuckles, pulling on the tape with a loud tearing noise. "Suck it up, kiddo."

He proceeds to fasten the tape around her wrists, pinning them against the armrests. Once he's done, he does the same with her ankles, his anxiety rising by the second and making her chest tighten as well.

"I'll be okay, Dad."

Rudy raises his head, fixing his gentle, blue gaze on her. "It's not too tight, is it? Doesn't hurt?"

She shakes her head, attempting a smile. "No, it's fine."

He kisses the top of her head before stepping out of the salt circle and heads to the table he put the lockbox on.

Riley breathes in and out slowly, trying to escape the heavy energies of the room. She has to focus on herself, her own feelings, in order to do this right. She can't get distracted. Which isn't easy with all that hair in her face.

"Wait. Jamie, grab my hair tie. It's in my pocket."

Although she can't see him because he's standing behind her, she feels a new peak of discomfort.

"I'm not putting my hand in your pocket."

"Dude, just do it."

He sighs audibly and bends over, slipping his fingers inside the tight jeans and making her stomach flutter. "I can't find it."

"Then, it's in the other pocket."

"Are you serious?"

"Please, Jamie-bear."

He searches inside the other pocket, his awkwardness turned up to the max, and finally pulls out the hair tie. He stands behind her, brushing the hair out of her face as he tries to make a decent ponytail. Riley is surprised at how gentle he is. She expected to have her hair pulled and tied too tight, but instead, James takes his time, making sure to gather each strand. She shudders at the pleasant little chills his fingers send down her back. Riley can't resist any longer and looks up at him. It's sort of adorable how focused he is. When his eyes meet hers, a flicker of a smile lifts his mouth.

The metallic clink of the lockbox being laid at her feet makes her look down. James leaves her side, stepping out of the salt circle, and stands next to Stella, his arms crossed against his chest and disquietude painted all over his soul.

Rudy searches Riley's face, waiting for her signal. "Are you absolutely sure you want to do this?"

Riley nods. Her mouth is too dry to utter a single word.

"Tell me when," her dad says.

She closes her eyes, dissociating from the anxiety, the fear, and the dread permeating the room. She needs to stay sharp. After a few deep breaths, Riley opens her eyes and nods once at Rudy. He unlocks the box slowly and opens it, then backs out of the salt circle.

The angry energy of the thing lurking inside annihilates the presence of the three other people in the room. Riley's aware of them, standing and watching silently, but her focus is now on the black mist pouring out of the box. Its shape thickens as it crawls out, its ectoplasm leaving prints on the floor. Riley's nose stings and her eyes water as the stink of sulfur overpowers her.

A black tendril curls around her thigh, its shape turning into a shadowy hand, as another one grabs her shirt, pulling its blob-like body up. A twisted head comes out of the mass, its eyeless face leaning close to Riley as if about to kiss her. Each groan and grunt makes her skin prickle, and she tightens her jaw to keep herself from shuddering. Thin, dark fingers brush her neck, irritating her skin, and part her lips.

"God, I hate this part..."

The shadow melts into her mouth and slides down her throat, gagging her. Riley wills herself to be patient, to just hold on, but soon her body tenses and her nails dig into the chair as she struggles against the ectoplasm choking her.

Finally, deliverance comes as she is dragged deep inside her own mind.

Riley blocks the demon, keeping it from taking control of her. They're two separate entities trapped in the same body. She needs to find a safe space, somewhere neutral, peaceful. She conjures Winter's Attic.

From pitch-black darkness, the bookshop materializes around her, the walls and the shelves filled with books surrounding her. The windows reflect a nonexistent sun. Riley looks around herself, amazed at how real everything looks, just like it did when she was possessed as a teenager. One thing is out of place, however.

The shape standing in the shadows at the back of the bookshop. It has taken a human appearance, but Riley can't make out who it is as it stands shrouded in darkness.

I want you, it says, the voice echoing in her head.

"I get that a lot."

Let me take you. Don't resist.

"That's not why I let you in."

It turns and disappears behind a row of shelves, its footsteps slow and steady on the imaginary floor. Riley walks down the aisle in front of her just as slowly, peering through the cracks of books and shelves to get a glimpse of the demon's form on the other side.

You trapped me inside a box. I didn't like that. My host and I were perfectly happy.

"Really? Then, why did you try to take me?"

Silence follows. The glint of an eye shines through the gap between shelves.

"Because you can't resist me, that's why. No terrestrial can. No matter how tasty their host is."

The demon rounds the corner just as she does, both of them again standing on opposite side of the aisle, dancing around each other.

"Does it hurt you that I'm getting married, my darling?"

Riley's heart misses a beat at the sound of Daniel's voice. It sounds exactly like him, down to the British accent. It's playing with her, trying to weaken her. "If that's what you think, then I guess you didn't look deep enough."

"Come on, darling. Admit it. You feel left behind. You're a failure. A lonely little thing who doesn't know how to express her feelings to the man she loves. For an empath, it's quite pathetic."

"Fuck you."

"Tell me, pumpkin." The sudden change of voice startles her. "Are you still scared of the shadow man?" Her dad's voice, normally soothing and reassuring, sounds deep and cold.

"Don't you dare take my dad's shape, asshole."

The prickling energy presses harder on her. She's letting it get to her head. She stops walking, listening to the crushing silence, when a hand brushes her shoulder. She swivels around and takes a step back, heart pounding.

"Am I the one you want to see, lovie?" a fake James says, cocking his head. "I didn't have to look deep. He's front and center in your mind."

"What's the name of your last host?"

"Why would I tell you that?"

"Why did she want you back?"

A sickening grin stretches his lips. "She and I had a very special bond."

"What horrible things did you make her do?"

"I didn't *make* her do anything. It was all her. I'm sure she misses me, but I have to say, I found a lot better. If only you would let me make one with you."

His familiar and human-like language isn't lost on Riley. Most shadows have a sort of simple, archaic language. The less they talk, the better they are. But this one has a way of conversing that is too natural for a creature of its kind.

"How long were you in her body?" Riley says.

The grin stretches. "I experience time differently than you humans do. Based on her memories, I would say a few months."

Riley's jaw drops. *Months?* No one can stay possessed this long. Even the worst people. Their body can hold for a few weeks, tops, until they're sucked dry and die, or stay permanently insane. The only person supposedly capable of feeding a demon for a lifetime is a celestial or a terrestrial, and that woman isn't one. Riley would have felt it.

"If you want to know things about her, Celeste, you'll have to look into my memories."

Riley balls her fist, standing straight, bracing herself for battle. It won't tell her anything. She'll have to pry it out of its head.

It steps in her direction, James's body looking even taller than he is in real life and dwarfing her. "You and I have to become one. You have to let me in."

Another step closer. Riley wills herself not to flinch.

Fake James leans forward, his beard scratching her cheek and his breath hot as he whispers in her ear. "If I win and take over, I promise I will lock you inside a good memory. I don't need you to suffer to feed off you."

A strong hand clamps around her throat at the same time as Riley presses her fingers against his skull. The bookshop melts around them, and the floor disappears under their feet, as she and the terrestrial's minds click together like two magnets attracting each other.

CHAPTER 13

The sickening, nauseating memories make Riley want to scream. So many people, tortured, dehumanized, and savagely killed. It makes her weak. She can't look at all of them. She skips through them as fast as she can, or she'll go insane. She has to find *her*. Her name, her identity before the demon breaks loose in Riley's mind and takes over. Stella would probably like to know about the other bodies–the astonishingly high number of bodies left to rot in the woods in various parts of New England, their bones washing down rivers and lakes and being eaten by wildlife–but there's no time.

Your name, what's your fucking name?

The entity's rage rises. Her hold on it won't last much longer, and she needs enough strength to kick it out of her body. It knows this and does everything it can to hide what she's looking for. She forces herself to navigate and skim through flashes of broken limbs, severed hands, eyes clawed out, and blades slashing skin. The spine-chilling shrieks and howls bounce back in her head and freeze her blood. Even from here, in a memory, it's like she feels their pain. Their despair. The panic consuming them as they understand the torture they'll have to go through before being delivered by death.

Riley stumbles into another memory. She's in a large room lit by portable spotlights. The smell of blood gags her. Everywhere she looks, her eyes fall on various weapons covered in gore. Knives. Rusty tools. A hammer. Scissors. Hooks.

No matter where she turns to or how many times she tries to jump into another memory, it's the same room appearing before her, only the screams are different, as well as the tools used.

Despite the sickening fear shooting through her limbs, she has to dig deeper. Farther. Before all this. But the past looks like it's scrambled. Even if this woman wanted to have that demon inside of her, it still did some damage to her psyche.

I can feel you getting weaker, Celeste, it whispers.

Riley searches frantically, her mind packed with the dreadful images.

Blink.

A gasp catches in her throat. Silence surrounds her.

Drawing shaky breaths, she stares into the mirror in front of her. She takes a careful step, then another, studying the face looking back. Deep creases. Wild gray hair. Acne scars. A crooked grin lifting her lips as she wipes the blood off her face.

"Who are you..." Riley whispers to the reflection. "How could you be possessed for so long without dying?"

The reflection doesn't answer. Madness dances in her eyes, and she starts giggling to herself. "That bitch had it coming."

Riley turns away from the mirror and exits the room, searching her surroundings. Black prints stain the floor. Ectoplasm. This was the day the killer was possessed, she knows it. Is this her house?

Riley follows the black goo into the hallway and stumbles into a living room. The dead body of a girl lies on the floor, blonde curls spilling around her head. Her bloody fingers are missing their nails. Raw marks are peppered all over her body, and Riley realizes they're burns, probably made by the still plugged curling iron next to her. Purple bruises are printed around her throat.

A piece of knowledge, crystal clear, washes over her. *Her first kill. And it happened the day she was possessed.*

With it comes a series of flashbacks, interactions the killer has had with the girl before killing her, and suddenly...

Her name.

I'm loose, Celeste. And I'm coming for you, the shadow says, sending a new spike of adrenaline through Riley.

Fuck. She's too scared, too panicked, the images she saw now branded in her brain. She needs to come back to herself, to regain control of her body.

Blink.

When she opens her eyes, she finds herself in a square room with a high ceiling, its walls gray and black. The strong scent of smoke burns her nose. In the middle of the room stands a large box, something resembling an unplugged, blackened freezer.

Got you.

"No..." She darts to the only door, pounding on it and pulling on the handle. The door doesn't move. "No!"

Have fun in there. I'll take over you now.

A bright flash of light makes Riley swivel around. Fire spreads around the room, its flames licking the walls. She can't feel its warmth as it burns through her, as though she's simply a ghost. Because it's not her memory.

A pounding sound makes her heart jump, and she fixes her eyes on the freezer in the middle of the room.

"Oh my God..."

Another blow lifts the lid just an inch, until the padlock stops it. The fire shines brighter, slowly swallowing the shaking freezer. Screams emerge from it, the pounding against the lid now frantic, the sound of it bouncing in Riley's skull.

Nausea gagging her, she slams a hand against her mouth and presses her back to the door, watching as the blaze envelops the box. The hysterical shrieks rise inside, their vibrations almost hurting her physically. She rips her imaginary hearing aids off, but the screeches are firmly planted in this memory, in her head.

She whirls back to the door, beating on it and begging to be let out. Each scream of the man inside the freezer fills her with dread, and soon, she finds herself crying and shouting for her dad, wishing he were here to save her.

Nausea lingers in Rudy's throat. Seeing his daughter like this, getting possessed, is torture. The good thing for now—or what he assumes is a good thing—is that she's still unconscious. The demon didn't take control of her body. It's contained. And it's been inside for a little more than twenty minutes.

James is crouching in front of her, just outside of the salt circle, and stares at her with worried eyes, often glancing down at his watch. Stella's fidgeting with the pendant around her neck.

"I shouldn't have convinced you to agree to this," she says, her voice clipped.

"You didn't," he answers, almost whispering as though afraid to disturb Riley. "She did." He takes Stella's hand and squeezes it gently. "Sorry if this was painful to watch."

Stella's older sister, Jane, was possessed when she was sixteen and was shot by the police after slaughtering her parents. Seeing Riley like this must have reminded Stella of painful memories she would rather forget.

She looks at him, then glances at Riley. "It's just that... I've seen possessed people, but I've never seen them *getting* possessed. I sort of thought it was, I don't know, different. Painless. I just can't believe Riley would go through this willingly after having already experienced it."

"She's tough," Rudy says, more to reassure himself than anything else.

"She's *crazy*," James says, truly speaking Rudy's mind. "And fucking stubborn." He stands up, exhales, and runs a hand through his hair. "Can I smoke in here?"

That's one of the ways James shows he cares. By becoming angry. And that's how he looks right now as his eyes are locked on Riley. Furious. Mad at her for doing something so reckless.

"Sure. And give me one while you're at it."

Rudy has been trying to decrease his cigarette consumption, and he's doing pretty good. Some days, he doesn't smoke at all. The end goal is to stop completely, but as dread gnaws at his insides, he gladly takes one.

Riley still hasn't moved. The seconds pass, each of them stretching longer than the last, trapping them in an endless wait.

"How long was she like this with the other demon? The one that possessed her when she was sixteen," Stella asks.

"More than an hour."

James glances at Rudy. "Should we try to do something? I'm getting worried."

Rudy makes no reply. Saying he's worried this time would be a fucking understatement, and the feeling of having a brick sitting in the pit of his stomach won't leave him until he knows Riley's fine.

"Do you think the blood inside the box is still enough to draw it out?" James says.

"It should be."

They keep their eyes on her, waiting, the basement now filled with gray smoke reflecting the yellow light after they stub their cigarettes.

Riley shifts. Rudy's heart jumps in his chest, and before he knows it, he stands at the edge of the salt circle, James and Stella at his sides.

"Come on, pumpkin. Kick it out."

"She's not gonna kill it?" Stella asks.

"Last time, she almost destroyed the fucking house," James says. "And she was in a special kind of mindset. Like, *really* pissed."

Riley raises her head with a gasp, opening deep black eyes, chilling Rudy's blood.

"No…"

She cocks her head and smiles. "Yes," the double voice says. The chair vibrates, grating against the floor.

"Untie me, or I'll knock this chair over so hard it'll kill her."

Rudy stays frozen in place, the words dying on his tongue, but he doesn't have time to process the situation as the demon shuts its eyes, seemingly shaken by a shiver.

Riley opens misty eyes, balling her hands into tight fists. *"Get out."*

The shadow is pushed out of her, fighting against the telekinesis driving it back inside its prison. James shuts the lockbox, the lid slamming with a metallic *clang,* as Rudy throws himself before his daughter, kneeling in front of her chair. She's panting and sweating, her head bowed. He cups her face, his heart pounding in his chest furiously.

"Riley? Are you okay? Answer me, kiddo."

"Yeah." She breathes out the word more than she says it and attempts a nod.

James kneels next to her and cuts the tape off with his pocketknife. "Never pull that kind of shit again."

She shakes her head weakly, a single tear rolling down her cheek. "I won't."

As soon as the tape comes undone, Rudy pulls her out of the chair, intending to help her up, but instead Riley drops on his lap and hugs him tightly, her head resting on his shoulders as she tries to catch her breath and calm her nerves.

Rudy holds her, because of course he does, the realization of coming so close to disaster making his body shake.

"Janice Kraft," Riley says in a quivering voice, not moving from her position.

Rudy glances at James. James glances back, frowning.

"What did you say?" Stella asks.

"That's her name. Janice Kraft. And I wish I didn't see what I saw."

"She was possessed for *months?*"

Riley's dad looks at her as though she's insane, and despite how close she felt to having a mental breakdown while looking at Janice Kraft's memories, she hasn't crossed that line yet.

"Yes. I know, it's crazy," she says, her mouth full of delicious, re-heated macaroni and cheese casserole. Nothing like cheese pasta for breakfast. Being forced to look at these horrors while keeping the demon mentally 'pinned down' has left her weak and sort of shivering despite the crushing heat.

"How is that possible?" James asks, his intense gaze on her almost intimidating, as though he feels like he *has* to stare at her to make sure she's real and alive.

"I didn't see everything. I didn't have time. But the demon said it had a special bond with Janice. It definitely damaged her, but I was right. She let it stay willingly." She puts her fork down and swallows her food, then looks at Stella. "I think she killed a lot more people than you think."

Her face darkens, but she doesn't seem surprised. "How many, do you think?"

"I don't know... Thirty, forty? More, maybe. And she didn't just kill them, either. She tortured them. Broke their limbs and mutilated them. She made damn sure they suffered until they died. That was all *her.*"

"Did you see anything else?" Stella says. "A location, something that could help?"

"I think she always tortures them in the same place, but I don't know where it is. I kept seeing the same room. Some sort of old, stone room... Like a basement maybe, but..."

"But?"

"Whatever this place is, it can contain a fire."

Stella tilts her head. "What makes you say that?"

Riley swallows. "At some point, I was stuck inside a room... with a man. He was locked inside a freezer, and the room was set on fire. He was being burned alive and he made these... *horrible* screams, and—" Her throat tightens, shutting her up. She sits back and places her trembling hands on her lap to hide them.

Thick silence swallows them, and Riley takes a deep breath to hold back the tears threatening to spill.

James's hand slides over hers, warm and reassuring. A mundane gesture that feels incredibly intimate as he threads his fingers with hers and brushes the back of her hand with his thumb. The touch, hidden under the table, feels secret, forbidden, making Riley's heart kick up a notch. She doesn't dare look at him, nor does he dare look at her, not when two other people are sitting across from them.

"She was feeding it," Rudy says, as if talking to himself. "That's how she could hold it for so long, because she was willingly feeding it to keep it inside."

"Why would someone want to do that?" James says, his hand not leaving hers. "Why would she want to live with a demon inside of her? That makes no sense."

"Did you get anything else on her despite her name? Her home address, maybe?" Stella asks.

Riley shakes her head apologetically. Just getting her name seemed like an impossible task as she swam through an ocean of murders.

"I'll see what I can dig up on this woman," she says. "Thank you for your help, Riley."

"Keep me updated."

"You're clearly traumatized. Forget about it."

"I'm not—"

"Your involvement in this is done. That was the deal."

She stands up, and James's hand withdraws quickly as though he's scared of getting caught. Stella doesn't add anything else and gently squeezes Rudy's shoulder before leaving the kitchen.

Although Riley wouldn't go as far as saying she's traumatized, the desire to stay in her dad's house huddled under a blanket and watch TV all day is overwhelming.

"You should go home and rest," Rudy says.

"No. I'd rather hang out with you at Winter's Attic. Can I take some of your casserole with me?"

Rudy chuckles, a sound that will always warm her heart. "Of course."

CHAPTER 14

Stella can't believe her eyes and still can't believe Riley's abilities. That stunt she pulled was more than impressive, if a little scary. Rudy was still shaking even half an hour later, though he tried to hide it. He always wants to appear solid and reliable for his daughter, but Stella has learned he's a lot more sensitive that he lets on.

Her eyes are fixed on the computer screen in front of her. Pictures and files on Janice Kraft fill it. She looks just the way Riley and James described her. Sallow, acne-scarred skin, drooping eyes, long, wavy gray hair sticking out in all direction like a madwoman. And she *is* mad. Those files prove it. The sixty-one year old woman either quit or was fired from dozens of jobs. She took many trips to the Mental Health Center of Greater Manchester and was diagnosed with antisocial personality disorder paired with a superiority complex. She went to jail many times too, but for reasons that are nowhere near close to murder. Extreme anger outburst, aggravated assault—which resulted in another trip to the health center—or driving while intoxicated.

These repeated trips to jail and the mental hospital suddenly stopped seven months ago when Janice seemed to have dropped from the face of the earth. No one has reported her missing, and Stella supposes that this woman has done a fabulous job at making each of her close ones run away from her. She simply vanished, which should coincide with her possession and her first murder like Riley suggested it. The bodies didn't start popping up right away, but evidently, there are a lot of victims they haven't found, and never will.

It's time to pay Janice a visit, thanks to the address found in her files. Stella can't tell her colleagues she's got a lead yet. What is she going to say, that her empath friend told her Janice was the culprit because she saw through a demon's memories? No thanks. She'll say she got the info from a tip line, and it'll have to do.

Stella writes down the address and leaves the station, jumping into her car and blasting the AC. Some things still don't make sense, and she reflects on them as she drives to the place. The bodies were found almost all over New England. Why? How? Where does she kill? Riley mentioned two rooms. A large one with many tools and portable lights, which would indicate the place doesn't have electricity. Then, a second that was set on fire. It's unlikely that her apartment is where she operates. Stella will find out in about an hour anyway.

She parks in front of a red brick building in Rochester and looks at the structure. Janice lives in an apartment, surrounded by neighbors and shops, which makes the possibility of her torturing and killing her victims here even more impossible.

Stella steps into the coat of hot air and walks to the entrance. The fresh temperature inside the lobby is a welcome sensation against her overheated skin. Janice's apartment is the number 14, on the second floor. To shake off some of the tension in her legs after the drive, Stella takes the stairs. She checks that her gun is tucked in its holster as she walks down the corridor to the door number 14. She can't provide proof that Janice is the killer the police have been looking for, but it doesn't change that she is, and Stella likes to stay on her guard. This will only be an interrogation unless things turn to shit.

She creeps to the door, a hand still on her gun just in case, and presses her ear against the wood, listening. It seems quiet inside. No footsteps or TV or water running. Complete silence. She straightens up and inhales, then knocks. Three short raps that bounce off the walls of the corridor. The silence persists on the other side. There's not even a shuffle that could indicate someone is secretly looking through the peephole. Stella knocks again, louder, already knowing this is pointless. When she's met with more silence, she heads to the door number 12. As she approaches, she can hear the TV blaring in the background. The walls seem thin here. She knocks.

A man in his fifties wearing an old tank top and blue shorts opens. He looks her up and down and smiles, raising an arm to lean his elbow against the doorframe. "Hello there."

His round face and gold tooth make her appreciate even more how handsome Rudy is.

She clears her throat. "Hello. Sorry to bother you. Do you know the woman who lives next door to you?" She raises a recent picture of Janice for him to look at.

He squints at it for a moment, then makes a small noise with the back of his throat. "Oh yeah, she lives here. Can't say I really know her. She's not the chatty type, and she's not around much."

"Not around much? When was the last time you saw her?"

He shrugs. "Uh, I think she was here yesterday. She pops up every few days, sometimes every few weeks. It's not like I pay any attention. I just know that her apartment is always quiet, and that's what matters to me."

"You don't hear her even when she's here?"

"Nope, not really."

"Do you hear the neighbor on the other side? The number 10?"

He nods. "Oh yeah, often."

"Anything else you can tell me about her? Any detail that stands out to you or that seems strange? Anything at all."

The light seems to come on in his eyes. "Wait, are you a cop?"

Took you long enough.

Normally, she says outright who she is. But this time around, the line between official police work and paranormal investigation is muddied. She reluctantly takes out her badge. "Detective Valdez."

The man whistles in admiration. "Never seen one of them badges before."

"So? Anything else you could tell me about her?"

"Well..." He thinks about it, scratching his chin. "She's always dirty."

"Dirty?"

"Yeah. I thought she left to travel for a job or something, but every time she comes back, she's dirty. One time I passed her in the staircase, and she stank real bad. I don't know what she does when she leaves, but I think she mostly comes back here to shower."

Stella pictures Janice leaving for days, hunting for a new prey, torturing them and dragging them through the woods, then coming back smelling like death. Is that why she went inside that bar? Was she following someone?

"Anything else I can do for you?" the man asks, smiling wider. "Would you like my number or something?"

"That'll be all, thank you. Have a good day."

She gives him a curt nod and turns away before he can add anything else, hearing him close the door. Her legs carry her back to Kraft's door. After a quick glance left and right, Stella tries the doorknob. It resists under her hand.

Two options are left. One, stake out in front of the building and wait for Janice to come back. She isn't possessed anymore and shouldn't give Stella too much of a hard time. Two, breaking and entering. She could do it quickly, discreetly, and later get a search warrant, saying she got the lead from the tip line. If she can convince a judge that a sixty-one year old woman is a suspect in multiple homicides, that is.

Stella decides to go back to her car and get the lockpicking kit she's got in the glove compartment, a little thrill coursing through her. She goes back inside the building, walking as quietly as possible, and crouches in front of the door after slipping on a pair of latex gloves. The first tool to go in is the tension wrench, and Stella inserts it into the bottom of the keyhole, applying pressure there. The pick goes into the top of the lock. She fiddles with her tools for a moment, frowning in concentration, as she applies pressure on the wrench and scrubs her pick back and forth and rakes the inside of the plug. Once all the pins inside the lock are picked, she turns the wrench, and the satisfying *click* of the door opening puts a small smile on her face.

She slips inside the apartment, shutting the door behind her as silently as possible. One thing she knows by now, the walls are thin here, and she needs to be as quiet as a mouse. It smells of sweat and grime in the narrow, dark hallway. The air is hot and unbreathable. Stella creeps through the small space, glancing into the first room to her left. A bathroom. Dirty towels lie on the dusty floor, smelling of mold, and grimy prints mare the white sink. A door farther ahead to the right leads to a bedroom. There isn't much to see here except for a stained mattress and a few clothes. Another kind of smell floats in there.

Stella picks up a shirt carefully, smelling it.

Iron.

It's faint. Because the blood has been partly washed away. It's hard to see on the black fabric, but when holding it up to the light, badly-washed stains of blood cover the shirt. Janice might have showered with them and called it a day. All the clothes scattered on the dirty, brown carpet smell the same. If she gets this search warrant, and she *will,* these would be enough to make Kraft a suspect and bring her in for questioning.

She could stop right there, but curiosity pushes her to see more. After chasing the murderer for months, here she is, in her private space, despite how little Kraft uses it. Stella tiptoes to the back of the apartment. The small kitchen reeks of rotten food. Dirty dishes fill the sink. Flies buzz around them. After a quick inspection of the drawers and the fridge, she goes into the living room, a place that smells far worse than the rest of the apartment and is a few degrees hotter.

Brushing her hair away from her sweaty neck, Stella looks around the room. Old, beat up furniture scatter the place along with empty bottles and chips bags. One thing stands out, though. A wooden chest, looking at odds with the rest of the place. It looks new. Clean.

The smell, already coating Stella's tongue, thickens as she steps toward it and crouches carefully. The pit in her stomach tells her that whatever's inside, it'll be a bigger proof that Janice Kraft is the killer they want.

She raises her finger to the latch and flicks it up. Slowly, she pulls the lid open, and a warm, sweet waft makes her wince as she stares down at the mess of eyeballs and teeth filling the chest.

CHAPTER 15

James is slumped on the couch in front of the TV. *Evil Dead* is playing tonight. It's annoying to watch it with all the commercials, but he has nothing better to do. It's not like he's really paying attention, either. He keeps thinking about what happened this morning. How things could have dramatically turned to shit. How panic-stricken he felt.

And how he let down his guard when he took Riley's hand.

He never should have done that. Rudy was sitting right across from them and could have seen. He'd probably be hella pissed if he knew James's feelings for his daughter.

A short rap on the front door startles him. He rises and opens it, illuminating Riley with the light emanating from his living room. She's standing there, holding a duffel bag.

"I dropped by my apartment to get some stuff," she says.

He steps aside and closes the door behind her, his heart picking up the pace. He doesn't know if he's thrilled or terrified that she's staying with him. He should have been more insistent about her going to Rudy's house. After what happened this morning, he's awkward as hell.

He drops back on the couch, acting casual. "Make yourself at home."

"Can I get a beer?" Riley asks after dropping her bag.

"Get me one while you're at it."

She grabs two bottles from the fridge and hands him one, settling on the couch in the same position as him, her feet propped on the coffee table. "Ah, *Evil Dead*."

"We can change the channel."

"I'm fine."

He picks up the remote and changes the channel to something random anyway.

"I'm *fine*, Jamie."

"I didn't want to see it."

He doesn't like her seeing more horrible things today. She was straight up scared this morning, which is the whole reason James let his guard down like an idiot, eager to come to her rescue.

He glances at her. She's still thinking about it, he can see it in her eyes. She's looking down at her beer, lost in her thoughts.

"Did you have a good day at work?" he says, trying to distract her.

"Yeah, it was good. My dad took extra care of me."

"What happened with Kelly exactly?"

She shrugs. "She wants a real relationship with me, and I can't provide."

"Ah. The emotionally impaired bit, huh?"

"I'm not emotionally impaired."

"No?"

"No. I just don't love her that way, that's all." She turns to him. "Why, do you also think I have a problem?"

The question sounds like a warning, and James decides to just shake his head. He wouldn't go as far as saying she has a problem, but he doesn't think she's ready to have any actual relationship with anyone. One more reason to stay away from her. If only they could have talked about what happened after Kelly's birthday, things would have been better. Clearer. Or something. He should have said something, but he didn't find the courage to do so, and the memory of that night has been clinging onto him for the past nine months.

It started out normally. He tried to make himself look presentable, because fake boyfriend or not, he was the one Kelly's friends would call gruff or rough or scary if he didn't make an effort. When he got to the club, he was a little surprised to see Riley wearing high heels, but other than that, nothing to make a fuss about. He always thought she was pretty without being attracted to her, and sure, she looked good with two strands of hair tied behind her head, the rest of her long mane falling into a wavy cascade over her shoulders.

What truly changed his perception of her was the kiss she planted on his mouth when he arrived. It jolted his body into shock, filling him with a warm rush he couldn't identify. Somehow, it hadn't crossed his mind that by pretending to be her boyfriend they would have to kiss.

The evening went on, and James tried to shake the feeling off. Riley eventually forgot Kelly's bitching friends and started having fun. And they drank. *A lot.*

After leaving the club, she could barely walk straight, and certainly not on those freakishly high heels from hell she was forced to wear. The night air was crisp, and snowflakes coated the streets like a silk blanket.

"I can't make it to my car with these things," Riley said, wincing and leaning on his arm.

"Your car? You're not driving. You're leaving with me, and we'll get your car tomorrow."

"You drank as much as me."

"I'm taller and bigger than you."

"Show off."

He cracked a smile.

"Where's your car?" she asked.

"Three blocks away."

She stopped dead in her tracks. "That's even farther than mine!"

"Come on, it's not the end of the world."

"Easy for you to say. The skin of your feet isn't being peeled off each time you take a step. I'd rather take them off and have frostbite. At least it would numb the pain."

He laughed, because she's always funny even when she doesn't mean to be, and backtracked his steps, standing with his back to her. "Come on, I'll carry you."

"Yay! Piggyback ride!"

She didn't wait before jumping on his back, the breath of relief she exhaled warm on his cheek. She fastened her arms around his neck, resting her chin on his shoulder, and a little shiver went through him as he hooked his hands behind her knees. After all these years of her sneak-attacking him and wrestling with him, this time felt different, intimate. Her face was close to his, in a way that he could easily kiss her if he turned his head, and it dawned on him that it was exactly what he wanted to do.

James focused on watching his boots crunching in the thin layer of snow, hyperaware of the way Riley pressed her thighs against his hips and how her breath grazed his cheek each time she exhaled. It might have been his imagination, but it didn't feel like she was just letting him carry her. She was hugging him tightly.

Once they parked in front of his place, James helped her out of the passenger seat, and together, they walked to the front door. When she stepped onto the porch, Riley's heel slipped in the snow, but he caught her before she could hurt herself. Somehow, she ended up with her back pressed against the door, hanging onto his shoulders, while his right arm was still hooked around her waist.

That's when he realized just how beautiful she was, laughing, with white snowflakes clinging onto her dark hair.

He tore his eyes away from her and fetched the keys from his pocket, fumbling to find the keyhole, as his heart hammered his chest so hard he thought Riley would feel it.

"Jamie."

He met her gaze, intent and locked on him, then looked down again, his hand shaking slightly as he tried to open the damn door.

"Kiss me," she whispered.

His heart missed a beat. James looked at her again, wondering if he had heard that right. Normally, the top of her head would barely be as high as his chin, forcing her to crane her neck when talking to him. But with those heels of hers, she only had to tilt her head back slightly for her lips to be inches from his.

"You're drunk," he said, clearing his throat. "We're gonna get you to bed."

As he dropped his head down again, Riley pressed a hand on his cheek, turning his face slightly. Her lips grazed his beard, then pressed against the corner of his mouth. A warm shiver shook him.

"Kiss me," she breathed out, turning his face toward hers some more.

"No. We shouldn't."

Riley teased him, brushing her lower lip against his own. His whole body shook with desire but stayed frozen into place. His hand tightened over his keys, the pain in his palm keeping him grounded and reminding him that kissing her would be the worst idea he'd ever had. Not only because Rudy would kill him. Not only because he was twelve years older than her. But because he had messed things up with every woman he had ever been with, and he wasn't ready to flush his friendship with Riley down the toilet because he was drunk.

But she won.

What threw him over the edge was the tip of her tongue grazing his lower lip before she bit it gently. His willpower disintegrated then, and his mouth nearly swallowed hers. He kissed her feverishly, pinning her harder against the door and tangling his fingers in her hair. She answered with a moan of satisfaction, melting against him. It only made him burn for her more. She gripped his jacket harder and opened her mouth to him, allowing him to taste her tongue.

A sense of self-loathing came over him. She was drunk, and he was taking advantage of her. His best friend. He suddenly pulled away from her, cursing himself for doing something so stupid.

"Don't stop," Riley said.

"You don't know what you're doing, Riley."

"I know very much what I'm doing."

"It's better we put you to bed."

James finally found the keyhole and unlocked the door. They stumbled inside, and he helped her to his bedroom. She would be a lot more comfortable there than on his couch.

"All right," Riley said with a smile, dropping onto the bed. "It's true I'm hammered. But we're talking about this tomorrow. Because I know you liked it."

James had prepared himself to talk about it, not really knowing how such a conversation would go, but in the end, they never did. Riley woke up and entered the kitchen the next morning, asking him how they got home since she didn't remember leaving the club and going to bed.

"I'm drawing a complete blank. I was so shitfaced. Thanks for lending me your bed, though."

He wanted to tell her. He wanted to know if she had acted only under the influence of alcohol, but didn't find the courage, reminding himself how wrong all of this was.

It's probably better that she doesn't remember. She made it easier for the both of them, really. James wishes he could have forgotten too. Instead, there's hardly a day that passes by without him thinking about that kiss.

"Maybe I *do* have a problem."

Riley's voice brings him back to the present. He turns to her, having almost forgotten what they were initially talking about.

"I probably have several, actually," she continues, staring down at her beer. "Liam and Miguel are right, I'm unreliable. I haven't been a good friend lately. I hurt Kelly's feelings. I never should have slept with her. I knew damn well she was waiting for more. I haven't even congratulated Daniel properly on his engagement, even though I *am* happy for him." She finishes her beer and puts it on the coffee table, sighing. "I should lay off the booze too. It's like I do everything I can to forget about my feelings for–" She stops herself, leaving him wondering what she wanted to say. "Seriously, what's wrong with me?"

She looks at him with sad eyes as if waiting for him to answer. She's slumped next to him, still wearing his shirt, her hair a little disheveled, and James can't find a goddamn thing wrong with her.

"Nothing, Riley. I think..."

"What?"

"You're burnt out. You need a week off."

Riley smiles. "I doubt a week off will change me."

The words tumble out of his mouth before he can stop them. "You don't need to change, lovie. You're perfect the way you are."

Her smile vanishes. She gazes at him with an expression he can't read. He should look away, but he can't.

She rolls to the side, cups his jaw with both hands, and kisses him deeply. This is a feeling he's been dreaming to experience again, and for a moment, he's stunned, wanting to melt under her, all of his focus fixed on their lips touching.

But guilt—and fear—jolt his body. He pushes her away a little harder than he intends to and gets off the couch, afraid he wouldn't be able to reject her a second time if she kissed him again.

"What the fuck, Riley?" he says, angry at her, angry at himself. He goes to the kitchen and rounds the countertop as if that would prevent her from reaching him.

Riley gets up, anxiety painted over her face, and takes a few steps in his direction, twisting her fingers nervously. "I-I'm so sorry, I—"

"What the fuck were you thinking?"

"I thought—"

"I'm twelve years older than you, for fuck's sake. I've known you since you were a fucking kid!"

"Well, I'm an adult now, Jamie."

James rests his hands on the countertop, dizzy with anger, frustration, and desire. "Your father will shoot me in the face."

"Is that what you're afraid of? My dad?"

"No, I'm pissed that you'd be ready to fuck things up between the two of us just because you're drunk and need comfort."

Now he's done it. Hurt her. The look she gives him is unmistakable.

"Is that what you think I'm doing? I'm not drunk, I've had *one* beer. I did it because I wanted to, and because I thought you wanted it as well."

"Well, you're wrong."

"Liar. There *is* something between us that is more than friendship, and you know it too."

He shakes his head, unable to admit it to her. The risks are too high. "You're completely mistaken."

"I remember."

James raises his head and squints at her. "What are you talking about?"

"Our kiss after Kelly's party."

"You *lied* to me about not remembering?"

"No. I genuinely didn't remember. It came back to me after a few days. I just didn't know how to tell you because I was really embarrassed, and the fact that *you* never brought it up didn't help, either."

His chest deflates. All this time... She remembered all along and played the pretend game just like him. "This doesn't change anything. I don't feel that way about you."

Riley's face hardens, her jaw working as she tries to conceal her emotions. "Your feelings don't match your words."

"Instead of analyzing me, you should take a look at yourself. You're depressed and confused, and you're looking for someone to reassure you. Well, guess what? I'm not your fucking consolation prize."

Her eyes shimmer a little, and he looks down, shame crashing down on him.

"I think you should leave..." he says. "Go to your dad's."

He hears her huff, a sound full of concealed tears and disbelief. "You're kicking me out too? Can't we at least talk about this?"

James doesn't answer and refuses to look at her, his jaw clenched as he tries to keep his composure. He's no empath, but he feels her anger as she backtracks her steps and snatches her duffel bag.

"If you're too drunk to drive, I can take you there," he says, his voice clipped.

"Fuck off, James."

He raises his head, startled to have been called by his name. He's almost never heard it coming from her mouth. Even when she calls him Williams, there's a hint of affection in it.

Riley opens the door and turns to him, her face hard and her brows furrowed. "Fuck all the way *off.*"

She steps out, and the walls shake as she slams the door.

CHAPTER 16

The weather channel keeps blabbing about the coming thunderstorm. The air is still so hot that it's hard to believe the temperatures will drop in a day or two. The strong winds they're talking about couldn't come soon enough.

Rudy sets the honey cakes on a plate when he hears a car coming up the dirt path. He looks through the window, expecting to see Stella's car, but it's the blue Dodge that strolls through the woods, its headlights casting dancing lights over the trees. What is she doing here at this time?

He exits the kitchen and opens the front door by the time Riley parks. He waits there, but she doesn't come out of her car. Uneasy and eternally concerned about her, Rudy walks to her instead. He opens the driver's door and crouches.

Riley's forehead is pressed against the steering wheel, but she turns to him, attempting a smile. "Hello, good sir. Would you have a room available for a lost traveler?"

"Of course. Today's special is a mac and cheese casserole leftovers paired with fresh honey cakes."

"Yum."

"I'll show you to your quarters."

He offers his hand, and Riley takes it, letting him pull her out of her seat and under his arm. No matter what's going on tonight, she needs comfort. He knows her enough to know that. And she doesn't need him to bombard her with questions. Yet.

Rudy takes the duffel back from the trunk and walks inside with her, where he fixes her a plate and gives it to her as she sits on the couch. She kicks her shoes off and rests her back against the couch's armrest, and Rudy does the same, facing her. It's what Riley jokingly calls their 'talking position.'

"Honey cakes," she says. "It's almost as if you knew I was coming."

He thought all these years he made these for her, but the truth is, it has become a soothing habit. Something he does to calm his nerves. Clear his head. After what happened this morning, and the thought that Stella is after a serial killer and she hasn't called him all day, he needed to focus on something else.

"I would have brought you a few tomorrow."

"Any news from Stella?"

"No, not yet."

"It's pretty late."

He nods. "She often works late."

Riley looks at him sadly. "You're not lonely, are you? It must be difficult for you to have her work so much."

"I'm fine, pumpkin. I admire and like how passionate she is about her job. Just like I am about mine. And I can't be lonely when I get to work with you almost every day."

That puts a small smile on her face. "I love working with you too."

She takes a big bite of the honey cake, and the both of them stay silent for a moment.

"Are you going to tell me what's happening?" Rudy says.

"Everyone hates me, that's what's happening."

"I don't believe that."

"I guess 'hate' is a strong word. Liam and Miguel are definitely disappointed in me, which led them to kick me out of the band."

Rudy raises his eyebrows, tilting his head. Those kids have been playing together for almost ten years.

"Kelly loves me but also doesn't really like me at the moment. And Jamie, well..." Riley pauses. "So... is it okay if I stay here for a little while? Just long enough to find a new place to live."

"This will always be your house, kid. You can stay here as long as you want."

This place screams her name. Rudy sees it in every wall they painted, every shelf they assembled, every hole in the walls they patched, every new floorboard they installed. They had such a blast ripping off the wallpaper everywhere.

"Did you know there's still a tiny blood stain behind that picture where you planted the nail in your finger instead of the wall?"

Riley chuckles. "And I still have that scar on my finger. But we renovated this place like pros."

"We sure did."

"Maybe I'll find another old place, and you can help me fix it."

Rudy nods. "Of course." He doesn't ask more questions. He lets her talk about what *she* wants to talk about. She knows she can be open with him.

"You and I should play music together in bars," she says. "We make a good duet. Just us and our acoustic guitars. What do you think?"

"Sure, that'd be nice."

She takes another bite of the muffin, lost in her thoughts again. "Did you know Daniel's getting married?"

"Yes. He called me."

"Really? When?"

"This morning at the bookshop. I was in the back room."

"Why didn't you say anything?"

"He was worried about you. He said you didn't seem to be taking it well, so I judged it best not to mention it. You'd had enough emotions for one day."

Riley picks at her honey cake pensively. "Did you also think the relationship he and I had was unhealthy?"

"Um... I wouldn't say unhealthy. That's a strong word. Daniel was always a great guy, and you two were in love and happy. But a little co-dependent, yes."

She nods, as if reflecting on the past. "It's true what he said. I didn't take the news well. But not for the reason everyone thinks."

"Why, then?"

She sets the unfinished plate on the coffee table and crosses her legs. "Ending this relationship was the right call. It hurt *a lot,* but it was the right thing to do. It took the both of us a while to move on—me, especially—but we eventually did. And we've stayed friends. We've kept that *closeness.* We still call or text each other nearly every day. I guess I had imagined that we would grow and move through life at the same time. But instead, he's moving without me. He found a purpose, love, stability. And me, I'm left behind. I feel... directionless. Like I'm still the same scared little girl everyone finds weird, and I don't know how to deal with it. I've tried to accept who I am, to embrace it, and I've tried to believe in myself, to believe I was here for a reason, but the truth is, sometimes I still wish I wasn't... *me*. I wish I wasn't an empath. I wish I could go through life like Daniel does. Just... simply. But instead, I complicate everything, and now my friends are turning against me, and soon I'll go back to what I used to be and what I've always feared. *Alone*."

A profound sadness crashes over Rudy, and he can't help himself. He shifts his position and sits sideways on the couch, pulling her by the arm. She moves too and rests her head against his chest, like she's done a million times, letting him stroke her hair.

"You'll never be alone because I'll always be here," he says.

"I'm scared, Dad. I've always wanted to be fearless, but I'm still scared. Demons still scare me. I'm a grown-ass woman, and I still can't swim. Do you know why I never set foot in my old house? It's not because I'm scared of relieving bad memories. I want to go there at times. But I'm scared Lance's ghost will be there. You'd think that after having to face him a few years ago, I conquered that fear, but I didn't."

"No one expects you to be fearless, Riley."

"I know. I'm the one who sets these expectations for myself. I don't want to disappoint people, which is what I've been doing lately."

Her voice thickens a little, and Rudy holds her a little tighter.

"What happened with James?" he asks.

It's not like he can't imagine it. The two of them have been acting weird for a while, and Rudy's not stupid. He knows his daughter better than anyone, and he knows why she moved on from Daniel. As for James, he knows the smartass pretty well too. His behavior around Riley has changed. He's more distant. Careful. As if he's afraid he'll burn himself if he gets too close to her.

Riley sits up, tucking her hair behind her ear. "Um... it's embarrassing."

"I won't judge."

She turns to the window. "Stella's coming back. She doesn't feel happy."

Rudy hears the car driving up the path just as Riley finishes her sentence. "Not happy how?"

"I don't know... tired. Frustrated."

"You think she caught Janice Kraft?"

She shrugs. "We'll know soon enough."

A few seconds later, the door creaks open, and Stella's footsteps pound the floor as she joins them in the living room. She stops and stares at Riley, her face tense. "What are you doing here this late?"

Riley opens her mouth, but Rudy speaks in her place. "She's going to stay with us for a while."

"Oh."

"I promise I won't stay long," Riley says apologetically, probably sensing Stella's clear annoyance.

Rudy turns to her. "You can stay as long as you want. This is your home." He glances up at Stella, almost challenging her to say otherwise. He's always been patient, easy-going, understanding, and he hopes she looks upset only because she had a tough day. But Riley always comes first, and he doesn't like his girlfriend making his daughter feel unwelcome in a home they built together. "It's not an issue, is it?"

Stella turns away and gets a glass of water in the kitchen. "Of course not."

She and Riley have always gotten along. Riley nagged Rudy for months to call Stella and ask her out. They respect each other. But Stella never had kids, and although she never said anything, Rudy knows she doesn't always understand the relationship he has with his daughter.

A gentle pressure on his arm makes him look to his right. Riley says *sorry* in sign language, looking guilty.

"You did nothing wrong," he signs back. He gets up and walks toward Stella. "Did something happen today?"

She leans against the sink, looking at him sternly, then glances over his shoulder at Riley.

Riley reads the room and shuffles off the couch. "I'm gonna put my stuff in my room. Unless you've changed it into a gym or something?"

"No, it'll always be yours," Rudy says, smiling.

He and Stella listen to Riley's footsteps echo up the stairs.

"You could have called me," Stella whispers, even though there's no way Riley would hear anything from that distance.

"She literally just showed up asking for help. What was I supposed to say?"

Stella doesn't answer and sighs in irritation instead.

"Does that bother you that much to have her here?" Rudy says, his own irritation settling in his stomach.

"That's what you think?"

"That's what it looks like."

"Then, I guess you don't know me as well as you think you do."

Rudy frowns, making no reply.

After almost a minute, Stella inhales, opening her mouth a fraction. "I know I seem cold at times. I'm not the warm, happy stepmother."

"I'm not expecting you to—"

"But I really *do* like your daughter. She went through something traumatic today because she wanted to help, and I don't want her to be affected further by this case, especially after what I found today."

"What happened? Did you find Janice Kraft?"

She glances at the hallway again. "No. I dug up everything I could find on her. She has a history of mental illness and aggressive behavior. I went to her place."

Rudy's heart leaps.

"She was gone. But... I entered anyway. And I found enough to get a search warrant."

"Sounds a little backward, but okay."

"Well, obviously, I didn't tell the judge I went inside. Problem is, we don't know where she is, and she might not be back anytime soon. She apparently has a habit of disappearing for days or weeks at a time."

He steps a little closer, feeling stupid for imagining things. "What did you find?"

Stella shakes her head in a way that doesn't sit well with him. "I'm not sure you want to know."

"Tell me."

"A pile of eyeballs and teeth. And there were... *a lot.* Didn't see any hands and feet, though. Two police officers are on stake out in front of Kraft's building. They'll arrest her as soon as she shows up. Her face will soon be on every news channel. I just hope no one else dies before they catch her."

Rudy pulls her in against his chest, tangling his fingers in her curly hair.

"I'm grateful for her help," Stella says. "And I also feel shitty she had to do it. Let's just not tell her about what I found. I don't want her to be further unsettled."

"Deal."

Footsteps thunder down the stairs, and Riley appears in the doorway, wearing flannel shorts and a tank top. She stands there, looking back and forth between them, and none of them need to say anything for her to understand.

"So, did you catch her?"

Stella untangles herself from Rudy's arms and tries to smile. "Not yet, but we will soon thanks to you."

CHAPTER 17

White side. Two bottom rows. Yellow plus. Done. Repeat. Riley mixes the colors on the Rubik's cube and does it again in the soft glow of her bedside lamp. Sleep has been eluding her for hours, and she has given up a while ago. Reading has proved impossible. Her guitar is still at her place. *Kelly's* place. Rudy's guitar is in the living room. She could get it, but playing the guitar isn't an option since she doesn't want to wake up her dad and Stella. So, the Rubik's cube it is, a healthy and quiet hobby that helps her clear her mind.

Something else would take her mind off things. Talking to the master himself.

Riley reaches for her phone and places it on the mattress in front of her, propping it up with one of the pillows. Then, she calls Daniel.

Natural, morning light fills the small screen, a nice contrast from the muted glow of her lamp. Daniel has clearly just gotten up, his golden brown hair still disheveled.

"Now it's my turn to call you in the middle of the night," she says. "Well, *my* middle of the night."

"Can't sleep, darling?"

"Nope. I hope you're sharp enough for a little race." She raises the cube in front of the screen. "I think today is the day I beat you."

"We'll see about that." He props the phone on what Riley knows is the countertop of his kitchen and goes off screen for a few seconds before returning, armed with his own cube.

She waits for him to finish mixing the colors. "Ready? I hope you've had coffee."

"I don't drink coffee."

"Then, you're doomed, Danny boy."

He smiles a bright smile that jumps out of the screen. They count up to three and start. Riley feels like she's going faster than she ever did, probably because she just did it a dozen times before calling Daniel.

"Done!" she says as soon as she finishes, looking at the screen just in time to see the expression of surprise spreading over his face.

"Well, bloody fucking hell."

"I won? Holy crap, I won!" She claps a hand over her mouth, remembering that she needs to be quiet.

"I mean, first time in nine years. And I literally just woke up, but sure, congrats."

"Bitter doesn't suit you, Sunny Boy."

This makes him laugh, that genuine laugh only he's capable of making. "Congratulations, my darling. The student has surpassed the master."

"Thank you."

He leans forward a little, frowning at the screen. "Wait, is that your old room?"

"I'm at my dad's, yeah."

"What happened?"

"Kelly and I agreed it was better not to live under the same roof."

He tilts his head. *"Really? You both agreed?"*

"No, she kicked me out."

Daniel nods. "Sounds about right."

"Go ahead, say it. It's not like I don't know it already."

"Nah, I don't wanna be that guy." A few seconds of silence follow this statement while he takes a sip of tea, and when Riley waits long enough, he adds, *"But."*

"Here we go."

"I told you sleeping with her wasn't a good idea. She's been into you since high school."

"I know, I know... Oh, and I don't have a band anymore. They finally had enough of me."

He opens his eyes wide, his surprise evident. "You're joking."

"Nope."

"I can't believe those guys. After all those times we rehearsed in your garage. And it was *your* dad who booked most of the shows."

"Heh, it's fine. It'll free me some time to..." Riley lets the sentence hang in the air, unfinished because, really, having more time to think about having lost her friends and pissed off James isn't something she looks forward to. "Oh, by the way, better hold on to your socks, because I'm going to give a killer speech on your wedding day."

His face cautiously lights up. "Yeah? I hope it won't be too embarrassing."

"It *will* be embarrassing. And I'm not wearing a dress. I was thinking more like a suit and a bowtie, but in a feminine sort of way."

He smiles wide this time, looking at her with an expression she can only interpret as gratitude. "Just knowing that you'll be there means the world to me." He pauses, the both of them looking at each other. "So... you're okay with it?"

She cocks her head, guilt spreading through her at the thought that she, for just a moment, made him feel bad. He was excited to tell her about his engagement, and she ruined it for him. "*Of course.* I want you to be happy, you know that. In fact, I take credit for your happiness."

"You can."

"My dad told me you called him this morning. Well, yesterday for you."

He nods. "I did. I still like to talk to him. He's a lot more supportive than my dad."

"You're the son he wishes he had."

He laughs. "What does that make you?"

"The daughter he always wanted."

"But what does that make James?"

"The child that was forced on him even if he didn't want it, but he grew to love him, and now he would never part from the jackass."

Laughter fills the room.

"Hey, can I ask you something?" Riley says. "It might sound weird."

"Of course, darling."

"Do you also think we were co-dependent when we were dating?"

A little laugh escapes his mouth. "Oh, absolutely."

"Shut up," she lets out.

"It's true. I mean, I don't know about you, but me, I was addicted to whatever you were doing when you were trying to soothe me. I tried to convince myself many times that I wasn't that fragile little boy who needed constant reassurance, but... well, I was. When I was back in England, I *missed* your touch. When I was with you, I craved it. Like a happy drug."

"Dude... that blows my mind." It was brought to her attention, more than once, that she was easily 'addicted' to bright energies like Daniel's, but she hadn't considered the fact that she could make someone addicted to her by constantly soothing them and taking away their bad feelings.

"Truth is, I actually had to learn to manage my anxiety after we broke up. And I think it'd be better for you if you weren't with someone who always needed reassurance. You also need to be taken care of at times."

"Once again, your wisdom is leaving me on my ass." Riley reflects on this, her thoughts turning to James. He rarely needs reassurance. And when he does, he doesn't ask for it. He likes to protect her. When he's not acting like a dick.

"Something on your mind, Riley?"

"Well... I don't know what you'll think about this, but... I may or may not have developed feelings for James."

Daniel throws his hands in the air, his mouth hanging open, but no words come out.

"Yeah, I know," Riley says.

"Well, *shit*."

"I told him how I felt. Sort of. I guess I could have been clearer."

"Wait, did you or did you not tell him?"

"I–" She pauses, barely remembering the conversation. "I let him know. For sure. And I kissed him, like, *three times,* and now he's being an ass about it. So, you know, I'm upset."

Daniel holds one hand up, slowing her down. "Woah, wait. Walk me through it all."

Riley tells him everything from the first kiss to the last, the unspoken feelings between the two of them all these months, and James's claims that she was utterly wrong, even though, despite having been shitfaced, she remembers clearly how much he had desired her.

"Bloody hell," he says. "I didn't see that one coming. What are you gonna do?"

"Honestly? Ignore the hell out of him. I have more important stuff to think about."

"Like what?"

It's a genuine question, but Riley has momentarily forgotten that she shouldn't burden his mind with that stuff. "Oh, nothing. Nothing important."

"Did something happen?" The smile is gone, and his eyes are filled with worry. "Tell me."

"Paranormal stuff."

"Can you elaborate on that?"

"Your anxiety will shoot through the roof."

"I have medication for that. Come on, tell me about exciting things."

She hesitates, then decides to give him a short version of the recent events. She exorcised a woman who happened to be 'sheltering' her demon, and now Stella's looking for her because she also happens to be a serial killer. "You might see pictures of her on the *'telly'* soon."

"Woah, you helped catch a serial killer, that's insane. I'm glad you're safe, my darling. Just stick to ghosts, all right?"

Riley nods. "Honestly, after today, I'm thinking I want a little break. I'll only be a librarian this week."

CHAPTER 18

"You sure you're okay?"

"Yeah, Dad. Go home and relax."

"James would come if you called him. I'll just call him."

"What? *No.* You are not calling 'Mister Smartass' to 'bodyguard' me."

Rudy cocks his head. "What's up with the air quotes?"

Riley drops her arms and takes a deep breath. The last thing she wants is to see James. The workday is over, and all she wants is to go to Krav Maga and blow off some steam. Moving back in with her dad, even temporarily, doesn't bother her, but there's one thing she never missed, and that's being supervised all the time.

"I'm just going to Krav Maga and then I'll come home, okay?"

Rudy locks Winter's Attic's door and turns to her, his energy spotted in gray anxiety. "You know I worry. You've seen some pretty terrible things."

"I know, but you can't watch over me all the time. And I don't need to see James right now."

"What's going on between you two—"

"Nothing," she answers too fast. "Nothing is going on. Something *could* be going on, but the fact is that James is a shithead, and therefore, nothing's going on."

"Okay…"

"And I'm tired of being the 'patient' one, you know? The one who listens and understands and gives him space when he needs to 'figure things out–'"

"Again with the angry air quotes."

"Well, I *am* angry. So, now it's *his* turn to marinate in his own juice, and *I'm* the one who needs space. I don't wanna talk to him, and I'm gonna get some exercise and stay even longer after that to beat the crap out of a punching bag." She pauses, remembering to breathe, and nudges Rudy toward his truck. "I'll see you at dinner."

"All right, all right." He turns back to her before opening the truck's door, pushing against her pressure. "Call me if you need anything."

"I won't because I'm okay."

Rudy sighs as he opens the driver's door and hops in. He rolls the window down and sticks his elbow out. "Do I need to punch him in the face or something? Give him the scary dad talk?"

This steals a small chuckle out of Riley. "No, it's fine. We'll work it out, it's just… I've got my wires crossed, that's all."

He looks at her in a way that she knows *he* knows, but he doesn't say anything. That's something she loves about him. He never meddles. Never asks too many questions about her private life. When she told him she was also attracted to girls two years ago, he just nodded, smiled, and said *Thank you for sharing that with me* before he went on with his day. Riley knows he'll be there to listen to her whenever she's ready to talk about it. Right now, though, she needs some time alone.

She stands next to the truck and leans in to kiss his hairy cheek. "I'll come straight home after the gym."

They part ways, Riley hopping in her car, and Rudy driving away. If she had slept more last night, she wouldn't have overslept this morning, and they would have carpooled.

The hour working out helps clear her head and releases the tension that has built up in her guts. After the class, she stays a few more minutes to beat the crap out of a punching bag, as promised. The room is emptying, the hearing aids are in their box, and Riley can experience these rare moments when she feels almost alone, not surrounded by so many vibrations. She can hear a little, but she focuses on her punches instead, tuning out the rest. She releases her anger and frustration and leaves the club after taking a shower, feeling calmer and more serene.

When she steps out, it's already night, and a hint of crispness finally seeps into a growing wind, blowing through her freshly washed hair. She checks her phone as she sits inside her car, throwing her duffel bag next to her, and all the previously expelled frustration flares up again at the sight of James's several missed calls and texts.

Riley, pick up the phone. I want to talk.

I'm sorry.

"Sorry, I need space. Like you when you're in a crap mood."

She pats her wet hair a few more times with her towel before putting her hearing aids back on. She could do without them, but she likes to have them while driving.

On the passenger seat, the phone buzzes again. Riley stares at it, her hand aching to take it and pick up. But she doesn't, and the phone eventually falls silent again.

Only for a few seconds.

A new text from James pops up.

Fuck it. I'm coming over.

Riley lets out a grunt of irritation and thrusts the phone back inside her pocket. Let him come, then. He'll crumble down when her dad shoots him his most threatening Death Stare. Hopefully, they won't find themselves on the same road at the same time, since he'll have to drive close to the Krav Maga studio to go to her house.

Riley exits the parking lot, the knot in her stomach tightening. What does he want? If it were him who needed space, everyone would tell her to just leave him alone. Why can't *she* be left alone for once? Some peace would be nice. A few days of no one expecting anything from her, whether it is to love or to listen or to come to someone's rescue.

The view darkens as she drives through that portion of the road that rises up and snakes through the woods. It's beautiful there in the fall, when the leaves turn into flamboyant reds and oranges and yellows. It's also treacherous in the winter, when snow and ice cover the asphalt and threaten to send your car flying over the edge of the cliff.

But on a warm night like this, it's dark and peaceful. Riley has driven here hundreds of times and knows each turn. A sliver of light pierces the sky in the distance. That thunderstorm is finally coming and will take away the suffocating heat New England's summers are capable of.

Everyone waits for warmth after months of snow but gets sick of high temperatures after only a few weeks.

Riley's skin breaks into a cold sweat, the hairs at the back of her neck rising. Something insidious and smothering overpowers her. She hits the brakes, suddenly too light-headed to keep driving, and looks around herself, her heart beating so hard it threatens to burst through her ribcage. Her panting fills her ears.

Only darkness surrounds her. No movement. No cars or human in sight.

Riley stares at the woods. There's something there, lurking in the dark, invisible, and it's colossal. Something far bigger and imposing than anything she's ever felt.

A car comes in the opposite direction, the headlights reminding her to move.

Clamping her trembling hands back on the steering wheel, Riley hits the accelerator again. The Dodge barely has time to thrust forward when the other car takes a sharp turn and crashes into her. The impact jars her, and before her mind realizes what's happening, the car backs up and lurches forward, again crashing into the driver's side and crushing the door. It doesn't stop this time. Its wheels screech as it keeps pushing Riley's Dodge across the road, toward the edge of the cliff.

Riley glances at the driver but can't make out their face. The compressing evil surrounding her is playing tricks on her, altering her lucidity. She can't take hold of her vehicle as the mad driver crashes against it and pushes it again, so hard that the Dodge makes a quarter of a turn, directly facing the precipice from which trees poke at odd angles.

Icy terror as sharp as razor blades seizes her as another shock jolts her car, bringing it closer to the edge.

She needs to get out. Fast. All reason and logic and strategy leave her. All she wants to do is open the door, just open the fucking door that's destroyed and crushed and just won't move.

The wheels screech behind her seconds before the car blasts into the rear of the Dodge again, pushing it over the edge.

Someone is strangling her, using some sort of sharp rope that digs into the side of her neck. It makes breathing difficult, but not impossible. Her head throbs angrily as she is being pulled forward. Her hair sticks to her face. Something warm trickles from her forehead to the bridge of her nose, and drips down. It never touches her mouth, which is weird.

Riley laboriously blinks, trying to force her eyes open. She's still in her car, but for some reason, her hair darkens the view of the steering wheel, and the blood drips down onto it.

A rush of panic, *someone's* panic, blasts through her core. Shouting follows. A familiar voice.

As Riley tries to move, her achy ribcage sends a jolt of agonizing pain through her, making her cry out. Her hand flutters to it, attempting to grab what's crushing her chest. The texture under her fingertips is familiar, and when Riley tries to pull it away, it resists, already pulled taunt by her body.

My seat belt.

A clear memory of what happened jumps back at her. She looks above the steering wheel, through the shattered windshield. Her breath catches in her throat as a sliver of panic shoots through her spine. Below the windshield is the front of the car crumbled against a tree. Below the tree and the branches and the leaves is nothing. A black sea of emptiness as the Dodge dangles on the edge of the cliff, only stopped by a miraculously placed oak.

Riley's body shakes in fear and in pain, and her lungs can't draw oxygen as she stares down. One movement, and the car could plunge into the abyss.

The voice above her doesn't relent, and she finally focuses on it. On the energy. The wild, uncontrollable fear.

"Riley, please, answer me!"

"Jamie..." His name comes out as a raspy whisper that he couldn't have heard.

An alarming noise paralyzes her. A frightening squeaking sound. Metal grinding against wood, slowly shifting.

Riley finds her voice. "Jamie!"

"Riley! Are you okay?"

She swallows, the patch of skin where the belt digs in around her throat tender and raw. "I've been better..."

"You need to get out. *Now.*"

"I-I can't move."

Another distressing groan from the car, making her gasp.

"Yes, you can. You *have* to. I can't reach you, you have to come to me."

The car isn't completely upright, but it's certainly too tilted for her liking. It draws all her blood to her head and makes her dizzy. If she unbuckles the seat belt, she'll shift forward–*drop* forward–and might give the car the nudge it needs to slip from the tree.

"I can't... I'm gonna fall."

"Lovie, listen to me. Can you hear me?"

She mutters a yes, grateful to have put her hearing aids back on. Even with them, straining to hear him only aggravates the pounding headache.

"Strengthen your legs. Push against the floor and hang onto the steering wheel when you unfasten your seat belt. Push as hard as you can so you don't drop."

It's not like she has a choice. The *something* is still out there, somewhere. She needs to get out before the car slips from the tree.

Riley does what she's told, pressing her feet down on the carpet and one hand onto the steering wheel. With her other hand, she shakily fumbles for the button and, after bracing herself, presses it.

The belt comes undone, and despite holding on as much as she can, her body still slides forward, shaking the car. The metal complains some more. She waits, eyes closed, clenching her teeth at the stab of pain in her ribs, expecting to tumble down the cliff, but nothing else happens.

"Good. That's very good," James says above her, trying to control the tremor in his voice. "Now you need to crawl up to the back seat."

"Really, is that all I need to do?"

"Come on, lovie, you can do it. I'm right here with you."

Riley has a moment of hesitation, not knowing how the hell she can turn and let go of the stability she found.

"Just grab the passenger seat with your right hand," James says, as though reading her mind.

Taking in a ragged breath, Riley reluctantly unlatches one of her hands and clamps it on the passenger seat, gripping the faux leather there.

"That's right. Now the other one."

Putting all the pressure on her shaky legs and blinking blood out of her eyes, she turns a bit more sharply than she wants, hanging onto the top of the passenger seat and finding herself twisted at an awkward angle. The car groans again as she lifts her left leg and slowly places it on the passenger's side.

"You've got this, lovie. You're doing great."

Riley finally looks up, horror freezing the blood in her veins. From here, James looks small, on all fours on the edge of the cliff, looking down at her. She's a lot farther down than she'd imagined. Even if she manages to get to the back seat, James won't be able to reach her. She'll have to exit the car. Climb onto the trunk. And then *maybe* he can pull her up.

The repeated impacts against the car have exploded most of the windows, and many holes have pierced the shattered rear windshield. That's why she can hear him okay.

"Shift your feet against the glove compartment and pull yourself to the back seat."

She nods, muttering to herself. "Okay. Right... Piece of cake."

She quickly wipes some of the blood seeping into her eyes and climbs between the front seats, her body feeling heavy.

James gives her an encouraging look, although the terror he feels is hard to dissociate from. "Go to your left. It'll be easier to get out through the window there."

Her heart flips. Riley knows that the overall goal of this operation is to get out of the fucking car, but each task drains more of her energy, and knowing there's more coming, *worse things*, leaves her desperate and sick.

She crouches onto the passenger seat, sitting on its back. She shuts her eyes and winces again, as more shifting and creaking paralyze her. She waits it out, then looks up at James for instructions.

"Now. You have to sit on the edge of the window, then pull yourself onto the rear windshield."

Her eyes flicker to the mostly shattered glass. "It will break under my weight."

"You won't stand on it. You'll have to leave one foot on the edge and hang onto the trunk with your hands."

Riley nods, shaking, and can't help but whisper a dozen *fucks* as she slides out of the window and sits on its edge. Lukewarm wind envelops her, whistling in her hearing aids and making her hair fly around her head. Now she has to pull herself out of the window, but she can't find purchase, so she reluctantly reaches for one of the big holes in the back windshield and curls her fingers around it. The glass digs into her skin as she puts pressure on it. She slowly emerges from the car and places her feet on the edge of the window. More groaning. More shaking. More fear crushing her and threatening to make her body collapse.

James says something, but his voice is snatched away by a gust of wind. If he weren't here, if he hadn't thought *'fuck it, I'm coming over,'* she'd probably still be stuck in the driver's seat.

Sliding one knee onto the windshield, Riley reaches for the top of the trunk with a bloody hand and grabs it. She pushes onto that knee, her other foot dangling in the air for a second, and the second bloody hand joins the first. The shattered glass digs into her knees, scratching through the jeans fabric. Riley ignores it as she flattens her hands against the side of the cliff and pulls herself onto a standing position on the rear windshield.

Her heart sinks. Explodes. Bursts.

She has to also get onto the crumpled trunk, where the plate is, and stand on it if she wants to reach James. This fucking moment will never be over.

The car drops a foot farther, shaking Riley. She lets out a cry as one of her feet bursts through the glass. She hangs onto the trunk, the blood pumping furiously in her head. James's terror mixes with her own, smothering her. The tree beneath her swings for a moment, and the seconds stretch until she thinks it'll never end.

"Riley, look at me. Look at me."

She tilts her head, her neck stiff.

"You're gonna be all right, okay? I'm right here." He reaches a hand down. "You just have to stand on the trunk, lovie. And then I'll be right here."

She swallows around the lump in her throat and pulls herself up with achy arms. The wind rises, shifting her hair and blinding her. The back of her shirt is cold, soaked with sweat.

Riley runs her hand over the cliff wall, only lit by the angry red taillights, searching for purchase. When her palm connects with a protruding rock, she grabs it, pulling herself up with the remainder of her strength. Her fingers sting. More blood seeps out of the cuts there, hot on her skin, but she refuses to lighten the pressure. One after the other, her feet move up the trunk, standing on one of the taillights.

The rocky wall grazes her chest and cheek as she flattens her body against it, the cramps in her hands increasing as they stay clamped on the cavities. The car shudders under her feet. Her breath comes out in short, unsteady outbursts.

"Take my hand."

James's voice, falsely calm but solid and reassuring, gives her the strength she needs to look up.

He's flat on his stomach, reaching down. "Take my hand, lovie. I've got you."

Heart in throat, Riley unclasps one hand, and runs it up the cliff. The tears pricking her eyes threaten to spill when she can only graze his fingertips.

"You have to jump," James says.

A shiver shakes her, and she clasps her hand on the wall again, closing her eyes and clenching her jaw. "I can't."

"Lovie."

She raises her head to look at him, the red taillights casting shadows across his features.

"Trust me."

He tries to reach farther down as he says this, hand open wide, ready to grab her. Riley lifts her hand again, trying to ignore the way the wind makes the car sway and groan under her feet, bends her knees...

And jumps.

For half a second, it doesn't feel like her body goes up, but like the car slides down, stripping her of the stability she needs to push up, but then James's strong fingers close around her wrist. Adrenaline shoots through her body, and Riley plants her feet on the wall, grabbing his wrist with her second bloody hand. She climbs up as he lifts her faster than she ever thought he could, and not ten seconds later, he hooks an arm around her waist, and she is dragged away from the edge of the cliff.

She collapses in his arms, her body agitated by uncontrollable shivers as she clings onto him desperately, ignoring the pain in her slashed fingers. James holds her close, his heart pounding hard enough for her to feel it, stroking her hair and back as though to make sure she's here.

He pulls away and slightly shakes her. "What the *fuck* did you do?"

She doesn't have time to answer before he pulls her back into a fierce hug that is meant to calm his nerves more than hers. They stay in that awkward sitting-hugging position for a while longer, breathing in each other's ear.

A metallic groan rises below. Riley's heart flips, and she tears herself away from James, shuffling to the edge of the cliff just as branches give in, and the Dodge slides off the tree, tumbling and rolling down the steep incline. Its headlights' beam sweeps over more trunks, and the car finally crashes onto its back far below.

Staring at the hint of red light painting the branches, Riley lets out a sad moan. "My car..."

James rubs her back as he kneels next to her. "What happened?"

"Someone pushed me."

She looks behind them at the deserted road except for James's Mustang. Whoever was here left, but the evil presence still permeates the air around them.

169

The *something* shifts inside the woods, just behind the tree line. Riley flinches, searching the darkness.

James's hand doesn't leave her back. "What is it?"

Thick shadows play tricks on her eyes, shifting and dancing. The hair on her arms rises. An icy chill crawls through her skin. Her stomach is nothing but a bottomless pit.

"We're not alone."

CHAPTER 19

James yanks Riley to her feet. He keeps an arm in front of her, putting his body between her and the forest, shielding her.

"What do you think it is?" he says, his voice low.

"I don't know... But it's enormous. We need to go."

He grabs her hand and pulls her to his car in a hurry, almost shoving her in the passenger seat, then hops in behind the steering wheel and starts the engine. The warding engraved inside the car—the doors, the trunk, the hood—helps Riley breathe a little easier, slightly muffling the presence outside, though she still feels it. It's too big to be hindered.

James glances at her. "You okay?"

Nausea still gags her. The piercing headache from where she smashed her face against the steering wheel pounds fiercely. Her slashed fingers stick with blood. But she nods.

She can't pinpoint the *something* and keeps sweeping her eyes over the road and the dark woods surrounding them as they drive downhill. James takes a turn, his headlights bringing into sharp relief the cars blocking their path.

"Watch out!" Riley cries out just as James slams the brakes, making the car screech to a stop.

A red and a gray car stand in the middle of the road. The drivers look right at them, a sickly grin stretching their lips. The gray car's hood is crumpled. One of the headlights is crushed.

"That's him…" Riley says. "He pushed me."

James's anger spikes, punching Riley's stomach. He reaches for the car handle, but she grabs his arm and pulls him back before he can exit the car, ignoring the searing pain in her fingers and the blood she's painting on his skin.

"Don't!"

He swivels back to her and stares. "I will *fuck him up,"* he says through gritted teeth, barely containing his anger.

"Something wrong is happening here. Like, really, *really* wrong."

Riley looks at the man in the car again. He hasn't moved. His own forehead is wounded, and blood snakes over his eyes and mouth and teeth.

Movement catches her eyes to the right. A dark shape shifts in the shadows, just behind the tree line. Then, another one to the left. And another, until several others worm their way into the headlights, crawling down trees.

Riley's stomach feels like it's melting as people step out of the forest, all their eyes fixed on her. The *something* is them. A dozen people or more, some evil, some worse, stand in front of James's car, blocking the way.

"What the fuck is going on…" James whispers.

Riley stares at their faces, her fingers still clenching James's arm. A young man with blond hair. A middle aged woman with dark brown hair and office type clothes. An older man wearing grease-stained jumpers. All of them looking normal, some of them with black eyes.

The something isn't one enormous presence. It's several bad people, many of them possessed.

One last shape walks out of the forest, her dark clothes too large for her, and her wild, gray hair framing her face. Janice plants herself in front of the car, smiling at Riley, her eyes as dark as night until she blinks, clearing them. "Come out, Miss Winter. I just want to talk."

She didn't even raise her voice, and Riley knows why. Kraft saw into her head, as much as Riley saw into Kraft's head. She knows Riley can read lips.

"She's possessed again…" she mutters in disbelief.

"What did she say?" James asks, his voice tight.

"She wants to talk to me."

"Don't you *dare* step out of this car."

Janice cocks her head, her eyebrows raised. "Not all of us carry a passenger here. The warding on your car can't keep the humans away. Come out now, or we'll drag you out by force."

Riley swallows, her throat so dry it's painful. "They'll get me themselves if I don't get out."

"They can't cross the symbols—"

"They're not all possessed."

James looks behind the car, his jaw working.

"You can't get out," Riley says. She doesn't need to glance over her shoulder to know that three new cars have stopped behind them, blocking their way out. "Not without running them over."

"Come out, Celeste," she reads on Janice's lips. "Or we'll kill him." Her eyes shift to James in a way that makes Riley's stomach turn.

They're surrounded. Their only escape option, driving *through* the mass of people, would lead to carnage, and even then, they might not make it out. They could fall off the cliff, or just be forced by the non-possessed people to get out of the car and be put down like animals.

Riley turns to James and takes his hand. "Jamie, I need you to stay inside the car."

His face falls, his eyes and soul coated with panic. "What are you—"

"She's gonna *kill* you. I know you're scared, and I know you want to protect me, but there's *no* way out of this. Let me talk to her."

"What do you think she's gonna do, Riley?"

"I don't think she wants to kill me."

"No? Did I dream the part where your car was pushed off the fucking cliff?"

A knock on the passenger window. Riley swivels around to look at the office worker-looking woman with dark hair. She straightens up and opens the door, waiting patiently.

"It'll be all right," she says.

James draws his gun and points it straight at the woman, leaning forward to protect Riley. "Don't fucking touch her."

The open door lets the evil vibes crawl inside the car, nearly choking Riley. She takes a shaky breath and lowers James's arm. "Stay inside the car. I mean it."

She exits the car and shuts the door before he can reply, plunging into a demonic energy so thick it's hard to breathe or discern anybody's feelings. She takes a few steps forward, staying at a safe distance from the car. The dark-haired woman stays close, too close, and Riley shoots her the Winter-made Death Stare as a silent warning to back off.

"I'm sorry about earlier," Janice says, her voice a lot calmer than when Riley exorcized her. "We didn't mean to push you over the edge. We meant to stop you and force you out of your car. But *someone* went overboard." She gives the stink eye to the driver, whose smile vanishes as he looks down sheepishly.

"What do you want?"

"I saw inside your head, Riley, just like you saw inside of mine. I know things about you. Very interesting things."

"Is that how you found me?"

Janice nods. "Well, of course. I don't know where you live, but I know where you do your Krav Maga thing. I know about this empty road."

A million questions swarm Riley's mind. "Who are you people?"

Janice's lips stretch into a wide smile. "It seems like you didn't see *everything,* the same way I don't know everything about you. I know enough, though."

Thunder rumbles in the distance, slivers of light tearing through the night sky. The vibes press harder against her as some of the possessed people close in on her. Riley keeps her eyes on Janice, her hand creeping to her pocket to feel the pocketknife there. It won't be enough against all of them, but it could buy her some time.

"I was very mad when you took my passenger away," Janice says. "I was *enraged.* And because of you I can't even go home now. But I'm willing to forgive you. Just because you're special."

The possessed ones take another step closer. Seven of them. Riley doesn't move, willing her body not to collapse under the pressure.

"I'll ask again. What do you want from me?" she says.

"I want you on the team, Riley."

Riley frowns, glancing around her and fixing her gaze on Janice again. "The team?"

"The Faceless wants to have you."

"The... Are you a cult or something?"

"Our master was very clear. Either we bring you back, or..."

Black eyes surround her, the demons dwarfing her energy with theirs.

Riley swallows. "Or what?"

Janice's smile fades away, and her dead stare locks on her. "Or we'll destroy you."

Riley strains to feel James's energy to reassure herself, to feel less lonely in an ocean of darkness, but she can't pierce through the cloud.

"Understand that I'm not the one making the rules, Celeste," Janice says. "The master does. And he already loves you. So much so that he wishes for you to come to him *willingly*."

A stiff scoff escapes Riley's mouth. "You just said you were gonna destroy me if I said no."

"We won't kill you. The Faceless thinks you're too *precious* for that." The disdain is evident as Janice looks Riley up and down. "He wants you to come to him. To surrender and give yourself to his being. I'm just here to make sure it happens."

They won't kill her, then. But Riley's stomach clenches at the thought that they could hurt someone she loves. Maybe James could leave her and save his life, actually drive through the mass of people blocking his way. But he won't do that.

Riley glances over her shoulder and signs with her left hand hidden behind her back, "Go away."

His face hardens, and he shakes his head no.

For fuck's sake, Williams.

She wants to tell him they won't hurt her—at least for now—but they will kill him if he doesn't move. She doesn't have time to sign any of it before Janice's voice, loud and clear, rises above the wind.

"What's it going to be, Celeste? I need an answer *now*."

The demons surrounding her tighten their circle around her. They lick their lips, shaking in anticipation as though ready to eat her alive.

Riley takes a step back, bumps into the car's hood, and takes her knife out, steeling her body against the upcoming attack. "That'll never fucking happen."

As if that single sentence is what they needed to be triggered, the shadows around her shriek and jump at her. One of the bodies crash into her, slamming her against the car. The knife's blade sinks in the man's flesh, but that doesn't stop him from clawing at her face. In a second, they're all on her, pulling at her hair and clothes and limbs, drowning her in their maliciousness.

James's aura is closer, a little brighter, but never reaches her. Riley can't see or hear him. In an attempt to get herself out of the hands grabbing her, she swings her knife and gives a kick to the body directly in front of her. This is enough to give her space to roll over the Mustang's hood and free herself.

An entity crawling over one of the cars blocking the road jumps from the roof, the man's body connecting into Riley with such force it presses the wind out of her. Her back hits the ground, and she doesn't have time to catch her breath when dozens of hands pin her down, their fingers firmly planted in her arms and stomach and thighs and ankles.

Janice Kraft appears to her left and bends over, a sadistic smile spreading over her face. "I was hoping you'd say no."

Riley tries to move, but the groaning, drooling monsters holding her have a firm grip on her. Whatever James is doing, or whatever *they* are doing to him, she can't see it, can't hear it, can't feel it.

"Please, don't hurt him," she blurts out, breathless, each word causing stabbing pain in her ribs.

Janice cocks her head. "Don't you worry about him. Worry about yourself."

Ectoplasm drips on Riley's neck as a demon bends over her, watching her with hungry eyes.

"You said you weren't gonna kill me," Riley says through gritted teeth, her head spinning from the malevolent touches.

"We're not." The macabre smirk stretches wider. "We're going to do exactly what you like to do to us."

The next moments are nothing but a big blur of pain and pressure and screams. *Her* screams. The pressure turns into pulling, making Riley think she's being skinned alive. Her voice dies as something thick fills her chest and is ripped out of her.

She catches a glimpse of purple light, then everything goes dark as the shadows annihilate the glow.

CHAPTER 20

James punches the man holding him and kicks another one, his one and only goal being to save Riley from whatever they're doing to her. A woman jumps at him as soon as he takes another step toward Riley and the crowd of demons holding her down. He shakes her off, throwing her to the ground. But they won't relent. All these people, these *humans* keep getting up and charge him again.

James looks for the gun he dropped earlier when getting out of the car. He was so eager to get to Riley when she was assaulted that he didn't pay attention to the people waiting for him and got disarmed. The gun is just a few paces away, and he lunges for it, snatching it off the ground. He spins around and pulls the trigger on the first person dashing toward him. The bang echoes, mixing with thunder, and the man collapses with a scream. James turns into a semi-circle, keeping the others at bay.

"No one fucking moves, or I swear I'll kill you all," he grunts.

A woman raises her hands in a peaceful gesture. She's the middle-aged, dark-haired woman who opened the door to

Riley earlier. She gestures at the others to stay back while the man moans, holding his injured arm. She takes a step forward.

James points the gun at her. "I mean it. Don't fucking move."

"We're not here to hurt you."

"Great. Fuck off, then. And let her go. *Now.*"

"It's better you let them finish what they've started."

James glances over at the mass of bodies hiding Riley from his view, but the non-possessed people stand between him and her. "What the fuck are they doing to her?"

"They're taking what belongs to them. To the master. She's not what you'd call a normal person. I think you know that."

James readjusts his fingers on his gun. "I have enough bullets to end you all. Demons can't possess dead bodies. I could easily finish this. So, tell them to stop."

"You don't want to do that. She could die if you interrupted them now, and that's not what we want."

His heart in his throat and sweat stinging his eyes, James looks again at the entities. They're bent over Riley, who has stopped screaming, and her silence worries him a lot more. "What is happening? Who are you people?"

"It'll be over in a minute. This is a delicate process. You'll both be free to go after this."

He stays frozen, his arm aching, caught between believing this woman and wanting to charge through the mass of people and demons to shield Riley with his body. He's useless. If Rudy were here, he would know what to do. But James isn't the negotiating kind, and he feels lost. Clinging to the last sliver of hope of saving Riley, he asks, "Is she gonna be okay?"

The woman gives him a reassuring smile—genuine or fake, he can't tell—and nods. "Yes. I'm really sorry about this, but she'll be fine."

A demon screech startles him. The humans suddenly scatter around. The woman, still holding her hands up, backtracks her steps, then helps the injured man up. Janice smiles at James in the distance while the shadows scurry away from Riley in all directions and climb into the different cars.

James's feet are nailed to the ground, and he can't bring himself to lower his gun, now aiming for Janice.

"We'll see you soon, I think," she says before turning away and climbing in the red car.

The cars in front and behind his Mustang scatter, and James darts on weak legs to Riley, throwing himself at her side and dropping his gun. His hands shake as he hooks an arm under her shoulders and lifts her up, gently patting her cheek.

"Riley, wake up. Please, wake up." His voice quivers too much for his liking. He doesn't know what the fuck is going on or what the hell they did to her. All he knows is that she's unconscious in his arms. The Mustang's headlights are in his back, casting his own shadow over her, and he can't even assess her injuries properly.

He shakes her not so gently, his jaw clenched. "Lovie, answer me."

Riley shifts.

Relief floods him, loosening his chest. He holds her close, exhaling slowly to control the ache in his throat. "Fuck... I was so scared."

A blow to the chest presses the wind out of him. He nearly falls back but catches himself, as Riley scrambles away from him, her eyes wild.

"Don't touch me!" she says, her voice thick with a panic he has rarely heard.

Startled, he stares at her for a moment before raising his hands. "Calm down, it's me."

She doesn't stop backing away until her back presses against a tree trunk. She stares back, wide-eyed and shaking. Something is wrong with those eyes. They don't reflect the light the way they usually do.

"Lovie, it's me. Are you okay?"

She presses a hand against her mouth as if nauseated, moaning behind it. "Oh my God..."

James rises to his feet slowly and takes one careful step in her direction. "What's happening?"

"Stay back!"

He freezes on the spot, confused, and raises his hands to show he won't make a move. "All right, all right. Can you tell me if you're hurt?"

"What did they do to you?" she sobs.

His racing heart flips unpleasantly. "To me? What do you mean? They did something to you, not me."

She breaks into tears. Not like she did two days ago. These are full on choked sobs, a sight he hasn't seen in years. Riley has concealed her emotions masterfully after breaking up with Daniel, and seeing her so dismayed breaks James's heart.

He crouches, trying to make himself look less threatening. "Lovie, you need to talk to me and tell me what's happening. Are you hurt? Do I need to take you to the hospital?"

She inhales between two hiccups, drawing her knees close to her chest. "Are you dead?"

The question leaves him speechless for a second, and a chill crawls down his back. "No, Riley, I'm right here before you. I think you hit your head badly." He reaches out to her carefully with one hand. "Let me take you to the hospital."

She visibly shivers at the sight of his hand, so he withdraws it.

"You're dead," she sobs, burying her face in her hands. "I don't know what they did, but you're dead."

"Riley." He swallows, choosing his words carefully and attempting to get a hold of the growing fear grinding his guts. "Why do you think I'm dead?"

"Because I can't feel you." She raises her head again, staring straight at him. "Your energy's gone."

The strands of light aren't enough to light her face completely, but when another blast of thunder splits the sky, a bright flash brings her face into sharp relief, and James sees what's wrong with her eyes.

They're brown.

Not silver.

The streaks of purple nonexistent.

Just a pure, simple brown.

The flash of light disappears, plunging them back into darkness.

"I promise you I'm not dead, Riley. They didn't do anything to me. Just stay put, okay? It-it's gonna be all right."

James slowly reaches for his phone with a trembling hand and brings it to his ear. She's too scared and perturbed for him to handle. There's only one person who knows how to talk to her.

The streaks of purple nonexistent.

Just a pure, simple brown.

The flash of light disappears, plunging them back into darkness.

"I promise you I'm not dead, Riley. They didn't do anything to me. Just stay put, okay? It-it's gonna be all right."

James slowly reaches for his phone with a trembling hand and brings it to his ear. She's too scared and perturbed for him to handle. There's only one person who knows how to talk to her.

CHAPTER 21

Rudy takes another turn, and James's Mustang comes into view. He pulls over and jumps out of the truck, heart in throat. At the sight of him, James–who was crouching a few feet from Riley–rises to his feet and meets him halfway.

"Is she okay?" Rudy asks, glancing at his daughter curled up against a tree, hugging her knees and burying her face.

James looks aghast and jittery, fumbling to choose the right words. "Something really fucked up just happened. All these people and demons came out of, like, nowhere. They threw her fucking car off the cliff! And they did something to her, and now she's hysterical, and I don't know how to deal with it–"

Rudy clasps a hand on his shoulder. "Calm down, boy. Tell me what happened. Slowly."

James takes a deep breath and gives him a disjointed story about being ambushed by cult-like people, half of them possessed, the others just plain human. "Janice Kraft was there. It's like she was leading them, and she was possessed again but in full control of her body."

Rudy nods, registering all this, and starts toward his daughter, eager to see if she's okay.

James grabs his arm. "Wait. They... They did something to her."

"What did they do?"

"I think... I don't know... They took her empathy. Or something..."

"They—How did they do that?"

James shakes his head, his jaw working. "I-I don't know."

Rudy glances at Riley, taking a deep breath. "I'll go talk to her."

"Be gentle, you're gonna freak her out. She thinks we're dead. Remember her first reaction to Grace four years ago?"

How could Rudy forget? Riley was terrified. He nods, clenching his teeth.

"It's the same now. She can't feel us. Look at her." He points at her. She's still curled up, her face buried as she hugs her knees. "She hasn't even looked up, she doesn't know you're here. Because she can't feel you. So, just... don't sneak up on her."

Tendrils of terror slither through Rudy's chest as he steps in Riley's direction. Despite the rising wind, he can hear her mumble things to herself, adding to his concern.

"This isn't possible... I'm losing my mind, I'm losing my mind... This just isn't possible..."

He crouches in front of her, at a safe distance, not daring to touch her. "Pumpkin."

She shoots up, startled, staring at him with wide, brown eyes. The sight of them makes his heart jump. He didn't expect this. Her forehead is stained with dried blood, an injury he hasn't been told about yet.

Tears spill and roll down her cheeks as her lips tighten, and she shakes her head. "No... Not you too... Please, not you..."

The urge to hold her and comfort her tugs at him, but he doesn't want to pressure her. "What do you feel?"

"Nothing."

"You can't feel my aura?"

"There's nothing. No feelings, no colors, no energy. The air is empty and quiet and *dead*. They took it away from me, Dad. I don't know how they did it, but they took it, and now it's like you're *all dead*." Her voice breaks again, breaking Rudy's heart at the same time.

So, James is right. She lost her empathy. Her sixth sense. Which is clearly devastating to her, and Rudy can't imagine what it must be like to lose a sense so suddenly. It's probably just as distressing to lose eyesight or hearing.

"Riley, look at me."

Her eyes, so unfamiliarly brown it hurts, fix on him.

"I'm here. I'm not dead, and James isn't dead, either. I can't imagine what it feels like for you, but we'll figure it out, kiddo. Together."

"How?" The question is loaded with disbelief, uncertainty, and fear.

"For starters, we'll go to the hospital."

"No hospital."

"Riley, you hit your head. You might have a concussion—"

"No. I can't... I don't want to see other people..." She pauses, looking at him with imploring eyes. "I don't want to be surrounded by dead people."

Rudy nods despite himself. He can't stand those watery eyes. "All right. We'll go home for now."

She peers at him with mistrust, as though wondering if he isn't a figment of her imagination, unmoving. "You're not lying, are you?"

"I would never lie to you."

"But you do, sometimes. When you want to protect me. I can't tell if you're doing it now. Please, don't lie to me."

He holds out a hand for her to take, willing it to stay steady. "We're going to drive home and figure things out from there. You trust me, don't you?"

Riley raises a shaky, bloody hand, placing her palm inside of his. He offers his second hand, and she takes it. Rudy gently pulls her to her feet. She doesn't take her eyes away from him, squeezing his hands as though making sure he's real, then breaks into tears against his chest in a way she hasn't done in a while.

He gently nudges her toward his truck, an arm wrapped around her shoulders, and glances at James. "Are you able to drive?"

James nods. "I'll see you there."

So, this is what loneliness feels like. Riley has never really experienced it. She was always close enough to someone to be able to feel them. Her dad on the first floor. James in his room. Kelly somewhere in the apartment. But this, this is disturbingly quiet. Quieter than when she takes her hearing aids off. Darker than when the lights are off. This is lifeless, empty.

Riley looks at Rudy. He's right here, next to her, as he sits on the couch with her and pats the blood off her forehead. But there are no colors. None of the anxiety or fear or stress get to her. His gentle, blue soul is nonexistent. He's just a man. Is this what people are? Bodies that disappear once you close your eyes?

When she woke up in James's arms earlier, her mind couldn't comprehend what was happening. Something was touching her, pressing against her, something warm and solid. It was *him*. But seeing him, without the intensity of his sharp, red, "Highway to Hell" style soul brushing against her skin sent her into panic mode, and her mind automatically made the link to Grace. If she couldn't feel James, then he was dead and brought back to life with her energy. Couldn't be anything else.

She was wrong, she realizes that now. These people... they took it from her. Her empathy. Her reason for existing. The thing she wished more times than she can count she never had. Now that it's gone, leaving a hole, a raw *tear* through her soul, she wants nothing more than having it back.

"I'm nothing without it..." The words escape her mouth without her knowledge.

Rudy peers at her with an expression that she thinks is concern. "What did you say?"

"I've tried for so many years to make peace with being what I am. A celestial. An empath. I've gone back and forth between trying to accept it and hating it, but I built my identity around it, and now... I don't know what I'm supposed to be."

His blue eyes are kind as they fix on her. She was struck by the color of those eyes the first time she met him. She always thought of them as being icy blue or light blue, but the official name for this color is baby blue. His soul was the same color, she realizes. *Is* the same color. It's not because she can't feel it that it doesn't exist. It can be streaked with darker blue or gray or red depending on his mood. But mostly baby blue. A soothing color.

"No one is just one thing, Riley. We all have several identities. Look at me. I'm a paranormal investigator and a bookshop owner. A musician. I was a husband, and now I'm a boyfriend. But my favorite identity is being your dad. As well as a grumpy man."

This gets a chuckle out of her, one that makes her eyes watery and blurs her vision. "What am I?"

"You're a good friend, a wonderful singer and guitar player, a cute librarian, and a kickass paranormal investigator, celestial or not. And you're my daughter."

She smiles a small smile at this.

James comes back into the room, startling her despite his thundering footsteps, making her wonder if deaf people are constantly surprised to see anyone.

He hesitates for a second, seemingly aware to have frightened her, then hands over a small mirror. "Per your request."

"Thanks."

Riley takes the mirror and looks at herself. Her hair is disheveled, which isn't a surprise. There's a cut on her forehead, slightly off centered, but the blood is gone. A purple bruise runs across her neck and onto her clavicle, caused by the seat belt digging into her skin. None of these things bother her much. For now, she's fixated on the brown eyes looking back at her, still red and puffy from all the hysterical crying. It's a neutral shade, slightly darker than Grace's eyes, but a lot lighter than James's. His eyes are so dark they look black if the lights are subdued, like now. Almost as dark as his pitch-black hair.

"Is this my natural eye color? Is this what I would look like if I weren't an empath?"

No one answers, and why would they? It's not like they know any better.

"Do you still have that book on empaths?" she asks Rudy.

He nods. "Yeah, it's on the shelf over there."

"There's that bit in it about empaths having rare eye colors," she says, still staring at herself. "Remember what Molly said all these years ago? The demons, benevolent or malevolent, could reincarnate into people. I always thought it was a soul, *my soul*. But now I'm thinking it was an addition to my soul. A fragment. An imprint."

"How come Alison's spell was killing you if this thing could be removed from you?" James says, sitting in the armchair.

Riley's eyes sweep from the mirror to him. It's so weird to see him so calm. He's probably not, but he looks like it. His energy was always like a stormy ocean, wild and unpredictable. Now it's just quiet.

Rudy exhales, scratching his steel-gray beard. "I don't know. She might not have had all the information."

"Janice saw some of my memories when her demon tried to possess me outside that bar," Riley says. "She knew 'transferring' my energy would kill me."

"How did they 'cut it out,' though?" Rudy says.

Riley nibbles on her lower lip, staring into the small mirror again, at those simple brown eyes. "They dragged it out of me. I suppose Alison's ritual wasn't precise and took *all* of my energy, or something. But the demons, they pulled it out the way I pull them out of possessed bodies."

James rubs his forehead, resting his elbows on his lap. "My head hurts."

"Do you feel tired or weak or sick?" Rudy asks Riley.

"Like I was after Alison's ritual? No. I mean, I definitely feel like shit. But not to the point that I think I'm risking kidney failure. I'm also kind of hungry."

James raises his head, frowning. "That makes *no sense.*"

"What makes no sense?"

"They didn't kill you. Why?"

"She said their master wanted me."

"Why?"

"Because I'm a celestial."

He rests both his elbows on his lap and leans forward. *"Why?* They took your power. They cut it out. They won. They have what they wanted. Why didn't they kill you? Why would they even ask you to go with them if they could do that from the beginning?"

Riley opens her mouth a fraction, thinking. He's right, that shit makes no sense.

"I think we'd need to know who this master is to answer these questions." Her dad turns to her and puts a gentle hand on her back. "For now, how about I fix you something to eat? We're not gonna solve this problem tonight. You might as well rest a little, and we'll talk to Stella as soon as she comes home."

Riley cracks a small smile and nods, as he gets up and heads to the kitchen. Even in all this chaos, it hasn't been lost on him that she's hungry, and she's grateful for it.

In the meantime, she decides to head upstairs, and takes a long, warm shower to wash away the dirt she's been dragged through and the feeling of having somewhat been violated. The dirt slides off her body and disappears down the drain. The feeling of being violated persists, clinging to her skin. The noise of the water fills her head, what she can hear anyway. All other sounds are nonexistent, all other feelings imperceptible. She's alone with her emotions, with the same high anxiety that gave her panic attacks when she was a teenager.

Riley turns the water off and dries herself quickly, then puts on fresh night clothes. It's a strange feeling, doing normal things when your life is falling apart. Despite the pain, the grief, the fear, you still need to shower and sleep and eat. Because life won't stop for you and your problems, no matter how fucked up they are.

She crosses the hallway, past the staircase, and goes into her room. Thunder lights the night sky in the distance, its rumbling too far for Riley to hear, even as she puts her hearing aids back on. The room feels weird. It's the same room. The same walls, desk, and bed. But it feels empty, only containing her, as though the others have left and are too far away for her to perceive.

I don't think I can ever get used to it.

A knock on the door makes her heart jump, and she swivels around, her wet hair slapping her face.

"Dude," she breathes out, a hand pressed to her chest.

James clears his throat. "Sorry. I tried not to sneak up on you."

"I guess that's my life now. Not hearing nor feeling people coming close to me."

He stuffs his hands in his jeans pockets and leans against the doorframe. "You feeling okay? I mean... despite everything."

She nods, even though she feels anything but okay. "Are you staying here tonight?"

"Of course. That's what we do in tough times, right? We stick together."

Riley looks down for a moment, focusing on her own messed-up feelings now that she can't feel anybody else's. She was mad at him. He was pissed as well. "You don't have to stay if you don't want to."

He cocks his head, his expression unreadable. Daniel told her years ago she needed to pay attention to body language. Expression cues. She's doing better, but James does too good of a job at hiding his feelings.

"Are you still mad at me?" he says calmly, though the question sounds loaded.

"No. If it weren't for you, my dead body would be in the middle of the woods right now, still strapped to the driver's seat." She pauses, a question burning her lips. "Are *you* mad at me?"

He slowly shakes his head. "No."

"Sorry for the meltdown earlier."

"That's all right."

An uncomfortable silence follows. She looks away again, twisting her fingers, not knowing what to do or say under

James's dark stare. She could never pinpoint exactly what he thought. She was never a mind reader, but feelings usually pointed her in the right direction. Not with him. Not really. Who knows what he's thinking now as his gaze doesn't leave her, his face blank and expressionless.

"It's probably not the right time, but I wanna talk about last night," he finally says.

Riley lets out a small chuckle. "You wanna talk? That's a first."

"Very funny."

"It's funny because it's true."

He cracks a smile. "All right, I deserve that. I just want to explain why I reacted the way I did."

"You don't have to justify yourself. I get it. Really. I shouldn't have done what I did. It was wrong, and I just wish we could forget it. I don't want things to change between us."

He doesn't move, doesn't answer, doesn't bat an eyelid. His dark eyes are still locked on her, his face unreadable.

She crosses her arms tightly against her chest, her fingertips digging into her bruised ribs, waiting. When he doesn't say anything, his mouth seemingly glued shut, Riley shrugs slightly. "Don't you agree?"

It's a bad way of asking *do you love me as much as I love you even if we don't know how to say it?* but the risk is too great to say it outright. It could potentially destroy a precious friendship. She was so sure of herself before. So sure of his feelings, but now none of it seems real. She might have projected her own desire onto him and imagined what she wanted him to feel, not what he actually felt. Like she told Daniel, she kissed him three times. James would have told her if he truly felt something for her by now, and Riley doesn't think she can handle another rejection. Not now. Not when she feels so vulnerable. The first kiss was a quick, unplanned one. The second one was nothing but a drunken impulse. And after the third, he clearly let her know he wasn't interested, even when she said she had feelings for him. No means no after all.

Still, she dares to meet his eyes, somewhat hoping he'll say three simple words, and she'll be able to run into his arms and let him sweep her off the floor to kiss her.

The answer is as painful as being stabbed in the heart, bringing new tears to her eyes.

"Yeah. Let's forget about it."

CHAPTER 22

Rudy steps onto the porch and closes the door behind him. Riley finally crashed in her bed after her anxiety skyrocketed again, seemingly at the same time she and James started avoiding each other.

Sleep keeps eluding Rudy. He's not particularly proud of himself, but he's craving a cigarette, and James happens to be smoking outside.

As if you didn't know.

James briefly glances at him, his expression stoic but his eyes somewhat sad, then returns to looking at the dark woods, exhaling a big cloud of smoke. By the time Rudy stands next to him, James holds out a cigarette for him.

"Thanks." He takes it, lights it, and relishes its taste, feeling guilty for poisoning himself and indirectly poisoning Riley as well. She might not have started smoking if he had never smoked in the first place. "I'm gonna ask you the same question I asked her because I'm honest. Do I need to punch you in the face?"

James gives him a side glance, raising an eyebrow. "I sure hope not."

"I don't like to meddle, but... she seemed upset with you earlier."

James looks in the opposite direction, shifting from one foot to the other. A clear sign he's uncomfortable. "You know I can be a dick."

"That's a cheap answer to a deeper problem. And you seem upset too."

James makes no reply and draws on his cigarette instead.

"Why are you scared of me?" Rudy says, offering a teasing smile. "Have I been mean to you? Should I hug you more?"

James's shoulders slightly relax. He hides his smile as he plugs the cigarette between his lips and doesn't meet Rudy's eyes. "I don't know, Rud. My old man intimidated me too for some reason, but I respected him. It's the same with you. A shrink would probably say something about me not wanting to disappoint the paternal figure."

And that's about the most open he's ever been, at least while sober. He's clearly distraught.

"You could never disappoint me, boy."

James looks at him.

"Piss me off? Sure," Rudy says.

"Figures."

"Amuse me because you think the first 'w' in our business name stands for Williams? Also yes."

"Okay, I got it. You can stop."

"But disappoint me? Nah. Never happened. Never will."

They stay silent for a moment, the both of them smoking and watching the distant lightning illuminating the dark clouds. It seems to be moving away for now.

"Are we sure it's not *Williams and Winters Paranormal Investigation,* though?" James says.

"Not in your wildest dreams."

"Worth a shot."

"Just so you know," Rudy says after another few seconds of silence, "if for any reason you ever feel like you can't talk to Riley, you can talk to me. I'm not gonna bite your head off."

James seems to chew on this for a while. Surely, he knows he can trust his old man of substitution by now. Rudy says nothing, waiting patiently, until finally, James inhales and opens his mouth. He doesn't have time to say anything when lights pierce through the trees bordering the dirt path. Stella is coming home. She apparently has a way of showing up just when someone's about to open up to Rudy. Now the moment's gone. They have things to talk about with her. Her case might have returned to 'normal' when Janice Kraft was exorcised, but not anymore, not when she has miraculously found a new passenger. It's paranormal, and they can't let the police meddle.

Rudy frowns when the car emerging from the woods isn't Stella's gray Sedan. James notices it too, dropping his cigarette and crushing it under his shoe.

"I've seen this car earlier," he says.

The car parks, and from it emerges a woman in her fifties with formal clothes and dark hair brushing her shoulders. She steps hesitantly toward them.

"She was there," James says, his voice clipped. "She was with them, I recognize her."

Anger rises in Rudy's guts, and he quickly looks around to see if other people are hiding and surveilling them.

"I'm alone," the woman says, as if reading his mind. "It's just me. I want to talk."

James's face darkens. "You've got to be fucking kidding me."

Rudy raises a hand as a silent request to stay calm. "Is this a trap?"

"No," she says. "I swear, I come in peace."

"In peace? After what you did to my daughter?"

"It wasn't me–"

"You fucking helped them," James snaps, taking a step toward her.

She takes a quick step back, eyes wide, clearly frightened by the giant. "Please, just... just listen to what I have to say and then I'll leave."

Rudy stands next to James. "Why the hell would we listen to what you have to say?"

"Because... Because I want to help. I've never wanted to be with the Faceless. They made me think they could save me, that I could be better. More powerful. But after what happened tonight, I just can't go through with it. I can help you find them."

Rage boils his stomach. "'After what happened tonight?' What about before when Janice Kraft slaughtered all those people? Did the other possessed people kill too? Did *you?*"

"No, I–"

"How did you even know how to find us?"

She audibly swallows, nibbling on her lips. "After we all left... I came back... I don't know why, but I came back. I wanted to see if she was okay... And then, I saw you, and I followed you.

It just… took me a while to gather the courage to come and talk to you. This isn't easy for me."

"What makes you think you're safe here?" Rudy steps closer, looking down at her. "How do you know I won't hurt you after what your *cult* did to all those people and to my kid?"

"Because… I…"

Rudy leans forward slightly, dwarfing the woman. "Get the fuck off my property."

"Please, you don't understand–"

"Leave. Now."

Despite how frightened she looks, she stands her ground and dares to meet his eyes. "Just let me talk to her."

His patience spent, he grabs her arm and shakes her. "Why on earth would I let you get close to my daughter?"

"Because she's my daughter too!"

Rudy stares at her. The world melts around him, and hot flashes flare along his back. "What?"

"My… My name is Madelyn Kennedy. In 1985, I became Madelyn Brooke by marrying Lance Brooke. And in March 1988, I gave birth to a little girl named Riley."

"Holy fuck…" James mutters behind him.

Rudy lets go of her arm and takes a step back. He looks her up and down, his mind racing. He hadn't noticed it before, but he can sort of see it now. The same dark brown hair, not quite black. The same brown eyes, now that he knows this should be Riley's natural eye color. Still, he can't help but say, "You're lying."

"It's the truth," she says, smoothing the sleeve of her blazer where Rudy grabbed her arm.

"Riley's mother killed herself when she was just a toddler."

"That's what I made Lance believe, but that's not what happened. They never found my body, did they?"

Nausea spreads through Rudy, making him feel hot. Rage still gnaws at his guts, but dizzying fear fills his chest, and it takes him a moment to understand why.

He's stupidly, selfishly scared this woman could steal Riley's love for him. Her mother, her *real,* biological, blood-related mother, the one who gave birth to her, is standing in front of him. It's not a fucking competition, and yet it feels like it.

"I'd like to talk to her," Madelyn says.

"You have no right to talk to her."

"I'm still her mother. I deserve—"

"You're nothing, and you don't deserve *shit.*"

A hand presses on his shoulder. "Rud."

Rudy shakes it off. "If you didn't kill yourself, that means you abandoned her."

"It's not that simple—"

"Where were you when Lance beat her up, huh? Where were you when he locked her inside a closet for hours? When he made her feel like she was less than nothing?"

Her eyes widen, and her mouth hangs open. "I-I didn't know—"

"Where the fuck were you when he tried to drown her?"

She takes a step back as if slapped in the face and presses a hand over her lips.

James grabs Rudy's arm, pulling him back a little. "Rudy."

Rudy turns to him, the anger making his body shake. "You should be fuming right now."

"I *am.* But I think Riley would want to know that her mother's alive."

"Like I said, I want to help you," Madelyn says, her voice muted and sheepish. "I understand if you don't trust me. I understand if you hate me and don't want to let me talk to her. But I can help you catch the Faceless. I can help get her power back."

Rudy forces a deep breath into his overheated lungs and glances at James for approval. Or support. Anything, really.

James gives him a tight nod, mirroring the same angry but worried expression. "I can keep an eye on her if you want."

"We still don't know if it's a trap—"

"It's not a trap," Madelyn cuts off.

"Shut up," Rudy snaps, then looks back at James. "I'd rather you keep watch from inside, just in case. She can wait outside."

"All right," James says.

Rudy turns back to Madelyn, quickly checking his surroundings again. "Wait here."

He returns inside the house, James at his side. Leaving his partner outside isn't an option. He needs to keep his kids safe and sound.

Rudy climbs the stairs and slowly opens Riley's bedroom door. For a moment, he sees an eleven-year-old version of her, sprawled over the bed just like now, her hair a dark mass spread all over the pillow. He used to check on her a lot back then, when she had just moved in with him, as though he was scared she would vanish. She had a lot of episodes of sleep paralysis and night terrors, and often ended up sleeping in his bed.

He feels the same eagerness to shield her now, protect her from anything that could hurt her, and he wishes Madelyn fucking Brooke hadn't shown up to his door. Worse, he wishes she was really dead. Not because he doesn't want Riley to meet the mother she never had, but because the mother in question happens to be part of a cult that tortures and kills people.

For the first time tonight, he thinks it might not be such a terrible thing that Riley can't feel his feelings. She might be shocked.

He sits on the edge of her bed, like he has so many times, and gently shakes her with a trembling hand. She shifts slightly, then lets out a cry.

Rudy lets go of her, realizing his mistake, and fumbles with the bedside lamp to turn the light on.

"Fuck," Riley says, shifting into a sitting position.

"I'm *so* sorry."

"No, it's okay, it's okay. I'm just not used to seeing a dark shape sitting on my bed without knowing it's you." She lets out a nervous laugh, exhaling. "What are you doing here? Are you okay?"

"Well, not really. Something came up."

"What's happening?"

He takes her hand, stalling as much as he can before announcing the life-changing news that he doesn't know how she'll react to. She looks at him, worried, but definitely not as worried as she would be if she could feel what he feels.

"One of the members of the cult is outside. She says she wants to help us catch Janice and the others."

"Holy crap... She's outside right now?"

"Yes. But that's not all. I need you to prepare yourself. This will be a shock."

CHAPTER 23

Riley stares at her dad, her mouth hanging open. "I... I don't think I read your lips well."

"You did. Her name is Madelyn Brooke. And she says she's your mother."

"My mother's dead."

"From what she says, that's just what Lance believed."

Riley's mind spirals out of control, unable to stay grounded now that she can't latch onto her dad's energy. Her heart pounds in her chest, and the words just refuse to leave her mouth.

"She wants to talk to you," Rudy says.

His expressions are slightly more readable than James's, but Riley realizes that she still can't guess what he truly feels. Is he as distraught as her? Scared? Confused?

Her body stiff, Riley gets out of bed and reaches for her bag. "I guess—" She clears her throat. "I guess I should put on proper clothes to meet her."

Two hands press against her shoulders. Rudy turns her around so they can make eye contact. He's scared, that's what he is. That's what he does when he's frightened, either for her or for himself. He seeks contact as though he's afraid she'll disappear.

"You don't have to talk to her if you don't want to. It's your decision."

"Well... I have questions, you know?"

He nods. "I understand."

"What do you think of her?" If she can't feel a thing, then his guidance is what she'll hang onto.

He seems to think about it for a moment, choosing his words carefully. "I don't trust her, but I don't want you to forge your opinion based on what I think. Trust your instincts, Riley."

The wise answer, as usual. One that makes her smile a little, nonetheless. "My instincts are shit at the moment."

"Don't underestimate yourself, kiddo. I have faith in your judgment."

Her thundering heart makes her nauseated, but she needs to get a grip before stepping out. "Can I have a minute? I need to gather my thoughts."

"Of course."

Rudy leaves her alone with herself and her swirling thoughts. The news is so big, so unexpected, that she doesn't fully comprehend it yet. She feels sluggish, tired, and the insidious migraine pounding her skull won't relent. She flexes her raw fingers as a way to distract herself and get her body to fully wake up.

Her mother is outside. Her mother is alive. After thinking all these years she had killed herself, here she is.

Riley fetches her black jeans, black tank top, and since the air is slightly fresher, a black jeans jacket. That's how she's the most comfortable. 'The woman in black,' Aiden called her.

She wants to appear strong. Fearless. Even if she's none of those things at the moment.

She puts her hearing aids on and climbs down the stairs on weak legs, then retrieves her black boots in the foyer, aware of James and Rudy's gaze on her as she walks past the kitchen's doorway.

Her hand hovers above the doorknob.

Her mother.

Outside.

A woman that must have rocked her to sleep, changed her diapers, maybe even breastfed her. Did she sing lullabies and read stories before bed? Or did she spend those two years of her life crying because Riley was, as Lance said, a nightmare and Madelyn couldn't cope?

Floorboards shift slightly under her feet. Although Riley's not an empath anymore and doesn't hear sounds well when they come from behind, she's become good at feeling vibrations, and those shifting floorboards indicate that one, maybe two persons are behind her, anxiously waiting for her to make a move.

Riley slowly turns and looks at the two men standing in the hallway. She forces a small smile on her face—one they return as a silent cheering—before stepping out.

Madelyn stands in the yard and clasps her fingers together so tightly her knuckles turn white. Riley recognizes her instantly. She met her earlier when she and James were surrounded by the cult. That woman opened the door for her.

She wasn't possessed, therefore she could approach the warding of the car without burning herself. She *must* be a shitty person to be part of a cult composed of murderers who torture and kill. Riley couldn't feel her aura before. There were too many of them, too many demons overpowering and overwhelming her senses.

The fact that she married Lance and left me—in addition to joining Janice Kraft—proves that she's an asshole at the very least.

"Hello, Riley. Thank you for talking to me."

Riley sweeps the dark woods with her eyes, making sure nothing sinister is hiding in there. Saying hello would be a start, probably, but her mouth is glued shut as she takes in Madelyn's physical appearance. Same dark hair, and same brown eyes. Lance said he didn't know where Riley got her eye color from, that her mother had brown eyes. That was when he and Hank had shown up to Riley's house and tried to kill her and Daniel.

Another thing Lance said when she was little. She asked him if her mother had loved her, and the answer was no.

"Could we maybe sit down inside and talk?" Madelyn asks.

"No."

"Oh. I thought—"

"Not here." This place has already been polluted by Lance, Hank, Terrestre, and Pepper's death. "Cindy's Diner in twenty minutes. I'll meet you there."

Madelyn is already sitting at one of the bright red booths in Cindy's Diner when Riley steps inside. She wanted to go to a place other than her house, but also wanted a peaceful setting. One in which she's created many fond memories. Her dad taking her here the day after they moved into their house. James making fun of her for liking vanilla milkshakes. Getting a late dinner with Daniel and their friends after going to the movies on a Saturday night.

Riley settles in the booth facing Madelyn, glancing through the window. The green truck is in the parking lot, with her dad inside. He couldn't let her go on her own. James was forced to stay behind, despite bitching about it, so he can fill Stella in on the details when she comes home.

"Can I get you anything to drink?" the waitress says.

"Coffee, please," Riley says, then raises her eyebrows at Madelyn.

"Um, tea's fine."

The waitress nods, a smile too big on her face considering the late hour, and saunters away. Madelyn and Riley are left staring at each other, none of them knowing how to engage the conversation. Madelyn looks different in the bright lights. The creases on her forehead are more present. Her eyebrows shine differently than her hair, as though they're a shade or two lighter. Residue of red lipstick cakes the lines of her lips.

Once the hot cup of coffee arrives, sliding in front of Riley, she takes a sip, the scorching liquid a welcome distraction from the awkwardness of this meeting.

Madelyn clasps her mug, looking down at the steam billowing from it. "You must have a lot of questions for me."

"I don't even know where to start."

"You must be angry. Like your father is."

Riley stares, not in anger and not to intimidate. She just does, making Madelyn wildly uncomfortable judging by how she averts her eyes, looking out the window, then at the cup of tea again.

"You wanted to talk to me," Riley says. "So talk."

Madelyn nods and swallows. "I'm sorry for what happened tonight. I had no idea you were the target. See, I'm just in training. I don't have my own demon yet. I have to prove my worth. When Janice talked about you and your abilities, the master said he wanted to have you. Of course, I thought about you when I heard her say your name, but I had no idea that Riley Winter was *my* Riley. I didn't make that connection until I saw you... Until I saw your eyes... I'd recognize those eyes anywhere."

"And yet, you let these people hurt me."

"I'm so sorry... They would have killed me on the spot if I had said anything. But I knew right there and then that this was wrong. I hate what they did to you, and I want to help you get it back."

She leans forward, reaching for Riley's hand. Riley leans back against the booth, putting both her hands on her lap, out of reach.

Madelyn tries to smile despite the rejection. "I knew you were special. I knew as soon as you were born."

"By special, do you mean a nightmare? Because that's what Lance said."

"No, no... Well, it was hard, yes, because of your lack of hearing. But that's not what I'm talking about. The doctors told me that all children were like sponges and mimicked their parents' emotions, but it was so strong with you. You'd cry when I was sad, you'd laugh when I was happy, and you'd scream when I was mad."

Riley's throat tightens. She takes another sip of hot coffee to try to loosen it up. She's not gonna cry in front of this stranger. "Why did you leave? My whole life I thought you were dead. I'd like an explanation."

"I never wanted to leave you. This wasn't what was supposed to happen."

"Then, what happened?"

"Your... Your father was a violent man."

Riley's jaw clenches so hard it hurts. "No *shit*." She leans forward sharply, a sensation she can't describe–anger, pain, distress, and bitterness all mixing together–twisting her guts. "Do you have any idea what he put me through? You left me alone with a monster."

Madelyn's eyes glimmer, and she shakes her head apologetically. "I'm so sorry, Riley... I wanted to take you away with me, but my mental health was degrading. I was depressed and suicidal. I wanted to leave Lance and take you with me, but my depression got really bad, and I had... very dark thoughts..."

"What kind of thoughts?"

"Oh, I'm not sure you want to know, sweetie."

"Don't call me that." Riley leans back against the booth, bracing herself for what she's about to hear. "What kind of thoughts?"

"Well... sometimes I thought that it would just be better if I drove into a wall or plunged the car at the bottom of a lake... with the both of us in it."

Riley closes her eyes for a second, forcing steady breaths in and out of her lungs. She glances out the window, the sight of her dad waiting for her outside in that faithful green truck reassuring.

"That's when I knew I wasn't just a danger to myself, but to you as well," Madelyn continues. "And I didn't want to hurt you, Riley. That's why I left. I didn't think Lance would do these things to you."

Riley turns her gaze back to Madelyn. "You said yourself he was a violent man."

"With me, yes. I was the one who took care of you. As long as I kept you away from him, he didn't touch you. When he got mad because of your crying, I would make sure I'd take the beating. Not you."

"Why did Lance think you'd killed yourself instead of fleeing?"

"Because I left him a suicide note." She lets out a sad chuckle. "Who knows? Maybe he kept it. Your father might have been a terrible man, but he loved me. I could see him holding on to some of my stuff and putting it in the attic."

Riley's stomach twists in surprise. "The attic? We didn't have an attic."

Madelyn cocks her head, her eyebrows raised. "Yes, we did. There's a trap door on the hallway's ceiling."

Riley searches her memories, cringing as she thinks about this horrible house, but can't remember an attic.

Madelyn shrugs. "Maybe Lance failed to mention it. He probably didn't want you to play up there and hurt yourself. Or make a mess."

The latter sounds more like him. He wouldn't have cared if Riley had hurt herself as long as he didn't have to pay for a doctor's visit. Still, this doesn't sound right. She couldn't have lived in this house for nine years and not know there was an attic. "You're lying."

"I'm not, I promise you. Look, I understand if you don't trust me. I understand if you hate me. But I *do* want to help you. I can tell you where the Faceless are hiding. I can help you get them."

Riley misses her empathy. A lot. And right now, she misses being able to tell if someone tells the truth or not. How can she know this isn't a trap? How can she know this woman is genuine? If what she said about having depression and faking suicide is true or not?

Rudy's words play on a loop in her mind. *'I don't trust her.'*

"Have you killed?" she asks.

"No."

"You're part of a cult that *butchers* people. I saw some of the things Janice did. Burning people alive, opening their gut, or cutting their limbs. Did *you* do that?"

"No, I promise you, no."

Riley suddenly leans forward, and her fist falls onto the table as if having a will on its own, shaking the cups. "But you're with them!"

Madelyn flinches, then quickly looks around at the people staring, startled by the noise. She bows her head and lowers her voice. "Listen. I didn't know what they were doing. One day, that woman, Janice, came to me. I was having a shit life, always being someone's pushover, and I was desperate and miserable. She said she could make my life better. She said she could save me. That I could finally have a family with people who loved me. In exchange, I had to do things for them."

"Yeah, that's the proper definition of a fucking cult."

"But I promise I didn't kill anyone. Only the ones worthy enough to have a passenger have to kill. To feed them."

Riley's patience is wearing thin as her anger thickens. "What kind of things did you do, then?"

"I just had to look for people. I didn't know what it was for, I thought they wanted to recruit more of us."

"But the people you chose were new targets, weren't they?"

"Yes. I had no idea, Riley, you have to believe me. But now I know what they're doing. And I want to stop them. I don't want to be part of this anymore, but if they knew, they'd kill me."

Riley chews on this. She'd like to stop them too. She'd like her empathy back. She'd like to punish them for what they did to all those people. But she has no way of knowing if Madelyn is telling the truth.

Actually, there's a way to verify some *things.*

Madelyn slides a piece of paper across the table. "Here's my phone number. You don't have to answer me now. But when you're ready to take them down, call me, and I'll tell you where they're hiding."

"How about you tell me now?"

"No. It's too dangerous. The place is big and crawling with evil. Trust me on this, you'll need my help."

Riley takes the piece of paper, the black numbers jumping off the white background.

Madelyn puts a five dollar bill on the table and rises to her feet. "Take your time to decide. But not *too* much time. Other people could die." She puts the strap of her purse onto her shoulder, then looks at Riley with watery eyes. "When all this is over, maybe you and I could..."

"Could what?"

"I don't know, get to know each other. Have coffee. I'd like to be part of your life... if you let me." She glances through the window in Rudy's direction. "Having a mother might do you some good–"

"Don't you dare," Riley cuts off, glaring daggers at her. "Don't you dare say anything about him."

Madelyn turns and walks out of the diner, taking with her all the answers Riley didn't get.

CHAPTER 24

The house on Normand Street looks just as terrifying as in Riley's nightmares. It looms ahead, daring her to come closer.

"Are you sure you want to do this?" Rudy says, standing next to her on the sidewalk.

Riley smiles, even though her face feels like plaster that's about to crack. "I'm guessing you're worried."

"Always."

"Yes, I do. And I need to do it alone. I'll be fine."

"Sure?"

"I'll send out smoke signals if I need anything."

Rudy glances at the decrepit house, then back at her. "Take the bag of salt. Could be haunted."

Riley nods and rounds the vehicle. She opens the compartment inside the bed of the truck and takes out the massive bag of rock salt hidden there. He's right. Lance could be here, roaming the hallways of the sinister house.

She carries the heavy bag under her arm and hesitantly steps back onto the sidewalk, facing the building she had sworn she'd never go back to. It's just a mass of rotting wood.

Its abandoned front lawn is filled with dry, unruly shrubs spilling onto the driveway and coming out of its cracks. The very same driveway she used to draw on using rocks. The windows are dark, looking like a multitude of dead eyes staring at her.

Riley has the unwelcome sensation that if she looked hard enough, she'll see Lance's gray aura standing behind one of them, waiting for her to come home. She wishes the building wasn't as threatening as she remembers. She thought it'd look smaller now that she's taller. It doesn't, and the sight of it makes her skin break into a cold sweat.

She briefly looks at the burgundy house to her left. A bright, luminous image of Grace and her luxurious strawberry blonde hair flowing in the wind jumps at her. A cherished memory from the first time they met.

'I wish I had strawberry hair,' she told Grace.

Riley turns back to the dismal house, keeping Grace in mind for courage, and walks the path leading to the front door, the windows' bleak stare seemingly locked on her. Her throat tight and her jaw clenched, she turns the handle. The door doesn't resist, opening with a lazy creak of its hinges. The inside is dark. Silent. Threatening. Waiting for her to step inside so it can swallow her.

She reaches for the flashlight in her jacket pocket and turns it on. Its beam of white light brings into relief the various graffiti and the mold that made its nest, casting dancing shadows across the walls. The living room is mostly empty, except for a few forgotten pieces of furniture. The couch is gone. So is the TV. To the right, the staircase looms like a stalker, and underneath it, a closet, its door open ajar as if trying to coax her into coming back inside. When Riley points her flashlight to it, the light fails to penetrate the vertical line of blackness. Adjusting the bag under her arm, she walks to it, the sound of her footsteps disturbing the eerie silence.

She lifts her foot, and gives the door a little nudge outward, certain for a second that she'll see the ghost of a little girl springing out of the closet, screaming that the monster wants to eat her, but the small space is empty except for flecks of dust dancing in the flashlight. It gives her chills just to look inside it.

'*The only monster I see is you,*' Lance had said.

"Dickhead," Riley whispers, and shuts the closet door.

Behind her and to the left-hand side of the living room is the kitchen. Riley takes a deep breath and walks to it.

She's not psychic. She doesn't communicate with ghosts easily. But before what happened tonight, she could feel spirits' energies, nonetheless. They're less palpable than the living. Their imprint is like mist. Without her empathy, though, she can't feel if there's a ghost in here. If Lance were present, haunting this house, she wouldn't be able to feel him unless he decided to show himself. And if there's one place he would haunt, it'd be the kitchen, where his violent death happened.

The room is bare of furniture. Plywood obstructs the back door, replacing the glass door. Riley pauses and listens, trying to ignore the wild pounding of her heart. Surely, Lance would show himself if he saw her. He'd probably throw shit around. Yet the house stays quiet. Only a few scratching sounds disturb the silence here and there. Rats, most likely.

Maybe Lance really *is* here, unaware of his own death, and he can't see her. Her dad told her once that some spirits keep living their lives after they die. They get up in the morning, have breakfast, go to work, thinking it's all real, when in fact their house might have changed. Their furniture is no longer there, and other people might be living with them. Both humans and ghosts can live in the same house, unaware of each other's presence. Someone could have built such strong rituals through life that they keep repeating those rituals through death. Is this Lance's case? Is he watching TV, sitting on a couch that's no longer there, waiting for Riley to come home so he can torture her?

Riley doubts it. He wasn't a man in love with his routine. He was bitter and angry. If he were here, he'd probably be stuck in his death loop, only snapping out of it for a good reason: her. If he's not here, endlessly falling through the glass door and impaling himself, he might be at the lake, where he died for the second time. Or maybe he moved on.

A salt line is poured across the kitchen doorway, nonetheless. She'll throw a handful at his face if he decides to show up and attack her.

Riley turns her back to the kitchen and crosses the living room. She climbs the first few steps of the staircase until it makes a bend. The second floor is drowned in shadows. Her legs feel weak. She doesn't want to go up. Doesn't want to see her room. Or *his* room. Rudy would be more than happy to take her hand and do this with her, but she can't ask him this. She needs to do it on her own.

Being scared isn't a good reason not to do something.

Riley repeats her dad's mantra to herself as she steadily climbs one step after the other, the wood complaining under her boots.

The humid, hot air upstairs is thick with dust, coating her tongue. The hallway stretches before her. The first door to the right is the bathroom. The next door to the left used to be her bedroom. The last door is the master bedroom. She pushes the door to her room.

The rest of the house feels the same, but this bedroom looks like it shrunk. She doesn't remember it being so small. It's bare of furniture, like the rest, but the memory of where her things were is clear in her mind. Against the left wall, in front of her, was the head of the bed. On the opposite wall from the door, the window, looking over the front yard. To the right, not far from the foot of the bed stood her desk, behind which she drew stick figures when Lance didn't bother buying her paper.

Next to the desk, the closet.

That one's still there, of course.

A question rises in Riley's mind, something she'd thought of before but could never quite formulate. *Can a demon split its imprint?*

When it left its ectoplasm in its wake, did it leave a part of itself as well? It seems weird, impossible even, but oddly plausible as she stands there, staring at this closet. Just because she killed most of Terrestre doesn't mean a tiny part of it didn't stay here, waiting to feed and grow stronger.

Riley shakes the thought away, suddenly frightened, and crosses the small bedroom in three long strides to pour a semi-circle of salt in front of the closet door without opening it. She glances through the window, making sure Rudy's still out there, and allows herself to breathe deeper when she sees him leaning against his truck, his arms crossed against his chest. He looks up and sees her.

"Everything okay?" he signs.

Riley gives him the thumbs up and picks up the bag before returning to the hallway. All the doors receive the same treatment; a semi-circle of salt in front of them in case something is lurking inside the rooms.

When she's done, Riley sweeps the beam of the flashlight over the ceiling, her mind screaming that this isn't possible, that she can't possibly have overlooked a trap door leading to an attic. She steps deeper into the hallway, walking toward Lance's room.

She freezes, hand raised, a chill running up her arms.

There it is.

A discreet trapdoor, blending almost perfectly with the white paint, turned dirty and gray after years of neglect. A discreet hook hangs from it. There should be a string there, but it's gone. It could be the reason she's never seen it. That and the fact that it's so close to Lance's room. She rarely ventured there.

Even if she jumped, she wouldn't be able to pull it down, and there's nothing for her to use. She backtracks her steps and goes inside her old room. After flashing her light through the window, Rudy looks up.

"I need your help with something," she signs.

She watches him walk the path leading to the front door, then strains to listen to his footsteps on the first floor. Guilt settles in her stomach. He shouldn't have to be here, either.

Not after what he went through to save her, and not after he found Ann Pritchett's body.

The stairs groan. Riley steps out of the room just as her dad steps onto the landing.

"You okay?" he asks.

"Yeah. I need help opening the trapdoor to the attic. It's too high for me to reach."

He follows her to the end of the hallway and frowns. "Are you sure this is a good idea? The wood might be rotten and unstable."

"I just... I want to see if what Madelyn said is true."

"Even if it is, you might not find what you're looking for, pumpkin. There's probably nothing up there anymore."

"I know, I know, but I need to try. This house is my only link back to her. If I were to find tangible proof of what she said, it'd be up there."

Rudy doesn't argue. He nods, his eyes reflecting the light. He reaches up, but despite his height, his fingertips are a few inches from the hook. "Come here. I'll lift you."

"Don't break your back."

"Can't promise anything."

Riley can't hold back a smile as she steps in front of him, turning her back to him. His arms circle her waist, and a second later, her feet leave the floor. Craning her neck, she slides a finger inside the hook and pulls down. The door opens easily, and Rudy puts Riley down gently, then pulls on the ladder. It unfolds swiftly, as though it hadn't been forgotten for years.

"Any sign of Lance?" Rudy says.

"No. But pour a salt circle around the ladder and stay inside it, just in case."

"You don't want me to come with you?"

"I'll be quick."

Riley climbs the ladder, feeling it shake under her weight, threatening to collapse. She peeks through the opening, her light catching flecks of dust in its beam. Her heart jumps in her throat. Someone is here.

She locks the light onto the tall shape to her left and lets out a nervous chuckle. Furniture, maybe a mirror or a wardrobe, covered by a white sheet.

"You okay?" her dad says below.

"There's stuff in here. No one has bothered cleaning this space."

"Maybe it belongs to the Pritchetts."

"But maybe some of it belongs to the Brookes."

Shelves, chests, dressers, and boxes clutter the space. The attic is spacious, the same surface as the other floors, its roof slanted on both sides.

A chilling, grim thought jumps at her.

This could have been my room. If Lance had been a worse psychopath than he already was, he could have locked me up there.

Riley pulls herself up, wiping her hands on her jeans, and looks about the space. It'll be a pain to look through all this clusterfuck. Unable to endure the suffocating heat a minute longer, she sheds her jacket off and gets to work.

Nothing is left unchecked. The sheets are pulled, the drawers are opened, the boxes are searched. It's mostly old clothes, junk, and cobwebs with the spiders in them. Some of the furniture is empty.

Riley crouches in front of a large trunk and unlocks it. Her breath catches in her throat.

Baby toys and clothes. Books. A handmade, knit blanket. It's faded, but a pale pink is still visible. A crib mobile with stars and clouds and a sun. Stuffed animals. Edward and Ann Pritchett didn't have kids. It can't belong to them.

A rabbit catches Riley's attention. She takes it and observes its graying fur. She doesn't exactly remember it, but it rings a little bell somewhere deep in her memories. It looks familiar and brings a sadness that makes her eyes burn. Why would you buy such a pretty thing to your daughter and then abandon her?

At the top of the small stack of toddler books, an envelope makes Riley pause. She takes it and turns it around. A name is written on it, still clear and visible. *Lance.*

Swallowing around the lump in her throat, Riley sits on the dirty floor, her back against the trunk, and opens the envelope. In it, a single sheet of paper, barely crumpled.

Lance,

I can't go on like this anymore. I'm tired. I'm beat up. Dead inside. I need to end it. Take care of Riley for me. Make sure she gets everything she needs and tell her I love her. She deserves better than you and I.

Madelyn

Riley stares at the letter, her hands and lips shaking. Her limbs feel heavy, as though lead is flowing through her veins instead of blood.

Something tickles her arms. Her first thought is that Lance is here after all, and he's going to try to kill her, but when she shifts the flashlight to her arm, a small, black spider crawls on it. Riley bends over and puts her arm to the floor, waiting for the spider to scurry away. When the creature finally decides to get off, she turns, shuts the trunk, and shoves the letter in her jeans pocket. She snatches her jacket off the floor, the air too thick to flow through her lungs properly, and hurries down the ladder.

It turns out that the oxygen on the second floor feels just as toxic and unbreathable, so Riley darts down the stairs and out of this fucking house, taking in a not so pleasant breath of humid air, feeling as though the dust and the grime and the darkness of her past still cling to her lungs.

"Riley?" Rudy joins her a second later, trying to catch her gaze. "Are you okay?"

She nods, still inhaling and exhaling as slowly as she can, eyes watery. "She was telling the truth." She takes out the letter and gives it to him.

He reads it, pointing his own flashlight onto it, and stays silent once he's done. He watches her, waiting for her to talk.

Riley looks the house up and down, hating it more than ever, but no longer scared of it. "I saw things that belonged to me up there. Baby stuff. There was that pink knit blanket... I wonder if Madelyn made it for me. I thought she didn't care about me to leave me, but now I think... I think she *did* love me."

Her dad stays quiet. Despite having lost her abilities, she guesses what he feels. The expression in his eyes as she turns back to him is unmistakable. It's the face he makes when he's scared. His jaw is set, the creases around his eyes deepening.

"What I don't understand is why she left me with him," Riley continues. "She could have put me up for adoption or something, right? But no. She left me here. I thought her death was tragic, but the fact that she lived and left me with this psychopath is a lot worse. All the horrible things that happened here could have been avoided."

She pauses, noticing the sadness growing in Rudy's eyes. Her own vision blurs.

"I wish I could burn this place to the ground. But you know what? I'm glad things happened the way they did. I don't understand them, and I *hate* them, but if it weren't for them, I wouldn't be your daughter." She inhales and quickly wipes her nose, a storm of emotions swirling through her. "And being your daughter is my favorite identity. I wouldn't be the person I am if it weren't for you, and you are my favorite person in the entire universe, and there is *no one* I trust more than you."

His eyes glimmer, but he stays silent, respectful as she blurts out everything she needs to take off her chest.

"So, as far as I'm concerned, Madelyn and her offer to be a part of my life can suck it because I already have the only parent I need, and I wouldn't change my shitty past for the world, even if I could."

He smiles, trying to find his words. "I was sort of afraid she'd steal you from me."

"Dad, come on. That could never happen."

"How about we go home?"

"Not yet. There's something else I'd like to do. Another fear that needs conquering, and I need you for this."

"What is it?"

She steps toward him and utters words she never thought would pass her lips. "Can you teach me how to swim?"

CHAPTER 25

The sun will rise soon, and the lake brings a fresh breeze. Rudy takes his shoes off but keeps his jeans and shirt. Riley does the same and sheds her jacket–as well as taking her hearing aids off–and stands next to him, surveying the dark water.

"Don't let go of me, okay?" she says.

"Never."

He takes her hand, and together, they step into the fresh lake. Riley's fingers tighten around his, but she keeps a straight face, doesn't say anything. Rudy walks backward and takes her other hand as the water rises to their stomach, then to their chest.

Riley blows a big breath through her mouth, trying to calm her nerves. "All right. What do I do? And please, don't feed me the 'water is your friend' bullshit."

That makes him laugh. "Water doesn't give a shit about you. It'll kill you if you can't control your body. It's your job to make sure you use it to your advantage. Come here."

The lesson he thought he would have taught her years ago begins, starting with showing her how to float. He makes her lie back, keeping a hand under her neck and the other under her lower back.

The first sunrays peek over the horizon, glowing with a shy orange light over the oil-like appearance of the lake.

"Can you read my lips?"

"Yes."

"Notice how you rise when you take a deep breath, and how you sink when you exhale. Find a balance to stay to the surface. Your breathing is key. If you panic, you'll hyperventilate and sink like a stone."

The sense of time means nothing to him as he gives his daughter her first swimming lesson. No matter that she's eleven or thirteen or twenty-five, teaching her something new always excites him, makes his heart swell.

The next step is to let her float on her own. Then, to show her how to stay upright and keep her head above the surface. Finally, to swim. She doesn't struggle for long, and soon, she looks like she's been doing it all her life. Like when he taught her how to ride a bike. Once she found her balance, she rode through the yard, laughing.

"Look, Dad, I'm doing it!" she yelled then.

It's exactly the same now.

"Look, Dad, I'm fucking doing it!"

Well, almost the same.

By the time they step out of the water, their clothes and hair dripping, the orange sun has turned into a warm yellow, its shine caressing their skin. They sit on the sand side by side, enjoying a view he'll never get tired of. The blue water stretching before them, the thick trees surrounding it, the rising sun.

"That's where my friends and I used to hang out in the summer," Riley says, a content smile stretching her lips. "I miss that. I miss them liking me."

He turns his face to her to make sure she can hear him and read his lips. "I'm sure they still do. It's not too late to work things out."

"Maybe." She looks ahead for a moment, her smile slowly fading away. "I'm in love with James."

"I know."

She frowns at him. "What do you mean, you know?"

"I've known for a while that something was up between you two. I've been waiting for it, in fact."

Riley stares. "How did you know?"

"Well, I didn't think of it on my own. It was Grace who planted the idea in my head four years ago. When I brought her back home that night, and she saw how over-protective James was with you, she thought he was your boyfriend. She told me that later. I remember I wasn't a fan of the idea, with him being older than you and all, but she said age didn't matter. After that, you broke up with Daniel, and you and James just spent more and more time together. Now it makes sense to me that you'd fall for each other."

She chuckles. "You're very perceptive."

"For a non-empath, I guess, yeah. I just know you two pretty well."

"You're wrong about one thing, though."

Rudy tilts his head. "Oh yeah, and what's that?"

"I fell for him, but he didn't fall for me. He doesn't feel that way about me. He made that clear."

"Ah. The 'embarrassing thing' you didn't have time to tell me about."

"Not sure I want to, honestly."

"You don't have to."

She thinks about it, then rests her arms onto her knees and exhales. "I kissed him the other night. He completely freaked out. I tried to tell him that I had feelings for him, but he was so pissed he didn't really listen to me. And then he told me to leave."

Which is surprising, considering that Rudy assumed James had been in love with her for a while now. "Did he say why he was angry?"

"We're talking about James. He's *always* angry."

"Sure. But he must have given you a reason."

"Something about how he's too old for me, how you'll shoot him in the face when you find out, and how I'm so lonely and desperate I just want to use him as a way to comfort myself. Those are all bonuses to telling me I was wrong to think he had feelings for me too."

"You weren't wrong, though."

She raises her eyebrows, a mix of hope and surprise flashing through her eyes. "What do you mean?"

"Pretty sure he's been feeling the same as you for a while now. He just gave you as many excuses as he could to keep you away. Probably because he's scared."

"What the hell is he scared of? It's *me*. He knows me."

Rudy puts on the most compassionate smile he can. "Sure, but you haven't really committed to anything serious these past few years."

"What does that mean?"

"I don't mean it in a bad way. You're young. Living your life and having fun. But in James's eyes, you're not ready for a serious relationship and you didn't get over Daniel."

"I *am* over Daniel."

"Does James know?"

"I mean…" Riley seems to think things over for a while, chewing on her lower lip. "I guess not… I acted really bummed when Daniel told me he was engaged. James tried to talk to me yesterday, and I just told him to forget about it all. Like an idiot."

"You guys need to sit down and talk things over."

Riley turns to him again, raising an eyebrow at him. "That doesn't bother you at all? You'd really be okay with us being together? Even with the age gap?"

"If it were another man, I'd shoot him on the spot, yes. But it's good old Jamie-bear we're talking about. I trust him. And you're an adult, you don't need your paternal's permission."

Her smile widens, her eyes sparkling. She hooks her arm around his own and lays her head against his shoulder, looking at the gleaming lake. "You're the best, Dad."

CHAPTER 26

James wakes up in Rudy's guest room. The orange glow streaming through the window tells him it's early morning, which means he didn't sleep more than two or three hours. His raw nerves kept him awake most of the night, and he couldn't stop pacing the house and making sure no one was outside, waiting for Rudy and Riley to come back home. He filled Stella in on the details when she came back, at least the details he knows about. He was pretty much left out of the loop on this one. He doesn't know what Madelyn and Riley talked about, and he got a text from Rudy much later, telling him they were going to the house on Normand Street. When James asked if they wanted him to join them, he got a simple 'no' back, and that was that.

Stella wasn't too happy to hear about the Faceless and was at least as pissed as him that Rudy and Riley had left to talk to Madelyn. She kept asking questions James didn't know how to answer, interrogating him.

"How many were they exactly?"

"Um, more than a dozen. Maybe even twenty."

"Can you give me a description of the people you remember?"

He blew out a big breath, not remembering much except for Janice, Madelyn, and the creep who pushed Riley's car off the cliff. He did his best to describe them, their cars, but the rest is pretty blurry.

"How did they take her empathy?"

"I don't know, Stella."

"What are they going to do with it?"

He shrugged. "How should I know?"

"Did they say who this master was?"

His already thin patience was spent by the time she asked that question. "If I knew that, don't you think I would have told you by now?"

"Where did Riley and Madelyn go? I'd like to question this woman."

"Riley didn't tell me."

"Well, Rudy's not answering his phone. When are they coming back?"

James did his best to keep his cool, but the nagging quickly made him turn to the bottle of whiskey Rudy had left on the counter. "I *don't know.* When they come back, you can ask them all this. I'm sure Riley will get more info from Madelyn."

He ended up drinking alone in his room between rounds of patrolling to make sure the outside was safe. Stella's a good woman. A good cop. She and Rudy go well together. But James doesn't feel particularly close to her, and Stella tolerates him at best.

What frustrates him the most is not being able to be by Riley's side. He said some horrible things to her the other night, and she was right to be mad at him. He deserved it. But after she almost died, after these dicks took something so precious to her, and after her biological mother fucking showed up to her door, it doesn't matter to him that Riley doesn't have feelings for him. It doesn't matter that she told him they should forget about everything. He just wants to be there for her, which he can't do if she keeps him away like this.

And to think he actually almost let Rudy coax him into opening up. That would have been a big mistake. And yet, he was ready to spill the beans.

He rubs his eyes, his eyelids feeling heavy, and rolls out of bed. It's half-sunny outside, and the dark clouds looming in the distance will be upon them soon. When he looks through the window, James notices Rudy's truck is outside. Weird. He didn't hear them come back, and the house is quiet.

At least, it is until the front door opens, and footsteps and voices fill the hallway downstairs. A pang of anticipation mixed with frustration tug at his guts. James jumps into his clothes and steps into the hallway just as Riley climbs the stairs. She emerges, her back to him, and James already imagines her expression. Tired. Sad. Scared, maybe. But when she turns and sees him, her face lights up, and she smiles a beautiful smile.

"Hey. You almost scared me there," she says.

He looks her up and down. Her clothes and hair are wet, sand sticks to her jeans, and her socks leave damp prints on the floor, but she doesn't seem bothered by it. "Where the fuck were you? I was worried."

"Sorry about that."

He exhales, trying to calm his nerves. "Well, are you okay at least?"

"Not gonna lie, last night was insane. Stella's questioning my dad frantically, but he refuses to answer until he's changed and has had coffee. That's hilarious. Definitely a scene you'd enjoy watching."

Her smile is contagious, and he can't hold back his own even when he tries to bite on it. "She drove me insane last night, thanks to you guys disappearing."

She laughs, and for a moment, it feels like they're friends again and nothing ever happened.

"Don't get me wrong," James says. "I'm glad to see you smile. I was afraid you'd be devastated. But... *why* are you smiling? And why are you wet?"

She looks down at herself as though she didn't realize her clothes were dripping, and chuckles. "Oh, right. I *am*. Devastated, I mean. It was a weird and emotionally draining night. It was utter crap, really. In fact, I've rarely had such a bad time in my life, and that's saying a lot. I've lost my empathy, which I feel like I'll never get used to, my biological mother randomly showed up and said she'd like to know me better after admitting that she abandoned me because otherwise she might have committed a murder-suicide, and worst of all, I'm grieving the loss of my car and I'll have to deal with the insurance company."

"Which is worse? Losing your car or dealing with the insurance company?"

"The insurance company hands down. *But.*"

He raises his eyebrows at her. "But?"

"I had the displeasure of visiting my old house last night. I've had so many nightmares about being back there with Lance's ghost waiting for me." She shrugs. "But he's not there, and all these terrible things I had imagined, well, they didn't happen. It's just a sad, empty house."

"A new fear conquered, then, huh?"

A smile plays at the corner of her lips. "Two new fears conquered, actually. I know how to swim."

That almost makes him angrier. "Seriously? That's what you were doing just now? You went for a fucking swim?"

"Yeah, at the lake," she answers, as though there's nothing more natural in these dark times. "My dad taught me. It's actually nice, being in the water. You know... when no one's trying to drown you. It was about time I learned."

She smiles wider, waiting for him to react, probably. If she could feel his anger and frustration, she'd try to pacify him, but she can't. Instead, she's feeling her own emotions, looking oddly content.

James is blown away, really. He'll always get amazed at how resilient she is. At how quickly she gets back on her feet after being beaten to the ground. Anyone in her situation would be sitting in a fetal position and rocking themselves back and forth in the shower, crying. But not Riley. She went out for a swim with her paternal, and that gets a small laugh out of James.

"Congratulations. Color me impressed."

"Ha! I appreciate the word play. Would work better if I could see your colors."

"I haven't been to the lake for a swim in forever."

"No, because you and I hang out all the time, and until now, I didn't want to go. Maybe we can go before it starts getting colder. Once we have sorted this clusterfuck, that is."

"Sure," he says. "So, how did it go with Madelyn exactly? How are you feeling?"

She holds a hand up and walks backward in the direction of the bathroom. "I'll enforce my dad's rule on that one, Jamie-bear. Not before coffee. Let me take a shower, and I'll join you guys downstairs in a moment."

His anger vanishes. He didn't think he would hear that stupid nickname come out of her mouth again. "All right."

He sees another flicker of her smile before she closes the bathroom door. Forced to wait despite the curiosity gnawing away at his stomach, James goes down the stairs, avoiding Riley's sock prints. Voices rise as he gets closer to the kitchen, getting a smile out of him when he enters it. Stella's giving Rudy an interrogation but gets no answers out of him. He already put dry clothes on and isn't dripping everywhere like Riley was.

James helps himself to the coffee and sits down, enjoying the scene now that he isn't the one being nagged. Despite how anxious Rudy can be, he always appears astonishingly chill, another thing James admires. When *he's* anxious or pissed, everyone will know it. He can't keep it down.

Riley comes down a moment later, wearing a black T-shirt and faded blue jeans, and settles next to him after getting coffee. Her freshly washed hair smells of berries, and he has to force himself not to look at her.

"Are you okay, Riley?" Stella says, looking worried this time.

Riley nods. "I'm fine."

"Will someone *finally* tell me what happened last night?"

"All right, meeting time," Rudy says. "I myself don't really know exactly what Madelyn told you."

He and Stella look at Riley from the other side of the table, and James now allows himself to do the same.

She takes a white paper from her pocket and places it onto the kitchen table, unfolding it. "Madelyn said she wanted to take down the cult of the Faceless. She knows where they are, but she didn't tell me. If we want to know, we need to call her back and let her help us."

"Help us do what exactly?" Stella says, in interrogation mode again. "I'd like to talk to this woman. How do you know she's not lying?"

"I don't know," Riley answers. "But this letter I found in my old attic proves that at least *some* of the things she said were true."

James leans over to read the note, but Stella snatches it before he can. She reads it silently, then drops it back onto the table, finally allowing James to read it.

"So, she left a suicide note but didn't actually kill herself," he says.

Riley nods, trying to act casual, but he sees the flicker of sadness flashing through her eyes. "She was clearly struggling with her mental health, but that's not the point. The point is that she's with the Faceless, and she said taking them down will be dangerous, but she wants to help."

"Do you trust her?"

"I don't know... But what choice do we have?"

"Has she killed?" Stella asks.

"I asked her, and she said no."

"And you believed her." It almost comes out as an accusation rather than a question, and that doesn't sit well with James. She needs to chill.

Riley lets out a long sigh. "I don't know what to believe, Stella. She says she's a new recruit and has to prove her worth before getting her own demon. Only the possessed ones kill to feed their passenger. Her job is to look for new targets to kill, although she said she didn't know what she was doing."

Rudy leans forward, resting his forearms onto the table. A strand of silver gray hair falls in front of his eyes, but he doesn't brush it away. "Where do they get their demons?"

"Um... She didn't tell."

"I know. I'm just wondering." He looks at James. "You said there were almost twenty people ambushing you, half of them possessed. If what Madelyn said is true, the newcomers could get their own demon anytime. I know we've dealt with a lot more shadows than the average, thanks to Riley's reputation."

"And our professional-looking website," she says proudly.

"Yes. But we know these things are actually quite rare compared to regular spirits. Janice could get her hands on a new one not even forty-eight hours after you exorcized her. Where did she find it? How is she able to provide a demon for every new recruit?"

James scratches his beard. "Maybe the bodies hosting the entities still degrade after a while, even when feeding them. So, they just move the demons from body to body. She might have stolen her entity from someone else in the cult. Since she gives the orders and all."

When Riley looks at him, James is still startled by her newly-brown eyes. "I saw Janice's demon's memories. The way they murder is so barbaric that it's more than enough food for the shadow to feed on without taking too much of their sanity."

"Terrestre said something when it possessed you all those years ago," Rudy says. "It said it would gladly destroy other shadows when it saw them. Could demons detect other demons easily, you think?"

Riley nods. "I think so. I feel them easily too. Well, I used to. I suppose it's the same for them. Like a shadow magnet."

James doesn't remember Terrestre having said that. He was probably too busy making sure he and Daniel weren't stabbed to death by the pieces of glass floating around them. But now that he hears this, a new question rises in his mind. "So, that's what she does when she's not murdering people? Finding demons to adopt?"

Riley shrugs. "I guess so."

"Call her," Stella says. "There's a lot of questions I'd like her to answer."

Riley makes no reply as she takes her phone out along with another small piece of paper with a phone number scribbled on it. She types each number, and when she's done, her thumb hovers over the call button, trembling slightly. "Excuse me, I'm just gonna..." She doesn't finish her sentence and pushes her chair back, leaving the room.

Stella sighs.

"It's hard for her," Rudy says.

"I know. I get it. I don't mean to be impatient. This is just so much bigger than I thought."

Rudy turns his icy blue eyes to James and gives him a short nod toward the hallway.

James stares for a moment, not sure what Rudy wants from him. Usually, the paternal is the one Riley needs in these kinds of situations. Someone to pacify her. But still, Rudy gives James another insistent nod, silently asking him to go with her.

James pushes his own chair back and exits the kitchen.

Riley's sitting on the second step of the staircase, the phone's screen reflecting its light on her face. Her eyes flicker to him as he approaches. "You know when you'd rather text a person than directly talk to them? That's how I feel right now, which is stupid because I talked to her yesterday."

James crouches in front of her, putting one knee down.

"What do I tell her?" Riley says, searching his face.

"Another meeting is in order. With all of us this time."

"Where? Here?"

"No. I don't like the thought of her being here in case we can't trust her. It's too isolated, and there's a bunch of demons in the basement. A public place, maybe."

"Winter's Attic?"

He nods, keeping himself from reaching for her hand. "That would work."

She looks down at the phone again and presses the call button.

CHAPTER 27

Riley presses the phone to her ear, her heart beating uncomfortably fast. It's fine, she already talked to Madelyn yesterday. They carried a whole conversation. So, why does the anxiety crush her chest a little more with each ringtone?

Because I can't stop thinking about the pink blanket and the stuffed rabbit.

She looks at James. With the way he's kneeling in front of her as she sits on the steps, their eyes are at the same level. Riley loses herself in the darkness of his irises until finally, Madelyn picks up the phone.

"Hello?"

Her mouth turns dry, and it suddenly feels impossible to talk.

James's eyes, deep and dark, don't leave her as he nods encouragingly.

"Hello?" Madelyn repeats.

"Hi. Um, it-it's Riley."

"Riley, I'm so glad you're calling. How are you feeling?"

I was feeling sort of okay until I talked to you again.

"Fine. Uh... I've been to the house. I don't know if you're aware, but it's been abandoned for years." Not that it matters, but the need to say it and ask about the baby stuff overpowers her.

"No, I didn't know."

"I found the attic. There are still... toys. And things." *Her* things. Things Madelyn used to care for a baby Riley until she vanished. Her jaw tightens. She keeps her eyes on James, seeking comfort.

"I knew Lance would hold onto some stuff, but I'm surprised it's still there after the house was empty all these years."

"Did you... used to knit?"

A soft chuckle on the other side. "I still do. Once, I made you a blanket. You loved it. You would sleep with it every night. It was pink."

The lump in Riley's throat swells. James doesn't look down, knowing she needs support. She can't talk about this. It hurts too much. "I'd like to meet again. *We* would like to meet. To talk about the Faceless."

"Of course."

"When are you available?"

"Well, I get off work at five."

"You have a job?"

"Yes, of course I have a job, Riley. I have bills to pay like everyone else."

The question tumbles out of her mouth before she can stop it. "What do you do?"

"I'm an administrative assistant for the Madison's Church in Manchester."

James must have heard it. He frowns, shakes his head slowly, and mouths, *"For fuck's sake."*

Riley's breath catches in her throat, and she presses her hand against her mouth. James presses his lips into a tight line to keep himself from laughing.

"You work at a church?" she says behind her fingers. The irony of it is just too much.

"Yes."

"What do you do exactly?"

"Oh, a lot of different things. I provide administrative support to the community life Pastor, I receive and direct calls, manage the calendar, and coordinate meetings and church-wide activities—"

The rest of what Madelyn says is lost. There is a divine moment of shared amusement as Riley and James stare at each other until tears prick at her eyes and she can't keep still any longer. She tightens her hand over her mouth, and James presses a finger against his lips to tell her to stay silent, but the two of them fall into an incontrollable fit of laughter they have to keep quiet. He gestures at her to keep it down but can't do the same, either. It occurs to Riley that she needs to stop looking at him if she wants to stand a chance to calm down. She grabs his forearm, digging her fingers into his skin as a warning to stop. That doesn't work, and he keeps laughing, but at least he bows his head down, allowing Riley to get a hold of herself.

"Riley?" Madelyn says. "Is everything okay?"

Riley wipes her tears and takes a deep breath before putting the phone back to her ear. "Yeah, yeah. That sounds awesome. Not sure your church would approve you being part of a demonic cult, though."

That sets James off again. His fingers close around her forearm as well, now the both of them holding onto each other, and he buries his face in his other palm, his elbow resting onto Riley's knee and his shoulders shaking, while she twists the phone away from her mouth to make sure Madelyn doesn't hear her laughter.

"We all have our secrets," Madelyn says. "Where would you like to meet?"

Riley exhales another breath to recover from her fit. "Winter's Attic. It's a bookshop in Manchester that my dad and I own. You'll find the address on the internet."

"All right. I can be there at five thirty. Is that okay?"

"Yes. You'll be alone, right?"

"Of course. I don't want the others to know I'm meeting with you. Secrecy is extremely important. They would kill me."

After hanging up, James pulls Riley onto her feet, still smiling despite himself as they go back to the kitchen.

"She'll meet us at Winter's Attic at five thirty today," Riley says.

"What's so funny?" Rudy asks, making Riley realize she's also still smiling like an idiot.

They glance at each other, and James says, "Madelyn works at a church."

A hint of a smile tugs at her dad's lips. "You're shitting me."

"It sounds like a bad joke, I know."

"Can you make it, Stella?" Riley asks her.

"Yes. I'll meet you all there."

"And I need to get some things at my place," James says. "I'll be at the bookshop before Madelyn gets there, all right?"

He waves at them and disappears into the hallway. Once the front door closes, Rudy looks at Riley, raising his eyebrows at her.

"What?" Riley says while Stella has her back turned, washing cups into the sink.

"Go with him," Rudy signs.

"What about work?" she signs back.

"I'm not opening today. I just pulled an all-nighter, and like the old man that I am, I need to get some sleep. You should rest too. But it's your chance to have a talk with James."

"Since when do you meddle? You never meddle."

He does the *go away* sign, shooing her away impatiently. With a frustrated grunt, Riley turns to the hallway and grabs her boots from the foyer, putting them on hastily. She darts out the front door, penetrating a morning wind saturated with humidity as dark clouds gather above them.

James's Mustang starts driving away. Riley bolts from the porch and runs before it rounds the house, jumping in front of it.

He hits the brakes, sending a cloud of dirt around the tires, and sticks his head out the window, frowning. "Do you have a death wish?"

"Can I come with you?"

His face softens a little as he hesitates. "Uh, sure."

Riley rounds the car and jumps in the passenger seat, buckling the seat belt, already regretting being here. She's not ready to have that talk. What is she going to say exactly? 'I love you?' Fuck. This was a mistake. Having this talk on no sleep can't bring anything good. She's not really good with words. Her dad could be entirely mistaken, and Riley's just about to be rejected another time.

It's not about being rejected. It's about being honest and fixing your mistakes.

Because she hurt him. Even if he doesn't love her back, the way she acted was shitty, either when she made him feel like she only kissed him when she was drunk, or when he tried to talk to her, and she didn't let him speak.

Neither one of them talk, making the trip painfully awkward. To ward off some of the discomfort, Riley turns up the volume of the radio. *Queen* is playing.

She glances at him. He glances back briefly, a small smile on his lips. Their laughing fit seems to have revived their friendship. Or maybe listening to *Queen* relaxes him a little.

Riley's stomach twists a little more the closer they get to his place. She keeps her fingers clasped together, threatening to make them bleed again. A few drops of rain occasionally hit the windshield, teasing them. If only those clouds could break already and alleviate the suffocating heat.

They drive by the road they were ambushed on, sending a flashback of herself trapped in her car as its nose pointed downward. Black tire marks are clearly visible on the gray concrete, showing the exact spot where that psycho crashed into her.

When arriving at his place, James parks in the driveway. Riley follows him inside, nausea gagging her as she inwardly tells herself to speak her mind.

"I'll go change," he says. "Make yourself at home. You know the way to the fridge."

"Okay."

The word is spoken so low that he doesn't seem to hear it as he leaves her in the living room and heads to his bedroom, then the bathroom. Riley sits on the couch, listening to the shower running, not knowing what to do with herself. Exhaustion is finally catching up to her, making her body sluggish and her eyelids heavy. She gives herself a series of slaps on the cheeks and rises to her feet, pacing the floor. This is stupid. Everything. They have better things to think about. Well, worse things, but important things.

On the other hand, they don't meet Madelyn until five thirty, and it's still pretty early in the morning. There should be enough time to say *I love you, you don't have to answer, I'm going to bed now.*

Riley stands in front of the sink, looking out the window. If he doesn't come out of the shower soon, her courage will wane.

The bathroom door opens a moment later, making her heart jump. She conjures the things she wants to say to him, but only a puddle of incoherent word vomit jumbles in her mind.

James emerges from the short hallway, his hair still damp, and heads for the fridge. He takes a bottle of water, then freezes as he meets Riley's eyes. "You all right?"

She's been staring. Her heart is in her throat, pulsing fiercely. She turns back to the window, her hands gripping the edge of the sink. If she has to say it, it'll be easier not to look at him. "I love you."

Her skin breaks into hot flashes as the words roll off her tongue.

Silence behind her.

She swallows. "I'm sorry if I made you feel like I didn't care, like I would only kiss you because I wanted to make myself feel better. I just... I didn't know how to tell you how I really felt. Honestly, it's fine if you don't feel the same. I was wrong to be mad at you for that. And if we can't be more than friends, at least I hope that we can get a fresh start because I can't stand the idea of losing you."

His silence stretches into eternity. She still can't look at him. She can't feel him. She wishes she weren't so miserable, but new tears already burn her eyes.

"Please, say something. Anything at all. Be honest. Just... talk to me."

Warm fingers brush her arms, making her heart pick up the pace. His breath tickles her hair. James turns her around, standing close and towering over her. He gently wipes a rogue tear from her cheek, his intense gaze locked on her. "I hate to see you cry."

The world disappears around her as his fingers graze her neck and settle under her jaw, his face inches from hers.

"I love you, Riley."

The words, spoken in a deep, low voice, send a shiver through her body before he bends down and presses his mouth against hers. His lips caress her lips, and soon Riley allows herself to run her hands over his chest and dig her fingers in his hair. His strong arms wrap around her, his hands moving across her back and tangling in her mane.

A flash of lightning pierces through the windows. The thunder shakes the walls a few seconds later. Clouds break, finally releasing their load. The rain falls hard, slapping the windows, the sound deafening.

Riley pays no attention to it. James lifts her effortlessly, sitting her up on the edge of the sink and allowing her to wrap her legs around his waist. He holds her closer, tighter, as he slowly runs his lips down her neck. The edge of the sink disappears from under her when he lifts her again and moves her away from it. She doesn't know where they are nor where they're going. She can't stop kissing him and tasting his tongue and biting his lips, burning for him.

Her back sinks into the soft mattress. She's not dropped or thrown onto it, but delicately laid down. Their clothes fly off their bodies. James's chest presses against hers, his breath hot on her neck and his beard rasping against her skin, as his hands explore her curves.

She opens her legs and pulls him closer, her fingers digging into his back as he melts onto her.

CHAPTER 28

The bell above the door tinkles as James and Riley burst inside, giggling, and their clothes dripping. Riley's wrapped in James's jacket, which is way too big for her. The vibe they give off feels vastly different.

"You kids are here early," Rudy says from behind the counter. "Stella's not here yet, and Madelyn shouldn't come for another thirty minutes."

James slams two pizza boxes onto the counter, ruffling his wet hair.

"There are towels in the bathroom," Rudy tells him.

"I think I'll grab one." He glances at Riley. "I'll grab you one too."

Riley joins Rudy behind the counter and sits next to him. "What's that? I don't have my hearing aids on."

"Towel."

"Yes, please."

James disappears into the hallway leading to the bathroom, and Rudy peers at Riley for a moment. Her face is relaxed. A smile tugs at the corner of her mouth. Her eyes sparkle. "You look happy."

She sheds James's soaked jacket and lets out a little laugh. "Well… I guess I am. Despite everything."

"Did you get some sleep?"

"Yes."

He doesn't add anything. Knowing she's happy is more than enough. Riley flips one pizza box open, and the smell fills the space, making him hungry. There's one thing he'd like to do first, though.

He puts a hand on her shoulder to signal he wants to make eye contact. "Be right back."

She nods, then shoves half a giant slice of pizza inside her mouth.

Rudy leaves her side and enters the hallway leading to the bathroom and the back room. James stands in front of the bathroom mirror, the door wide open, while he dries his hair with the towel.

"Come here for a sec, boy," Rudy says, beckoning him to the back room. "I'd like to talk to you."

James turns to him, looking puzzled for a moment, but follows Rudy, towel in hand. "Everything okay?"

Rudy shuts the door, enjoying the flash of panic lighting James's eyes, and crosses his arms against his chest. "Something you wanna tell me?"

"Uh… weren't you the one who wanted to talk to me?"

Rudy frowns and takes a few steps forward, enjoying himself way too much as he makes himself look threatening and gives his best Death Stare. "Quit being a smartass and spit it out."

James swallows and holds his hands up. "All right, listen, I understand you're pissed. I promise you this is *very* recent, okay? I only started having feelings for her a few months ago, but not before that. Not when she was younger, and not when she was, you know... underaged..." He closes his eyes and winces as the word passes his lips, as though it tastes bad and threatens to make him gag when it rolls off his tongue.

"Mm-hm."

"I swear this is true, Rud. And I would never hurt her, you know that."

"You better not. Because I'll kill you."

"Trust me, if I hurt her, I'd kill me too."

Rudy looks him up and down. "Do you love her?"

James squares his shoulders and stands tall, daring to hold Rudy's gaze. "Yes."

Rudy closes the distance between the two of them and pats his cheek, finally allowing himself to smile. "Good."

Confusion paints James's face again. "What, seriously? You're... cool with this? I thought you'd want to murder me. I thought you *were* going to murder me right now."

"I trust you. And I trust you with her."

"You were fucking with me just now, weren't you?"

"Yes. Gotta maintain the intimidating dad vibe."

James nods, a smile playing at the corners of his mouth. "Well done. I nearly shat my pants."

Chuckling and happy with himself, Rudy opens the door and starts down the hallway. "Don't forget her towel."

When he and James return to the bookshop, Stella's there, standing across from Riley.

His daughter's eyes flick to him, her eyebrows raised. "What's happening over there?"

"Nothing."

"I might not be an empath anymore, but I'm not stupid."

"Everything's good, pumpkin." He stands next to Stella, who gives him a tight smile, and he kisses her. "Not eating?"

"No. I don't want to be sluggish before an interrogation."

Riley freezes mid-bite, tomato sauce dripping down her chin. "I did not think about that."

"At your age, you're always sharp," Stella says. "Wait until you hit your thirties."

They eat, at least most of them do, and the closer they get to five thirty, the quieter the room becomes, the heavy rain replacing the chatting.

A figure stands on the other side of Winter's Attic's door. A woman with dark hair holding an umbrella.

Rudy leans toward Stella, speaking in her ear. "Your time to shine."

The bell above the door tinkles, announcing Madelyn's arrival.

The sign on the door is flipped to *closed*. The lights are turned off in the bookshop while everyone is huddled in the back room. Madelyn has been seated on a chair right in the middle of it. Stella stands in front of her, arms crossed, while the others loom on the side of the room.

James stands next to Rudy, who's behind Riley, his hands on her shoulders as though to keep her stable. Rudy's the one he's keeping stable, Stella knows that perfectly well. Being in this room with his daughter's biological mother makes him feel uneasy. He talked to Stella a little about it this morning after James and Riley left the house. He said he had no real reason—no right—to be jealous. He's not, not really. He's wary. Afraid Riley could become taken with Madelyn only because they share the same blood. Afraid she'll be more disappointed and hurt than she already is.

Stella can't even imagine what it's like for him, or what it's like for Riley. For now, it's time to ask Madelyn some questions, and hopefully, James will keep his mouth shut.

"There's no need for an interrogation," Madelyn says, looking at Riley instead of Stella. "I told you I wanted to help."

"Eyes on me," Stella says, bringing Madelyn's attention back to her. "I'm Detective Stella Valdez, and I've been working on the case your cult created by murdering all those people. I looked you up. You go by the name of Charlotte Caldwell. Administrative Assistant at the Madison's Church. Fifty-six years old. No partner, no children, but a cute apartment in Nashua, New Hampshire. Nice place. You didn't have a life on record until you got a parking ticket in Boston at the age of forty-three, which is pretty much your only offense. Not much going on in your life, is there?"

"I believe you don't have the right to run someone's background for personal matters."

She's right. Running backgrounds as a service for someone is a big no-no. But when it comes down to paranormal cases, Stella often needs to do illegal things she could be fired for. "You admitted being part of a cult who kidnaps, tortures, and kills people. This is hardly personal matters, Miss Caldwell. Or would you like me to call you Mrs. Brooke?"

"You have no actual evidence of my involvement. I didn't kill anyone. I didn't even *know* they were killing until very recently."

Stella nods. "Maybe. I don't have a way to verify your involvement yet, and this is admittedly not a 'normal' case we're talking about, but if you're worried about this not being legal, then maybe taking a blood test to prove you are indeed Riley's biological mother will make it official. Especially if the tests come back negative. Because then, you'd be an identity thief."

"It won't be negative." She looks at Riley again. "If this is what I have to do to prove that I'm telling the truth, then I'll do it. Just say the word."

Stella snaps her fingers in front of Madelyn's face, again catching her gaze. "Oh, you bet we will. For now, why don't you tell me what made you join them? Were you bored? Did you need some thrill, some sense of importance?"

"I..." Madelyn takes a deep breath, squaring her shoulders. "Yes. Maybe. My mental issues didn't vanish after I left Lance. I thought being away from my daughter would make me feel better because she would finally be safe from me, but..." She turns to Riley again, her eyes watery. "But there wasn't a day I didn't think about you and miss you. So, no, I wasn't happy, and I spent my life being sad and depressed, taking medication every day and letting people walk all over me."

"You work in a church. It's hard not to laugh at the irony," Stella says. "Was it a way of redeeming yourself?"

Madelyn takes her eyes away from Riley and looks up at Stella. "I thought it would feel good. I thought it would make me feel better to turn to God and the church. It didn't."

"So, what happened, then? How did Janice Kraft enroll you?"

Madelyn tightens her hands together, her knuckles turning white. "I was at the church after work one day. I sometimes like to stay a few more minutes, and I sit, praying for my daughter. Praying that she's okay. And this woman showed up and sat next to me. She started talking to me. She said she understood me. She knew what it was like to be invisible to other people. That she, too, was undermined and mocked or just ignored. And she said she could make it all better. She said I could have a better purpose and do things that really mattered."

"And what was that?"

"I didn't know exactly... She talked about having a family, support, and never fearing money issues again."

Stella cocks her head. "And you believed her? Just like that? Didn't it strike you as suspicious?"

"Of course it did. I didn't believe her. Until she showed me her eyes. They were... so black. When she talked again, her voice was different. It was her demon talking to me. Telling me the reward would be infinite. *That's* when I believed."

"Riley said your job so far was to find people. New targets. Tell me more about that."

"Well... I find someone who fits any of the criteria and have to find out where they live or work. Then, I give the Faceless the address. They do the rest."

"What are the criteria?"

Stella already knows the answers. The only things the victims had in common was some sort of success in any area. A big, happy family. Money. An important career. Physical attractiveness. But she wants to hear it from Madelyn's mouth. She wants to be proved right.

"I had to find the type of people who would look down on me," Madelyn says in such a low voice it's hard to hear her. "Someone who would feel superior. Above everyone else."

Stella glances at Rudy. His icy blue eyes glint in the low light as he nods. She was right.

"And you seriously thought you were supposed to recruit new people?" James snaps. "How stupid are you?"

Stella glares daggers at him. He can never shut up.

Madelyn turns to him as well, her lips pressed into a tight line. "You would make a great target, Mr. Williams. You're just as condescending as the rest of them."

"How do you know my name?"

"Janice saw a lot of things in Riley's head."

"Stop it, you two," Stella orders, getting Madelyn's attention back. "How many people do the same job as you?"

"We're not that many yet. About nine or ten."

"Do you know their names or where they live?"

Madelyn shakes her head. "No. I only know they're all over New England. Janice said it was important to spread out."

Which played in their favor. By spreading out, it's too hard for the police to pinpoint where the murderer might live or kill. It drove Stella crazy, having the same murders repeating themselves hundreds of miles from each other.

"So, all the possessed people kill, then? Not just Janice?"

"That's correct. Yes. The possessed ones have to feed their demons."

"Why cutting their hands and feet? Why pulling their teeth and eyes out and slashing their faces?"

Madelyn looks down at her hands again, wincing. "I don't know. Like I said, I never killed. Janice gives the orders."

"Not this master you have talked to Riley about? Who is this person?"

"I've never met the master. Janice takes orders from him, and we listen to her."

Stella sighs, shifting from one foot to the other. "What does he want with Riley?"

"Isn't that obvious? He wants her because she's so powerful."

"Janice already took her empathy. Why doesn't this man run away with it?"

Madelyn shakes her head. "I-I don't know..."

"You're lying."

"I'm not! I *don't know*. Janice just said that once we've got Riley's imprint, we would be unstoppable. I *wanted* that until I understood that this Riley Winter they were talking about was my daughter, Riley Brooke. Then... it just felt horribly wrong."

Riley noticeably flinches at the sound of her former name, her back pressing a bit harder against Rudy. He wraps an arm across her chest, holding her tighter.

"I hate what they did to you, Riley," Madelyn says. "I want them to pay for hurting you and manipulating me. I don't care what happens to me after that. I don't care if you never speak to me again. But for now, I'm here, and I can tell you where to find them."

"Where are they?" Riley says, her voice falsely calm.

"The abandoned bunker in Westland."

The image of the old, decrepit bunker jumps to Stella's mind. She and Rudy have hiked over there many times. There are trails and ponds and fields. One of these fields holds an abandoned bunker from World War II. It doesn't look like much, just a stone structure, with a single, locked, metal door.

"No one can get in there," Stella says. "It's been condemned for years."

"Well, that's where they are. And that door was open for me every time I went there when they called us for meetings. I think that's where they kill, but I haven't gone down the tunnels."

Riley holds her hand up. "Wait a second. *Meetings?*"

"Well, yes. We have to be there when Janice calls us all. Usually with a text that we have to delete afterwards. We never speak over the phone. We go there to get our orders and our next missions and to tell her about the new target we found. But we only meet in a room close to the entrance. I've never been deeper into the bunker, but I know that's where you'll find Janice and the master, whoever he is."

Stella takes a deep breath to calm her nerves. Of all the bodies that have been found in diverse woods, none of them were in Westland. Nothing ever pointed her in that direction. This abandoned bunker is simply a relic from World War II, a structure that always loomed in the background of everyone's mind. "How many possessed people are there?"

"Eight, I think." Riley's voice snaps Stella's attention away from Madelyn. "There were eight, including Janice."

Madelyn nods. "That's correct. The Faceless are very young. It started with Janice and the master. And now she's trying to grow, but it's not too late to stop her. The possessed ones sometimes meet up without us. If I figure out when their next meeting is, we could go there and only have to worry about them instead of all the cult."

Stella looks at the three paranormal investigators. "Does this sound doable to you? Take on eight demons at the same time? Plus a master that we know nothing about? I can help, but I'm not a pro in this area."

James glances at Rudy, raising his eyebrows in a silent question. Rudy looks back.

Riley bites on her thumbnail. "When they assaulted me, I couldn't do much. I'm even more useless now."

"That's why you need me," Madelyn says, standing up. "I could create a diversion so you wouldn't have to take them all on at the same time. The tunnels... they have a lot of hiding places."

"I guess we could pull it off if we're prepared," James says, his voice low as though he's talking to himself. "Some of our EMF detectors have a silent mode. They can show us if they pick up a signal without making any noise, which will play to our advantage if we want to be discreet and ambush the shadows. We've got tons of amulets, UV light sticks, salt... and guns. If push comes to shove, of course."

"Do we even have enough lockboxes lying around?" Riley says.

"No. But I can call the guy who makes them for us."

"Why do they meet without you?" Rudy looks straight at Madelyn, his face cold in a way Stella has rarely seen.

"Excuse me?"

"Why do they have meetings with the non-possessed like you, and others without you? What do they do during that time?"

His suspicious tone isn't lost on Stella. She can almost feel him boil. His jaw is set, and his body is tense.

"Well…" Madelyn hesitates a moment. "Like I said… They kill there."

"So, you're suggesting we wait for them to torture someone? Or maybe you want to find them some bait?"

"No, of course not… But what other option is there? I don't know how they get inside the bunker, so I can't get you in without them. We have to wait for them to come."

He takes a sudden step forward. "You're sick."

"If we act fast, we could get them before they kill. Trap them. This is the only way."

"I don't trust a fucking word you say, Madelyn."

Riley takes his arm gently. "Dad."

"I don't care about whether you trust me or not, Mr. Winter. I'm just trying to help my daughter."

"*Your* daughter?"

"*Yes.* I know I've made terrible mistakes. I wish I had never left her behind, and I wish she hadn't ended up with someone as gruff and disagreeable as you. She deserved better–"

"She's *my* kid. I'm the one who raised her, who taught her how to ride a bike and who comforted when she had nightmares. So, don't you *fucking dare* talk to me like that."

A murderous flash glints in Rudy's eyes, and Stella steps forward, a hand outstretched toward his chest. "Rudy, calm down."

"I understand why you're part of that cult," he says through gritted teeth. "You're pathetic and a poor excuse for a human being. Now get the hell out of my bookstore."

Madelyn takes a shaky breath, clearly intimidated by the giant who just yelled at her, and glances at Riley quickly. "I'll call you when I have more info." Without saying another word, she storms out of the room.

The rain has calmed down, reduced to a quiet drizzle, but the wind has picked up the pace, snatching at the lighter's flame and keeping Rudy from lighting the damn cigarette. Finally, he succeeds, taking a deep breath of the wonderful poison. His hands still shake. A headache pulses at the back of his skull. He stands with his back to the wall in an attempt to escape the rain, facing the street with its glowing lights as the day darkens.

The bookshop's door opens, and Riley steps out, hugging her arms to protect them from the wind. Rudy can't look at her. The way he acted was stupid, as though Riley's his property, a thing he possesses and not a human being who makes her own informed decisions.

She stands next to him, not talking for a moment.

"I thought you quit smoking," she says after a while.

"I'll quit again after this whole thing is taken care of."

"I'll quit with you."

"Good."

He brings the cigarette to his lips again, his hand trembling slightly less.

"I've rarely seen you this angry," she says. "If I could see your colors, you'd be all red right now."

"It's cute how you still use colors even if you can't see them."

She chuckles, then fixes her eyes on him, her features softening. "It's not a competition, Dad."

"I know. I'm sorry."

"If it *were* a competition, she wouldn't even be allowed to enter it. Thinking about her leaving me hurts, yes, but in the end, she's nothing to me. You're *everything*. And you taught me not to give a shit about what people think, so stop giving a shit about what she thinks."

He meets her eyes this time. "I've raised you right."

"Yeah, you did."

"Do you think we can trust her? Do you want to go along with this plan of waiting for someone to be kidnapped?"

"Hell no. My instincts are a bit blurred at the moment, but I trust your judgement. And while I think that ambushing the cult is perhaps our only option, no, I'm not fond of the idea of waiting for someone to be killed. We need to be at the bunker *before* they show up. If we can't find a way inside, then shit will have to go down outside."

Rudy conjures the memory of the bunker. It sits in the middle of a clearing, which means there aren't many places to hide. Attacking in an open area would be messy and dangerous. Carrying all these lockboxes will be awkward as hell. "That just won't work. We can't take them all down at the same time. Even with amulets around their necks, I suspect they're quite strong. We need to be inside the bunker and set traps."

"But we've seen the door, though. No one can get in. Maybe demons give their humans super strength or something, but we don't have that."

He smiles at Riley. "Or."

"Or?"

"They use another entrance Madelyn just doesn't know about."

"Can there be an entrance we've never seen?"

"Yes. On the roof. The rusted ladder that used to be there has long been broken. If we can climb, maybe we'll find something there."

Riley considers this. "Sounds like wishful thinking, though."

"Maybe it is. But I think our next move is to go and check it out before we come up with an elaborate plan. If we know what to expect, we'll be able to prepare ourselves better."

"We can check right now."

"No, it's too late, and it's dark—"

"No, Dad." She chuckles, fishing her phone from her pocket. "I can literally check it out on my phone right now."

He frowns, feeling as though he just aged another ten years in five seconds. "How?"

"Google maps. You know, the satellite view? The bunker is exposed, right? There are no trees hiding the view?"

"I don't think so. It sits in the middle of a field."

"Then, it shouldn't be a problem."

She types quickly on her phone, and Rudy leans over her shoulder to watch what she's doing. These kids and their smartphones. They know how to look up everything. Rudy can barely find the website to his favorite pizza place and still hangs onto the flyer to have their number handy.

After a few magic taps of her fingers, Google maps shows Westland, the woods, the trails, the ponds, and the bunker. The small gray dot is surrounded by grass. Riley zooms on it and lets out a sigh of disappointment as the flat roof looks desperately plain. "There's no entrance there."

"It was wishful thinking after all."

"Not necessarily." She does something he doesn't understand, dragging a small, stick figure onto the screen. The view changes, showing a trail surrounded by trees.

"What did you do just now?"

"I put on the street view." When she clicks somewhere, the view seems to jump forward, showing them another angle of the path. "The problem is that the trails don't go to the bunker. You have to walk through the grass for that, so I can't look at it on the screen. But look at the front door. It clearly hasn't been forced, so I think you're right. They found another way in and then opened from inside. We need to go there ourselves. If they got in, then we can get in too, super strength or not. Probably."

He smiles at her, filled with pride. "You're a smart girl."

She smiles back, then seems to choose her words carefully. "I hate to say this, but... we sort of need her."

Rudy makes no reply. He's aware they need Madelyn's help, but that doesn't sit well with him.

"She could call them once we're ready to take them on. Invent something to bring them into the bunker without having to wait for them to find a new victim. And maybe she could help with the exorcisms."

He sighs, looking at the rain and the cars driving by, their tires splashing on the flooded road.

Riley smiles that playful smile of hers and gives him a small nudge of her elbow. "Going on a hike tomorrow, then? Just to check things out?"

"Did someone say hike?" James steps out of the bookshop, his eyes sparkling. "I used to hike all the time with my dad when I was a kid. Sounds like fun. Also, you can't leave me alone with Stella like this."

Riley giggles, and Rudy can't hold a chuckle.

"She scares you?" he says.

"Yeah."

"You're right to be scared," Stella says, grinning and closing the door behind herself. "So, how do we move forward? Do I need to take the day off tomorrow?"

Riley turns back to Rudy, her eyes a different color, but her gaze the same as it always was as she looks up at him. "What's the plan, boss?"

CHAPTER 29

The trees clear, letting the strong wind slap Riley's face and whistle in her hearing aids. The dark clouds hang low above their heads, and the tall, yellow grass is flattened by the gale.

Rudy turns and signs, "It's over there."

She's grateful for him using ASL because she wouldn't hear him talk from that distance. She follows him and Stella, then feels strong hands clasping on her shoulders and pushing her forward. She tilts her head to look at James.

"The wind's gonna knock you out," she reads on his lips.

She chuckles, ready to say she's not that fragile when another gust of wind nearly makes her lose her balance. The woods gave them a nice cover, but in the open field, they're completely exposed and at the weather's mercy. James hooks his arm around her waist to keep her stable, and Riley turns to face him, walking backwards.

This new dynamic between them feels weird. Wonderfully weird. Hand holding. Ear whispering. Back rubbing. Stolen kisses. Sneaking into his room last night even when they slept at her dad's house. Lying in bed face to face while she traced indistinct patterns over the black hair on his chest. It makes her happy and dizzy and fills her stomach with butterflies.

She looks up at him, unable to keep herself from smiling despite all the shitty things that happened these past few days.

At least one good thing happened this week.

"Kiss me," she says.

He frowns. "In front of your paternal? Are you kidding?"

"He's cool with it."

"Doesn't mean I wanna kiss you when he's here."

She wraps her arms around him and hangs onto his neck, making herself heavier than she is, which doesn't stop him from walking. "He's far away and not looking."

He flicks his gaze above her head to make sure of that, then he bends over to kiss her, the warmth of his skin a welcome change from the damp wind.

They resume their walk, his arm still hooked around her as he helps her not get knocked over.

The bunker appears ahead. A not so tall, round stone structure covered in graffiti. Broken steps lead to a large, metal door. Just like Rudy said, a broken ladder gnawed by rust hangs onto the side of the building, at the bottom of the wall. It looks to Riley as though you could catch tetanus just by looking at it. Thankfully, they won't have to get close to it since they already know there's nothing to see on the roof.

Riley climbs the stone steps leading to the door. It looks as clean as she saw on her phone the day before. It hasn't been forced. When she grabs the handle and shakes it, the door stays firmly in place, tightly locked.

"We definitely can't go this way," she yells at the others above the screaming wind.

Rudy looks at them all, his steel-gray hair disheveled. "Look around. See if you can find anything that would show us how they got in."

Riley rounds the structure, her eyes darting from place to place, analyzing the building. On the other side, she meets James, who's crouching in the high grass.

"Did you find something?" she asks.

"There are windows here."

She crouches next to him, looking at what he's showing her. Narrow windows, covered in dark grime and hidden behind the grass, run the length on the wall.

James knocks on the glass. "I'm surprised no one has broken them yet. They look pretty solid, though." He runs his fingers around the edges, prodding, trying to find a way to open them, but the windows don't move. "If we can't open them, then that's not our way in."

"I'll keep looking around."

She kisses his cheek, then leaves his side and walks further back. The high grass brushes her knees, their wet tips soaking her jeans. The air is uncomfortably lukewarm, making her shirt stick to her back.

Riley turns in a circle, looking at the bunker and its surroundings. Nothing but grass and trees in the distance.

Until something else appears in her vision farther away. It's almost completely hidden in the dry meadow. She walks to it, wiping the thin layer of sweat coating her forehead. It's a small stone structure, made greenish by moss, not higher than her knees. Some sort of rectangular post with a tiny air vent, standing next to a larger square. Wild grass and ivy cling onto its surface, covering it almost completely.

Almost.

Another type of gray, the metallic kind, peeks through the branches. Riley lifts the plants, realizing they're a lot looser than she expected them to be, and starts pulling them off the structure, revealing the metallic panel. A smile creeps onto her lips, as she feels oddly excited by this discovery. On each side of the panel, two rusty latches are clamped, keeping it closed.

She turns around, waving at the others. Rudy sees her first.

"Over here," she signs.

He calls for the others, and the three of them walk through the grass in her direction.

"Look," Riley says. "It looks like a hatch, doesn't it?"

"It does," Rudy says. He steps close to it and tries the latches. When he digs his fingers under them, they move slightly under the pressure. "You have your pocketknives?"

Riley reaches for hers at the same time as James, who starts working on one latch while her dad takes her knife and works on the other. Sliding the blade under it, he lifts the knife handle and pulls on it, using his body weight to apply more pressure. James does the same. It looks hard, the latches resisting, but little by little, they slide outward.

Riley turns to Stella, eyes wide. "This is so cool. Isn't that cool?"

Stella cautiously smiles. "Until we see what atrocities await us there."

"True, but, I mean, it's a secret passage." Riley grabs Stella's arm, shaking it gently. "A *secret passage,* Stella!"

This gets a small laugh out of Stella.

One latch opens with a metallic grind, the other follows. The two men exhale and chuckle proudly, nodding at each other.

"Go ahead, open it," Riley says, barely containing her excitement.

Rudy lifts the hatch, and all four of them bend over to stare inside. Darkness stares back at them. A long, black tunnel leads down, rusty ladder steps fixed into its wall.

"Woah," James breathes out.

"That's the way they use to get in," Stella says. "Their strength enables them to open these latches."

Rudy searches his backpack and takes out a flashlight. The beam barely cuts through the darkness, but it's enough to highlight the portion of the wall that broke off and makes the passage even narrower. "They probably have one of them go in there and open the door to the others. Someone thin. Being possessed and having your demon crawl onto the walls for you surely helps."

Riley nods to herself, staring into the black pit. "I'll go."

Three pairs of eyes fix on her.

"No," her dad says. "I'm not letting you go in there alone."

"Dad, look at this." She takes his flashlight and bends over farther. "You see where the wall collapsed? You and Jamie won't fit in there. I will. And no offense, but I'm the most athletic."

Rudy sighs, obviously not happy with any of this, and turns to James. "Please, tell me you're on my side."

Riley raises her eyebrows at James, and for a moment, he looks at them back and forth.

"I hate this. When you guys force me to take a side, I mean. I-I don't know, okay? Riley's got a point, she looks like she can fit in there, but I also don't like the idea of having her go down there alone." He clears his throat. "Stella?"

She looks inside the tunnel for a moment as though calculating. "I'll go with her."

Rudy's face falls.

A smile spreads on Riley's lips. "All right, a mission for the girls! I like that."

"Take your knife back," Rudy says, his chest deflating. "And the flashlight. You have your phone?"

"Yes. Not sure about the signal down there, though. Listen, this place should be empty for now, and it's not like we're going to check it out yet. We'll look for the door and open it for you guys."

"Stay on your guard."

Since the tunnel is tight, it's impossible for her to carry much without being stuck. Riley tucks her gun in the inside pocket of her jacket and wraps an amulet around her neck. The rest—UV light sticks, a small bag of salt, an extra amulet, an EMF detector, a lockbox, and two flashlights—will be dropped inside a smaller backpack once she's climbed the ladder. Not that there should be any demons in here at this time, but her dad likes to be extra careful, as always.

Riley sits on the edge of the hatch and slips her legs inside. Finding footing on one of the rungs, she lowers herself inside the tunnel, grateful to find cover from the growing storm. Silence fills her hearing aids. Straining to hear any suspect noises, Riley cautiously makes her way down, her fingers clasped on the old ladder, her back scrapping against the wall. The descent is slow, plunging her into thicker shadows.

The portion of the broken wall is a bit tricky. Riley presses her chest as tightly as she can against the rungs and, with her hands firmly clamped on one step, squirms her way down, letting her feet hang in the air so her body weight can pull her down. The strained muscles in her arms start to burn, but she keeps her breathing steady. There's an uncomfortable moment when the pointy corner of a brick digs into her shoulder blade and her chest refuses to slip through the narrow passageway. Riley exhales slowly, rotating her body slightly to the right to free herself.

Blackness swallows her. She raises her head, but the thick clouds have annihilated any light above. Even if there were any, the three heads looking down at her anxiously would hide it. A few raindrops slap her face, announcing the return of the downpour.

Riley lowers herself again and prods at the wall with her foot, searching for purchase, her arms on fire. Her heartbeat kicks up a notch as she doesn't find any. The lower half of her body is no longer surrounded by the tunnel.

New noises surround her. Echoes. Dripping water.

Lowering herself on shaking arms, she looks down, trying to see the floor. It's too dark. Her strength spent, Riley takes a deep breath, bracing herself for impact, and lets go.

A thought flashes through her mind. *You crazy idiot. You're gonna break your legs!*

Her feet connect with a concrete floor a lot sooner that she was afraid of, echoing deep in the tunnel stretching on both sides of her. Riley lands surprisingly well, in a crouching position, and a small laugh escapes her mouth as she stands back up.

"She sticks the landing." Her voice answers back to her, traveling through the empty space. Riley looks up. "I made it!"

Someone answers something, their voice snatched away by wind and thunder, and a second later, a backpack tumbles down the passageway and drops at her feet. Eager to get some light, Riley rummages through it and lets out a breath of relief as she turns the flashlight on. She directs it upward, watching Stella make her way down just like she did. From here, it looks a lot narrower and trickier.

"I hope you're good with pull-ups," she tells Stella, her voice again echoing around her. "Because a few feet down, the ladder disappears."

Stella lands almost as well as Riley and grabs the second flashlight.

"We're okay!" Riley yells at her dad and James above. "Will meet you guys at the entrance." Although she doesn't hear the answer, she sees a thumbs-up. She puts the backpack on her back and studies the passageways stretching on both sides. "Which way do you think we should go?"

Stella sweeps her light both ways, her face as composed as ever. "Isn't there something that strikes you as weird?"

Riley snorts. "We're in a military bunker where a cult of people possessed by demons murder their victims and answer to the commands of a master. So, I mean, yeah, that's weird even for us."

"I'm talking about the smell."

"What smell? There's no smell."

"Exactly. If demons were often crowding this place, shouldn't it reek of sulfur?"

Riley exhales, looking around herself again. "Not if the entities are well fed and concealed in their vessels, which they seem to be... Which in return means we're dealing with evil people holding very powerful shadows. Which, you know, sucks."

"Better get a move on then. The door was this way, I think." She points to their left.

The tunnel leads to nowhere but thick blackness, the beams of the flashlights casting dancing shadows across the arched walls and ceiling.

Riley nods. "All right. Let's go."

The two of them walk side by side, their footsteps disturbing the silence. The stone walls are a sickly beige, and water leaks have stained them, infiltrating each crack and crevice.

"This bunker dates from World War Two, right?" Riley says.

"Yes. This one was made for blast protection in case of a nuclear attack."

"How do you know?"

"There are several types of bunkers. They weren't built for the same purpose. This one could also protect from radiation. That's why it's buried deep and is steel reinforced. Not all bunkers contain large pipes and tunnels like this one. The latch we came from is a secondary exit. They all had one."

The tunnel bends to the right. Riley takes a peek, lighting the area before walking in. As she advances, a shiver runs through her, and her breath plumes in front of her. A cold spot.

If she still had her empathy, she'd be able to tell which kind of energy it is, good or bad, angry or sad. Now she doesn't feel more than what Stella does. There're not alone, but they can't see anything. Just an uneasy feeling of being watched. They glance at each other but don't stop.

As they make progress through the corridor, the cold spot disappears, and the temperature comes back to normal.

"This place must be haunted as fuck," Riley says.

Stella stops and looks at Riley. "You felt it too, right? The cold spot?"

"Yes. My guess is that if the Faceless kill in here, it must hold *a lot* of lost souls, and potentially a bunch of negative imprints. These are extremely violent deaths. I wouldn't be surprised if many of those victims still lingered here."

Stella shivers a little and resumes her walk. "That's fucked up."

Riley follows, picking up the pace to walk by her side. "I'm sorry, did I upset you?"

"No. Why?"

"I don't know. I never know what people feel anymore, but you seem a little... tense."

"You didn't upset me, Riley. I'm just angry that even if we took that cult down, even if we gave the victims justice, some of them will be forever trapped in this horrible place. Don't spirits who had a violent death become violent?"

"Well... not *all* of them. It really depends on how they were as living people. Some of them are stuck on loops, relieving their death. Others don't even know they're dead. Others don't haunt the place they died in. They might be attached to their house, an object, or a person."

Stella keeps walking fast, her shoes pounding the floor, the sound bouncing against the walls. She clearly doesn't want all that knowledge, and guilt fills Riley.

"We can cleanse this place later," she ventures. "We could come back and make sure the spirits leave. Give them peace."

Stella makes no reply. That would be a long shot, and Riley knows it. A place this huge, haunted by dozens and dozens or more spirits, wouldn't be so easy to cleanse. And if she's right, many unfound bodies are left to rot in the woods, and some ghosts can't move on until they're found and have a proper resting place.

At the end of an endless tunnel with several doors on each side, a staircase leads to a lower level. To the right, another corridor with doors. They turn right.

"Since my instincts are crap lately," Riley says, "what do you think about Madelyn?"

"Well, her story checks out so far. She could have faked her own suicide. Her body was never found. She just vanished, leaving a note behind. And she seems eager to get that blood test done, which points to her telling the truth."

"But? Why do I feel like there's a *but* coming?"

"Just don't get too attached."

Riley cocks her head, her eyes darting from Stella to the darkness in front of her. She doesn't want to get attached to Madelyn, but still, seeing her biological mother has been emotionally straining. "Why?"

"I don't like how eager she is to please you. I don't like how gooey she becomes around you."

"Well, she's my mother—"

"She didn't give a crap about you until now, Riley. And chances are, if she hadn't randomly run into you, she never would have looked for you."

Riley stops walking, as though Stella's words have punched her in the stomach. She's been so preoccupied about thinking of the reason Madelyn abandoned her in the first place that she didn't stop to think about this; if Madelyn wasn't part of the cult, they would have never met. She seems to have known that Lance was dead. When did she find out? Why didn't she look for Riley when she realized her child had become an orphan?

Stella stops and turns around, the halo of her flashlight blinding Riley. "I'm sorry. I didn't mean to sound harsh."

"No... It's all right. You're right." She forces her legs to work again, though they feel heavy.

Did I get attached? Just a little?

No. Or maybe yes, a little. Although she's reluctant to admit it, the sight of the letter and the baby stuff did something to her. She's not attached to the fifty-something woman, but she's softened by the mental picture of the young mother who knitted a pink blanket and bought a fluffy rabbit for her daughter. The idea tightens her throat, forcing emotions onto her that she refuses to feel.

"Why would she act like this, then?" she asks. "Why would she say she wants to be a part of my life?"

"She probably feels guilty. Or she doesn't want you to think badly of her."

"But like you said, she could have stayed hidden."

"She *should* have." The words are spoken through a clenched jaw.

"Are you... mad?"

Stella stops walking and looks at Riley in a way she has never looked at her before. "I know I appear to be a cold woman."

"I've never said—"

"I know I'm not motherly, and it's true that sometimes I feel a little left out when you're around your dad because he loves you so much and you guys have such a special relationship. I'm not jealous. I miss my parents. I miss my sister. I lost them way too early, and I guess that's why I became so antisocial and distant."

Riley scrambles to find what to say. "I wouldn't say antisocial—"

"But yes, I'm mad. Not just because this person who was absent your whole life dares giving parenting lessons to your dad, but because I really like you, Riley. I've liked you since the moment I saw you wearing that ugly sweater at the hospital, holding your father's hand. I've liked you since the moment I understood you and your loved ones survived what my sister and parents didn't."

Riley stares at her, both stunned and confused. She's always liked Stella. Always thought she was a badass cop. She thought she had her figured out, but evidently, she was wrong.

"It pisses me off because Madelyn felt the need to dump her guilt on you. She's trying to coax you into liking her because it makes *her* feel better about herself. She should have left you alone."

Silence stretches between them, only perturbed by rogue raindrops dripping onto the ground.

"Now I want to hug you," Riley says. "You know I'm a hugger."

A reluctant smile tugs at Stella's mouth. "I'm not the hugging type."

"And that ugly sweater you speak of belongs to my dad."

"I've never seen him wear it."

"I stole it from him when I was eleven. It was during our first winter at our house. We were watching a movie, I was cold, but my lazy ass didn't want to go to my room upstairs, so I went into his room instead and grabbed that sweater. It's been mine ever since. My comfort sweater. You should steal one too, he won't mind."

Stella nods, resuming her walk down the tunnel. "I'll think about it."

"I've always liked you too," Riley says, catching up to Stella. "Just so you know. Jamie and I were with my dad when he called you to ask you on a date. We were cheering him on."

"He sounded stressed."

"He was. That was hilarious."

"All that being said…" Stella pauses, choosing her words. "I know I'm not your go-to person, but I'm here if you ever need something."

Riley bumps her shoulder with hers to make up for the fact that she's not allowed to hug. "Same."

After one last turn, the floor rises up into a steep incline and leads them to a metal door taking up most of the wall. The front door. A thick bolt keeps it tightly shut. Thankfully, the cult coming in and out of this place have opened and closed it several times, and it doesn't give Riley too much of a hard time when she pulls on it with both hands. The door opens with a loud screech of its hinges, scraping on the stone floor.

CHAPTER 30

The storm has redoubled outside. Heavy rain blurs the woods, its water mistreated by the whistling winds. Thunder cracks the sky open. Rudy and James are soaked to the bone by the time the bunker door opens, revealing Riley's wide smile. She steps aside to make way for the both of them.

"You guys took your sweet time," James says, ruffling his hair and splattering water on the others.

"This place is a maze." Riley squints as splotches of water hit her face. "Dude, stop it."

Rudy's more worried about her and Stella being okay. "Did you see anything? Run into any trouble?"

Stella smiles and gives Riley a side glance. "We're fine. We didn't search any of the rooms, but we saw a staircase leading to a lower level."

"Did you smell anything?"

"Neither blood nor decay nor sulfur," Riley says. "There are cold spots, though. Place is haunted."

James eyes the tunnel descending into the shadows. "Doesn't surprise me. We might have more than demons to worry about here."

Rudy adjusts the straps of his backpack. "Let's search the place. Once it's done, we can elaborate a plan and call Madelyn. Did you take your EMF detector out?"

"No," Riley answers lightly, as if she's not standing in a place where God knows how many people have been killed.

He stares at her, knowing he's giving her the Death Stare without even trying.

"Dad, it's fine. We came straight for the door."

Rudy makes a dissatisfied noise at the back of his throat and takes his EMF sensor out of his pocket. He closes the door, and flashlights in hands, the group advances through the darkness. Their footsteps fill the tunnels as they move forward.

Each room they see stands empty. A series of barren and hollow stone rooms. The bunker has an eerie atmosphere, as if something too thin for them to see floats in the air, coating every surface, as well as Rudy's skin. As they take the staircase leading downward, unease seeps through his chest, tightening it more as he walks with the rest of the group behind him. His skin breaks in goosebumps, and his heart, quiet until now, starts beating furiously. His EMF sensor makes its high-pitched whirring, a few quick bursts at first, then an uninterrupted buzzing.

Riley's voice behind him startles him. "I don't feel so good."

He turns to her, and her face is an exact reflection of what he feels. Her eyes are wide in the dark, the flashlight shaking in her hand.

"Me neither," he says. He searches Stella's faces, as well as James's, and none of them looks serene. "Is it the same with you guys?"

Stella nods.

James does the same, his jaw working. "This place gives me the creeps. I usually don't feel like this, I can't explain it."

It's fear.

A deep, sickening dread filling them. Something primal. Rudy looks at Riley again since she's the closest to him. Her pupils are dilated, making her eyes look almost entirely black. "Fight or flight mode."

"But why?" Stella says. "We didn't see anything."

"Just because we don't see it doesn't mean nothing's here. I believe we're dealing with negative imprints left by the people who died here. And there were *a lot*. Their negative energy has built up to something so powerful we can all feel it."

Riley wipes a tear away from her cheek. "Well, shit. They were really fucking scared."

He wraps an arm around her shoulders and resumes walking down a new tunnel. "I know. Let's try to shake it off."

"Isn't that how demons are created?" Stella asks behind him.

James answers. "Demons used to be simple ghosts, who used to be real people. Evil people. But yeah, they certainly would love a place like this. They can feed on negative energy without possessing a human. It's not as good, but it works."

"That's how Terrestre got stronger," Riley says, still shaking a little under Rudy's arm. "The bad energies in my house fed it until it became strong enough to possess Lance."

Stella sighs. "It's still so abstract to me."

Rudy swallows down the overwhelming fear. "The spiritual world is complex, and even *we* don't have all the answers." He tilts his head toward his daughter. "You okay?"

"Yeah, yeah."

He lets go of her, the EMF detector still buzzing in his hand, flashing an angry red. He turns the sound off before losing his mind.

An insidious smell burns his nose. The dread in his chest makes him sick. It's so strong it prickles at his skin and leaves a bitter taste in his mouth.

James's hand falls on his shoulder, stopping him. "Look at this."

Another doorway stands a few paces ahead to the left of the corridor. It doesn't look like the others. At its base, black stains tarnish the stone floor. Rudy freezes, heart in throat, sure for a second that this black pool is ectoplasm, and the shadow will stand on two feet and attack them.

But the stain remains still, and he realizes the smell is familiar.

"Something was burnt here..." Riley says, stealing the words from his mouth. "Or *someone*." She leaves his side too fast for him to hold her back, throwing herself in front of the doorway. "This is where she did it... This is where she burned that man in the freezer. I saw it in her memories. I recognize this room."

Rudy stands next to her, the negative imprints of this place still making him shake, and he looks inside the room. She's right. The walls and the inside of the door are covered in soot and smoke residue. It's a striking contrast from the other rooms. They were empty and white. Bland.

This one smells like death, coating Rudy's tongue. In the middle of it stands one single piece of furniture; the freezer Riley was talking about. It's large enough to hold a person. He takes a few steps toward it, his boots sinking in the gunk covering the floor.

"Don't open it!" Riley cries out, her voice thick with panic echoing around them.

Everyone visibly startles, Rudy included.

"I wasn't going to," he says.

She exhales, squaring her shoulders, and clears her throat. "Sorry, I'm just... I don't like this room. I remember being stuck in it."

The ceiling is high above them, stretching up to the first floor. Remnants of steel shelves cover the walls, going almost as high as the ceiling, glinting through the ashes.

"That's the room I was looking into when we were outside." James's voice makes Rudy turn. "Look, it's got those narrow windows up the wall. I couldn't see inside because they were too dirty. Now I understand why."

A freezing breeze brushes Rudy's neck, making the hairs there stand on end. He turns to it, seeing nothing but darkness. The crawling in his skin redoubles. When he looks down at the EMF sensor, now on silent mode, the violent red still flashes over its screen.

"Let's move on," he says, a cloud of condensation escaping his mouth. "I have a feeling we'll hate what we see if one of these spirits decides to show themselves."

Taking the lead again, Rudy directs his flashlight in front of him, the negative energies of this place still smothering him. Dread. Pain. Those are the imprints people left in here before dying. Their fear still lingers, almost palpable.

No one talks as they walk. Cold spots make their breath plume. Disembodied voices whisper in their ears, some of them screaming for help, but they're so far away, so deep into this other realm that Rudy barely hears them. Their echoes brush the edge of his awareness before fading away.

A double door looms ahead. Another kind of scent, one that is bitterly sweet in the worst kind of way, has replaced the burning smell. Rudy's eyes fall onto the red-brown smear staining the handles.

Riley grasps his arm. "There's something in there."

"I wouldn't be surprised. This place is crawling with ghosts."

"No, something else. Don't you feel it?"

Rudy attempts to dissociate himself from the dripping energies of this place, his nerves on fire, but can't pinpoint what she's talking about. Her fingers feel tight on his arm, and her stare is fixed on the door.

James stands next to her, searching her face with concern. "What is it?"

"It's... I don't know. It's familiar but unlike anything I've ever felt. I think..."

Rudy raises his eyebrows, forbidding himself to interrupt her even if he thinks he knows what it is. She wouldn't feel it otherwise.

"I think it's a part of me," she says. "My empathy. I'm feeling my own energy."

"Let's go get it back," Stella says.

Rudy holds his hand up and keeps his voice low. "Not so fast. We might not be prepared for this. If Riley's empathy really is there, then it might not be the only thing we'll find."

James takes out his own EMF sensor, the screen flashing the same angry red light cutting through the darkness.

"Problem is… the place is so haunted we won't be able to know what's in there before we step in."

Riley takes a slow step forward, seemingly mesmerized by the door. "It's like it's pulling me in… Like it's calling to me."

Rudy places himself in front of her, blocking her way. "Listen to me. You have to stay *sharp*. Understand? Stay behind me at all times." His eyes flicker to James. "You stay behind us."

"Maybe I should go first, Rud."

"*No*. I can't take the risk."

"What if something attacks you?"

"Then, it'll attack me and not you."

Stella draws her gun. It wouldn't help against paranormal entities but would come handy if someone's in there. "I'll walk after you. Riley, you stay behind me and in front of James."

Riley shakes her head. "I can take care of myself."

Rudy cups the back of her head and kisses her forehead. "I don't give a crap. I'm the old man, and I give the orders."

"Hm… Fair enough, Dad."

Rudy checks that everyone's in line and has their firearm at the ready, also making sure that his daughter is safely tucked between Stella and James. Then, he turns to face the door, UV light stick in one hand, gun in the other, while Stella lights his way over his shoulder with her flashlight.

Raindrops drip somewhere, their *ploc* sound echoing around them. He keeps his eyes on the double doors ahead, straining to listen for any other noise. He reaches for the handle, wincing at the dried blood smears, and hooks a finger around it.

Rudy pulls it open. His heart flips as he catches motion deep into the room. A brief flash of purple before it's swallowed by shadows, as though it had never existed. It could be his eyes playing tricks on him. After going through a haunted tunnel and feeling so tense, it's not impossible. Still, it's better to stay alert.

Slowing his breathing, he takes a look to the left, then to the right. Raising one hand, he motions the others behind him to follow. Just a few steps so Stella's light can penetrate the dark room. It highlights sparse furniture. Spotlights. Red-brown tables. Shelves with various tools scattered on them. Even the floor has a peculiar color here.

And the smell. The sweet, putrid smell of blood coats the roof of his mouth.

The tables aren't red. They're covered in blood. The tools glint in the dark, the blades of knives and axes reflecting the light back at him.

Riley gasps behind him. "This is the room I saw in her memories."

"Shit…" Stella whispers. "This is a torture room."

Rudy steps deeper into the space, followed by the rest of them. It's large. Larger than any room they've seen, and it's cluttered with shelves, tables, hooks, and tools, all of them sticky and grimy with gore. A saw lies among knives and axes, resting next to a sledgehammer.

"It's here somewhere," Riley says, her voice low. "I can feel it."

James clears his throat, wincing at the view. "Should we really look for it now? I know it's important, but our goal was only to get familiar with the space."

"I don't like being here," Stella says.

Rudy nods, his neck stiff. "Me neither. Let's take a quick look around and get the hell out. Stay close to me, Riley. Stella, stay close to James."

While James and Stella edge toward the right side of the room, Rudy and Riley go left. They can still see each other, and Rudy likes to keep an eye on everyone.

"Do you still feel it?" he asks Riley.

"Yeah, but... sometimes, it's muffled. I don't know exactly where it is. And I still feel terrified, which doesn't help."

Her voice quivers slightly. This place messes with their senses.

A tool rolls off a shelf, clattering onto the floor. Rudy stops dead in his tracks, putting a hand behind himself to stop Riley as well. She turns her light to the tool—a knife—just in time for them to see a flicker or red disappearing behind the shelf.

Rudy snaps his fingers, the sound echoing in the room and catching James's attention.

"Don't move," he signs.

James nods.

A muffled bump followed by a growl coming from deeper into the room startles Rudy. He stares into the darkness, again catching a glimpse of that purple glow. That light is gentle, nothing like the violent flash of blood red he saw seconds earlier.

Another growl, low, the sound dragging and grating at Rudy's nerves. It feels closer too.

Riley raises her light toward the motion. "It's there."

They're not prepared for whatever's hiding in the smothering shadows. Rudy motions to his group to back away when the double doors behind them blast open. The shape of several people stand in the doorway.

Lights flicker around them, coming from portable spotlights scattered around the room. Tools rattle onto metal tables and shelves. Janice Kraft stands in front of her group. Rudy knows it's her. Stella has shown him pictures.

She shows her yellowed teeth as she smirks, stepping inside the room. "What a surprise. I knew you would come to your senses, Riley. I just didn't think you'd do it so fast. Welcome home."

Lights flicker faster, blinding them.

Rudy puts himself in front of his daughter, shielding her and raising his gun.

"I'm afraid you're not invited to this party, Mr. Winter," she announces loud enough to be heard over the deafening clatter. "Your gun doesn't hold much power here."

"It can kill you all, that's how much power it has."

Her face falls, her dead eyes fixed on him. "Leave now or die."

Electricity buzzes around him. The fear and dread rise, the disembodied voices around him screaming, crying. The energies feel more chaotic, prickling at his skin and yelling at them to get out.

And they're right. Never mind exorcising demons, never mind the growling *thing* scurrying behind shelves at his back. They're not ready for this, and the cult will kill them and take his daughter.

Riley's hands press against his back. "Dad, you need to go."

"I'm not leaving you here."

"Then, die," Janice says.

The rest is nothing but a big blur of flickering lights, weapons flying, and demons screaming and splitting their heads open.

There are gunshots coming from his left. After the deafening demonic shrieks stop, Rudy opens his eyes in time to see four men charging him, their eyes pure black. Killing these people wasn't part of the plan, but it's kill or be killed. Despite the dizziness, he raises his gun and shoots.

Riley has dropped her flashlight, and her gun echoes next to him. Two men fall to the ground, the other two still running. Rudy fires again, hitting his target, but the body still slams into him. They both fall to the floor, and he gets a glimpse of Riley being violently pinned against the wall.

The shadow screams in his face, clouding his vision. Rudy presses the tip of the gun against the man's chin and shoots. Blood and brains spray out of his head, and the body falls motionless on top of him. Rudy pushes it aside, quickly scrambling away before the entity inside slithers out. Strong as it must be, it could bypass the amulet and try to possess him.

Pride fills him, momentarily taking over the dread, as he realizes that Riley has overpowered the man attacking her, flipping him onto his back and pressing a UV light stick against his neck. The man struggles and tries to claw at her face, screaming at the light burning him.

Rudy glances at the other side of the room. Stella shoots someone. James kicks a man, sending him crashing against a wall. Sharp objects fly their way, threatening to slice through them.

Janice still stands in the middle of the room, clearly enjoying the scene. The floor shakes under Rudy's feet, and an idea flashes through his mind.

Shoot her in the head. Now.

She won't let Riley leave, and the other entities answer to her.

Ectoplasm pours out of the man Riley's keeping down. She skips to her feet, searching for the others, and a heavy brick settles in the pit of Rudy's stomach when Janice's black eyes find her. Her face is dark, bitterness creasing her skin.

The sledgehammer flies through the room, smacking Riley in the stomach. She lets out a choked cry and stumbles back, hitting the wall and holding her mid-section. After that comes a knife. A huge, sharp, bloodied knife. Rudy throws himself on front of her and aims for Janice.

The shot echoes above the racket, and Janice cries out, falling to the floor as she holds her leg.

More demons are coming. The rumbling around him makes him dizzy, crushing his chest and weakening him. When he glances around the room, looking for James and Stella, red eyes look back at him in the far corner of the room. Two wide, round rubies flashing, fixed in the middle of a deformed, black head.

The *beast* disappears again, taking with it this purple, glowing orb.

Rudy grabs Riley by the arm and drags her out of the room. "Everyone, *out!*" he shouts to the others.

A little relieved to see them catch up to him, he lets himself breathe easier as they step out the door. But something won't let him. Something tight and deep. Dark spots edge his vision. A thick liquid coats his throat.

"Dad..."

Riley clasps his arm, her eyes wide and her mouth half-open as she stares at him.

Rudy sluggishly follows her gaze and looks down. The knife that was thrown at her is embedded deeply in the middle of his chest. As though his brain had waited to be notified with a visual reminder, pain blooms from his wound, the blade scraping against his organs as he tries to breathe. A cough escapes him, splattering his lips with blood.

Riley catches him before he hits the floor, hooking her arms around him. "Oh my God, no, no, Dad!" She twists to look behind herself, but Rudy's vision is decreasing already. *"Jamie!"*

Things happen behind him. A wild chaos of screams and gunshots fading into the background. He thinks he hears Stella cry out. James shouts *Fuck* before yelling at Riley to get out.

"I'll take care of Stella, get him out of here, *now!*"

Rudy would smile if he weren't coughing blood again.

Good call, boy.

Riley gets a flashlight from God knows where—she must have picked up hers—and her shaky beam paints the arched walls as she drags him through the bunker, her breath unsteady and ragged.

"Hold on, Dad... Please, please hold on."

Rudy fights to keep his eyes open, willing his weak legs to support him a little longer as he tightens his arm around Riley's shoulders. He has to do it, not for himself, but for her. *She* has to get out of here. This place isn't safe for her.

Climbing the stairs takes a lot more time than needed. The tunnels, seemingly never-ending, threaten to be his dying place. He doesn't want to stay here. He doesn't want to cross over and be stuck in a place full of lost souls. He doesn't want to become one of them.

"I don't wanna die here..."

"Dad, don't say that." She tries to keep her voice steady, but it's already thick with sobs. "You're gonna be okay."

"I want to be outside. Not here... Not with them..."

Finally, they reach the front door. She fumbles with it for a few seconds before unlocking it and bursting outside, her arm still tightly hooked around him. The knife in his chest moves a little more, carving inside of him and sending agonizing waves of pain. The afternoon light is hidden behind clouds and rain.

"I-I need to sit."

"No."

She keeps pulling him, unrelenting. The adrenaline must give her a lot of strength to carry most of his weight like this. They make it across the field, to the edge of the forest, when she finally lowers him to the ground, resting his back against a tree.

Her rapid, erratic breathing fills his ears as she looks at the knife planted in his sternum and the blood soaking his shirt.

"Oh..." Thick tears roll down her cheeks. Strands of dark hair have broken free from the ponytail and fly across her face. "Okay... You'll be okay. You'll be okay. I'm gonna–"

She doesn't finish her sentence and grabs her phone. The next minute is filled with her voice talking to a 911 operator.

"Riley." Rudy raises a hand that seems to weigh a ton and takes the phone away from her ear. "They won't be here on time."

Her eyes widen, and she shakes her head, pressing her lips together. "Of course they will be. They're coming, and they're gonna take care of you."

His mind sends him flashes, pictures of past times. Images of Grace. How he met her. The day they got married. He and Riley working on their house together. Christmas with their ugly sweaters. She and James laughing together.

He needs to be quick. He's fading away.

He brushes a strand of hair away from her face. "It's too late, pumpkin. I'm okay with this. I've had a good life."

Her eyes fill with fresh tears. She shuffles closer to him and places a gentle hand on his cheek. "No... I can't... I can't lose you, Dad, I can't lose you..." Her voice breaks, breaking his heart at the same time.

His breathing becomes more labored, rasping against the blood coating his throat. "You'll be okay. You have James. You two will be good for each other."

"I can't live without you," she sobs.

Rudy offers a smile, though it's a shaky one. "I won't be far, kiddo. I'll be with you whenever you pick up your guitar. I'll be there when you make honey cakes. I'll be riding with you whenever you drive my truck. And I'll be holding you when you wear my sweater." He pauses, taking in a ragged breath. "I saw your energy, Riley... I saw it down there. Your true colors. You're purple. Not a sad or an angry purple. But a beautiful mix of baby blue and pink. *You're* beautiful. You shine as bright as a shooting star."

The light fades. His own light.

"Adopting you is the best thing I've ever done, and I'm so proud of you. I love you."

Riley's shoulders shake, but she forces a breath into her lungs before she answers. "I love you too, Dad. I love you so much."

"Tell Jamie I love him too, please."

She answers with a shaky nod.

"And Stella as well."

"Okay…"

"But you'll always hold the first place in my heart. Come here."

Rudy pulls Riley against him. He wants to feel the weight of her head against his chest as he fades away. He wants to comfort her while she cries, like he has always done. It makes him happy that it's the last thing he gets to do.

His pride. His little girl.

He holds her here, running his fingers through her hair. "It's gonna be okay, pumpkin…"

Weightlessness and oblivion take him.

CHAPTER 31

Rudy's hand falls motionless behind Riley's head. The rise and fall of his chest cease. The slow beating of his heart stops.

Her cheek pressed against his chest, her fingers clasping his shirt, and her vision blurred by fat tears, Riley doesn't move. Doesn't breathe. Because it's not real as long as she doesn't look. It can't be. If she were still an empath, she would have felt his light go out. But she's *not* an empath. Not anymore. She can still pretend. Pretend her dad's asleep, just resting. Pretend she didn't just lose the most important person in her life. Pretend this is nothing but a fucking nightmare.

If she raises her head and looks at her dad's dead body, she will lose it. Truly become insane. It's safer to stay here, tucked against his still warm body. James and Stella didn't come out of the bunker yet. Maybe they're dead too. Maybe Riley should throw herself back inside and kill herself.

This is not happening.

This can't be happening.

Of course not. The ambulance will be here soon. They will take him and realize he's not gone yet. Everyone will be happy.

Her body achy and shaking, Riley slowly pushes away from Rudy, blinking tears away to look at his face. "Dad…"

No answer. The rain slaps against the trees and the wind blows strongly, snatching her murmur away.

"*Dad.*"

Nausea settles in her stomach. A blanket of despair wraps itself around her, heavy and suffocating.

A choked sob falls out of her mouth, followed by another, followed by a desperate moan, and soon, her own wailing fills her ears. A sound that comes from deep inside her guts, something inhumane that she never thought she could produce.

Riley slips an arm under his neck, bringing him closer. Her cheek pressed against his forehead, she rocks him back and forth, just like he did to her after saving her life when she was a kid, only *she* looks like a maniac. The screams and the sobs choking her make no room for air to flow through her lungs.

A humongous, deformed shape emerges from the bunker ahead, its footsteps slow and unsteady. They've killed Stella and James. They succeeded in destroying her. Because this is what Janice meant when she said that. She never intended to harm Riley physically. She wanted to take everything and everyone she ever loved.

And this master, this creature living in the depths of the building, has come to collect her.

The shape comes closer. It's blurred by rain and tears and has an odd body, something resembling a cross, with a mop of hair dangling to one side. A glimpse of red eyes shine in her direction.

Riley clings onto Rudy, holding him closer as if shielding him.

The monster comes into focus, piercing through the sheet of rain, lit by thunder. James limps toward her, carrying Stella, who seems unconscious, her head tilted back and her hair hanging down. The red eyes aren't eyes, but blood streaking James's face, pouring out of a gash running downward, over his forehead and cheek. He drops to his knees and places Stella on the ground as gently as he can.

"Jamie..." Riley sobs, her voice hoarse. "Please, do something..."

He shuffles to Rudy, sees the knife, and the range of emotions crossing his face are too numerous to analyze. "Oh... fuck, no, fuck..." His hands hover above the knife for a second, but then he draws them back, wiping the water and blood off his face.

"Do something, please," she begs, her voice breaking again. "You have to do something, *please, please.*"

His dark eyes, wild with grief and fear, find her, confirming this new reality, that her dad is dead, and there's nothing he can do about it. He looks down at Rudy again, lips trembling, and gently presses his fingers against his neck, searching for a pulse.

"Rudy... Rud, don't do this to us, man..."

His cracked voice is barely audible to her, but she keeps her eyes trained on his lips, hoping, *waiting* for him to tell her she was wrong, and her dad is alive.

Instead, a shiver shakes his body, and he presses the back of his trembling hand against his mouth, a tear rolling down his cheek and mixing with blood. The expression of pain spreading over his face is nothing like she's ever seen coming from him.

This nightmare isn't a nightmare after all.

The following hours are a blur of tears, people, bright lights. The paramedics have to pry Rudy out of her arms. James helps them holding her back. The only thing that eventually forces her to calm down is when they threaten to take her away and drug her.

Stella is taken away too. Riley doesn't know what's happening with her. She doesn't know what went on inside the bunker after she left with her dad and can't understand why the Faceless haven't followed them outside. It's not like James, hurt as he was, could have taken them all down. Them, and the monster with flashing eyes.

They're moving. No. They're *being* moved. Riding in the back of an ambulance. Her world is reduced to that sickening swaying that makes her feel like she's on a boat. That and James's arms around her. It's not a nice touch. It lacks the reassuring quality her dad was capable of. It's not comforting, the beating of his heart pounding directly against her temple like a stubborn headache. He's not holding her, he's *clinging* onto her, his hands too tight around her and his fingers digging into her skin in a desperate attempt to console her. All it does is make her want to push him away and scream at him to fucking let go of her.

But she can't. The tears keep spilling from her eyes despite her being quiet, and her body is limp, devoid of energy, like a rag doll.

The movements continue. Get out of the ambulance. Faces stare at her. James's arm too tight around her shoulders. Enter a cold hospital. Doctors. Police. Hundreds of questions.

If Stella was awake, she'd know what to do. But she's not. She's not dead, either. At least Riley doesn't think so.

Then, she's being seated on a chair. She's there for what feels like hours. A lifetime. Shivering in her damp clothes, her hands limp on her lap. She's alone this time, and she has no idea what she's waiting for. Someone told her, but words and sentences are distorted and muffled.

Her eyelids feel heavy. They keep closing despite her wanting to stay awake, coaxing her into sleeping.

When she opens them, James is kneeling in front of her. The gash has been cleaned and sutured. It will leave a scar. He takes her hands, his fingers just as cold as hers, and looks like he's trying to talk, but his lips tremble and he can't look at her.

"Is my dad okay?" she says before really thinking about it.

He raises his head, confusion painting his misty eyes. "Riley, your dad... You don't remember?"

"I... I know, but I mean... Didn't they... save him?" Her throat tightens and her teeth clench just at the absurdity of her own words. She doesn't make sense, just grasping at straws, in complete denial.

He shakes his head, his jaw working. "No... He's gone."

Riley stares at him, wanting to shout at him to stop lying, even if she knows he's not.

"They—" He clears his throat in an attempt to ward off new tears. "They put Stella in a coma. She was hit in the head pretty badly and has a brain injury."

But she's not dead.

The thought is almost cynical, as though it would have been better to have Stella die and her dad in a coma. Guilt crashes over Riley. Because it's true. She would have preferred her dad to live, even if it meant losing Stella. It's a shitty, horrible, selfish thing to feel, but it isn't something she has control over. It just is.

"We should get some rest," James says.

"I want to go home."

"My place is closer to the hospital. If they call about Stella, I think it's better to–"

"*I want to go home.*"

This is the loudest she's spoken since wailing over her dad's dead body. Faces in the waiting room briefly turn to her. She sees their movement at the edge of her vision but keeps her eyes on James, frowning and clenching her fists as she gives him the Death Stare.

He nods. "All right. Let's go home."

CHAPTER 32

James's hands are so tightly clamped onto the steering wheel his fingers cramp. He was able to get his car back, but Stella's car is still there, parked at the beginning of the trail they took on their way to the bunker. They never should have gone there.

For the past few hours, he's done his best to keep his emotions down, but his willpower will fail soon. Tears he'd like to hold back keep wetting his eyes, and his clenched teeth ache as he tries to control the squeezing of his throat.

Rudy's dead.

His business partner of eleven years. His friend. His substitute dad. A man he's looked up to since the moment he met him. The thought that he'll never get to stare into those mesmerizing and somewhat intimidating icy blue eyes fills him with a dismay that leaves him weak and shivering.

But he has to stay strong. For Riley. She's sitting in the passenger seat, her face turned to the window. Quiet and weakened by grief. He'll do anything for her. Anything to appease her pain. But the idea of being inside Rudy's house *without* Rudy makes him queasy. It'll be empty and cold.

When they were inside the bunker, he saw that Rudy was injured. He saw the way Riley was helping him walk. But James hadn't imagined he would find him dead a few minutes later. He was too busy keeping demons away from him, especially when Stella was knocked out cold, struck in the head by a hammer, and he had to run away from the place while carrying her.

Riley's hysterical, heart-wrenching wailing while she held her dad still echoes in his head and will haunt his nightmares.

"He loved you."

Snapped out of his thoughts, James glances at her. "What?"

She wets her lips and inhales. "He wanted me to tell you he loved you. He wanted to make sure you knew it." She turns away again, her face hidden by dark hair.

"Did he... Did he say something else?"

He missed it. He wasn't there during Rudy's final moments. He wasn't there to listen to what he had to say. He wasn't there to hold his hand. His stomach clenches, making him sick and nauseated.

"He, um... He said—" Riley sniffles, the words stuck inside her throat. She takes a shaky breath. "Sorry, I can't right now."

James makes no reply. She'll talk when she's ready to talk, but the guilt of not having been there to begin with claws into his chest. Rudy could have directly told him he loved him. And James would have said it back. He loves him more than his own father. Michael was a good dad, the only one of his family who actually cared about James, but he died long ago.

Twenty-five years ago.

Rudy welcomed him into his business, into his family. He made James feel wanted and needed.

A sudden exhaustion settles over him, shrouding him like a blanket. He doesn't want to sleep. The day after a tragedy is always the worst. It feels like a bad dream.

Riley straightens up in her seat and leans forward as James pulls onto the dirt path. "What's that over there?"

He squints through the windshield slapped by a rain reduced to a slow tapping for now. A light glows in the distance. The black clouds seem unnaturally low. They're moving fast too.

Those aren't clouds... It's smoke.

The car darts forward as he pushes his foot onto the accelerator. The glow brightens as they get closer. The house slowly comes into view, giving them the full display of a horrible scene, and James slams the brakes.

The house burns like a torch, its ferocious light bleeding onto the fields and the woods around it. High flames brush the edge of the sky. The windows have exploded, and fire bursts out of them like burning limbs.

Riley fumbles with her seat belt and throws herself out of the car. She takes a few wobbly steps toward her house, and James goes after her, afraid she'll do something stupid. She doesn't. She stares at the fire, an expression of frozen terror hanging onto her face, and falls to her knees.

Heat waves graze James's skin, burning the cut on his face. He stands there, his hands too numb to grab his phone and call 911. What are they going to do, really? It's too late. That shit has been burning for a while, and nothing inside will be salvageable.

"The truck," Riley says, scrambling to her feet. "I have to save his truck."

A sliver of panic shoots through his spine as Riley scrambles to her feet and darts toward the truck, too close to the burning house. "Riley, wait!"

She doesn't listen to him and throws herself at the driver's door, trying to open it. It resists under her fingers.

"Riley, you're too close to the fire, get the hell out!"

He grabs her arm, but she shakes him off and pushes his chest. "Don't touch me!"

The roaring fire is deafening, seemingly melting his clothes onto his back.

Riley pounds at the window, punching it several times, the sharp bump of her knuckles against the glass audible above the inferno. She gets tired of it quickly. Breathless, sweat coating her forehead, she looks around her in a panic. Her eyes dart to the garage door, but it's a no-go. It's in flames as well.

James makes to grab her hand again, eager to drag her away from the smothering smoke. "Riley, you need to leave it!"

"Just leave!" she yells at him, pulling away sharply. "I'll follow you, but I have to take my dad's truck. There's a spare inside, I know it!"

Her brown eyes reflect the orange light, making her look fierce, and James doesn't want to insist. He can't leave without her, though. He won't.

She rounds the truck, turns into a circle, searching the ground, then ducks down. She comes back with a large, heavy rock in her hands, and before James has the time to say anything, she throws it against the window, smashing it. She brushes the glass away quickly, unlocks the door, and jumps inside. Just like she thought, the spare key is inside the sun visor and drops inside her palm as she pulls it down.

"Go *now*," she says.

The truck roars to life, and Riley drives away. James glances at the house one last time, his heart breaking as all the memories he has here burn away.

 The green Ford truck pulls over ahead. It's hard to remember Riley's in there, and not Rudy. James parks behind her on the side of the road, that same road snaking through the woods, not that far from where her car crashed.

Riley kills the engine but doesn't get out. The back of the vehicle is only lit by the Mustang's headlights. Why she decided to stop here, in the middle of nowhere, he has no idea. It can't be good. His chest is tight, his lungs scorched from the smoke. James opens the door and walks on weak legs in the truck's direction.

Riley steps out too, the loose strands of hair flying in the wind. He wants to hold her, reassure her, *anything*, but the way she looks at him is hollow, and he doesn't dare move.

"They took the lockboxes in the basement," she says.

He frowns. "How do you know?"

"Why would they go to my house if not for this?"

"But how did they know—"

"They know *everything*. I thought Janice had only seen a few of my memories, but clearly, she knows *a lot*. Her human friends waited for us to leave so they could bypass the symbols and raid my house."

"This doesn't make any sense. Why didn't they just attack us while we were there if they knew your location?"

"Because they want to destroy me. They want to take everything from me to make me miserable, and—" She looks down, planting her hands on her hips, bracing herself for something already twisting James's stomach. "You need to get as far away from me as you possibly can. Leave. Now. Just drive and don't look back. Go somewhere I wouldn't know where to find you. If I know where to find you, they'll know too."

James does a double take, not believing what he's hearing, but Riley looks him in the eyes now. She's not kidding. She's got that set, stubborn expression of hers.

"I'm not leaving you, Riley."

"Don't you understand, Jamie? You're next. They took my empathy, my dad, Stella, and my house. Oh, and my fucking car too. Who do you think they'll come after now? They're probably pissed that you got away earlier."

She's right, but James shakes his head, clenching his jaw. "No. You and I are staying together."

She takes a sudden step forward. "I'm *not* giving you the choice, you idiot. I don't care about your pride and your tough guy act or your love for me. Just fucking go!"

"I don't care what happens to me," he says, his voice rising in frustration despite himself.

"*I* do. *I* care. So, just—" Riley closes the remaining distance between them and shoves him hard enough to actually make him move.

"Stop it. We can still do something. We can take them down."

But she doesn't stop, her eyes full of tears as she pounds his chest and shoves him toward his car. "It's *over.* They fucking won, and we can't stop them, and they're going to kill you so just *go the fuck away!*"

She finally steps away, panting and brushing hair from her face. She glances at him for a moment, walking backward. "Just leave." Riley turns away and hops in the truck.

It disappears into the night, leaving James alone in the dark. The rapidly cooling wind snatches at his clothes and his weak body. Riley left him. She left. Gone. Rudy's dead. Everything is fucked. A dead weight settles in the middle of his chest. Driving will be hard. *So* hard. He wishes he could go to sleep forever.

James drags his feet to his car, limbs trembling.

The drive to his place is painfully slow, and a few times he thinks he's about to go off road. The exhaustion is spreading like poison, now paired with soul-crushing loneliness.

Once inside his living room, he sheds the damp jacket and drops it on the floor. He heads to the kitchen and grabs a whiskey bottle from one of the cabinets. Bottle and glass in hand, he sinks into his couch, pours himself a drink, and gulps it down. Whiskey fills the glass again. Then, again. No amount of alcohol will take the pain away, but let's hope for some numbing.

He brings the glass to his lips again and suspends his movement. The ticking of the clock is deafening, pounding in his brain. Behind it, complete silence, a poor analogy for his loneliness.

Rudy's dead.

Riley's gone.

Something fractures in him, and James breaks down into sobs.

Riley stares at the condo from the truck, the rain soaking her arm and jeans as it seeps through the broken window. The house is lit. Kelly's home. The clock on the dashboard says it's barely five. Is it really that early? Riley can't remember what time they got inside the bunker, or what time they got out. It was some time around noon, but the sky was so dark that it felt like night already.

She wipes her tears again. How can she still be crying? No human can hold that much moisture in their body. Her mouth feels dry, her eyes should be dry too. Riley looks at her face in the rearview mirror. Her skin is pale and pasty, and her puffy eyes are dark-rimmed.

A flash of red catches her attention. Someone sits behind her. Her dad.

Riley swivels around, heart hammering her chest. She swallows, staring at the empty seat. The red thing is still here, though.

"Oh…"

A new wave of sobs escape her at the sight of Rudy's plaid jacket draped around the seat. She unhooks it, and presses it to her chest, burying her nose in it. It smells like him and will soon be soaked with tears.

Everything he owned has been destroyed. The floors he walked on. His books. His guitar. His clothes. The letters she wrote him when she was a kid. The picture albums.

But his favorite jacket is here, in the truck he could never part with, and Riley will cherish it forever. Leaning to the side, she opens the glove compartment in the hopes of finding something else, but despite a few old CDs, there's nothing more personal.

His wallet.

She has it. They gave it to her at some point in the hospital, and she placed it in her pocket without really thinking about it. Riley takes it out and opens it hastily. In one of the see-through flaps, three small pictures are tucked.

The first one makes her chuckle. It's a portrait of her taken during picture day at school when she was eleven. It was the year Rudy became her legal guardian. She looks like a dork on it, but he kept it in his wallet all this time. The picture underneath shows a young couple posing in front of Winter's Attic. Him with baby blue eyes and brown hair, her with a long, blonde braid going down her waist and holding a key up in a *we just bought a bookstore* gesture. The corners of this picture are yellow and crinkling.

"I hope you're with Grace, Dad. I hope you're happy."

The third picture gives her the final blow. The quality is not even that good. It's slightly off and tilted. But the smiles on it seem to jump out of the image.

Her dad's last birthday, when James and Riley gave him the brand new smartphone he didn't really want. Rudy decided he wanted to have barbecue despite it being February. The yard was buried under three feet of snow, which didn't seem to bother him as he grabbed a shovel and dug a trench from the front door to the back of the house so they could access the barbecue. Stella took that picture. James and Riley are on either side of Rudy, and he has his arms wrapped around them, as though wanting to ward off the cold and protect them. That day, he was wearing that red plaid jacket Riley's now clutching, and she had Grace's navy blue, knit hat on her head.

She has hundreds of pictures in her phone, but none of them feels as special as these three. To think he actually went out of his way to print this picture. It was a happy, cold day filled with laughter, snow crunching under boots, and delicious smells of burger patties taunting them.

My house is gone now.

Shoving the pictures back inside Rudy's wallet, Riley exits the truck, holding the jacket tightly against her, and walks the driveway to the front door on numb legs. The doorknob resists under her hand, so she reluctantly knocks and waits, shivering like a leaf in the wind.

The door opens a moment later, and Kelly stands on the other side. Her blonde curls spill over her shoulders, and she wears that cute, oversized pink shirt with the Care Bear she likes to use as a nightgown.

"Hey, what are you—" She frowns, searching Riley's face, and takes a step forward. "Riley, are you okay?"

Despite how hard she tries to keep a straight face, Riley is forced to realize her cheeks are drenched again. Before she thinks it through, the words she dreads to say seep out of her mouth. "My... My dad is dead."

Kelly opens her eyes wide and gasps, clasping both her hands over her mouth. "Oh my God."

"My house burned down... I-I don't know what to do now."

Kelly utters another *Oh my God* loaded with sobs and wraps her arms around Riley's neck, holding her in a fierce hug. Riley sinks into it, her legs on the brink of collapse. Kelly seems to feel her friend wobble and pulls her inside, shutting the door behind them. She makes Riley sit on the couch and kneels in front of her, rubbing her arms and brushing her hair back.

"What happened?"

Her body is exhausted, the tears burn her eyes, and the past few hours make her want to scream and puke, but she manages a few words, telling Kelly that her dad was killed, *murdered,* and the word feels dense and barbed as it rolls off her tongue, leaving a bitter taste in her mouth. It's actually surprising that Kelly can understand anything in this massive mess of word vomit.

After another long, needed hug, Kelly rushes into the kitchen, sniffling and shaking, and comes back a minute later. She places a blue pill inside Riley's palm. "Take a Xanax."

"I don't want a Xanax—"

"Just take the damn pill."

She nearly forces it into her mouth, and because Riley has no energy left, she swallows the thing with the water that is given to her. After this, Kelly pushes a cup of tea between her hands. There's more incoherent babbling and sobbing, but she tries to drink the tea, grateful for some warmth.

Once she thinks she's calm enough, she fights the crushing fatigue to talk. "Kelly, you need to leave. We need to leave."

"What are you talking about?"

"I can't... I can't let them come for you too."

"Riley, you're scaring me."

"You *should* be scared. They will do whatever they need to get to me."

Unless I do what they want.

The thought brings a temporary comfort, as if it would solve everything, but it wouldn't. It would make it a lot worse. Maybe not for her friends, but for so many other people who would be killed because of her.

"Maybe I should kill myself."

"What?"

Riley startles, realizing she spoke out loud. Her mind is clouded, the room spins, and she'd like to sleep even if the clock claims it's not time yet.

"Let's get you to bed," Kelly says, as though reading her mind. "You're not thinking clearly, you need some rest." She pulls Riley off the couch and leads her to her room. "I'll call the guys, okay? We're gonna take care of you."

Riley reluctantly lets herself be put to bed. She's still clutching her dad's jacket, has been all this time, and curls up to the side, letting Kelly's warm body behind her and the gentle strokes in her hair lull her to sleep.

CHAPTER 33

Time has stopped. That's what it feels like to Rudy. The world has disappeared, buried under three feet of glinting snow, and the woods look like they're holding their breath. The three pairs of footsteps pounding the floors of his home make him smile as he tears his eyes away from the window and resumes preparing the burger patties. This barbecue will be epic.

Every snowstorm, James and Riley like to huddle here with him before they're snowed in. Now the fresh white powder has coated everything. Their cars won't be able to move for the rest of the day. But the clouds are gone, leaving place to a fantastic, crisp blue sky. Rudy couldn't have asked for a better birthday. He has the people who matter near him, as well as everything he needs to make a barbecue. He made a big coffee pot, something big enough to keep them warm outside.

"You're not going through with this *insane* idea of having barbecue outside, are you?"

James's voice makes him turn, and Rudy raises an eyebrow at him. "Watch me."

"You can't even reach the thing, and even if you did, there's no way you'll be able to light it up."

"You're scared of a little cold, Jamie-bear? You're from Vermont, for Christ's sake." Riley slips inside the kitchen, her hair everywhere and wearing her night clothes, wrapped in what she calls her comfort sweater. She giggles and elbows James as she passes him. "We'll get you a hot water bottle and a blanket."

"My house, my birthday, my rules," Rudy says.

"Happy birthday, Dad." His daughter stands on her toes to hug him and kiss his cheek, and Rudy already knows this will be his favorite part of the day. She looks at him with a bright smile, silver eyes sparkling. "Fifty-five and super handsome."

"I agree," Stella says from the hallway before she emerges.

Rudy gets another warm hug and kiss, from her this time.

Riley turns away. "Eww, I'm standing right here!"

He gives James a slap on the shoulder as he walks past him on his way to the foyer. Time to shovel some snow.

A playful smile plays at the corners of James's mouth. "Do you also want me to kiss you, or…"

Rudy puts his boots and jacket on, chuckling. "I'll take a rain check on that."

James answers with another chuckle. "Happy birthday, man. Do you need help?"

"I'm okay, boy." A faint smell stops him for a second. Did he leave something on the stove? An insidious, burning scent floats about the space. "Do you smell that?"

But James has gone inside the kitchen with the others and doesn't hear him. They're talking cheerfully in there. If something was burning, they would notice. Shrugging it off, Rudy gets out into the crisp air, shovel in hand, squinting at the glorious morning sun. Let the digging begin.

It takes him a while to dig the trench from the front door to the back of the house, plowing through three feet of snow, and it takes him some more time to actually figure out where the barbecue is hidden. He finds it after stabbing the snow a few times with the shovel and works on making a clearing large enough for the four of them to stand. He'll get the camping chairs out. It will be fun. The snow he has to shovel out amounts to something so high it almost looks like an unfinished igloo, but the final result is quite satisfying.

Rudy plants the shovel in the ground, exhaling in relief, his back aching but his heart full. He unzips his jacket, letting the icy air flow inside, and wipes sweat off his forehead. Sure, he's been exercising, but he shouldn't be so hot.

Orange light, as bright as fire, catches his eyes. He swivels to the house, and his breath catches in his throat. The sky is nearly black, and his home burns like a torch.

In one blink of an eye, the dark blue house is back, standing tall and sturdy under a clear sky.

Rudy releases a shaky breath, not sure about what he just saw. Exertion has messed with his head, and he'll feel better once he gets this thing going.

By the time he's back inside, everyone is dressed and bundled up into warm clothes, ready to follow him and grill some meat. James gets the folding table from the basement. Stella gets the camping chairs. Riley brings up the charcoal and lighter. Rudy brings the food out.

He was right. This is epic. Even James admits it. The snow-caked woods surround them, and the nature is quiet, except for their chatting and laughter. They'll be stuck in here for the rest of the day, but they don't mind. They're together, eating burgers in the winter sun. This calls for a picture. Not one of these shitty-ass pictures Riley takes from her smartphone. A *real* picture taken from an actual camera. One he'll get developed later.

Stella offers to take one of them three. With both his kids at his sides—because yeah, they're both his kids—Rudy feels happy, complete, serene. The three of them flash their most brilliant smile, and Rudy knows this picture will be the one he'll want to carry around.

"Let me see," he tells Stella.

She gives him the camera, and he looks at the small screen.

His smile vanishes. He squints and brings the camera close to his face.

Behind James, Riley, and him, the house glows orange. He looks up, wondering what could have caused such a weird glitch. They were facing the sun, so the angle is wrong. Rudy studies the picture a little longer. On it, it almost looks like his home is on fire.

"That's because it is, love."

Rudy whirls around, the sound of Grace's voice startling him. She stands in the snow, wearing her favorite summer dress. The white one with the sunflowers.

He shakes his head. "You're wrong."

"I know it's hard to accept. You'll get there."

Staring too long at the snow glowing in the morning sun makes bright spots cloud his vision. Rudy smiles, working on the burger patties. This will be a great birthday and knowing that James and Riley are snowed in with him and Stella makes his heart swell.

James doesn't think Rudy's serious about the barbecue. Of course he is. It'll be epic.

Riley hugs him and kisses his cheek when she comes into the kitchen. "Happy birthday, Dad. Fifty-five and super handsome."

The cold bites his face as he gets out, shovel in hand, and digs a trench starting from the porch and going all the way to the back of the house. It takes a while, but he does a good job at clearing an area big enough around the barbecue for them four.

Everyone helps, bringing up a table, chairs, and charcoal from the basement. Rudy carries out the tray holding the patties and throws some charcoal in the barbecue while James and Riley drink coffee, laughing and teasing each other. Something's up with these two. Rudy wonders when they'll finally stop tip-toing around the subject and just admit it. Grace was right. She knew something was up long before they did.

Rudy turns on the gas lighter and freezes. He hasn't lit up the charcoal yet, but it already smells like it's burning. The scent of charred wood overpowers him, scratching at something in the back of his mind. Some sort of wall that's there, hiding something cold and terrifying and ominous he doesn't want to see. He turns to look at his house, convinced he'll see it completely destroyed, burnt to the ground.

The dark blue house stands tall and sturdy under a bright sky.

Rudy fires up the barbecue and grills the patties. Stella gives him a cup of coffee, and he hooks an arm around her as he listens to James and Riley arguing like two kids about God knows what.

"Dad, tell me I'm right. I'm right, right?"

"You said 'right' three times," James says. "I can't believe Daniel thought you should be a writer."

Riley shoves him. "Shut up, Williams."

When she turns back to Rudy, his stomach drops. He lets go of Stella and takes an uncertain step toward his daughter.

"Why are your eyes brown?"

But then she changes. She's not longer bundled up in a warm coat, Grace's navy blue beanie on her head, and her dark hair shining in the sun. She's kneeling next to him, her ponytail messed up, her eyes red, and tears flooding her cheeks.

"I can't live without you…"

Barbecue time. Yes, in the middle of winter, after a storm has buried them under three feet of snow. It'll be a great birthday, surrounded by the people who matter to him.

Riley kisses his cheek.

Stella kisses his mouth.

James jokes, asking if he should kiss him too.

After clearing a path for them and firing up the barbecue, the four of them chat and laugh, bathing in the glorious sun reflected by the pure white snow. Fresh fallen snow always has that magical effect on him. Later, it'll turn to ice or melt and become murky. But this, right now, is perfect. It warrants a picture. A *real* picture. Not one of these shitty-ass pictures Riley takes with her smartphone.

"My smartphone actually takes pretty good pictures, you know," she says.

Rudy shakes his head. "My birthday, my rules. I'll get my camera."

He rounds the house using the freshly made path and stomps the snow off his boots on the porch's steps.

"Riley, you're too close to the fire, get the hell out!"

"Don't touch me!"

James and Riley's voices, desperate and full of fear, make him swivel around. He sees her shove James and punch his truck's window repeatedly, each blow scraping her knuckles raw. The sky is dark, and the smell of scorched wood burns Rudy's nose. Bright flames invade the edge of his vision, a searing heat seeping through his clothes.

He turns back to his home, walking through the hallway to get his camera. The wall at the back of his mind is crumbling. The house flickers, one second normal, one second burnt to the ground.

Rudy goes back out, grateful to feel the crisp air bite his skin. Stella takes their picture. Several, actually, but the first one she took of him with James and Riley is the one he'll want to carry in his wallet. He'll develop the others and put them in the photo albums.

A weight settles in the middle of his chest. He ignores it, knowing it's just anxiety trying to get the best of him. Not today. Not on such a perfect day with his family. But the weight doesn't go away. It pierces through him, seemingly carving into his heart and lungs. Rudy looks down.

The long knife is planted so deep he can't see the blade anymore. It's not a stupid pocketknife in the shoulder this time. It's a butcher knife, slicing through him like a pig and coating his chest with sticky blood.

A gentle hand rests on his arm. "I'm so sorry, love."

Grace is wearing one of her favorite summer dresses. The white one with the sunflowers. He peers at her and her venetian blonde hair flowing in a nonexistent wind. She has never looked more beautiful. Rudy should be surprised to see her, but he's not.

"Aren't you cold?" he says.

She smiles that soft smile of hers. "No. Neither are you. You just *think* you are. Your mind is conjuring all your senses to recreate this memory and make you feel like it's real."

Rudy lets his eyes sweep over the snow-caked woods, his home, his girlfriend, his kids. "This was my last birthday, then."

"It seems like it was a good one. A happy one." She glances at James and Riley, who keep chatting and joking just like they did on that day. "I was right."

"Yeah. They're together now. He'll take care of her now that I'm gone."

Grace's face glows. "I doubt Riley needs to be taken care of. That's what she thinks now, but she'll realize soon enough that you made sure she'd be able to take care of herself. And she will."

"Have you been stuck here all this time?"

"I'm not stuck. I was waiting for you. Time doesn't mean anything to me anymore."

He takes her hand. Her fingers are warm and soft around his, just like they always were. "I've never felt you."

"I've never shown myself. I fade in and out. And I'd rather do what you're doing now, live a past life with you, pretending to cook and laugh and go to work, than haunt you. Sometimes, I invent things that didn't happen. A life where I didn't die, and you and I adopted Riley together."

He smiles, blown away by her beauty. "I would have loved a life like this." Rudy desperately tries to hang onto the illusion of the biting cold, the blue sky, and the sparkling snow surrounding him, but already, the air feels warmer. "Did my house burn down?"

She cocks her head, sadness filling her eyes, and nods. "You were there when they came."

Thunder splits the sky open. The gale blows through the trees, making them sway. Any trace of snow is gone. Black smoke chokes the air. His home is nothing but a charred mess. He does remember now. He was standing in the kitchen making beef patties and hugging his daughter and girlfriend while the Faceless beat his door down and let themselves in. His mind rewinds to that moment. Those were the non-possessed people, easily crossing the warding of the house meant to keep demons out. They knew exactly where they were going, crossing the hallway and opening the door to the left, the one leading to the basement. Down the stairs, they headed to the back wall on the right side, toward the shelves holding the lockboxes, and took them.

They could have stopped there. But taking with them all these entities was apparently not enough, and they coated every surface of Rudy's home with gasoline.

And he didn't pay attention to it because he was busy having barbecue.

"I hope you don't stay tethered here, Rudy, but I sense you're not ready to go yet."

No, he's not ready to go. Because as he stares at the smoking foundations of the house, an enormous beast lurks, its round, red eyes flashing in the dark. Its heavy footsteps—its *paws*—send ashes dancing in the air each time they stomp the ground. It's not really here. It's a memory of what Rudy saw deep in the bunker. He didn't have time to understand what it was then, but now he knows. It was the reason they were so affected by the imprints there. It's something James and Riley have never encountered before.

Rudy and Grace have. It was different. Smaller. Probably less harmful, not powered up by a heavily haunted place and evil people possessed by shadows.

But he knows how to get rid of it.

"I know what you're thinking, love. You might not have as much impact on the living world as you would like."

"Maybe. But I also know I'll never be at peace if I don't help them. Warn them."

Grace gazes at him with her doe-like eyes.

Rudy tightens his fingers on her hand, angry and more determined than ever. "I might be dead, but I won't fade until I watch over my kids one last time."

"I'll wait for you, then."

"Or you could help me. We could do this one last thing together."

His words have lit a spark in her eyes. "What do you want to do?"

"First, I need to find Riley and James. I need to go to them. How do I do that?"

"Just think really hard about them. Focus on one."

Rudy gives one last glance to his house, the lovely home he fixed and took care of with Riley, before closing his eyes. All his thoughts turn to her. The overwhelming need to see and help her takes over him, filling him with urgency.

When he opens his eyes, the room around him confuses him. It's not what he expected. The angle is wrong. The door isn't facing the bed, but is on the right side of it, facing the window. This isn't James's bedroom. It's Riley and Kelly's place, and Rudy didn't think she would be here. But she is, sleeping in her bed, curled up and looking fragile as she holds his jacket.

Rudy kneels next to her, brushing a strand of hair away from her face and shaking her gently. "Riley, wake up."

She doesn't shift.

"You think you're touching her, but you're not. Not really," Grace says behind him.

Rudy glances at her, and when he looks back at his daughter, the strand of hair he brushed away is still there, falling across her face, untouched.

"How do I manifest? I've seen tons of spirits impacting the living world and do insane shit. Why can't I do that? Do I need to focus or learn or something?"

"Neither, love. We mostly have an impact when we're upset or feel any type of strong emotions."

Chatter rises from the living room. Kelly isn't alone. Maybe James is here as well. Rudy kisses Riley's forehead and heads to the hallway leading to the front of the house. Liam and Miguel are here. They seem to be waking up, the both of them sprawled on the couch. Rudy looks at the clock in the kitchen wall to the left. It's almost four in the morning.

James is nowhere to be seen, and that doesn't sit well with Rudy. Why? Did something happen to him too? It has to be it, or he and Riley wouldn't have split up. This makes no sense.

"It was Daniel," Kelly says, her voice small, gesturing at her phone as though it's enough for them to understand what that was about.

Liam rubs sleep out of his eyes with his fingers. "Man, for a moment I thought this was just a horrible nightmare."

Kelly crosses her arms against her chest as if cold, the tip of her nose and her eyes red from crying. "I can't wrap my head around this."

Rudy feels touched by this, not because they're talking about him, but because they all came to be close to Riley and support her. They're good kids. But they won't be much help right now. Although they know about W&W Paranormal Investigation, seeing actual paranormal activity would freak them out more than anything. He needs someone who's experienced. Someone who will understand.

All of his focus falls on James.

You better be okay, boy. Please, be okay.

The next thing he knows, Rudy stands in James's living room. It's dark, and the smell of whiskey strikes him. The bottle, almost empty, lies onto its side on the coffee table, alcohol dripping onto the floor. Although passed out on the couch, James still loosely holds the glass in his hand.

A sigh of relief seeps out of Rudy. He sees the scar on James's face, making him realize, *remember,* he has no idea what went on inside the bunker after he was stabbed and Riley got him out. He doesn't even know if Stella's okay. He can worry about it later, and he will, but right now, he needs to wake James up.

He bends over the couch. "James, wake up."

"I know it's hard to understand, but you need to feel strongly, love," Grace says, standing in the middle of the room. "If you do, you may touch things, and he may possibly hear you as well."

Dismay fills Rudy. He *needs* to do this. He has to be able to help them. If he doesn't, he won't be able to move on.

His mind wanders through memories. How the cult attacked his daughter, almost throwing her off a cliff. How Madelyn told him Riley deserved better than Rudy. How they burned down his house. Despite himself, flashes of the good times, the *best* times, jump at him. His birthday. Christmas with their ugly sweaters. The day they chose the name of their business. How he taught Riley how to swim, and they sat together facing the lake.

This gives him the push he needs. He reaches for the bottle and gives it a soft push. It rolls off the table and crashes onto the floor.

"Wake up, Jamie."

CHAPTER 34

The shattering noise of the bottle snaps James awake. He sits up, looking down at the floor, heart beating fast. He must have dreamed. It can't be. But the words echo in his mind, loud and clear, as though just spoken close to his ear.

Wake up, Jamie.

James could swear the voice belonged to Rudy. The familiarity of it was unmistakable. He stares at the broken bottle. He must have kicked it. Right?

And yet, a chill crawls down his back, and a cloud of condensation escapes his mouth as he exhales. The cold air seems to have thickened around him, filled with something he can't see.

Realizing the glass is still in his hand, James puts it down onto the coffee table. There are two possible scenarios. One, his ass is dead drunk. Two, Rudy's in the room with him. The possibility of the latter fills him with mixed emotions. Some sort of happiness and reassurance, but at the same time, Rudy doesn't deserve to stay tethered to this world.

Slowly rising, his mind swirling, and his brain still soaked with booze, James clears his throat. "R-Rudy? Are you here?"

The whiskey glass slides off the table and crashes onto the floor.

"Holy crap..." A new cloud of mist plumes out his mouth as he speaks. "Rud, I'm so sorry... I should have done better, I should have been there for you... Are you stuck? Why are you still here?"

Dizzying silence follows, ringing in James's ears.

An idea rises at the back of his mind. "Hang on a sec."

He turns on the lamp next to the couch and stumbles into the small hallway, where he opens the closet door. There's a lot of crap in there, but thankfully, what he's looking for is something he used very recently and lies on the top shelf. The Ouija board. The one he used at Mrs. McCarthy's house. Not all spirits interact with them. But Rudy just might. The fact that he's not stuck in his house or in the bunker where he was stabbed is already a good sign. He's self-aware and reaching out.

James grabs the box and brings it back to the living room. He settles on the floor, ignoring the whiskey and the shattered glass under the coffee table. Crossing his legs, he unfolds the board and places the planchette on top of it, blood pulsing in his ears.

He places his fingertips above the planchette, barely grazing it, and takes a deep breath to clear his mind. "Rudy, are you here?"

Despite having been a paranormal investigator for nearly twenty years, the feeling of the planchette moving under his fingers still startles him slightly as it slides over the **YES**.

A small laughter falls out of his mouth, followed by the tightening of his throat. "I'm so sorry I couldn't protect you or save you, man..."

The planchette slides over the board again, briefly stopping over some of the letters to form a sentence.

NOT YOUR FAULT.

James inhales, blinking tears out of his eyes. He imagines Rudy sitting across from him, cross-legged just like him.

"Are you stuck? Do you need help moving on?"

NO.

"Then, what—"

James doesn't have time to finish when the planchette moves again. It goes extra slowly, as though Rudy wants to make sure James can follow closely and make a mental note of each letter it stops on.

E

G

R

E

G

O

R

E

"*Egregore?* What does that mean?"

IN BUNKER.

"You mean the creature we saw down there?"

YES.

James stares down at the board and the planchette hovering over the word *yes*. His drunken mind scrambles to conjure memories from the torture room. It's not that he doesn't remember, it's just that Rudy's death has taken the lead in his thoughts and feelings, annihilating the rest. There was something down there. Something he didn't have time to see or understand. It wasn't a demon nor a spirit.

But Rudy seems to know.

The planchette moves again. **GET BOOKS WINTERS ATTIC.**

James chuckles. "Why would I go there to read books when I have the internet right here?" He scrambles to his feet and grabs the laptop resting on the countertop inside the kitchen. He sits back on the floor, his back against the TV stand. "All right, let's see what this Egregore thing is."

A shiver spreads through his right side, and the screen of his computer glitches for a second. Rudy's next to him, watching over his shoulder.

What James reads rings a little bell somewhere deep. "Wait, I remember you told me about this. You encountered one when you worked on a case with Grace, right?"

On the Ouija board next to him, the planchette slides to **YES**. Turns out he doesn't need to put his fingers on it for it to work. If people knew this, a lot of fake spiritism séances wouldn't be able to happen. Like the one he had with Mrs. McCarthy. What a dumb idiot he is.

"Right, that's how you know."

These aren't spirits or demons. They're made up by an idea. A non-physical entity that arises from the minds and emotions of people. Most likely a large group of people, like, say, countless people being murdered in the bunker. Their feelings leave an imprint, and these feelings will later be the reflection of the Egregore. Its attributes. Which means that it can pretty much look like anything, its appearance only limited by human imagination, and be either good or bad or neutral or all these things. The one lurking in the bunker looks like whatever Janice Kraft made it up to be, and its nature most likely reflects hers. But it was scared, hiding, still impacted by the fear permeating the place and making *them* scared as well.

James keeps reading, something in his mind not quite clicking just yet. "But *why?* I mean, I get how it was born, but what does that have to do with Janice Kraft, the cult, and..." He raises his head, looking at nothing but empty space. "What the fuck does it have to do with Riley? I get it, usually, sort of... but now—"

The lamp light flickers and dies, plunging James in darkness. No moonlight pierces through the shroud of clouds and rain battering the windows.

"Rudy?"

The scraping of the planchette on the board makes him look down. He tilts the computer to shine some light on it, and what he sees sends blood rushing through his numb body.

GET OUT.

James leaves the laptop on the floor and shuffles to the front door, staying low. He leans just enough to peek through the window above the couch, squinting through the sheets of rain.

People are outside. And they're walking toward his apartment.

"*Shit.*"

Riley was right. Of course she was right. If he couldn't stay with her, he should have gone somewhere else, even a crappy motel, instead of coming back here. The idea was to get some stuff, but then he stumbled upon a whiskey bottle and drank himself to sleep as a pitiful attempt to numb his pain.

Heart in throat, he looks for his gun. It's not on the countertop. He crouches in front of the couch, feeling cushions with his hands, searching for cold metal.

Glass shatters, and heavy footsteps hit the carpet in his bedroom. Someone has broken in already.

A loud bang on the door makes the walls shake. Then, another, louder.

"Fuck..."

When his hands touch nothing but the couch, James pats the floor next to it and under the coffee table, cutting himself on the broken shards. Finally, the reassuring coldness of the gun connects with his whiskey-coated palm.

He grabs it and skips to his feet, whirling around just as three men emerge from the hallway and the front door opens with a blast, letting in three others. They stop as he raises his gun, their eyes glinting in the white light of the computer on the floor. Rudy turned off the light to help him hide, but James wasn't fast enough.

He's fucked. It's clear as day that he's fucked. They know it too, or they wouldn't give him such a sticky, drooling smile. But he's got Rudy by his side, and maybe he'll be able to help.

James steadies his hand. His muscles ache, his head is still foggy, and a drop of sweat rolls down his temple. "What are you waiting for, assholes? Come at me and see if you like it."

Riley wakes up with a start, sitting up straight in her bed, as if pulled out of sleep by an invisible force. She stares at the empty room, panting. The coldness lingers for a moment, and a chill filled with urgency courses through her body, making all her hairs stand on end. She touches her bare arm. It felt like someone grabbed her, and the skin is still slightly cold there.

All of it subsides, except for the erratic beating of her heart. She throws the covers aside. Having no idea what she's doing, she puts her shoes on and grabs her jacket on the desk next to the window, putting on the hearing aids and taking her gun. She safely tucks it inside her breast pocket before she heads out but stops cold at the sight of her friends in the living room. It's the dead of night, but they're all awake too.

Liam sees her first and rises. "Riley, you're awake."

Miguel follows.

"Guys... what are you doing here?" It feels like it should be obvious, but her confused mind is filled with an urgency she can't understand.

"I called them," Kelly says from the couch.

Liam wraps his arms around her, and Riley remembers what happened, how she got here, and the reason for their presence. Her body turns numb in a second, and she lets herself be hugged and passed to Miguel's embrace.

"What time is it?" she says after they let her go. It's a stupid question, but for some reason, it seems important, like she has somewhere to be but she's already late. "How much did I sleep?"

"It's four fifty in the morning," Miguel says. "Come and sit with us."

"I don't—I can't."

"Why not?"

She opens her mouth, but the answer stays stuck in her throat. A coldness sticks to her back, as though a hand is pushing her and nudging her toward the exit. A crippling anxiety—no, *dread*—clings to her chest.

Kelly gets up, suddenly. "Ah, finally." She heads to the front door, ready to open it.

The memory that the cult came to her dad's house and burned it down sends a wave of panic through Riley. "Don't open the door!"

They're here for her. They came. And they will kill everyone.

"It's okay, Riley, it's just—"

"Wait!"

She takes a few steps forward, ready to shut that door to whoever's on the other side but stops dead in her tracks at the sight of the man stepping through the threshold.

His golden brown hair and clothes are soaked. He brushes wet strands away from his forehead before his dark blue eyes find her. He looks sad, devastated even, as he steps in her direction, but Riley steps back, a hand ahead of her as a way to stop him.

"What the *fuck* are you doing here?" she says.

Daniel freezes, confused by her reaction. "Riley, I—"

"No, no, no. You don't get to be here! Why—" She turns to Kelly. "Why did you call him?"

"Well, I thought..."

"She called me to tell me about your dad," Daniel says. "I'm so sorry, my darling. I jumped on a plane as soon as I hung up the phone."

Riley swallows the dread choking her, feeling as though she's about to have a mental breakdown, which shouldn't be possible since she pretty much had one earlier. "How the fuck did you get here so fast?"

"I got lucky with my flight—"

"You shouldn't have come here. *This* is the exact reason I broke up with you in the first place, so you wouldn't be in danger. So you would be safe in England. And now here you are! You decided to come back right in the middle of this clusterfuck!"

Her friends glance at each other.

Daniel inhales and focuses back on her. "I–"

"Did Kell tell you how my dad died?" She can't even remember if she even *told* Kelly what happened. "He was *murdered* by a cult of people set on destroying me, and as if I didn't have enough to worry about, *you* decide to show up! What the hell, man?"

He and the others look stunned for a moment. He opens his mouth a fraction, but she cuts him off again.

"You need to leave."

"What?"

"In fact, you *all* need to go and be where I'm not. As simple as that. All of you, just go, drive away together, and make sure you're going to a place I have no idea about or they will find you and they'll hurt you and–"

"What happened to your eyes?" Daniel closes the remaining distance between them, his gaze boring deep into hers. Realization fleets across his face. "You didn't know I was here. You didn't feel me coming."

She exhales, this short outburst of anger already seeping out of her and leaving her shivering. "No, Sunny Boy. I can't feel you."

He wraps his arms around her, pulling her into a tight hug. She lets him do it, realizing how much she misses that bright energy of his, realizing how 'normal' he seems at the moment. How normal they both are. James might have been right. Their friendship now established, they'll always be fond of each other and have that strong bond. But would they have formed such a deep connection if she hadn't been an empath and couldn't have felt the brightness of his soul?

"I'm so sorry about your dad, my darling... I'm so, so sorry."

A new wave of tears ready to be set loose, Riley hides her face the best she can, pressing it against his wet shirt.

"Riley." He pulls away enough to look at her with misty eyes. "What the hell is happening? Why is James not here?"

Riley rubs her face, wiping tears away and gathering her thoughts. "James, uh... Yeah, I told him to go. He's gone."

"No, he's not."

"What do you mean?"

"He's home. My cab drove by his place on the way from the airport. His car is parked in the driveway, and his light was on."

Her jaw drops at the same time as her stomach. "No... He wouldn't..." She's already fumbling frantically to get her phone out of her jacket pocket, knowing the dread she's feeling is linked to James. She calls him and presses the phone to her ear with a trembling hand.

It rings. Once. Twice.

"Come on, Jamie, come on..."

Three, four times.

Click. *"This is James Williams, leave a message after the—"*

Riley hangs up and calls again but is kicked into his voicemail one more time.

"For *fuck's sake,* Williams!"

Daniel's hand presses on her shoulder. "I'm sure he's fine, darling, he might just be sleeping."

Riley cups his face, urgency digging into her guts. "Do you trust me?"

She can't feel what he feels, but the way he looks at her tells her he understands this is serious. "Yes, of course."

"I need you all to go. Now. I have to leave, but I need to know you'll convince them to get the hell out and hide somewhere. Stick together. Can you do this for me?"

He nods, and that's all Riley needs. Because she trusts him too. She gives him a tight smile and kisses his cheek before storming out of the apartment, ignoring her friends as they call her name.

The drizzle persists, soaking her shoulders and the top of her head by the time she's in the truck and sits in the equally soaked seat. She drives as fast as she can to James's place, the rising cold inside the truck numbing her fingers. Rudy's words resonate in her mind.

'I'll be riding with you whenever you drive my truck.'

He's here. She knows he's here. If she looked into the rearview mirror, Riley's certain she would see icy blue eyes looking back at her. The thought is oddly reassuring. His words were true. He kept his promise.

"I got the message, Dad. I'll save him. I promise I'll save him."

Although just a few minutes away, Riley lets out a shaky breath as she reaches James's place and hits the brakes, making the truck screech to a halt along the sidewalk. She jumps from it and runs up the driveway. The Mustang is here. The light is out.

"Jamie!" she yells.

The door opens as she knocks on it. Riley looks at it, noticing how the doorknob is messed up and the wood is splintered. She bursts in, panic driving her, and turns on the light. Her breath catches in her throat.

The whole place is an absolute wreck. The coffee table has collapsed, as though someone fell on it. The TV's on the floor. A spot on the wall is fissured, dark blood clotting between the cracks.

"No…"

She bursts into the hallway and turns into the bedroom. It's empty as well, and the broken window lets rain and wind pour inside the room. Riley checks the bathroom, afraid this last room will hold James's dead body. The harsh light turns on.

The bathtub is empty.

They took him.

Riley darts back to the living room, her eyes sweeping across the space to find a clue when her phone rings in her pocket. Without thinking about it, she takes it out and picks up.

"Kell?"

"There are people trying to break inside the house!"

Kelly's panicked voice sends ice running through Riley's core, and by the time she starts talking, she's already outside, running toward the trunk. She wants to ask why the fuck they haven't left but there's no time. "Are the doors locked?"

"Y-yes. But I think one of them went around the house."

The windows.

"Where are you right now?" She jumps in the truck and starts it, already driving away.

"Locked inside the bathroom."

"Kell, did you see how many there were?" Her voice is oddly steady now. Her fight or flight instinct has taken over. And she's gonna fight. They fucked with the wrong person.

"I saw two… but I'm not sure—" She lets out a small cry.

"Kell? Kelly, are you there?"

Her words, barely above a whisper that Riley has to strain to hear, send ice coursing through her veins. "They're here…"

Riley parks in front of her place. She hasn't made it to the porch when she freezes, staring at the two shadows standing on each side of the door. They can't go inside the warded house, so their vessels left them outside. Their eyeless shapes are turned to her, the black ectoplasm undisturbed by the weather.

They make no move. They won't, not when Riley has become 'normal.' They both have perfectly suited hosts for them.

Swallowing around the lump in her throat, Riley makes her way to the front door, drawing her gun. She keeps an eye on the demons following her movements, anxiety gnawing away at the pit of her stomach. Once she reaches the threshold, she bursts through the door.

A man is pointing a gun at her friends, who are sitting on the couch. A quick glance at them tells her they're physically unharmed.

The man sees her and aims at her. "Come with us now, and we won't kill them."

Instinct and furor driving her, Riley raises her gun and shoots him.

He stumbles back with a cry, the blood from the hole in his shoulder spraying the wall behind him. Riley lunges at him and punches his throat. He claws at his neck, making choking sounds, and she kicks his ankle, sweeping his leg from under him. As soon as his body hits the ground, Riley plants a knee on his chest and punches his face.

"You don't—" another blow, harder, "give me—" then another, *"orders!"* His nose breaks under her fist, spraying blood on her face.

A scream rises from deeper in the apartment, making Riley realize Kelly isn't on the couch with Liam, Miguel, and Daniel. They barely have time to get up before Riley jumps to her feet and darts through the hallway, footsteps following her. What she sees when entering her room sends lava through her body, making her head throb.

A man is pinning Kelly on the bed, trying to rip her underwear off.

Riley hooks her fingers in his collar and yanks him back, half strangling him before he crashes against the wall. She's vaguely aware of her friends getting Kelly out of the way when the butt of her gun connects with the man's forehead, stunning him. But she's far from done. This motherfucker deserves everything that's coming to him.

She grabs his hair, smash his face against the dresser, and shoves him hard enough to make him fall to the floor. The way he looks at her, with eyes as wide as saucers, as he scrambles back when she walks to him is quite satisfying but isn't enough to extinguish the fire running through her.

Riley raises her foot and drops it on his stomach. He lets out a cry, holding his midsection and rolling over. She grabs his collar again and pulls him upright, only to throw him onto the bed a second later. She straddles him before punching his face.

As he lets out another cry, Riley clasps her hand against his chin to force his mouth open and slides the tip of her gun inside.

"Suck on my gun, *bitch.*"

The man whimpers, shaking under her, his face coated with sweat and blood.

"Do you like it, dicksplash? Huh? Do you like to feel as scared as she was?"

More helpless whimpering follows as tears roll down his cheeks. She presses the gun a little farther, enjoying seeing him gag on it, before she takes it out and presses it against his forehead.

"Where is he?"

"W-who...?"

"Don't play dumb with me," she spits through gritted teeth. "Where's James? Is he dead? Did you kill him?"

The man swallows, pausing his panting for a second. "No... He's at the bunker. They didn't kill him."

The bunker. I don't want to go back to that godforsaken place.

"Why the fuck did you come here, then?"

"Janice told us to get you."

"Is Madelyn in on it? Did she lie to me?" He looks at her with confusion for a second, and Riley presses the gun harder against his skull. "Answer me!"

He shuts his eyes, wincing, trying to find his words. "You mean Charlotte? Yeah, she's a traitor all right. We know she tried to help you. If Janice hasn't killed her yet, then she will soon."

Riley's facing a new choice now. To kill him or not to kill him. He's a murderer. A rapist. He doesn't deserve to live.

The man seems to sense the shift in her when she fastens both her hands onto her gun and clenches her jaw.

"Wait... Please... Don't do this..."

"You don't get to beg like a little bitch. Not after the things you've done. Did you stop when my friend struggled? Did you stop when your victims cried and screamed? How about when my dad was killed?"

"No, please, please..."

"Go to hell."

As if having a will of its own, her finger slides over the trigger, fastening around it. This will feel good.

"Riley."

The voice forces her to look to her right. She meets Daniel's imploring eyes.

"Don't do this, darling... I know you're angry, but this isn't who you are."

It's not just him that keeps her from pulling the trigger. It's Miguel, standing behind Daniel, scared and shocked. It's Liam, holding Kelly tightly in his arms, while she still shakes, her cheeks covered with tears. It's the fucking bathroom door behind them, splintered and smashed. They're here because of her. Because they wanted to be there for her, and she abandoned them. They shouldn't have to see someone die before their eyes.

A hard blow to her wrist shoves the gun away from the man's face. Riley feels his clammy hand clasp around her throat before the room spins and her back hits the floor. She quickly jumps back to her feet, aiming at the man jumping from the bed and throwing himself through the window. She pulls the trigger. The shot echoes, quickly followed by a scream.

Riley darts to the window, jumping above the bed, and sticks her head out. She hit him, but he's still running away, limping, his leg stained with blood. She raises her gun again, but the rain makes it impossible to see clearly, and a second later, her target is gone.

"Shit."

Back inside, Riley crosses the room to her friends. "You guys wait here." She walks through the hallway and into the living room. The guy she knocked out earlier is still here, passed out on the floor. Outside, a shadow lurks. Just one. The other has reentered its host.

Her friends were 'lucky,' sort of. The cult didn't think they'd all be here, which is probably why they only sent two men. They thought they would only find Kelly. It does nothing at soothing Riley's raw, angered nerves. She walks back to the hallway, quickly searching everyone's face.

"Are you guys okay?"

Kelly leaves Liam's arms and steps close to Riley, choked by sobs. "I-I'm so sorry, this is my fault... I wanted to pack a bag before leaving and then they were here, and–"

Riley pulls her into a hug, wishing she could appease her. "Shh, it's okay. It's not your fault, Kell. You're safe now. You guys are safe." Still holding Kelly, her gaze flickers to the others as she's trying to assess who's the calmest. "Which one of you can drive right now?"

"I could," Daniel says, "but I don't have my own car."

Miguel gives him a nod. "I can. Where should we go?"

"Somewhere you think I wouldn't be able to find you. You guys stick together, okay? I'll call you when I know it's safe."

No one argues this time. They follow her to the front door, Kelly holding her arm tightly. Riley peeks outside, noticing the cloud of ectoplasm to the left side of the porch. It hasn't moved, waiting silently for its host to come back and claim it.

"Everyone, be quick," Riley says.

"What about him?" Liam says, gesturing at the man lying on the living room floor.

"We don't have time for him just now."

The group stays close to her as she escorts them to Miguel's car. Miguel hops in the driver's seat. Riley ushers Liam and Kelly onto the back seat.

"What are you gonna do?" Daniel asks, his hair and clothes and face dripping with water as he looks at her.

"I have to save James."

He takes her hands, squeezing them too tightly. *"Please,* be careful."

A quick glance to her left is enough for her to realize that the shadow, stretching high into a humanoid shape, is slowly advancing toward them.

"I will. Go."

He gives her hands another squeeze and rounds the car, hopping in the passenger seat. Riley watches the car drive away, some of the weight crushing her chest vanishing, and slowly turns back to the demon hovering above the ground.

There's a pull, a heaviness settling over her body. Her feet are rooted to the grass, and her arms are numb. The shadow, exercising its power on her and paralyzing her, stops in front of her. It's tall, taller than James even, towering above her and blacker than black.

Riley swallows, willing her body to relax as much as possible, and lets her eyes sweep over the gigantic form in front of her, staring up at its faceless head.

"Let's get this over with."

CHAPTER 35

The throbbing headache battering his skull slowly brings James back to consciousness. They got him good. Rudy did help. He threw shit around and hit a few of them, but it wasn't enough.

The blow he took at the back of his head feels like it's splitting his brain open. His jaw pulses. His bruised chest aches each time he draws air into his lungs. His hands and feet feel numb.

James opens his eyes, but blackness surrounds him. A chill crawls over his skin, the coldness of the place settling into his bones. Water drips and echoes around him.

A growl disturbs the silence somewhere to his left. James tries to move, but his ankles and wrists stay rooted to the cold surface he's lying on, and he understands why his hands and feet are so numb. Thick restraints are tied around his limbs, pinning his arms by his sides and keeping him from moving.

The room smells of rain and rot and blood. He's in *that* room. No doubt about it.

Red eyes cut through the dark. James stares at them, holding his breath. Underneath, thin strands of purple light peek through the ocean of darkness, swaying and fading in and out as though the Egregore rolls the orb over its hands like a cat playing with a ball of yarn.

Forcing air into his lungs, James tries to remember the things he read about this creature. He shouldn't fear it as much as he should fear Janice Kraft.

A metallic door opens to his right. Footsteps fill the room, their echoes bouncing against the walls and James's skull. Lights are turned on, making him wince and blink. It comes from those portable spotlights scattered on the floor.

The Faceless march into the room, standing in a circle around him. A series of random people looking more frightening than ever. They keep immobile, standing straight, their lifeless, black eyes fixed on him, undisturbed by the creature lurking in the background. There are more people than when he and Riley got ambushed. And they're all possessed. Every single one of them.

Janice steps into the room, slowly advancing, a smile spreading on her lips. Her gray mane is more disheveled than ever, her large, loose clothes moving like a robe around her. A limp is clearly noticeable. Rudy shot her leg before he got killed.

"Finally awake I see, Mr. Williams."

James makes no reply, clenching his jaw instead. There's nothing to say, really. They will torture and kill him. The end.

"I was told you gave them a hard time," Janice continues, standing next to the table he's strapped on. "Some of them are badly hurt. It doesn't surprise me, that's why I sent so many of them to fetch you. You're quite violent, aren't you? I remember clearly how you mistreated me a few days ago."

"Stop listening to yourself and kill me already."

"Yes, yes, I will absolutely kill you, James. But not just yet. I want to wait for Riley first. She needs to see you die and hear your screams."

"Riley's not coming—"

"Of *course* she is." Janice cocks her head and smiles as if he's stupid. "I've been informed that she knows you've been taken. She's coming, all right. And once she gets here, I will have accomplished my task of bringing her to the master."

"You have no clue what you're dealing with, do you?" Now *he* looks at her like she's stupid. "This thing you're calling your master doesn't give a crap about you, and it's not gonna reward you with anything. It's just giving back whatever you're projecting onto it."

The slight twitch in her eye pleases him. "You're confused, Mr. Williams, and you better watch your mouth. This is a god we're talking about, and he will—"

"It won't do shit because it's not a fucking god."

With baffling rapidity, Janice grabs a knife, slams her hand onto his forehead, and presses the cold blade under his jaw, so much that he can feel his blood pulsing against it. "You're my favorite type of target, James, you know that? Beautiful on the outside, but so arrogant and sure of himself. You think you're so superior to me?"

She turns the knife, and slices downward on the side of his neck. Hot blood coats his skin as the pain makes him grunt.

"I wish I could take my time with you. I wish I could skin you alive, but we don't have time for this because Riley will be here soon. Don't worry, though, I have a very special treatment for men like you."

She smiles a sick smile, showing yellowed teeth, then leaves his side, the knife still in her hand.

"Is that why you kill?" he says, the cut on his neck pulsing fiercely. "You don't like pretty people? You're pathetic..."

"Do you know who my first kill was? One of the pharmacists handing me my prescriptions. Always so manicured and blonde, her face covered in makeup."

"That's not a crime."

"No. But she always acted like she was better than me. Always gave me this top to bottom look, like I wasn't worth being looked at. Like I was just trash. Always rolled her eyes when I asked if all my meds were really in the bag." She looks at him, the spark in her eyes making his skin crawl. "So, one day, I followed her home. Almost strangled her, but there was nothing fun about it. I wanted her to *see* me. To know what I was doing to her. I didn't kill her just yet. And wouldn't you know? Her house was haunted by a dark presence. That's when the demon took my body. Before I could do what I wanted to her. But see, the shadow was smart. It let me regain control of myself so I could finish what I had started."

Nausea pounds the back of his throat. This girl, whoever she was, probably was a good person. A Daniel or Grace level of goodness or the shadow would have possessed her while it could. Instead, it took Janice, and it probably wasn't smart at all. It let her regain control because it simply wasn't strong enough to take over such an evil person yet. It's only once she started feeding it that it grew and made a comfy nest within her body.

"I finished her." She chuckles, a sadistic sound sickening him. "You wouldn't believe how much she endured. I took her manicured nails out, one by one. I burned her skin with her beloved curling iron. I broke each of her fingers. And the best part? My demon helped me carry her into the woods. It made me crawl up the trees to leave without a trace. This little torture session did wonders at feeding it."

"*Shut up.* Just shut your fucking mouth, you monster."

"Don't act so self-righteous, Mr. Williams. You're no better than me. I'm sure a demon would be delighted to possess you. My shadow and I are very close to each other. I'm so glad to have it back."

When she blinks, her eyes turn black, a statement that her demon is indeed here somewhere, watching. Riley was right. They took the lockboxes in Rudy's basement, and Janice got her precious passenger back, as well as a demon for each member of the cult.

"After killing her and not getting caught," Janice continues, "I knew I could do anything I wanted, only I needed a safe place for this. Taking the risk to leave hair or pieces of clothes behind me in different homes was too risky. That's how I found this place. And then *he* came to me."

A growl echoes. Janice looks at something to James's left, awe spreading over her face. From where he is, he can't see the creature lurking behind the circle of people surrounding him.

"It was so small and fragile. So scared and sad, like my victims. But I helped him. I made him stronger. And now he's magnificent."

"What does it want with Riley's empathy?" It doesn't matter much now that he's going to die, but he has to ask.

Janice's face darkens. Bitterness tightens her lips when she turns back to him. "I wanted to kill her after she took my demon. She was so cocky, just like yourself. She's everything I've always hated. I despised her for the things I saw inside her head. She thinks she's such a special being. A *celestial*. I *had* to take this thing away from her, give her a taste of what it's like to be useless and forgettable. She's not so special now, is she? And the best part is that this energy of hers, this piece of soul, it gives us access to all her memories. It was quite useful. I wish I could have kept it for myself... I've tried to make it mine, but it won't latch onto me... If I can't have it, then neither can she. It will die with Riley once I kill her."

James's heart misses a beat, making a painful flip in his chest. His body tenses, and he pulls on the restraints keeping him nailed to the table. "What do you mean, kill her? You said you didn't want to kill her."

She raises her eyebrows, a smirk playing at the corners of her mouth. "Have you never told a white lie? Why on earth would I want her in my growing community? Every demon would fight for her body, and she would destroy everything I've built. We're all equals here. We don't need her *celestial* poison."

"No offense, but you're not making sense, lady."

"And what is it that your small brain cannot process?"

"You said you wanted to get Riley back to your master willingly. Why?"

A chuckle falls out of her mouth. "Our community is made of terrestrials. You can't imagine the pleasure it gives me to know that a celestial could be so far damaged that she'd be ready to give herself to us."

"She won't give herself."

"Not yet, but soon. And when she does, that's when I'll finish her."

He might have a small brain but there's a hole in her story, something she's not even aware of. She said the Egregore wanted Riley, but Egregores usually don't want stuff of people. Either it's just Janice projecting her desires onto it, or it developed a will of its own when it got its hands on Riley's energy. That would explain why it didn't attack or do anything when they showed up. It was too busy playing with its new celestial toy, only it can't use it without the host that comes with it. "You're being manipulated. What you call your master is actually an Egregore. It's not a demon, it's not a spirit, and it's definitely not a fucking god. It was never human. It's no more than an imprint created by energies and echoes left behind by people."

"You don't know anything."

"I know *this*. The energies left by the spirits of the people you murdered have created a new being. An Egregore. It's *you* who fed it into being so big by bringing torture and fear into this place, and it's *you* who made it into being a god. All this time, it was only a reflection of your projections. Until now."

She takes a sharp step toward him and presses the knife against his chest. "Go ahead, speak. I dare you."

The blade digs into his shirt and the skin underneath. He's going to die anyway, so fuck it. "It only mirrored your emotions and desires. It has become what you made it out to be. But once it saw into your memories, once it got Riley's empathy, it knew it wanted *her*. A creature like this will always latch onto the biggest energy in the room, and when she gets here, the brightest will be her, not you. It will discard you as soon as it gets what it wants."

She slices through his skin. Razor-sharp pain blasts through his chest, and James can't hold back a cry. He tries to sit up, but several pairs of hands fall onto his chest and shoulders to keep him down. A hand clasps over his mouth, muffling his grunts as Janice moves the knife further down and makes another cut across his stomach.

She brings her face close to his, her eyes glinting with madness. "Maybe I have some time for you after all. You're a liar, and I'll make you regret all the things you've said. My master will feast on your pain."

Janice leaves his side and turns away. Black eyes stare down at him, the grasp of their hosts unyielding.

"Let's see what you think of this."

Janice's voice makes him tear his eyes away from the demons. His heart picks up the pace, fast and beating away at his chest. She dangles a sledgehammer under his nose, drags it over his body slowly, then stops on his knee. No matter how much he braces himself and clenches his teeth as she raises it, the hammer falling onto his knee sends an agonizing blast of pain rippling through him, snatching a muffled scream out of him. The hand clasped over his mouth tightens, not quite covering his nose but almost.

She strikes him again.

And again.

Each time, the hammer feels like it's seeking deeper into his tissues, smashing his bones.

His stomach convulses, and through the agony and the torment, James has the crystal clear knowledge that this is how he's going to die, puking from the pain and choking on it because of the hand keeping his mouth shut.

"Let him breathe," Janice says.

The hand lets up just in time for him to turn to the side as his stomach revolts. He coughs, each time shivering from the pain, leading to him puking some more. James lies back down, drawing shaky breaths.

Fingers tangle in his hair and wipe sweat off his forehead. He feels Janice's breath against his cheek before she licks the tear rolling down his face.

"Oh, I do love to get some tears out of a tough guy like you. You're probably not feeling so hot right now, are you?"

A metallic screech snatches her attention away from him. A small thing to be grateful for.

"What a *nice* surprise," Janice says. "Didn't I tell you she'd be coming?"

Shuddering and sick to his stomach, James wills himself to open his eyes. He looks to his right, following Janice's gaze. "No..."

Riley stands in the doorway, as stiff as a plank. Her eyes, a deep obsidian black, is the last thing James sees before passing out from the pain.

CHAPTER 36

Riley's vision clears after the ectoplasm leaves her mouth. She takes a deep breath and blinks at the dirty lights, the concrete floor cold under her knees and digging into her palms.

"Are you with us?"

Janice's voice makes her look up. The woman stands in front of her, the rest of the cult forming a wide circle around Riley. Dozens of them. James is nowhere to be seen.

"Can you hear me?" Janice yells, leaning over.

Riley bites back on her anger and fixes her gaze on Janice. "Yes. Where's James?"

"How was your demonic ride? Enjoyed it? I was surprised to see you show up like this. My brother here told me what you did to him, but he didn't see how you got your hands on a passenger. You're quite feisty, aren't you?"

Riley glances at the 'brother.' It's the man who assaulted Kelly. "I'll tell you what happened. The other guy you sent is unconscious in my living room. To be honest, I don't even know if he's alive. As for your other *brother*," she grins defiantly, "he pleasured the tip of my gun."

The man looks down. Janice's face turns cold as she glares daggers at him.

"He barely got out alive," Riley adds. "That's what you get for fucking with me."

"Is that so? Let's see what *you* get for fucking with *me*."

Riley vaguely hears a metallic, squeaking sound before a man breaks through the circle of people, throwing Madelyn to the floor. She falls with a cry and curls up, shaking. Her bruised face bleeds, and her eyes shimmer as she looks at Riley.

"I'm so sorry..." she sobs. "They caught me after our meeting..."

"Indeed," Janice says, nodding. "She admitted to telling you about this place, so we knew you'd be coming. It's not her fault, really. I should have known she wasn't fit to be with us."

She nods at the man who threw Madelyn to the floor, and in two quick steps, he's next to her and grabs her hair, forcing her on her knees, and holds a knife to her throat.

"But finding Mommy dearest might have been a blessing in disguise," Janice says.

"What more do you want?" Riley snaps. "You wanted me to come here? I'm here. Just let her go."

"Ah, but you didn't come for the right reasons. You're just looking for your boyfriend."

Riley clenches her teeth, slowly rising to her feet and glancing around her to see if anyone will jump at her. No one moves. "Tell me where he is."

"Are you ready to give yourself to the master?"

"*Fuck off.*"

"Still better than us, I see. How about we play a game, then? Maybe that'll convince you."

Janice nods at someone to Riley's right. A woman takes a step forward, raising a smartphone for her to see. The screen shows one of the bunker's rooms. Riley's stomach churns. On the right side, narrow windows run along the blackened wall just under the ceiling. Under them, a series of metal shelves. In the middle, a large freezer. It's open.

James is inside, unconscious.

Riley's lips start to tremble. "Is he—"

"Dead? No, no. Not yet. I hope you don't mind, we took a few of the cameras in your bookshop while you weren't there. Don't worry, though, we didn't burn the place down. For your house, it was different. We needed that *wow* effect because we knew you'd go back there. That's why we let you go. But it's not like you'll ever set foot in Winter's Attic again now, will you?"

Janice's voice blurs into the background. Riley's fixed on what she sees on the screen. A man enters the camera's view and closes the lid over James. He hooks a padlock to keep it shut, then picks up a gas can, spreading its content all around the room.

Icy terror shoots through Riley's body, fastening its claws on her. "What are you doing? Let him out!"

"If you want a chance to get him back, you have to play by my rules."

All the anger Riley has felt before crumbles down, desperation filling her and taking its place. "Please, let him go. I'll do whatever you want. I'll be part of your cult."

Janice crosses her arms against her chest, thinking. "Mm. I'm not convinced. Being part of this community requires to make tough decisions, Riley. If you want to save him, you'll have to prove to me that you're capable of it."

"What does that mean?"

"You have to choose between him and your mother."

The man fastens his hand on Madelyn's hair, pressing the blade tighter against her throat. She lets out a feeble moan, her eyes imploring Riley.

"Which one should we kill, Riley? Mommy? Or *Jamie-bear?*" Janice says. "You have ten seconds to make a choice."

Her breath catches in her throat. She takes her eyes away from Madelyn, staring at the phone still held up for her to see the room James is held in. The *burning* room. Her hands start to shake as her breathing rasps against her dry throat.

"See, the funny thing is that he won't burn in there. He'll cook. Which will take far longer to kill him. To make it even, we'll make sure Madelyn suffers for a long time too, should you choose her." An irritating chuckle escapes Janice's mouth. "Hell, maybe I'll make *you* torture her." She pauses, watching Riley, enjoying herself. "So? Choose now or lose them both."

"Wait, no—"

"*Now.*"

"*Madelyn,*" Riley blurts out despite herself.

Madelyn lets out a sob, shutting her eyes. When she opens them, she gives a shaky nod. "It's all right, sweetheart. I understand. It's the right choice."

Riley might still be able to find a way to buy some time. She doesn't want Madelyn to die, but she can't lose James.

Janice peers at Riley. "Figured you'd say that." She takes her phone out, writes a quick text, and looks back up, nodding at the phone the other woman is holding.

Riley gasps, panic blasting through her chest. On the screen, the man standing on the threshold strikes a match, flicking it off before shutting the door.

"No!" she screams, and already hands and arms fasten around her, holding her back while she shrieks and thrashes, desperately trying to pull herself out of their grasps to flee the room and save James.

As though things couldn't get more horrible, Riley hears sounds in between her screams, coming out of the phone.

Frantic pounding on the lid.

Grunts.

And most terrible of all, James screaming her name.

Her pleading and begging get lost in between her sobs and wailing. He's right there. *Right there,* in the next room, and she can't get to him, can't save him. She keeps thrashing, ignoring the way the demons' hands dig into her skin and pull her hair. In all the chaos, her jacket is ripped off, making her think she can slip through them, but all it does is making them clamp their strong fingers harder around her arms, hard enough to bruise them.

The image on the camera glitches and turns black.

Riley's legs buckle under her, and the arms and hands let go of her. She's left weeping, curled up on the floor and holding her head.

"He should have placed the camera higher," Janice says. "I would have loved to watch some more."

A new pair of hands, gentle this time, stroke her back and her hair. "Oh, sweetheart, I'm so sorry..."

Madelyn's touch and voice do nothing at soothing Riley. The thought that James is still in that box, pounding away at the lid while screaming her name, makes her want to die.

"Riley." Madelyn pulls her up into a sitting position and cups her face, making Riley look into her eyes. "You have to surrender. You have to tell her you're giving yourself, or she'll find other ways to hurt you. She'll find your other friends, and she'll kill them too. Just *give up*."

Trembling and sobbing, Riley stares into Madelyn's face. The aging lines. The fading lipstick. Her eyebrows. Those eyebrows that are slightly lighter than her hair.

She freezes. A profound feeling of disgust at being so naïve crashes over her. Her dad's words once again flash through her mind. '*I don't trust her.*'

"You're not my mother..." she whispers.

Madelyn blinks at her, tilting her head. "W-what are you talking about?"

"You dyed your hair..."

"This isn't the moment to talk about—"

"I thought maybe it was because you had gray hair. But your eyebrows aren't gray. They're light brown... You dyed your hair to make it look like mine." Things unfold in her mind, as crystal clear as ever. How the trapdoor to the attic of her old house opened so swiftly, as though it had been opened recently. When she held her dad's pictures in her hands, they were wrinkled, especially the oldest one. She remembers how it had surprised her that the letter she found in the attic was so smooth, so oddly clean after so many years. "You wrote that letter... and you put it there to make sure I'd find it so I would trust you."

"I... No, that's not—"

"You saw into my memories. You know everything about my past, and you *used* it to get to me."

"You didn't even know there was an attic—"

"You only had to visit the house to find it. That's why you mentioned it to me... so I would go there and look and believe you." Blinking tears away, she shuffles away from Madelyn, her body sluggish and heavy. She directs her gaze to Janice. "Was that all part of your plan to destroy me?"

Madelyn reaches to her. "Sweetheart, I promise—"

"That's enough, Charlotte," Janice says. "The cat's out of the bag. I must say, the fact that your mother's body was never found helped us amazingly."

Rudy's words still play in Riley's mind, stuck on a loop. *'I don't trust her. I don't trust her. I don't trust her.'*

Madelyn—Charlotte—sighs and rises to her feet, wiping blood off her face. The fake bruises are smeared away, revealing healthy skin underneath. "Your father was onto me. I'm glad he's dead."

Riley plants her palms onto the concrete, feeling herself falter. Her dark hair dangles in front of her face, blocking her view of the evil surrounding her. "Why?" The question is stupid, and her broken voice sounds pathetic.

Janice's legs enter her line of vision as she kneels close. Catching Riley's chin between her fingers, she makes her look up. "Do you remember when we met, and you stole my demon? I said I was going to destroy you then, and I always keep my promises. All my life I was disrespected. Mocked. Pushed around. And they all paid for it. But you... Giving you the same treatment just wasn't enough. I just... *hate* you so much... You have no idea how it felt like when my passenger, the one that had stayed with me for so long, didn't hesitate a second to discard me when it saw you. That really hurt... The truth is, Riley, I never wanted you to be part of this family. I've had a lot of fun with you. I've got my revenge. I've enjoyed stripping you of who and what you loved the most, like you did to me.

"You might not have completely surrendered, but I have you exactly how I want you. Alone and broken. Knocked out of your celestial cloud. Now it's your turn to die." She leans closer, brushing Riley's hair away. "Oh, how I'm going to enjoy slashing that pretty face. I'll make you as faceless as possible. When I'm done with you, you'll be reduced to no one. *Nothing.*"

A beastly growl resonates in the cold room.

Janice lets go of Riley's face and stands. "Master, I've accomplished my mission. We can kill her now."

Another growl, meaner and sharper, makes Janice step back.

Slow footsteps fall onto the concrete, coming closer. Riley raises her head, peeking through the strands of hair getting in her eyes, as the creature separates itself from the shadows. Its skin is black, but the edges of its body are blurred, the way demons and spirits are. They're intangible. In the middle of its enormous head flash two wide, round eyes, their bright red light fixed on Riley. It plants its gigantic, clawed hand onto the floor as it advances, holding a purple orb with the other.

'*I saw it down there. Your true colors. You're purple. Not a sad or angry purple. But a beautiful mix of baby blue and pink.*'

Riley doesn't budge, too tired and empty and beat up to make a single move, mesmerized by the bright ball of energy the beast is holding delicately, as if afraid to drop it and break it. When it brings the orb close to her, Riley feels the warmth emanating from it, caressing her face. Her eyes sweep over the gigantic creature bending over her. This is no monster. She doesn't know *what* it is, but she's seen enough evil in her life to know that this spirit isn't one of them. It's impressive, yes, but not scary.

The clawed hand rotates the orb, lowering it and pushing it onto Riley's chest.

"Master, wait!" Janice cries out.

The creature raises an arm, nailing her to the floor.

The purple light, warm and soft and full, presses against Riley's skin. It travels over her and through every fiber of her being. The walls seem to throb around her. The demons' energies grate at her skin. Evil fills the room, and in the background, lost souls. Ghosts, unable to move on, their imprints brushing at the edge of Riley's consciousness.

Janice screams something.

Riley doesn't hear what. Doesn't pay attention to it. She rises to her feet, still facing the creature, and raises a hand to touch its face. Echoes of fear and pain blast through her.

Her mouth forms words without her knowledge as she stares at the beast, taking away its feelings and giving it hers in return. "You don't have to be this way. Now you're anger. Revenge. Justice."

The thing closes its red eyes, its growl low and subdued, and when it opens them again, they have turned a bright purple.

"You're death."

She brushes her fingers on it, purple light spreading from her touch, dozens of tendrils weaving over the black mist and mixing, *fusing* together.

"You're me."

The shape of the head and hands and feet blur until nothing but a giant purple cloud is left. It advances, swallowing her, warming her, filling her with its current. Her body feels light, her hair is no longer wet and levitates as though under water.

Their conscience fuse, their powers blending into something she's never felt before, not even when taking over Terrestre. She has the ability to touch demons. Demons have the ability to make lifeless objects move.

But this.

This will do anything she wants it to. It has become the attributes she gave it, powered up by her celestial soul. The materialization of her desires and furor.

Riley slowly turns. The cult's fear is sharp and pleasing. When a few of them—Charlotte included—scramble away and run, the door shuts with a loud bang, making Riley smile. She didn't even have to do anything. She just wanted that door closed, and closed it is.

Aside from the dozens of people in the room with her, Riley can see other occupants. A crowd of lost spirits, some watching her and drawn to her, some unaware of what's happening around them. All of them bear terrible scars, all of them are covered in blood.

No, not all of them.

Five men are entirely burnt, their melted skin black. What if James is one of them, and she can't even recognize him?

A feeling far more terrible than furor and dread takes hold of her, making her heart and her energy pulse. Each pulse beats against the walls, the ceiling, and the people in the room, as though the vibrations travel through them too. At a simple request of her mind, all the bodies fly up to the ceiling. They scream as they crash onto it, stuck in awkward positions.

"Janice."

Terror flashes over Janice's soul before her body falls back to the ground. The pulsing keeps beating at the objects and the structure around them, steadily pounding. The ghosts seem thicker, more present with each blast wave.

"Come here."

Janice's body rises as though lifted by an invisible hand, and is pulled toward Riley, her feet dragging on the concrete. Riley opens her palm, catching Janice's throat. Her face is bloody from her fall, her nose swollen and twisted.

She beats against Riley's grasp uselessly, panting. "You stole it from me!"

Riley brings Janice close to her face, her anger burning brightly in the pit of her stomach. "You killed my father."

Another energy wave beats against the bunker, jarring it. Dust rains on them. Cracks form inside the walls and run through the concrete.

"You killed my boyfriend."

The ground shakes. People scream. Ghosts become restless. More of them become self-aware, their eyes turning to Riley and the people stuck on the ceiling.

"Stop!" Janice cries out, struggling under the unyielding grasp. "You're gonna kill us all! If you don't stop, even *you* will die! We'll all be crushed!"

Riley tightens her fingers around her throat. "You succeeded, Janice. You destroyed me. I don't care about dying. All I care about is making you suffer. I will hurt you, then kill you, then my spirit will still be tormenting you after death. I'll torture your empty soul for thousands of years until there is *nothing* left of you."

Angry spirits gather around. Their faces slashed. Their hands severed. Their skin burnt. They reach out to Janice.

Rage and disgust flow through Janice's veins, transferring through Riley. She spins the old woman around, hooking her arm around her throat.

"I want you to see them. I want you to see the people you killed."

Janice lets out a strangled cry when she sees the ghosts for the first time. Her victims look at her with dead eyes, at least for those who still have them. A young girl Riley has seen before in Janice's memories steps through them. Pink aura. Long, blonde curls. Angry-looking bruises around her throat. Bloody fingertips with no nails. Burns over her neck, face, and arms.

Riley unhooks her arm, and Janice falls to her knees, letting out hysterical shrieks. Riley ignores her for now and turns her attention to Charlotte. She stares back, her body tightly pressed against the ceiling. Riley walks under her, still surrounded by her purple orb, and looks up.

"You *have* killed, haven't you?"

"No! I swear I've never killed!"

The words sound wrong. "Lies. Were you one of the people who burned my house down?"

Charlotte sobs. "No... I swear."

"Lies again. You're even possessed. You..." She looks at each person stuck on the ceiling like pathetic bugs. "You are all so dark. You will die here, and the people you killed will be on the other side, waiting for you."

A few of them whimper. Others are taken over by their demons. Their black eyes stare at her, and furniture starts flying in her direction. Tables and hammers and knives and scissors, all crashing and bouncing off the purple cloud enveloping her.

She shakes her head. "I don't think so."

Riley closes her eyes, reaching out to the shadows within the humans. She pulls her hand into a fist, mentally pulling the entities out of their hosts. The view she gets as she opens her eyes is beautiful. Black ectoplasm pours out of open mouths, falling like rain. Janice is curled up on the floor, surrounded by her victims, while she pukes and chokes on her demon.

Riley fuses the shadows together, resulting in a gigantic mass of ectoplasm. This is what it looks like. But this isn't what it feels like. She discerns each entity in it. Janice's demon, the one Riley let herself be possessed with. The others, the ones she exorcised after being contacted through W&W Paranormal Investigation, are here too. Like the small, pathetic shadow who possessed the little kid.

The blob implodes at her will. Just the desire to annihilate it is enough to make it shrivel on itself.

"No!"

Janice's scream is so loud that even Riley can hear it above the racket of metallic objects rattling against the concrete floor and her energy pounding away at the bunker.

"No! Stop it! Not my demons!" She scrambles back to her feet, grabs a pair of scissors, and throws herself at Riley.

With a flick of her mind, a knife flies through the room and stops in front of her. Janice sees it, panic widening her eyes, but she can't kill her momentum, and impales herself onto the blade. The scissors drop from her hand, but her hateful eyes never leave Riley as she inches forward, bringing the unwavering blade further inside her chest.

"I... hate... you..."

Riley peers at her, a woman so evil and so sick she doesn't even realize she's hurting herself more by keeping moving forward. "Likewise."

Her mind drops the knife, and Janice falls on her stomach, impaling herself further. Blood sprays out of her mouth, splattering the floor. She isn't dead yet, which is good. She needs to suffer more. They all need to hurt, to see their death coming.

Riley will destroy this place and bury all its suffering and its negative imprints.

But first...

She lets the bodies drop to the ground. As she feels the energies flow through her, using the creature, no object touches the floor. Not even her own feet. The bodies painfully get back up, wobbling around as if blown by a strong wind. It's not wind. It's energy, pulsing like a steady heartbeat.

Their terrified shrieks fill the room, competing with the deafening current pushing and battering the walls. They *see* their victims. Each shock wave rippling through the room brings them into relief, into existence, into flesh and bone. And they're angry. Eager to get their hands on their murderers.

Wider cracks run up the walls, snaking and slithering to the ceiling, until concrete blocks fall, crushing the skull of a man like a watermelon. Good riddance. The flickering ghosts seize knives, hammers, scissors, hooks. They slash through their murderers relentlessly each time they take substance. The man who assaulted Kelly gets stabbed in the eyes repeatedly. Madelyn—Charlotte—is slashed in the back by a saw. It's a fireworks show of blood painting the walls and choked screams filling Riley's head.

Clenching her hands into tight fists, Riley gathers her strength and her hatred. Being good doesn't matter. It doesn't mean anything. Getting rid of the Faceless does, and dying will be her punishment for murdering the ones that aren't killed by ghosts.

The purple light around her brightens and spins, bringing into it the few demons that aren't dead yet, melting their blackness into this tornado.

"Let's wipe the slate clean."

More screams grate at her nerves as the ground shakes under their feet.

CHAPTER 37

A few minutes earlier...

The pulsing of his destroyed knee and the gash on his chest isn't what pulls James back to consciousness. It's the heat. It's strong, enough to give him hot flashes and make him sweat. Shaking and blinking at the darkness surrounding him, he raises his hands, but his fingers only meet with a hard surface. It's warm too. He's in a box. A tight one that squeezes his shoulders and threatens to suffocate him.

The freezer.

The image of the room with its walls blackened by smoke and its freezer standing in the middle of it jumps in his mind, clear as day.

Panic sets its claws into him, and James pushes the lid, his breathing quickening. The lid moves up just an inch before it resists above his palms, letting only a thin strand of light peeking through the opening. The room was dark when he saw it the first time. Now a bright orange glow is visible through the gray smoke seeping through the opening.

He's going to burn alive.

Sharp terror shoots through him, as his fists are already pounding at the lid above him. Each blow sends blasting pain through his bleeding knuckles, but he doesn't stop, panic driving him. His voice has a will of its own as the heat increases, and he finds himself screaming for Riley, begging to be let out. More smoke seeps through the crack each time he beats on the lid. It fills the hot space around him and scorches his lungs.

Between two punches, the lid flies open. Through the smoke and the flames, James catches the faintest outline of a man, a flash of blue eyes piercing through the blaze.

After looking at the empty space for a second, stunned, he pulls himself onto a standing position, leaning against the edge of the freezer for support as his right leg sends currents of screaming pain running up his body.

Fire and smoke surround him. A barrier of flames stands between him and the door. Even if it were open, he wouldn't be able to reach it. Through the sound of the blaze, shattered glass makes him looks up. Up the shelves, one of the narrow windows is broken. *Has been* broken. Because Rudy's still here somewhere, watching over him.

He'll have to be fast. With shredded knuckles and a pulverized knee that may or may not be broken but is so swollen and painful it makes him want to puke, it will be challenging.

James jumps out of the freezer. The landing sends another crippling blast of pain, and he collapses onto the ground. He scrambles back to his feet and tries to avoid the flames inching closer to him. The heat and smoke make him sweat and cough, but he doesn't stop and reaches for the shelves, praying they'll be sturdy enough to support his weight. The metal is hot under his fingers, but he climbs, nonetheless.

The heat is unbearable, sizzling his skin. His rasping breathing becomes labored. He coughs, nearly losing his grip. The smoke coats his mouth and tongue and lungs. The view of the window above him blurs. He's not losing consciousness, not yet. The pain is so sharp that it's enough to keep him awake for now, but the smoke burns his eyes and makes them water.

The ascension is long. The shelves creak. The fire is already cooking him. The pain makes him shiver.

He throws his hand up again and gasps as his fingers connect with fresh, damp weeds. He grasps them and pulls himself up. The narrow window feels like it closes around his chest as he slides through it, keeping him from bringing air into his lungs, but after more pulling, he's outside in the fresh air, under the battering rain soaking him and washing the smoke away.

James crawls away from the bunker, panting, and collapses in the divine moisture of the grass. He can die now. Dying here is fine. It's better than the oven. Adrenaline is seeping out of his body, weighing him down, and the pain in his leg comes back with a vengeance, fierce and pulsing, and he finds himself crying again. Crying from being so miserable. Crying from losing Riley and Rudy. Crying because he's not dead, and not feeling a thing would be so much better.

Get up, son.

Rudy's voice echoes through his head, cutting through the constant tapping of the rain. James can't move, his face pressed against the grass.

Get up, Jamie.

Wincing from the pain, he rolls onto his back and lets water wash away his sweat. "I can't, Rud... I can't... I can't save her. I'm sorry."

A faint rumbling travels through the ground like a shock wave. A steady beating pumping under his back. James fights to open his eyes, and in the darkness, he can almost perceive the rain shake for half a second, its vertical decent perturbed by the weird vibrations. He squints. Each time a current ripples through the ground and the air, a familiar shape comes into view, highlighting a red plaid jacket, steel gray hair, and light blue eyes, then disappears again.

Until another shock wave comes, and Rudy's here again, kneeling next to James, a hand on his shoulder. He keeps blinking in and out of the darkness, the rain falling through him, the pressure of his hand on James's shoulder fading and reappearing at the same time as him.

"What the fuck is going on..." James mutters.

You need to

"...get up, son."

The voice, at first only in his head, now clearly fills the air as Rudy reappears.

James swallows the feeling of nausea and nods, then rolls onto his side. A long, sturdy branch conveniently lies on the grass within grasp.

"Thanks for that," he says, reaching for it.

His leg throbs as he battles to put the stick upright and haul himself up. Rudy tries to help him, but his grasp on James's arm vanishes into thin air every couple of seconds. Finally, he stands, his good leg trembling wildly under him. The idea that he has to round the bunker, cross it, and go down the stairs fills him with dismay. But he has to. And if he can't save Riley, then he'll die with her. Maybe he'll get to hold her one last time.

The thought gets him moving. The high weeds cling to his ankles, seemingly trying to hold him back. The branch sinks into the saturated ground. The rain and the dark make it nearly impossible to see. The only thing that keeps him moving is the slowly blinking shape of Rudy standing before him, leading the way. Surrounding him is a blue halo, as light as his eyes.

That's his color. His soul. For the first time, James understands what Riley has felt her whole life. He sees it as much as he feels it, a warm and reassuring presence. He doesn't know how it's possible, nor does he know what the hell is happening in the bunker, but something gives Rudy substance intermittently.

James faces the bunker's door. It's open wide, ready to swallow him. A shiver runs through him, and his grasp on the stick tightens. He's scared. Scared of what else they could do to him. Scared of what they'll do to *her.* The blue halo reappears inside. Rudy's soul is like a beacon guiding James.

He limps his way inside, clenching his teeth to hold back his grunts as he walks down the incline leading him underground. He follows Rudy's light, pausing when it dies down and plunges him back in the cold darkness of the bunker. Each time, he waits, panting and feeling as though he'll collapse, but when his friend's soul cuts through the shadows again, soft and gentle, it gives him a small regain of energy that makes him take a few more steps.

It could be his imagination, or the pain making him hallucinate, but the air around him thickens. It almost feels like electricity. Rudy's shape stays a few seconds longer each time he blinks to life. Each pulse of energy lasts longer. A steady beating that he doesn't just feel anymore but hears. It's in the walls and the ceiling. It's in the vibrating floor and going up his stick. It's in his guts.

James stumbles and loses his balance, his body weak from exhaustion. Sickening pain shoots through his knee as he crashes onto the floor, and he can't contain a scream. Then, he's in the dark again, alone and shivering and nauseated, coated with sweat.

"I can't..." He shuffles to the wall and rests his back against it.

The blue light fills his vision again. Rudy, kneeling in front of him, wraps his arms around him to pull him up, and for a moment, it almost feels like a hug. It *is* a hug.

"Come on, boy."

James grabs onto Rudy and holds him tighter than he ever had, gripping the plaid jacket he wasn't wearing when he died, the one that's always been his favorite. James is on his feet and holding the stick just as Rudy fades. A few seconds later, he's here again, and James follows him through the corridors and down the stairs that threaten to make him fall and kill him.

The arched hallway seems to pulse and undulate around him. Other spirits fill the space. They also blink in and out, matching the shock waves. Some pay attention to him, others don't. They're all walking to the room at the end of the corridor, attracted by what's inside.

The floor shakes harder. Dust rains on his head.

"There's no stopping what's happening," Rudy says, looking back at him. He looks serene, composed, just like he always was. "But you two can get out before this place collapses on you."

James opens his mouth, but the rippling energy dies down, making Rudy fade. The dread crushing his chest grows as he approaches the door. A high-pitched ringing seeps through it. He keeps limping toward it, moving in a straight line and just guessing where he's going since there's no light to guide him for a moment, when he understands what the noise actually is.

It's no ringing. Those are screams. Terrified shrieks that belong to a crowd of people.

Another ripple shakes him and the structure. Ghosts keep advancing. James can see their souls too, and for a few seconds, the hallway is filled with blue and red and green people walking. None of the colors are alike. Rudy's baby blue feels unique next to the other shades.

Blinking ghosts that look like lanterns.

For fuck's sake. He could almost laugh.

A glimpse of bright, warm yellow catches his attention to his left. He freezes where he is, staring at Grace.

She smiles a brilliant smile, her long hair floating around her. "It will be okay, James."

James tightens his grip on the stick, clenching his teeth to hold back new tears. He would like to tell her how sorry he is that she had to die a second time and that he can barely sleep since it happened, but there's no time. He walks faster to the door. Grace's energy is just like Riley described it. It feels like a warm blanket around his shoulders, giving him strength.

The handle resists under his palm.

The 'lanterns' around him fade, leaving him in the dark, but when another blast runs through the bunker, the door opens before him. Rudy stands on the other side and turns away from James.

James looks in the same direction, and what he sees freezes his blood. In here, the ghosts blink but don't quite fade anymore. All these colors, all these souls stained with red crowd the room, beating, slashing, and stabbing at the Faceless. Most of them are dead, some are being tortured. Their screams make him dizzy.

In the middle of the room is the biggest, brightest orb. The only one to be purple, *this* kind of purple. The energy blasts come from it. It looks like a gigantic beating heart, pulsing and sharing its blood to the spirits around it. Riley is in the center of it. Her feet don't touch the floor. She's floating, her long hair hovering and gently moving around her head. She looks up but doesn't really see. Her eyes, flashing purple, stare into nothingness.

Paralyzed and hypnotized by the magnificence of this scene, James does nothing but stare, his mouth hanging open.

The heart beats. The walls crack more, their dust clogging the air and their blocks of concrete crashing onto the floor. The rumble snaps him out of his trance.

Rudy's eyes fix on him again. "We can't reach her. You have to do it."

James moves through the spirits and the people screaming, trying not to get knocked out each time Riley sends a ripple through the room. Two steps forward, one step back. His shoes stick in viscous blood.

"*Riley!*" he screams, but his voice gets lost in the deafening rumbling and shaking and shrieking.

Something grabs his ankle and pulls his right leg. This sends another blast of pain through his knee and makes him fall in a pool of gore. The grasp doesn't leave his ankle, and he turns around, a sliver of fear shooting through his heart as he meets Janice's crazy eyes. She coughs, spraying blood onto his leg, as her clawed fingers cling onto him and plant themselves in his wound, making him cry out. She pulls out the knife planted inside her chest. The blood pouring from the hole soaks him, warm and tacky. She raises the blade, ready to strike.

The image of her hammering his leg sends stomach-churning anger through his body, and he rolls over, catches her wrist before she brings the knife down, and punches her face with all his strength. His bloody knuckles hurt, but the feeling of her jaw shifting and cracking under his fist fills him with satisfaction.

"Fuck you, you old hag!"

Janice doesn't relent and tries to claw at him again.

Pink light catches James's eyes. He looks to his left, his heart jumping as he sees the dead girl standing next to him. The marks on her body show she was severely tortured before dying.

Janice's breath catches in her throat. "No..."

The girl reaches down for the knife, straddles Janice's back, and stabs her in the neck over and over again. James turns away from the scene as Janice drowns in her own blood, her body twitching.

He attempts to shift back to his feet. He can't. The closer he gets to Riley, the more the air and the ground vibrate, rippling against his skin. He has no choice but to crouch, which for him is half-crawling as he drags his leg behind him.

"Riley! You need to stop!"

His voice still can't rise above the chaos. Riley hasn't moved, her palms open at her side, the energy around her steadily pounding away, protecting her from the debris falling from the ceiling.

He raises a hand, reaching out for her. If she could feel him, she would stop. If only she could. But the mix of the Egregore, the ghosts, and the evil left in the room annihilate James's presence to her. He has to touch her.

His fingertips pierce through the purple aura. It's warm and soft, but something's not right. He goes deeper, his heartbeat fastening and furor rising through him. This energy is filled with anger. It's transmitted to the ghosts, making them commit murder.

James can't let it consume him. For the first time in his life, *he* has to be the calm one, the one who can pacify her.

He inches further, entering the sphere of hatred and fighting to stay focused. "Riley, *stop!* I'm begging you!"

He breaks through the purple light completely, feeling its force pushing him away. The ground shakes harder. The structure will bury them all.

With the last shred of strength, James pulls himself to his feet and grabs onto her shoulders.

The shift of the vibrations around him is instant, jarring. The pulsing stops. The lit ghosts vanish. The orb around Riley fades, and her feet reconnect with the floor. She blinks, and when her silver eyes fix on him, wide and confused as though he's the last person she expected to see, James's heart swells with hope and love.

"Jamie..."

His legs buckle under him. Riley tries to slow his descent and hooks her arms around his chest but falls to the ground with him.

Biting on another scream of pain as his knee touches the floor, he takes a shaky breath. "We need to get out."

She looks around, her eyes darting over the bodies and other things he cannot see.

The sound of stone cracking above their heads announces the imminent collapse of this place.

Riley runs her hand over his face. "Can you walk?"

No, he can't. Coming here was the worst torture he had to endure, and now he's just tempted to push her out of here.

Riley hooks her arm around him and tries to lift him, with no result. "Jamie, you have to get up."

"I've heard that before... Listen, you... you have to go."

"I'm not leaving you here—"

"Just go. *Please.*"

A grunt to his right makes them turn. Madelyn is alive, one hand missing and blood pouring from the stub. She staggers to her feet, carrying a dagger. The hatred filling her eyes when she sees them is foreign to James, telling him she was worse than she led on.

"If we're not getting out..." she snarls, "you're not getting out, either."

Dagger in hand, she darts to them. James makes to protect Riley, but she needs no protection. In a second, her face hardens, and that bright, purple bubble is here again around them, sending a new blast of energy. The wave flickers through the room, highlighting the ghosts, highlighting Rudy standing between his daughter and Madelyn.

She lets out a strangled gasp as he reaches forward and grabs her throat, stopping her sharply in her momentum, and raises her off the floor.

"I've never trusted you," he says.

The earth shakes, the vibrations grating at James's wounds. The rumble is deafening, and a horrible crack splits his ears as the ceiling collapses. Riley throws herself on top of him, pinning him to the ground.

The last thing he's aware of is her weight on his body and her arms around him in a last effort to protect him.

Hold on. Please, just hold on longer. Just a little longer.

Riley inwardly repeats the mantra to herself, to the imprint of energy that fused with hers, willing it to keep protecting them from being crushed to death. But her mindset has changed. Why is it that she's the strongest when she's angry? She should be the strongest *now*, when she knows that James and she will die if her bubble of energy disappears. She can't let it happen. She thought he was dead before, burned alive in that freezer, but he's here, and he came back for her.

But she's drained. Her entire body shakes and hurts.

Hold on. You're still strong. We can get ourselves out of here. Please.

Her purple light is enough to see in the makeshift cave. James is unconscious under her. Rubble and stones have piled over them, burying them. If her orb disappears, this air pocket she created will be gone.

Riley strains on her arms and legs to push herself up onto a half-plank position, feeling the weight of the concrete over her energy. "Come on... He will die if you can't do this... He will *fucking die.*"

The orb expands some more, pushing up. Riley clenches her teeth, focusing the remaining of her strength onto a single thought. *Dad is dead. Jamie will die too.* She repeats this to herself, begging, no, *ordering* the entity melting into her to just do this one last thing. There are small remnants of demons somewhere. They're almost spent, like her.

Stones move. Rubble of concrete shifts. She keeps pushing, straining and grunting.

"Just... fucking... *do it!*"

A weight lifts off the bubble as rocks fly outward, creating an opening and letting another kind of darkness, a lighter gray, pierce through the cave.

It's outside.

Riley dares look up, the shaking of her body redoubling, and lets out a relieved sob as she looks at the opening she created. Other rocks have shifted downward, closing in on them, but the slanted debris should be climbable.

If James could walk.

Riley swallows, forbidding herself to cry once more, because she cried way too many fucking times, and this isn't the moment to give up. The purple light around her is waning, slowly blinking, on its way to die and leave her. She crouches behind James and hooks her hands under his arms.

"Come on, give me some strength... Just for a little longer," she tells the entity.

She starts pulling James out of the hole, then onto the pile of debris, grunting each time she has to drag his body. She's aware of other souls around her, but she's not strong enough to give them substance anymore.

The energy enveloping her thins rapidly.

And dies, completely spent.

The gray-blue light of pre-dawn swallows her as she keeps pulling James, now relying only on her own, miserable strength. It's better he's unconscious for now. If he were awake, it would hurt him to be dragged like this over a mountain of rocks digging into his body.

Her legs burn, her arms ache, and her breathing is out of control. She blinks sweat out of her eyes and gives another pull. Her feet touch nothing but air for a second, and she falls onto her back, James collapsing against her chest. The feeling of the high grass on her exposed skin fills her with relief, and a laughter falls out of her mouth.

Riley sits back up and again hooks her arms around James's chest, dragging him away from the collapsed bunker. The stone structure to her right is still intact. It looks like only the big room and part of the tunnel sunk into the earth.

She stops pulling, panting and crying despite having forbidden herself to do so. She sits there, holding James tightly and stroking his hair with a shaky hand.

"We made it out, Jamie-bear... We made it out."

No wind blows through the wet grass. The rain has stopped. Strands of sunlight peek at the horizon, bathing the woods and the fields in a golden light.

A familiar soul catches Riley's attention. She raises her head, looking at the faint blue shape standing in front of her. She was never psychic, but feeling energies is her thing. She wishes she could see him as clearly as he appeared before and hug him as fiercely as she used to.

Next to him, a yellow light.

Riley sniffles, trying to smile. "Thank you for your help, Dad. I'll be okay. *We'll* be okay. You can be with her."

James shifts slightly, his eyes still closed as he winces from the pain, barely conscious. "Riley... Riley, don't leave me..."

Riley strokes his face and kisses his forehead. "I'm not leaving, Jamie. I'm staying with you. I'll take care of us."

CHAPTER 38

Riley pauses and takes a deep breath, looking at the rows of seated people watching her, all of them wearing black. Daniel sits in the front next to Molly, who has flown in for Rudy's funeral. Next to him is Miguel and Keenan, then Liam, and at the end of the row, Kelly. James's wheelchair is posted next to her, his right leg in a cast, and she's great at taking care of him while Riley stands here, doing her speech. He shouldn't be here to begin with. He's in too much pain. His eyes are dark-rimmed and a thin layer of sweat shines on his forehead. The doctors fought him tooth and nail to have him stay at the hospital, but James is the sole definition of stubbornness and got his way. Riley would have done the same thing in his place.

The two of them were lucky to have been in a place often visited by hikers. A middle-aged couple walked near the bunker about an hour after Riley pulled James out of the rubble. They called 911.

All the members of the Faceless are dead, including the guy Riley beat up in her living room. Brain hemorrhage. Riley doesn't even feel guilty about it.

James's knee is broken. Shattered, more like. God knows how he managed to get out of the burning room and retrace his steps to find her. He'll need months of physical therapy to walk normally again.

Stella sits just behind Kelly, wearing dark sunglasses and hiding her tears. Riley had to announce to her the devastating news at the hospital after they woke her up from the induced coma. Once let out of the hospital, she cleaned up the mess, as usual. A cult of dozens of people was responsible for the murders, torturing and killing people inside the Westland bunker, until a freaky accident killed them as the ceiling crashed on them. Case closed.

The rest of the room is filled with people Riley doesn't know well, or not at all. Some faces are familiar, others she's never seen. Paranormal investigators. People her dad helped and advised.

Riley puts a rogue strand of hair behind her ear. She tried to tie her mane into a braid, but it's not holding up as well as the one Grace did for her a few years ago. She adjusts the long, black sleeves covering her arms. The air has finally chilled.

"My dad told me that we had several identities. We're not defined by just one thing. He was a wonderful singer and guitar player. A husband. A boyfriend. The best friend you could ever have. A hard worker." She pauses. "A sexy librarian."

A quiet chuckle runs through the room, lighting up faces.

"But mostly, he was the super dad everyone wished they had. He was *meant* to be a father. He was just so good at it. He told me his favorite identity was being my dad, but the truth is, I'm not the only one he adopted. Not really."

Her gaze finds Daniel. His eyes shimmer with tears as he looks back at her, a smile stretching his lips. Daniel, who still gave

Rudy personal calls years after he and Riley broke up. He felt closer to him than his own dad. Miguel and Liam always felt comfortable around Rudy, after being intimidated by him at first. But they loved him. Kelly was fond of him as well, always running around the kitchen whenever he visited Riley to make him a cup of coffee.

And James. He doesn't smile now, he can't, but his eyes are gentle. He found a substitute father in Rudy, and Riley knows her dad treated him and loved him like a son.

"He had a way of taking you in. Of making you feel welcome, and heard, and loved. Safe. That's how he made me feel my whole life, and when he died, I..." She swallows and exhales, regaining control of herself. "When he died, all I could think about was 'what am I gonna do?' Living without him felt impossible. But I know the answer now. I'll be okay. Because my dad taught me everything he knew. He gave me the tools I needed to survive without him." Another much needed pause before finishing this speech. The image of the two of them sitting in front of the sparkling lake fills her with both incredible happiness and sadness. "I have no regrets. When I think about the last moment we shared together, just the two of us alone... it was *brilliant*. And that's what I'll think about every time I think about him."

Riley turns her face to the right. The people in the audience must think she looks at Rudy's open casket. Really, what she does is acknowledge the blue glow next to her, the energy she latched onto to stay composed. A feather-light, almost imperceptible hand rests on her shoulder.

"Goodbye, Dad. We love you. And we'll miss you."

A brilliant sun shines over the lush cemetery as Rudy's casket is lowered into the ground. If he had known he would witness his own burial, he would have laughed.

After the grave has been filled, he stands next to his daughter, watching and listening to people giving her their condolences. Molly hugs her with a *oh, dear,* and paranormal investigators chit chat with her, telling her how they met Rudy.

Riley gives everyone a gracious smile, nodding patiently. The brown undertones of her hair shine in the sun, and the purple glint in her silver eyes reflects the light. Rudy tilts his head, watching her closely. Something has shifted in her. Changed. He wonders if she can feel it the way he can. She looks taller, even though she's not, and older, even if her face still belongs to the same young, beautiful woman she is.

Once the mass of people clears around her, Stella steps forward. She takes her sunglasses off, finally, and Rudy can look at her dark green eyes one last time.

"I think I'm gonna go now," she says.

"Are you sure? I have this thing at my apartment if you wanna come. There'll be food and drinks."

"No, thank you. I need to be alone. I'll go back to my friend's place." She gives Riley a small pat on the arm. "I'll see you around."

Riley catches her hand. "Hey, I know you're not the hugging type, but you'll have to humor me for a second."

She wraps her arms around Stella's neck, catching her curly hair in the embrace, and Rudy's heart swells as Stella hugs his daughter back.

"You know where to find me if you need anything," Riley says after pulling away.

Stella finds her smile. "You too, kid."

Rudy watches her leave, hoping she'll be okay, wherever she goes. Hoping she'll get over him and fall in love again. He wants nothing but happiness for her.

Grace's hand, warm and soft, finds his. "Are you ready, love?"

"Just a moment."

Daniel comes over and hugs Riley as well. "Beautiful speech, darling. I'm impressed you could go through with it without falling apart."

She chuckles. "Ah, well, I've cried a lot these past few days, but... I wanted to do this right for him."

"I would have been proud of you either way," Rudy says, knowing she can't hear him.

She feels him, though, and briefly glances in his direction before turning back to Daniel. "When is your flight back?"

"In three days." He pauses, gazing at Rudy's grave farther away. "I liked what you said about him being sort of like a dad for all of us. He taught me how to shoot a gun. Whenever I called him, he was always interested to know how things were going for me. I really did love him. I wish I'd told him."

Riley smiles, again glancing toward Rudy. "Don't worry. He knows."

"Likewise, Danny boy."

Daniel glances over his shoulder, looking at James in the distance. He's still in his wheelchair, shooing Kelly away as she tries to make him take the painkillers the doctors gave him when all he wants is to light a cigarette. Even in the face of disaster, he doesn't like it when someone tries to take care of him.

Daniel looks at Riley again. "It makes sense."

She raises her eyebrows at him. "Mm?"

"You and James. It makes sense."

Her eyes shift to James. "I think so too."

James catches her looking and signs, "Tell her to stop pestering me."

Kelly sighs loudly. "You're, like, *super* old. Stop acting like a baby."

It makes Riley and Daniel chuckle.

A few years ago, James promised Riley he would learn sign language. He kept his promise. He did a lot more than that. These two will be okay.

An appeasing sense of peace settles over Rudy. He's fading away.

Before he does, he kisses Riley on the cheek. It feels real to him. He can really feel the warmth of her skin and her hair under his hand.

She looks at him, at his shape, grazing her cheek with her fingers. Her eyes glimmer, but the corners of her mouth lift into a discreet smile. Raising her hand, she signs the only important thing to him. "I love you."

He raises his hand too, hoping she can perceive it, and signs back before vanishing. "I love you."

CHAPTER 39

November 2013

Riley pulls Rudy's truck up a dirt path bordered with trees. They're on the other side of Minley Falls, and the woods are different here. They're surrounded by maple trees and hemlocks and oaks, their leaves flamboyant shades of red and orange and yellow. James watches them through the window, admiring their beauty.

"Are you gonna tell me where we're going now?" he says.

"Patience, Jamie-bear, we're almost there."

He peers at her for a moment. Her eyes sparkle, and a smile plays at the corners of her mouth. She's excited about something. She has been for more than a week, but she refused to tell him anything until he got out of the hospital.

Three months. Three goddamned months of hospital food and physical therapy. Riley came every day after working at Winter's Attic and stayed with him during her days off. W&W Paranormal Investigation has obviously taken the back seat. She'd sit next to him on his bed, reading him her favorite books to distract him from the pain while he laid his head against her shoulder. She used her empathy on him to help him relax and cope.

He has officially never loved anyone as much as he loves her.

His knee is almost okay. He still walks with a crutch most of the time, and the wheelchair is in the back of the truck if he needs it. James hates this fucking wheelchair. He'd rather hurt than sit in it. He's stupid like that.

"We're here," Riley says, showing a bright smile.

She turns right, and the trees clear. A large wooden cabin sits in the middle of a clearing, old and decrepit.

James frowns at it. "What is this place?"

"Come on."

She jumps out of the truck and trots around it to get to his side. James opens his door before she can, but she has already grabbed his crutch and is ready to help him out.

"Are you hurting? Do you want your wheelchair? I can take it out."

"No, I'm fine."

"Are you sure? The doctor said you shouldn't push yourself too much."

"I'm okay, lovie." He slides off the seat and takes the crutch, shivering in the unexpected cold. "Just tell me what we're doing here."

"Are you cold? Do you need my jacket?" Riley's wearing her dad's red plaid jacket, the one with the gray hood Rudy liked so much, which is way too big for her, but for some reason, it looks good on her.

"I'm *fine*."

"Okay. Sorry, I worry."

"You sound like your dad."

She's changed since Rudy died. She's still grief-stricken, of course. Will be for a long time. But she's calmer, more grounded. The type of vibes she gives off strongly reminds James of her dad's, as though she took his place now that he's gone. As though a part of him has taken root inside of her. A certain quiet and stability emanate from her. Even the way she walks and carries herself are different. Sturdier.

James wanted to take care of her, to step up for her. But in the end, she's been the one taking care of him this whole time.

She walks to the cabin and steps onto the large, square deck stretching before the front door. She fetches a set of keys from her pocket and opens it. James limps the two steps to the deck, leaning on his crutch and wincing at the low, steady throbbing in his knee, then follows her inside.

Riley turns around, arms outstretched. "Ta-da!"

He frowns again, looking around. It's a shithole. The large room is bare of furniture, dusty, and strangely smells of mildew. The old and faded floorboards creak precariously under his weight, threatening to break. To the right is an old kitchen sink he wouldn't dare put his hands in. To the left sits a fireplace surrounded by bricks fixed inside the wall. A bit farther on the same side is a door. Through the grime and the overall grayness of the place, James makes out two other doors on the back wall, and one on the right, past the kitchen area.

"What am I looking at?" he asks.

"It's our house. I bought it for us. Surprise!"

"You *what?*"

"I bought it with the insurance money and what my dad left me." Her smile is unwavering as she keeps her gaze on him.

"What about your dad's house?"

"It's beyond repair. We would have to destroy it completely and build something new. And maybe we'll do that, someday, but..." A flash of sadness flits over her face. "I can't bear to have another house on the property. If I built something on it, I would want to build the exact same house, but it wouldn't be the same house. There wouldn't be that bloodstain where I hammered a nail into my finger instead of the wall. It wouldn't be the same floors my dad walked on. The couch we watched TV on wouldn't be there. His guitar and the picture albums would be missing. The place just wouldn't carry his presence." She pauses, looking around the space, and fixes a smile on her face again. "I thought it'd be better to start fresh. To have *our* own place and make new memories." She moves deeper into the room. "My dad taught me everything. I can paint, patch up walls, redo the insulation, install a new sink, a bathtub, and put new floors–"

"I don't know, Riley..."

She stands before him and takes his hand, threading her fingers with his own. "When I moved in with my dad, our house didn't look that much better than this. Well, it did, but it still needed a lot of work. And we fixed it together. We bonded over this. By working on the house, we worked on ourselves, on our relationship. By fixing its holes and tears, we were healing ourselves from our traumas. The house was *us*. And it was amazing and safe, and I want to do the same with you. I want a place that screams James and Riley. I want us to build something new together."

James looks into her eyes, reluctantly touched by this and feeling himself give in. "All right, show me."

A gleaming smile splits her face, and she leads him across the left-hand side of the living room to open the door past the fireplace. "Here's the bathroom, and here..." She opens the first door on the back wall. "That's the master bedroom."

The bedroom is quite large with a big window to the left, giving them a view of the fiercely colored woods outside. James catches himself thinking that this place must be incredible in the winter, when the trees are buried under the snow, and everything is quiet. Before he turns away, motion catches his eyes outside. It looks like branches scraping against the glass, but the trees aren't close enough for that.

The thick sticks move up, filling the window's view, and the head of a deer appears. It turns its head, its black eyes fixed on them. When it exhales, condensation mists over the glass.

Riley chuckles apologetically. "Get used to him. I gave him carrots every time I visited this place. We need to find a name for him."

"He better not shit on the deck."

"Look at you. Already protective of this place." She shows him the two other rooms. "This will be Daniel's guest room for when he visits."

"Figured he'd have his own room."

"Well, *obviously*. And this one, well, maybe an office or a music room. I'm thinking maybe I could use it to, I don't know, write or something."

James smiles. "You're thinking about writing?"

She shrugs. "I don't know. Maybe. I've been writing a little since my dad died. It's soothing. I know it's stupid."

He brushes her cheek. "It's not."

She clasps her hands together, craning her neck to look up at him with hope. "So? What do you think?"

A piece of ceiling falls behind her. It crashes on the floor with a dull *thump* and sends a cloud of dust floating about the space. Riley keeps her eyes on him, actively pretending she didn't hear it.

"I don't know... It feels a bit empty."

"You're right," she says. "I agree. I'm thinking... German Shephard."

"I was thinking more of a..." He clears his throat. "A tiny human."

She cocks her head. "Really? I had no idea you wanted kids."

"Me neither. I guess I was never with the right person to even think about it, but now..." He feels stupid for mentioning it in the first place. He should have shut his mouth. The slow throb in his knee messes up with his brain. "I'm sorry. Forget I said anything."

"No, no! It's fine, it's just... I've never thought about it before, but..." She looks at the empty room again, maybe picturing a kid's room like James already has, and smiles. "Maybe. You know, one day. I think... *yeah.*"

"Yeah?"

"Yeah." She cups his face and stands on her toes to kiss him.

James has to bend over, which strains on his knee, but the warmth of her lips against his own makes it worth it.

He wraps an arm around her shoulders, keeping her close to him, and peers at the living room. It might be a shithole for now, but he can picture it. Fixing the walls and the floors. Painting. Drinking beers and eating pizza while they take a break, a portable radio blaring some rock music lying on the floor. Furnishing the house the way they want. The fireplace looks quite nice, actually. Rustic. And he can already imagine cozy winter nights, the two of them huddled on a couch close to the fire.

"So, this place is us, huh?" he says.

"Yes."

James looks down at her. "And you really think we can make it great?"

She smiles that beautiful smile of hers, her silver eyes boring into him. "I think it'll be amazing."

Vermont. August 1988.

James jumped into his clothes in a hurry and opened his bedroom door a crack, scanning the hallway for any signs of Charles. He lowered his gaze to make sure no rusty nails had been laid on the floor for him to step on. This had happened before, and the scar under his right foot where one nail had pierced a hole was still here to remind him to be careful.

The coast was clear.

James crossed the hallway to the door opposite his room and burst inside the bathroom for the fastest teeth-brushing session of his life. Though his black hair stuck out in all directions, he didn't try to flatten it, and darted out of the room. He slowed down as he passed Charles's bedroom, making sure the little shit wasn't in there waiting to ambush him or something. He always felt stupid for being so wary of his brother. He was twelve, and Charles was only six, yet he lived with a constant dread squeezing his guts, always wondering what Charles would come up with to make James's life more difficult.

Or physically painful.

Chances were that he wouldn't try anything today. Not when their dad was home. He usually pulled those kind of stunts whenever Michael was gone. Still, better to be careful.

Charles wasn't in his bedroom. James skipped to the end of the hallway and turned right to climb down the stairs, barely containing his excitement.

Today was the day. He would spend the whole weekend with his dad camping in the woods, just the two of them.

He skidded on the landing marking the bend of the staircase and walked down the remaining of the stairs, careful not to stomp on the creaky steps, or his mom would get angry at him again for making so much noise. He had to be careful. He didn't want to be yelled at or punished. Not today. He would be the perfect son so he could leave with his dad for two days.

He glanced left and right as he walked by the dining room and his parents' bedroom, then made sure that the closet before the kitchen was locked. Charles liked to hide in there. As he neared the front of the house, hushed voices rose from the kitchen to his right. James slowed his pace, straining to listen to his parents. He peeked through the doorway.

His mother stood at the sink, her dark hair tied into a low bun, as she aggressively scrubbed the dishes. His dad stood next to her, his back to James.

"We are *not* taking Charlie to see a doctor," Eleanor said.

"Ellie, this isn't normal. Something's wrong. How can you not see it?"

"He's just a little kid! He doesn't know what he's doing!"

"I've explained it to him, but—"

"What about Jim, then, huh?"

Michael bowed his head and let out a long, dragging exhale, his black hair reflecting the morning light of the window above the sink. "Not this again..."

Eleanor snapped her head toward him. "No? Your devil child is out of control."

"He's also *your* kid. Don't you forget that. And he's *fine*. Being restless and loud doesn't make him abnormal."

"He's the one we should take to a doctor."

Michael took a sharp step in her direction. "Jimmy doesn't torture and kill little animals, Ellie!"

Eleanor's shoulders slumped, and she stopped scrubbing the plate she was holding.

James held his breath, realization striking him. He had seen his dad pick up dead birds in the backyard a few times. One time, it was a mouse. Its insides had been torn out, and when James had asked about it, Michael had told him not to worry, that a crow had probably gotten to the mouse and not finished its dinner. But it had been Charles's doing. Like it probably was whenever James found insects, beetles or grasshoppers, cut in half or missing all their legs.

Michael inhaled deeply, looking out the window. "I found the antifreeze open in the shed this morning. If he's not slicing them open or crushing them, he's poisoning them. Are those healthy games a six-year-old should be playing?"

A clatter to James's left made them swivel around. Charles had been playing with his trucks in the living room, but James hadn't seen him before despite the large opening facing the kitchen. He'd been too curious about his parents' conversation. He turned back, warmth rising to his cheek as he met his parents' eyes. His mother's face hardened at the sight of him, but thankfully, his dad came to his rescue before she could open her mouth and scold him.

"Hi there, Jimmy. Ready to hike?"

James smiled. "More than ready! Let's go!"

Michael frowned, though a ghost of a smile hung on his lips. "Not before you have breakfast, buddy. You can't go hike on an empty stomach. Sit."

James sat down and wolfed down the food his dad gave him, wanting to be out of here as fast as possible. His greatest joy in life was hiking with Michael. The both of them knew the Willow Hills Forest like nobody else.

"Are you serious, Michael? Eleanor snapped, spinning around.

Michael ruffled James's hair and raised his eyebrows at her.

"You can't possibly go hiking now. You're sick," she said.

"I'm fine."

James looked up from his plate and peered at his father's face. His eyes were still dark-rimmed and slightly swollen. A thin sheet of sweat shone on his forehead. He had been tired these past few days, often coughing and going to bed early.

"Are you sure, Dad? I don't want to make you sicker..."

Michael smiled and crouched next to him. "Hey, I promised you we'd go camping just the two of us, didn't I?"

He did. The week before, for James's twelfth birthday, and this had been James's favorite gift. "Yeah."

"I always keep my promises, and a little cold won't stop me. Now finish your breakfast and join me outside when you're ready." He briefly glanced up at Eleanor. "I need to clean up the toolshed a bit."

James got his hair ruffled again before his dad walked out of the house. When he looked at his mother, he found her staring at him, her blue eyes cold and her lips pressed into a tight line.

"He needs to rest, and you'll just make him worse."

James looked down, shame pressing down on him. His appetite vanished. All he wanted was a break from his brother. And his mom. Faint memories told him she used to be a good mom. She used to hug him and sing to him and read him bedtime stories. She'd make him pancakes with funny faces for breakfast, using whipped cream to make the hair and fruits for the eyes and mouth. She would tend to his scrapes and give him magic kisses when he hurt himself. They'd make his birthday cakes together.

But all that stopped after Charles was born. This special treatment was reserved for him now.

James drank his orange juice and forced himself to finish his breakfast. He would need energy to walk the whole day in the woods and keep up with his dad. After he was done, he brought the dishes to his mother. She didn't spare him a second glance as he left the kitchen.

Charles, sitting on the floor in the living room while playing with his trucks, raised his head as James put his hiking shoes on. "Can I come?"

"No."

"Why not?"

James opened the door. "You're too young."

"I'm not!"

"Yes, you are! You're just gonna drag us down!"

Charles threw his toys through the room, and James had to duck down to avoid one of them. The trucks banged against the wall and fell with a clatter. His brother dramatically pushed past him to run to his mother. He threw his arms around her legs and buried his face in her dress. "Jim is being mean to me!"

Eleanor wrapped her arms around him and glared daggers at James. "Why can't you be nice to him?"

"*Me?* He just threw his toys at me—"

"Just leave. Out of my sight. *Now.*"

Anger flared in James's chest, leaving a bitter taste in his mouth. He walked out and slammed the door shut with a grunt. He took a deep breath to slow the shakes of his body and crossed the front yard in the direction of the toolshed facing the house.

Forget about them. You'll spend the whole weekend with Dad, and it'll be the best.

Something clattered in the toolshed ahead, making James freeze for a moment. Something was wrong with that noise. It hadn't been just a clatter. Something else had fallen down, something much heavier, slumping to the floor. A lump in James's throat swelled, and he resumed walking, a little faster this time.

"Dad?"

No answer came.

Breaking into a cold sweat, James broke into a jog and skidded to a stop at the shed's doorway. A sliver of panic shot through his spine. Michael lay on the floor, unmoving, next to a few tools scattered around him.

Nailed to the ground, James swallowed. "Dad..."

Only silence answered him.

He dragged feet that felt like bricks and crouched next to his father, gently shaking him. "Dad, please say something."

Not even the sound of his breathing reached James's ears. Michael's skin had turned a sickly gray. The circles under his eyes looked more reddish than black, and his lips had lost all their color. His jaw was slack, the way it was when someone was deeply asleep.

Fear choking him, James bolted out of the shed and sprinted back to the house. He burst inside, screaming for his mother. Already tall for his age, he was nearly the same height as her, and Eleanor visibly flinched as he darted in her direction and grabbed her wrist, pulling her toward the door.

"Something's happening to Dad! You need to come now!"

"Jim, what are you—"

"He's unconscious!" he yelled.

Fear fleeted over Eleanor's features. She shook his hand off and burst outside. James followed her, heart beating so fast he thought it was going to explode. His mother would know what to do. She would wake his dad up and take care of him.

She let out a shrill cry when she reached the shed's doorway and hurried at her husband's side. She shook him and patted his cheeks frantically, her hands trembling as she begged him to wake up. James watched as she bent over him, listening to his breathing.

Michael would wake up soon. He would get up and say he got dizzy for a minute, then everything would be okay. Because he couldn't leave. He couldn't leave James alone with a mother who didn't love him and a brother who only cared about torturing him. It just couldn't happen.

"What's happening?" Charles said, standing next to James and looking inside the shed. "Is Daddy sick?"

James made no reply, the lump in his throat strangling him, and his eyes burning as he waited for his dad to move. To talk. To do anything to show he was alive.

His world shattered as Eleanor's hysterical wailing filled his head.

About the Author

Amélia is an emerging suspense and horror writer who loves anything creepy and has always been drawn to the supernatural in particular. She loves ghosts, abandoned houses, tattoos, coffee, rainy days, scary books, and fluffy sweaters.

Although from France, she lives in Huntington Beach, CA, with her husband Christophe and her daughter Kara. The years spent living in New England before moving to California are a great inspiration and often impact her writing.

Subscribe to her newsletter to make sure you don't miss anything: https://www.ameliacognet.com/

Made in United States
Troutdale, OR
12/27/2024

27361801R00257